For my mom,
who likes this book best

Dreaming Death

A PALACE OF DREAMS NOVEL

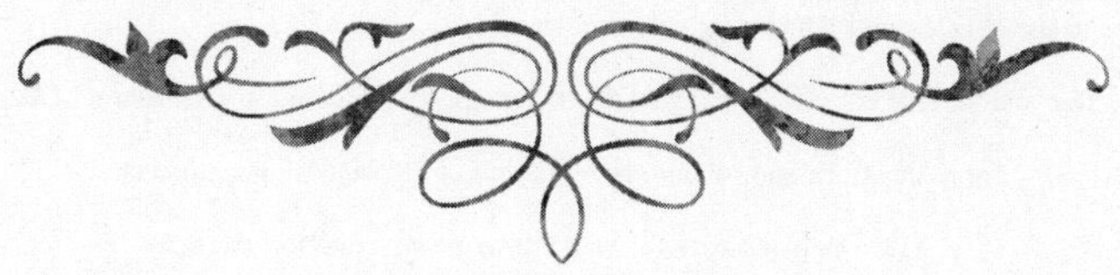

J. Kathleen Cheney

A ROC BOOK

ROC
Published by New American Library,
an imprint of Penguin Random House LLC
375 Hudson Street, New York, New York 10014

This book is an original publication of New American Library.

First Printing, February 2016

For more information about Penguin Random House, visit penguin.com.

LIBRARY OF CONGRESS CATALOGING-IN-PUBLICATION DATA:

Names: Cheney, J. Kathleen.
Title: Dreaming death: a palace of dreams novel / J. Kathleen Cheney.
Description: New York City: New American Library, 2016. | Series: Palace of dreams; 1
Identifiers: LCCN 2015036283 | ISBN 9780451472939 (softcover)
Subjects: LCSH: Psychic ability—Fiction. | BISAC: FICTION / Fantasy / General. | FICTION / Fantasy / Historical. | FICTION / Romance / Suspense. | GSAFD: Fantasy fiction.
Classification: LCC PS3603.H4574 D74 2016 | DDC 813/.6—dc23 LC record available at https://protect-us.mimecast.com/s/EJGvBqc2Ln5aCR

Printed in the United States of America
10 9 8 7 6 5 4 3 2 1

Designed by Tiffany Estreicher

PUBLISHER'S NOTE
This is a work of fiction. Names, characters, places, and incidents either are the product of the author's imagination or are used fictitiously, and any resemblance to actual persons, living or dead, business establishments, events, or locales is entirely coincidental.

Penguin
Random
House

Praise for the Novels of the Golden City

The Seat of Magic

"[A] killer sequel . . . intriguing and fun, the mystery unfolds like a socially conscious tour through a cabinet of curiosities." —*Kirkus Reviews*

"Mesmerizing." —*Publishers Weekly*

"Those who enjoy alternate history—Edwardian- or Victorian-era historical fiction with a touch of magic and mythology—will be delighted with this story." —*Booklist*

"This second entry in the Golden City series is even better than its predecessor. Readers will be completely enthralled with the characters and the organic development of their relationship . . . a sheer delight." —*RT Book Reviews*

The Golden City

"Cheney's alternate Portugal . . . provides a lush backdrop for an intricate mystery of murder, spies, selkies, and very dark magic. A most enjoyable debut." —Carol Berg, author of the Novels of the Collegia Magica

"[A] masterpiece of historical fantasy. . . . The fascinating mannerisms of the age and the extreme formality of two people growing fonder of each other add a charmingly fresh appeal that will cross over to romance fans as well as to period fantasy readers." —*Library Journal*

"Pulls readers in right off the bat. . . . Oriana's 'extra' abilities are thoroughly intriguing and readers will love the crackling banter and working relationship between Oriana and Duilio." —*RT Book Reviews*

"An ambitious debut from Cheney: part fantasy, part romance, part police procedural, and part love letter to Lisbon in the early 1900s. . . . [The author] does a lovely job connecting magical, historical, and romantic elements." —*Kirkus Reviews*

Books by J. Kathleen Cheney

ACKNOWLEDGMENTS

I want to thank all the people who've read and commented on various versions of this book throughout the years. Thanks especially to the participants and teachers of the Speculative Fiction Writers Workshop at the Center for the Study of Science Fiction, including James Gunn and Kij Johnson, who read the first bits of this. Also the members of Critters, several of whom touched one chapter or another. Thanks to the members of Codex who pored over specific words, especially Melissa Mead, Beth Cato, and Megan E. O'Keefe, along with Laurel Amberdine, who patiently reads everything. And finally, thanks to the editors who've touched this book: Jessica Wade, Isabel Farhi, and Danielle Stockley, who made this a much better book. You are all amazing!

DREAMING DEATH

J. Kathleen Cheney

CHAPTER ONE

Liran Prifata's dove gray uniform jacket lay to one side, his shirt tangled with it, pale blotches on the bare dirt. The rain pelted down, and the wind in the picked-over field tore at him. He was chilled to the bone, too numb to fight any longer.

Two of the men grasped his arms, pinning him on his knees like an animal to be slaughtered. The rain softened the ground into a muddy quagmire. Blood mixed with the water dripping from his chest, staining his trousers, all color leached out in the dark. A third man in a dark jacket leaned over him, light glinting off a curved knife as he sliced and cut again. Liran felt no pain, but the numbness scared him more than being captive. He wanted to scream, cry out for help. His throat wouldn't answer. His lungs could hardly find the air to breathe, much less cry out.

What are they doing to me?

The man in the dark jacket spoke as he worked, words that meant nothing in Liran's ears. He'd heard no names, seen nothing unusual about their clothes, no marks on the coach that would help his fellow police identify these men. The men didn't even hide their faces from him, but they had neither marks nor scars to distinguish them in his mind.

This had to be blood magic. He'd never seen it before, but there was no other name for what they were doing, letting his blood fall onto the earth. The Pedraisi did this in their fields, some ancient fertility rite. It was illegal, and forbidden by the temple. *God won't permit this,* he told himself. *Not here in Noikinos. He will send someone to save me.*

His tormenter stepped back and held up a lantern to survey his handiwork. Another man, the fourth one Liran had seen in the coach, came closer. Liran tried to focus on that face, to sear it into his memory, but he couldn't make out the man's features, hidden beneath the hat the man wore to stave off the cold rain. A fifth man huddled in the distance, face turned away as if he was ashamed.

Now that he'd bled for them, for their magic, surely they would let him go. They would leave him there, and someone would find him. The farmer would come to find out who had desecrated his wheat field to appease a false god.

The fourth man gestured sharply, and the man with the knife came close again. He made a single sharp movement, the blade slashing across this time, a flash in the darkness.

That hurt. Enough to reach through the numbness, enough to tell Liran it was no shallow cut like the others. He gasped feebly, and then he was falling. He landed on his side in the shorn remains of the field's wheat. Feet squelched away in the muck.

Darkness gathered at the edges of Liran's vision. *Why me?*

Warmth gathered in his soul, belying the dark and cold. He had the sense of a presence like hands resting on his shoulders. An angel had come to take him to the promised heavens.

CHAPTER TWO

Shironne stood on the balcony outside her room, wishing the wind could sweep the night's tattered images from her mind. The dream haunted her. Down in the city, someone had died.

She clutched her heavy robe about her, grateful for its warmth. Winter had come early to Noikinos. The chilly wind carried up with it the damp and earthy scent of the mews behind the house, the smells of horse and hay and manure.

Dry leaves rattled and sighed in the crisp breeze. The trees planted along the side of the house would cling to them until spring, when the softer whisper of new leaves would replace the rusty winter sound. When she'd been able to see, she'd thought the brown leaves unattractive. Now that she was blind, she listened to them instead, their rustle providing a clear demarcation of the edge of her family's property. Somewhere nearby pennants snapped and chimes tinkled, although she couldn't tell which neighbor had brought those from the temple to safeguard his home.

The cook spoke with a tradesman in the back courtyard, the clink of metal and glass underlying their voices and echoing off the yard's stone walls. Likely the milkman, Shironne decided. The distant noise of carriages and horses spoke of morning traffic—sounds of normalcy.

No one knows yet—no one but me and him. It had been one of *those* dreams.

At first, she hadn't known they weren't her own.

There was a man up at the palace who dreamed of death, deaths that were really happening. He involuntarily spun out those dreams, sharing the victims' fear and pain with the world. For most who could sense his dreams, that meant little more than a vague sense of fear and an occasional headache.

As in everything else, I have to be the one who's different.

Colonel Cerradine knew who the dreamer was, this man who inflicted his nightmares on her. The colonel had always refused to tell her anything about him, though, not even his name. Lacking any better label for him, Shironne had settled on the Angel of Death, a nickname the colonel's personnel seemed to find both apt . . . and ridiculous.

She rubbed one hand with the other, her left thumb smoothing along the scar that ran across her right palm. The souvenir of a foolish childhood accident, it served as a constant reminder that she too often let curiosity get the better of her.

But every time she woke from one of these dreams, she wondered about him. *Who is he? Why does he do this?*

The colonel had warned her that pushing to find that answer too soon could be dangerous for her. What he hadn't told her was *why*. What harm could there be in meeting someone whose dreams she already shared? After all, those shared dreams, however unpleasant, had given rise to her unusual vocation.

The angel's dreams gave her a purpose beyond simply finding a husband . . . or joining the priesthood, as was expected of Larossans who developed powers. When her powers had abruptly manifested when she was twelve, the chance of finding a husband had disappeared. Shironne had to consider other paths, but the priesthood didn't seem appealing either; selling charms and prayers in the temple wouldn't suit her temperament at all, she'd insisted. That infuriated her father and shocked the priests who more than once had come to talk to her mother about it. After all, they asked, what else is a girl child to do with her life?

Shironne was terribly grateful that her mother supported her decision to find another path, and that those dreams had shown her one. Those dreams always meant there was death, and she could do something about that. She could help find murderers.

Thus had begun her strange career with the army.

The man who had the dreams often couldn't remember much about them. She *could*. That had seemed odd at first. Then she'd grasped that his dreams were like paintings laid before her in her sleep, but the Angel of Death didn't see them that way. Instead, his mind was the canvas on which they were painted.

She stepped back inside her bedroom, closed the door after her, and drew the curtain shut. Not certain how long she'd stood on the balcony savoring the breeze, she crossed to the mantel and carefully felt the delicate hands of the clock. Her mother had removed the glass, making it possible for Shironne to read the time with her fingers. It was almost eight.

Her bedroom door opened, and Melanna pelted into the room, bare feet slapping against the wooden floor. Melanna's steps came toward her, her bracelet tinkling, and then her arms clasped about Shironne's waist in a fierce hug. The top of Melanna's head almost reached Shironne's shoulder. Her youngest sister was on her way to being as tall as their mother one day, if not taller.

"I had bad dreams," Melanna complained, quickly turning her loose.

Shironne set a bare hand atop her sister's coarse hair—a trait certainly not inherited from their mother. Whenever she touched another person, she could feel more than their emotions. She could actually feel the thoughts buzzing around in their heads like swarms of bees, sometimes formed into words she could catch, other times not. She found only a vague sense of Melanna's nightmare, but the girl rarely remembered anything specific from the angel's dreams. Their mother didn't either.

Even Shironne's memories of the dreams were unclear, as if she'd seen everything through a heavy veil. She knew she'd witnessed a murder. It was *always* murder, even if it didn't seem that way at first.

The faceless victim hadn't been able to fight back, and his captors—there had been more than one; of that Shironne was sure—had cut his skin. Then they'd let him die. It had been cold and raining, somewhere near the river. A field, perhaps, although she wasn't sure why she'd drawn that conclusion. But each detail might help the army find a murderer, or murderers in this case, so she needed to report them.

"I have to find my gloves," she told her sister. "Then we can go down for breakfast."

"Can we read first?" Melanna asked.

Her youngest sister had acquired a lurid novel from a lending library that was *their* secret. It wasn't one her governess, Verinne, would find acceptable. The book was full of Pedraisi witchcraft. It had witches who made stables go up in flames and others who could call birds from the air. Larossans possessed a variety of powers, but those were pure nonsense. Even so, they made for an entertaining tale. The story also had an unlikely romance between the heroine and a handsome young Larossan man who worked in her father's stables, whom Shironne strongly suspected would turn out to be the missing son of a lord or wealthy landowner.

Melanna did most of the reading but would spell out the longer words so that Shironne could tell her how to pronounce them. "Not now," Shironne said. "When Verinne takes her nap you can come to my room."

Melanna huffed out a dramatic sigh and slipped away from Shironne's grasp. A second later, Shironne heard her sister bound onto her mattress. Shironne returned to her bed and sat, locating her gloves on the table next to her bed, just where she'd left them. While Shironne tugged on the gloves, Melanna continued to jump on the bed, one particularly large bounce telling Shironne her sister had flopped onto her back.

Shironne reached out to the table again and found her focus. Pure quartz: she could trace along the perfect lines within the stone, even through her gloves. She'd used this stone as a focus for some time now and was as familiar with it as she was with her worn clothes. It was still endlessly fascinating. When she concentrated on it, all the other sensations that assailed her faded away: the feel of fabric against her skin, the hints of smoke on the air that brushed her face, the lingering traces of the last item she'd touched. She could shut out the constant barrage of others' emotions and simply follow the emotionless lines of the stone, clearing the clutter from her mind.

She concentrated on it a moment longer, chasing away the dragging grip of last night's dream. Then she pulled her attention back. "Are you ready to go down?" she asked her sister.

Melanna promptly clambered off the bed, and together they headed downstairs to the kitchen. It wasn't proper for them to eat in the kitchen, but they did so anyway, since Cook was nearly a part of the family, having come from their mother's childhood home with her.

Pausing at the base of the kitchen stairs, Shironne heard the customary oofing sound Cook made when Melanna ran to hug her. Then came the scrape of the bench when Melanna sat down at the table. The room smelled of baking flatbread and spices. Shironne went to join her sister pulled out the chair at the head of the table, and settled there.

"Is Kirya around?" she asked Cook. Kirya Aldrine was actually an army lieutenant the colonel had placed within their household to ensure the family's safety, but the young woman spent most of her days working as maid for Shironne's mother and her sister Perrin.

Since Mama was in mourning, her garb wasn't complicated. Until a year had passed, her tunic, trousers, and petticoats would all be of undyed silk and wool. She didn't wear any jewelry save for the bracelet that helped Shironne hear where she was. That made Kirya's assignment as maid easier. Perrin, on the other hand, was to be presented to the elite of Larossan society at the turn of the year in the hope of contracting a brilliant marriage. She got to wear bright colors, the cuffs and hems of her tunics and petticoats were heavily embroidered, and Mama had given Perrin the jewelry she no longer wore. Working on Perrin's wardrobe *did* keep Kirya busy.

Cook's worry spun about her at the mention of Kirya. "I think she's up with your mother. Should I send for her?"

Shironne realized that Cook must think something was wrong. "No. What about Messine?"

Filip Messine, another lieutenant, primarily watched over Shironne. He escorted her to her various assignments for the army. In his false identity here, though, he served as a groom in the mostly empty stable. The Anjir family had limited funds at the moment, so there were only the two old carriage horses there. They could spare Messine for an errand or two.

Cook's worry faded to relief. "Oh, you want a messenger. I'll go call him." She walked to the outside door and called out into the courtyard before returning to her cooking.

A moment later, Shironne heard the door open again, followed by the jangle of bells and Messine's familiar footsteps. Shironne turned her head that way to hear him better. Although she could *sense* where the members of their little household were when she concentrated, the various bracelets and bells each wore made it easier for her to locate them.

Messine came closer, clutching his concern tight about him. He was trained not to bother others with his emotions. For Shironne, that made him pleasing company. "Miss Anjir, did you need me?"

"I need to send a message to the colonel," she explained. "I had a dream. Someone died, and the Angel of Death dreamed it."

CHAPTER THREE

Hard hands pulled at Mikael Lee's arm and hauled him to his feet. "Where the hell have you been?"

Mikael blinked up at Kai's stern features. He concentrated on breathing as the room spun about him. His lungs ached. It felt like someone had jammed a knife in the base of his neck and a spike through his head.

He didn't dare answer Kai's question the way that came to mind, but the rumpled bed behind him should have made it obvious. He'd been *there* all night. He'd been dreaming.

He was at the Hermlin Black, his favored tavern in the Old Town. The clumsily carved bed with its faded yellow bedding looked familiar. An icon of the Larossans' true god sat in the corner, the statue's lap draped with a trio of grains for luck. Mikael had seen that one before. Synen, the inn's owner, must have dumped him in this room to sleep off his intoxication and keep him away from the other patrons.

Mikael rubbed his aching temples. At least he was alone this time, something to be grateful for. Synen understood that he came to this tavern to get himself drunk, *not* to find a companion for the night. That was why he ended up here most nights that he dreamed. Since Mikael always promptly paid his bill, Synen took good care of him.

Kai waited, arms folded over his chest, a pillar of inky blackness. Like Mikael, Kai had mixed heritage, part Lucas and part Anvarrid.

That wasn't uncommon, since the two peoples had formed a close relationship two centuries before, when the Anvarrid invaded the country. Most children born between the Six Families and the various Anvarrid Houses tended toward the fair appearance usually associated with the former. Kai had come out of the womb looking like an Anvarrid. He was tall with dark hair and dark eyes. His pale skin was the only trait he'd inherited from his Lucas mother, and that only served to make his hair look darker. It was hard not to see him as Khandrasion of the House of Valaren, even though Kai never answered to his full name. Or he never had in Mikael's presence.

Unlike Kai, Mikael had inherited a muddy mess of Lee Family and Vandriyen House bloodlines, with hair slowly darkening over the years from blond to brown, and eyes of a bright shade of blue particular to his father's ancestors. He'd also inherited his father's tendency to freckle, but *not* the man's height. While most Larossans might consider him of average height, he was short for either a man from the Six Families or an Anvarrid. No one but his father had *ever* called him Mikoletrion; he simply didn't look Anvarrid enough.

As Kai towered over him, Mikael took in a shaky breath and in a voice that sounded papery and thin asked, "What time is it?"

"Where are your boots?" Kai snapped in return. He didn't wait for an answer. His dark eyes flicked toward the room's bare wooden floor and he swooped down to retrieve something. A second later he jammed Mikael's boots against his chest. Mikael clenched his jaw to keep from gasping. He managed to grab the boots from Kai and sank back onto the rumpled bedding to put them on, a flare of nausea making him break out into a cold sweat. He hadn't registered that he'd carried injuries out of his dream until that moment.

Lowering his head to lace his boot hurt, but Mikael did so anyway. While he worked a knot out of the leather laces, Kai towered over him like a dark storm cloud. The sensitives up at the fortress actually referred to Kai that way behind his back.

Still kinder than anything the sensitives say about me, I'll bet.

"Where's your overcoat?" Kai asked.

Mikael had his uniform jacket on still, halfway unbuttoned and horribly wrinkled since he'd slept in it. His overcoat was nowhere in sight. "I don't know," he answered truthfully. "I'm sure I wore it down here last night."

Without waiting for further explanation, Kai turned to the room's other occupant, Elisabet. She'd stood at the open doorway the whole time, a silent presence. Mikael hadn't actually seen her there, but he'd never questioned her presence either. He'd known she was somewhere close. As Kai's primary guard, Elisabet went wherever he went. Or should.

"I'll go find it," Kai said. "Stay with him." Before she could argue, he swept out the narrow door, the skirts of his hooded overcoat swirling dramatically behind him. Drama was one of Kai's inborn skills.

For a moment, Mikael just breathed. He'd never known why Kai disliked him so intensely, but mornings like this one didn't help their working relationship. A hand touched his boot and Mikael realized he must have closed his eyes again. He opened them to see Elisabet kneeling before him. She lifted his foot onto her black-clad knee and began lacing his boot for him as if he were a child. "I can do it," he insisted.

"You're too slow," she said in her low, rusty voice. "He's in a foul mood. It's not quite ten."

When is Kai not in a foul mood? Mikael watched Elisabet lace his boot, hoping fervently that Kai didn't return before she finished.

Elisabet was truly one of the most beautiful women he'd ever seen. High cheekbones hinted at some Anvarrid blood, but otherwise she looked Family-born: pale eyes and pale hair, tall and broad shouldered. Her features were calm and even, her neat braids falling forward as she worked. He caught the faint smell of oil from at least one gun on her person. Dressed in her formal blacks, she was the perfect guard, never letting her emotions get the better of her, never reacting to the vagaries of her charge.

Life is simpler for those who know where they stand in the order of things.

Unlike Mikael, Elisabet knew where she stood. She was Lucas, which meant automatic acceptance among the Lucas Family. He was an outsider, sent to the Lucas elders by the Lee elders four years before in the hope that they could tame his dreams.

She was a First, which meant she oversaw her yeargroup and thus had companionship. He was alone, forced by the elders to live up in the palace rather than in the fortress below, because they hadn't found any way to tame those dreams.

She was a guard. She watched Kai's back during most of her waking hours, and when other duties forced her away from him, her Seconds, Tova and Peder, took over. It was a simple calling. She need only keep her charge alive.

Kai had no business walking away from her. If she was annoyed with him for that, it didn't show. It said something that she'd let him go alone—both that she felt this tavern was secure at the moment, and that Kai *needed* to be alone.

She lowered Mikael's foot to the ground and rose, setting one hand under his arm to help him up again. *Too fast.* Mikael swayed, and Elisabet laid a hand against his chest to steady him. She drew her hand back with a film of red staining her palm.

Oh Hel. Heat prickled through Mikael's body, nausea welling in his empty stomach. He'd bled through his uniform jacket. He could smell it now that he knew it was there. Fortunately, there didn't seem to be any blood on the yellow bedding.

Elisabet glanced down markedly at her red-stained hand, and her eyes flicked up to meet his.

Mikael shook his head. He didn't want Kai to know he was actually bleeding. Kai would see it as weakness. "Don't mention it to him," he asked of her. "Please."

One of her gull-wing brows arched upward, but she wiped her hand on her black trouser leg. It wouldn't show there any more than it did on his uniform. She gestured for Mikael to precede her out of the room.

He obeyed, walking along the narrow mezzanine above the floor of the tavern and trying to button his jacket and then tighten the sash about his waist. At this hour, the tables below were all empty. That explained why Elisabet thought it was secure; the tavern's outer doors must be locked.

Mikael made his way down the stone steps, doing his best to move normally. All of this would pass: the tightness in his lungs, the pain in his head and neck, even the blood seeping through his garments. It would be gone in a matter of hours. That was one reason he needed to get back up to the palace. He needed to see his spontaneous injuries for himself.

And change into a clean uniform. That too.

The main serving room below smelled stale, scents of flat beer, sweat, and spicy food making his stomach heave. Lit with tallow candles—this building predated the piping of gas out to this part of the city—the yellow plastered walls were marked with soot from the great wrought-iron sconces. Like the majority of buildings in Noikinos, this one was white outside but brilliantly colored inside, with bright tapestries on the walls, red cloths over the old tables, and golden temple pennants bearing the sigil for fortune hanging over the doorways.

Synen was notably absent; the man avoided Kai, having heard enough snide commentary on his tavern from him. Mikael made his way down the stairwell, not touching the rail. It was always a bit sticky. As they reached the base of the stairs, Kai strode through the swinging doors from the kitchen with a mass of black wool over his arm. He barely spared Mikael a glance, just tossed him the coat as he passed on his way toward the heavy exterior door.

"Wait," Elisabet ordered.

Kai actually did as he should this time, moving to one side of the doorway. She drew her pistol, unbolted the door, and surveyed the street to make certain the area was still secure. A large unmarked coach waited outside, a driver in royal livery sitting atop the box and a groom on the tail. Since the coach took up most of the narrow street—they *were* in the Old Town—the morning traffic had to find another way around.

Once satisfied with the safety of the situation, Elisabet had Kai climb into the coach first. Mikael followed, and she entered last, settling on the forward-facing bench next to Kai. Once she shut the door, it was dim inside. The shades were drawn, likely to keep Kai out of strangers' lines of sight. Elisabet sat erect on the bench, pistol across her lap, her eyes closed. She wasn't here to interact with them; she was listening to the situation outside. The groom riding the coach's tail surely had a rifle with him, but Elisabet was the one who was ultimately responsible for Kai.

Long ago, before the Anvarrid had come, the Six Families had been pacifists, living quietly in their buried fortresses. When the Larossans migrated onto their lands, the Families welcomed them and taught them how to farm in the colder climate. The Anvarrid invasion, a far more brutal introduction, forced the Six Families to change just to survive. Now they served to protect whichever Anvarrid House ruled each province. Here in Lucas Province, that meant the House of Valaren, the king's household.

Following the Anvarrid invasion of Larossa, assassinations had run rampant as different Houses fought for control of the new senate and, thus, the country. Two centuries later, the Houses predominantly used other means to seize control, usually legal maneuvering. Instead, the rising strength of the Larossan citizenry—who made up the majority of the country's population—was now seen as a greater threat to the Anvarrid. A Larossan "nationalist" had taken a shot at the king late in the previous year, evidence that there were those who had anti-Anvarrid sympathies and were daring enough to act on them. Although Kai hadn't been confirmed as the king's heir yet, as a member of the House of Valaren he still made an excellent target and thus was not permitted to leave the palace without at least one guard.

Since Elisabet was required to watch only Kai's back, not his,

Mikael appreciated her earlier show of consideration. He was equally glad that Kai hadn't seen it; Kai would have taken it the wrong way.

Mikael rubbed at the sore spot on his neck with fingers that tingled. The throbbing in his head had eased some already, and he was breathing better now. "Did they feel the dream at the fortress?"

Kai leaned back against the coach's leather squabs and folded his arms across his chest. "Of course they did."

Kai *hated* all of this. Kai disapproved of Mikael's drinking to mute his dreams. He disapproved of the fact that Mikael had dreams in the first place, and that he inflicted the horror of his dreams on the sensitives—those who could *feel* another's emotions—in Kai's year-group. Kai hated coming down into the city to find Mikael and drag him back to the palace, and he made no secret of his low opinion of Mikael's discipline.

Mikael shifted his heavy overcoat off his lap and onto the bench next to him. Getting himself thoroughly drunk might blur his dreams, further reducing the effect they had on the sensitives, but the hangover afterward never helped his disposition.

As the coach began to move through the streets of the Old Town, Mikael lifted the shade with one hand and peered out the window. Most of this part of the city dated back to the days before the Anvarrid, old buildings with simple slanted rooftops made to shed snow. Many were in questionable repair. The Larossans had favored plainer designs than the fanciful buildings the Anvarrid introduced on their arrival, but these were constructed of the same pale granite seen all over this part of Lucas Province. In some lights the city of Noikinos gleamed pink, at other times white or gold.

Elisabet shifted on the bench, drawing Mikael's attention back inside the dim coach. She was trying to reach a compromise with her coat; he recognized that movement from personal experience. While on duty, a guard usually stood. The steel plates in a guard's overcoat made it nearly impossible to sit comfortably—not to mention the knife digging into her back. Usually she carried a rifle while on duty as well, but she'd left it behind at the palace. It would have been ungainly in the coach. And while he didn't see her pistol in her sash, Mikael had no doubt that every time she left the palace, Elisabet went well armed. *He* didn't even have his knife with him.

Mikael preferred the sword himself, a *tidy* weapon, and the reason he identified as Hand-to-Hand. Very few guards chose a rifle as their principal weapon; in close quarters it could become problematic. But Elisabet was an expert marksman—she'd won marksmanship prizes at the summer fairs before—so he didn't question her choice.

Like both Mikael and Kai, she wore the Lucas uniform, with a high-collared jacket and trousers and vest all in unrelieved black. Swirls of black soutache trim on the sleeves and chest of her jacket marked her rank and assignment, the designs meaningless to most outside the Six Families. Mikael's rumpled jacket shared one of those markings, the swirl for First on the right shoulder, but he had the pattern for Daujom—the king's private intelligence service—on the left cuff. Elisabet and Kai both had the chest pattern for Rifles, compared to Mikael's Hand-to-Hand, marking them as among the Lucas Family's distance shooters.

The one thing none of those trim patterns reflected was that Kai would take off those simple blacks most afternoons, shedding the Lucas side of his bloodline. He would don an Anvarrid over-tunic—the ankle-length tunic that the Houses favored, usually fitting tight to the waist, but left unsecured below to allow room for the full trousers or skirt worn with it—and become the king's heir. Kai's tunics were heavily embroidered in the burgundy-and-brown hawk pattern that belonged to the Royal House, the Valarens, making it clear that he was the king's heir, even if not yet approved by the senate.

The coach slowed and then stopped. Mikael glanced out again and saw that they were at the edge of the palace grounds, waiting to pass through the sentry post at the fence line. After a moment, the coach's door was pulled open and a sentry stepped up onto the step to peer into the gloom.

She was an older woman, her blond braids threaded with gray. The trim markings across her chest identified her as a sentry. She leaned into the coach to get a better look at them, her eyes likely slowed by the dimness inside. She nodded once to Elisabet, then surveyed Kai. Like all sentries, she kept her face expressionless, even when she turned her eyes on Mikael. Even if he didn't recognize *her,* Mikael suspected she knew exactly who he was.

All the sensitives knew him. Or *of* him, to be more precise.

Her position, serving at the entry to the palace grounds, meant that she was a sensitive. The treaty required that all sentries controlling access to the Royal House would be. That afforded the Lucas Family multiple opportunities to gauge the intentions of visitors. *That* was what the Six Families had offered the Anvarrid to retain their place in the country following the invasion. They provided protection for the Anvarrid. In return, the Six Families kept their buried fortresses.

The sentry took one last look at Mikael, stepped down, and shut the coach door. The driver started the horses moving, heading around the palace grounds to the back courtyard entrance. As they moved on, Mikael raised the blind slightly to prepare his eyes for the sunlight outside. It might be cool this morning after the rain, but the sky was clear and the sun bright.

"I'm sure Father will want to talk to you," Kai said after a moment. His father, Dahar, ran the Daujom, the office out of which they both worked.

Mikael dismissed the accusing tone he heard in Kai's voice. "I'll clean up first and then go to the office."

"Good." Kai turned his head to gaze pensively at the closed shade on his side of the coach, fist held to his mouth. Evidently that conversation was over.

Mikael rubbed his temples, wishing the headache away. He didn't know what had been bothering Kai of late. He suspected it was some difficulty between father and son, because Kai had recently been making every excuse possible to get out of the office of the Daujom and away from his father. It would be more irritating, Mikael supposed, if Kai actually shirked his duties, but he did get his work done, often staying in the office long after his father had left for the day. Thus far, Mikael hadn't complained.

As soon as the coach stopped, Elisabet slipped out and waited for Kai. After he stepped down, Mikael climbed out, hitting the buff-colored flagstones with a semblance of normalcy. His breath steamed out in the chilly air. He could put on his overcoat but didn't want to transfer blood to it, so he just drew in a breath through his nose and did his best to ignore the cold.

The palace rose above them, an ornate creation unsuitable for the climate in which it existed. It harkened back to the palaces the Anvarrid had built in their homeland, a much warmer place from which the Cince had driven them. The pale granite of the palace walls rose in four stories that wrapped about the wide courtyard. Large onion domes capped each corner of the rooftops, and smaller ones sat atop the sentry turrets. Stone railings ran along the flat portions of the rooftops, and there sentries stood on duty, the black of their uniforms stark against the white walls and blue sky. As the palace stood at the highest point in the city, exposed to the cold wind, most of those sentries wore their hoods up at the moment, hiding their faces.

Not that Mikael could tell them apart at a distance. All sentries, male and female, wore identical uniforms. They wore their hair in the same style, braided away from their faces and falling to the middle of their backs. The uniformity was a tactic meant to intimidate, one all of the Six Families employed. But the Lucas Family *thrived* on conformation and perfection and carried the practice to greater heights than the other Families, perhaps because they guarded the king rather than the master of a province.

Mikael sighed. *How many of those sentries did I wake last night?*

He stilled his mind, not wanting to agitate the sensitives any further. He cast a glance up at the windows of One Above—the first floor of the palace—and spotted Dahar holding back the heavy black draperies, watching them. Mikael nodded once toward the window. Dahar returned the gesture and disappeared as the drapes fell back in place. He would make his apologies to Dahar later, after he went to his quarters and bathed.

Kai and Elisabet had already disappeared under the white stone of the arcade, so Mikael followed. Inside the palace there was only a single pair of sentries at the doors to contend with—a man and a woman, both years older than him. He wished good thoughts at them, hoping not to annoy them further this morning. Neither looked directly at him.

The back entry hall of the palace wasn't its most impressive hall—more of an intersection point for the wide stone stairwells coming from the upper floors—but light from a series of stained-glass windows spangled the white marble floor in a rainbow of colors. Like the Larossans, the Anvarrid favored colors, but darker and richer ones, so the walls were hung with tapestries of battle scenes wrought in jewel tones and highlighted with gold threads. The runners in the halls were thick wool and silk, muffling Mikael's footsteps, and had been created especially for this palace in muted shades of beige and brown so as not to distract from the brilliant tapestries. Delicately crafted iron lanterns hung from chains in the arched stone hallways. They were rarely lit now since gas had been piped in to light the palace, but were retained because of their beauty. In the summer, the outer doors and windows of the palace could be thrown open to allow wind to sweep along the hallways, but in the winter, the abundance of glass made these halls icy.

The opulence of the palace provided a stark contrast to the utter simplicity of the Lucas fortress located far below these halls. There the Lucas Family lived in a domain without sunlight, with endless gray walls and floors, with minimal decoration and painted floorcloths rather than fine carpets. It was a different world down below. And centuries underground had turned the Six Families paler than any of the peoples who surrounded them now. When the Anvarrid conquered Larossa, they had given the Six Families the nickname *termites.*

Truthfully, Mikael would rather live below instead of in this sparkling palace. Unfortunately, the Lucas elders found his dreams worrisome, and thus he lived up here, on Two Above, the wing of the palace that housed members of the Daujom. Kai and Elisabet had already gone up the stairwell to the left, probably to retrieve Elisabet's rifle from the armory, so Mikael made his way up behind them.

Once he reached his quarters, Mikael fished out his key. It was, thankfully, still in his jacket pocket. The room wasn't large, but it gave him privacy he wouldn't have had in the fortress below.

As a child in Lee Province, he'd regularly moved between his grandfather's wing in the Vandriyen Palace and the Lee fortress beneath it, his mother's world. With most yeargroups housing between twenty and thirty members, the children's barracks there were crowded, always full of noise and activity. By comparison, the palace seemed stifled and formal, quiet and dull. He missed the bustle of being in a yeargroup, but he would never have been able to hide the truth of his dreams from them for long.

After dumping his overcoat on the end of his bed, Mikael went to the window and drew back the heavy draperies to let in some light. From the chest at the end of his bed, he grabbed one of the old stained towels he kept for just this purpose and set it next to the basin on his table. He stripped off his jacket first, folding it so the laundry wouldn't notice the blood across the front panels. His shirt was blotched with drying blood, though, undoubtedly ruined. Mikael pulled it off over his head and rolled it up. He'd send that down to the quartermasters later to be cut up for scrap. Using the icy water left in the basin, he took the towel and gingerly patted his chest clear of blood.

After one of his dreams, he would often wake with injuries that mimicked the victim's. Most of the time they were restricted to bruises, but his false injuries sometimes bled through the skin, as if he were sweating blood. It happened only when a dream was particularly frightening or urgent, or when he felt a closer tie to the victim. Last night's dream had been one of those.

When he looked directly downward, he could see a wide band of bruising across the lower part of his rib cage, also oozing blood in a few places. The skin had broken in several spots when Kai hit him in the chest with his boots. But when it came to the injuries running across his collarbones, he couldn't see what lay beneath his chin.

He grabbed his shaving mirror with one hand and held it at arm's length, trying to understand what he saw. Left in a string of reddish purple bruises was lettering, running from the end of one collarbone to the other. Someone had carved a message into the victim's flesh, a message now reflected on Mikael's skin. But the markings were already fading. It had been too many hours since his dream.

Left alone, he would have slept on until the false injuries healed completely. He'd slept more than a full day after one of his dreams before, so there was value to Kai waking him and dragging him back to the palace, even if Kai didn't know that. This way Mikael got to see the injuries before they faded away.

He turned his head and angled the mirror to peer at the spot on his neck where it felt like he'd been jabbed by a knife. The tiny wound there was still tender to the touch. That transferred injury hadn't bled, which made him suspect the victim's injury might have come from some manner of poison. That might explain the alternating numbness and tingling of his limbs too, and the tightness in his lungs that made him feel fifty instead of twenty-three. A dart? Perhaps an injection?

He'd known it was murder before, without any doubt, given the ritualistic cuts made across his chest. But if there was poison involved, that indicated careful planning. A memory surfaced, no more than a flash, of someone watching as the victim died.

He went to his writing desk and pulled out his journal and ink, angled the mirror this way and that, and tried to record what was left of the unknown word across his chest.

The letters looked foreign—Pedraisi. Having grown up in one of the provinces that bordered the country of Pedrossa, he was familiar with the appearance of their alphabet, even if he didn't read the language. He could speak a few words of it, but that was all. Many Larossans had blood ties back to Pedrossa, though, since both their peoples had come here centuries ago from the same part of the world. There were people in this city who *could* read and write that language, but also those who traded across the border or had old family ties. The city had its share of Pedraisi immigrants as well, blending in among the Larossans.

Mikael blew on the ink to dry it and then angled the mirror to look at the word again. *What does it mean?*

It had to be blood magic, sacrifice to a foreign god, asking for . . . *something*. Although blood magic was illegal in Larossa, it was still practiced. Some Larossans secretly begged favors of the old gods, even while being faithful to their true god. Most of the time it was harmless. A prick of a finger to cause a man to fall in love, or cutting the thumb to dab blood on a pennant meant to bring success in business. Or luck in cards, tiles, or any of a hundred other endeavors. There were a multitude of tiny ways that blood magic still appeared in day-to-day life among the Larossans, only most saw no harm in those small actions, no disloyalty to their true god.

Ending someone's life in this way, however, clearly crossed the line. Murder, even in the name of religion, was as unacceptable to the Pedraisi government as it was to the Larossan one.

Mikael couldn't begin to guess what those letters were meant to convey. He hoped that in time his memory would supply more, enough details to make sense of the fragments of the dream he *could* recall.

He always did his best to keep an open mind when he considered his dreamed murders. Sometimes something that seemed clear turned out to be completely wrong. Even so, if he could figure out what that word was, that might tell him who'd killed whom, and why.

CHAPTER FOUR

"So Shironne says we're looking for a man's body," Cerradine summed up Messine's words. "Near the river." They walked along the hallway toward his office in the army's Administration Building, his heels loud on the hard marble floors.

All of the buildings in this area of Noikinos were comparatively new, as the entire Seychas District—including Army Square—had been built where an old slum had been razed before Cerradine was born. As befitted the rising importance of the Larossan army at the time, the buildings surrounding Army Square were fine, with marble-floored hallways and wood paneling on the walls. Paintings of past generals gathered dust in niches along the walls, some festooned with aged pennants, their tips stained with those generals' blood.

"In a field," Messine said. "She didn't know what sort of crop, but she thought it had already been harvested." Still wearing the livery he wore in his false position at the Anjir household, the young lieutenant shook his head.

Although the young man had been working at the Anjir household for months now, it always surprised Cerradine to see him dressed as a servant, in that simple brown tunic and black trousers. He was accustomed to seeing his personnel—*Cerradine's children*, as the general often called them, only halfway in jest—in the blue and brown uniform of the army. Messine had volunteered to take the post, though, and had been diligent in watching over Shironne.

The young man followed Cerradine into his office at the end of the hall, a brown box of a room with wood paneling, a wood desk, and wooden chairs. The only brightness came from a framed map of the country hanging on one of the walls. Messine waited patiently as Cerradine puffed out his cheeks, contemplating Shironne's information again. It wasn't much to go on.

The Laksitya River curved along the city's edge for miles, and for miles in either direction from that, much of the land was cultivated. He wasn't a farmer, but he couldn't imagine any crops would still be in the fields, not with winter coming on. The hints of the body's location they had were nearly useless. And the death might not concern the army anyway. The location she'd described, however vaguely, suggested that when the body *was* found, the investigation would fall under the jurisdiction of the local police.

That had been a thorn in his side for years now. The army served the Anvarrid government of the country, not the local municipal government, a wholly Larossan body that controlled the day-to-day functions of the city. The local police, however, were notoriously corrupt, a condition on which the current police commissioner and the city's council turned a blind eye. Anyone who wanted a crime hidden, even a murder that smacked of blood magic, as Shironne's description hinted, need only pay off the correct officials to have a case disappear. As head of the army's intelligence and investigations office, Cerradine had made a point of wresting every case away from the local police that he could.

Cerradine turned back to young Messine. "Would you go down to the morgue and bring Kassannan back? And tell Aldassa to come talk to me."

"Yes, sir," Messine said sharply, and ducked out of the office.

Cerradine sat in one of the chairs in front of the desk and stretched out his long legs. He didn't want to waste his resources chasing a crime they couldn't even prove had happened. The office's personnel were already stretched thin. A number of them were currently off investigating the disappearance of one of their compatriots near the Pedraisi border, in Andersen Province.

Even so, while people were murdered in this city every day, only a select few deaths played out in Mikael Lee's dreams. There had to be some significance to that fact; there always was. And Shironne Anjir was always dragged into them.

Over the last four years, Shironne had regularly picked up on Mikael's dreams, even though he shouldn't have bothered anyone at that distance. Shironne was a profound sensitive, though, possibly the strongest of her generation. Beyond the normal ability to sense others' emotions, she could read information by touch, a very rare power. So while a medical examiner could tell him *information* about a man's death, Shironne could touch the dead man's mind. She could even pick out thoughts or memories, so long as the man in question hadn't been dead too long.

The true question, though, wasn't why Shironne was intercepting Mikael's dreams. It was why she'd become a touch-sensitive at all.

Most people looked at Shironne and saw an average Larossan girl. She was small and brown, like most Larossans. She dressed as a Larossan and lived in a Larossan household, but Cerradine knew Madam Anjir's secret. Shironne's mother was the child of an affair between a wealthy Larossan businessman's wife and the previous king, Khorasion of the House of Valaren. Madam Anjir was thus half-Anvarrid and a member of the Royal House, even if she chose not to acknowledge that fact. And she *was* a sensitive, but not a particularly strong one. Shironne's youngest sister, Melanna, also showed signs of developing into a sensitive, although she was nothing special in that way either.

So why Shironne? Why had she suddenly developed a power so crippling that she'd come close to starvation because she couldn't tolerate the impurities in food on her tongue? She'd been unable to don clothing at first, and even now kept her garments to a handful of well-worn items to which she'd become accustomed. Over the four years since her powers had first emerged, she'd learned to compensate for them. She'd slowly become accustomed to touching things again, although, when possible, she preferred to have the minimal barrier that wearing gloves provided. She was, as far as Cerradine knew, the only touch-sensitive alive . . . or at least the only one who had survived to adulthood.

That the Royal House had any sensitives in it at all was a result of centuries of intermarriage between the Anvarrid and the Six Families. That was how Shironne had inherited the few drops of Lucas blood that ran in her veins. But none of the Lucas children had her profound powers. And although many shared the *emotions* in Mikael's dreams—fear, helplessness, and anger—Shironne came out of those dreams with *details*. Details that Mikael himself often didn't recall.

Deborah, the Lucas Family's Head Infirmarian and his own foster sister, claimed that Mikael's dreams were a gift that ran in his father's bloodline, the House of Vandriyen. The Lucas Family had extensive records of the talents of different Anvarrid Houses, and over the last few years, Deborah had become an expert on those as she hunted for a way to tame Mikael's dreams . . . and to figure out the puzzle that Shironne Anjir presented.

Aldassa peered around the corner of the office door. "Orders, sir?"

Lieutenant David Aldassa was one of the many workers in this office whom Cerradine had managed to snag for the army before the Daujom could hire him. When half-Larossan children raised by the Lucas Family finished their three mandatory years of service as sentries, they usually left the fortress. Joining the army was an appealing option for them. Since they'd been raised to military discipline, they often advanced through the ranks quickly. Cerradine had even won grudging permission to hire young women, a saving grace for many of them, who would not have fared well when dumped into the Larossan populace without any family. Most knew little of Larossan culture, religion, or society. Most didn't even know how to find a place to live, clothing to wear, or food to eat.

Not having had such an opportunity himself when he'd come out of the Lucas Family, Cerradine had never regretted acting as an advocate for those young men and women. And David Aldassa had the best organizational skills of anyone Cerradine had hired for his office. He rarely forgot anything and always seemed to have the information needed in every crisis. "Go see if you can borrow a few squads to comb up and down the banks of the river."

"Body, male, unknown name, possibly blood magic?" Aldassa asked, proving that he already knew about Shironne's dream.

"That's the one," Cerradine told him.

Aldassa nodded once. "Right away, sir."

The young lieutenant had no sooner disappeared from the office doorway than Captain Kassannan appeared, looking like he might be Aldassa's older, and larger, brother. "Colonel?"

Like Cerradine and Aldassa, Kassannan was taller than most Larossans, a facet of their shared Anvarrid heritage. Kassannan showed more of his Larossan blood, though, with darker skin and a heavier build. Cerradine took after his late father. He'd inherited the man's height and leanness. Unfortunately, his father had passed on his prematurely white hair as well. Cerradine was only forty-four, but people often thought him far older on first sight. At thirty-six, Kassannan had not a single strand of gray in his hair.

"Sorry for dragging you up here, Aron," Cerradine said, "but I wanted to ask if your friend still worked at the city's morgue." Kassannan was a field surgeon, but he served as the army hospital's medical examiner, shut away in the hospital's basement morgue. He worked with Shironne more than anyone else did currently, so he would better grasp the meaning of the details she'd provided.

"Harinen? He does," Kassannan said. "Do we need his help?"

"Did Filip tell you about the latest dream?"

Kassannan nodded quickly. "On the walk over."

"Can your friend let us know if the man shows up there?"

Kassannan's mouth drew to one side as he seemed to consider making a macabre joke. He apparently thought better of it. "I can go down and talk to him. He should be there if I go now."

Cerradine was grateful for the captain's willingness to get involved in things that weren't *his* affair either. "If you will."

. . .

It was nearly noon by the time Mikael reached the office of the Daujom on One Above. When he unlocked the door, he found no one within. Dahar must have gone off to seek his lunch. Mikael locked the door behind him and went to sit on the edge of his desk, letting loose a sigh of relief. He didn't have to worry about his loud emotions bothering the sensitives when he was doing something as unexciting as reading files. He unhooked the high collar of his uniform jacket and contemplated the piles of paper on his desk.

Across the entryway from his own, Kai's desk was completely cleared, everything neatly tucked away where it belonged. Mikael's desk was a mess by comparison, even though nothing *secret* lay in view. This office was the public face of the Daujom, the place where Anvarrid House members filed complaints against one another, or railed at the Lucas Family for some imagined slight, so Mikael and Kai had to be prepared to deal with outsiders on short notice. Thinking of that, Mikael hooked the collar of his uniform jacket again. He needed to look official.

Dahar also had a desk at the far end of the office, a monstrosity carved of mahogany that rested near the black-draped windows. He rarely sat at it, though, preferring to pace the black and gray patterned floorcloths that separated the three desks. Over the years, Dahar had done his best to make this office into an extension of the fortress below, stripping away the bright colors, soft carpets, and wall hangings.

He's doing his best to make me *into a secretary.* Sighing, Mikael plucked the paperweight off the largest pile and lifted the top folder. Even though paperwork wasn't his favorite occupation, he'd become reasonably proficient at it.

He settled behind the desk and read through a series of letters copied from House Hedraya, already deciphered by the back office. Nothing there was particularly striking, although Lord Hedraya did plan to block the vote on Kai's confirmation as the king's heir in the spring. Instead of outright battles or assassinations, that was how the Anvarrid Houses fought now—machinations in the senate. Mikael made a note of the letter's contents and cited the source, then set that file aside to have the back office tuck it away. Everyone expected Lord Hedraya to attempt that, so the information wasn't surprising. And as Kai's confirmation was months away, it didn't pose an immediate concern.

That was the Daujom's primary function, to keep the king abreast of what happened in the various Anvarrid Houses. Many of the Daujom's workers were of Larossan descent, placed as servants where they could gather information on members of the senate. Others worked in the back office, sorting through every scrap of mail sent out by those households. It would be read, deciphered if necessary, copied if pertinent, and then usually sent on its way. But the personnel in the back office of the Daujom forwarded anything they thought might warrant attention to Mikael and Kai to determine if it should be brought to Dahar's attention and, thus, the king's.

As if in answer to that thought, a key rattled in the office door. Mikael glanced up in time to see Dahar letting himself in, a scowl on his face. Dahar had the tall, lean build common among the Anvarrid. He had dark hair worn short, olive skin, and bright green eyes that left little doubt as to his heritage, but as often happened with younger sons of Anvarrid rulers, he'd been passed off to the Lucas Family to raise. When Dahar's elder brother became king, he'd asked Dahar to come live in the Royal House's wing of the palace. Even so, Dahar persisted in wearing blacks—the uniform of the Lucas Family—just as Mikael did. If that offended the king, the man had never said so.

Dahar favored Mikael with a narrow-eyed gaze. "You dreamed last night."

No point denying that; Dahar had likely had bad dreams. "Yes, sir."

"Do you remember anything?"

"Not much, sir. I'm sure I'll hear when the body is found, though." He had a standing arrangement of a financial nature with one of the newspaper writers down in the city. The man sent word as soon as he learned of any curious murders. That had saved Mikael a good deal of legwork in the past.

Dahar strode over to Mikael's desk, picked up his paperweight, and stared at the river stone as if he'd never seen it before. "I've already received word from Jon that they're keeping an eye out for the body."

Jon would be Colonel Jon Cerradine, the head of the army's investigations branch. That he'd already sent out feelers about the death meant that the army's pet sensitive had picked up enough detail from the dream for them to know where to look. Mikael sat up straighter. "Should I go down and see them?"

His duties with the Daujom did *not* include investigating crimes against Larossan citizens. The Daujom's investigative jurisdiction extended only to crimes involving the Six Families or the Anvarrid Houses. But the army often collaborated with the Daujom because Cerradine and Dahar were old friends.

The Lucas Family, as part of their treaty, took in orphaned children of half-Anvarrid birth. It was a relic of the invasion, after which hundreds of children born of rape were abandoned either in temples or on the streets. Larossan women still took advantage of it on occasion, claiming that an unwanted child had been fathered by an Anvarrid master. Therefore, a handful of children were left at the gates to the palace grounds every year. Jon Cerradine had been one of those children, born to a housemaid in the home of the current Lord Hedraya's father. When that housemaid died, her six-year-old son was handed over to the Lucas Family like an unwanted puppy. He'd thrived there, though, and had become best friends with another boy thrust into the same yeargroup—Dahar.

Dahar sighed. "Put it off until we know more, Mikael."

"Yes, sir."

Dahar set down the paperweight and paced the area between Mikael's desk and Kai's. That meant he had more to say, but Mikael didn't know how long it would take him to get around to it. He returned to his paperwork, peering at the file on Hedraya once more.

"Has Kai said something to you?" Dahar asked abruptly.

Mikael paused in the midst of closing up the file. "No, sir. Kai doesn't confide in me."

"Something has gotten under his skin." Dahar scowled.

When is that not the case? "Perhaps you might ask Elder Deborah," Mikael suggested. "He's more likely to talk to his aunt than me."

Dahar shook his head. "I talked to her this morning."

He'd likely *yelled* at her. The two of them didn't rub along well, mostly because Dahar had been married to Deborah's sister. Deborah was Mikael's sponsor, though, the adult who'd taken responsibility for him when he'd first been sent to the Lucas Family by the Lee elders. Even though he was an adult and no longer required a sponsor, he still went to talk with her regularly. He respected her, even if he didn't always agree with her. Not only did she and Dahar argue over Dahar's children; since Dahar was Mikael's employer, they often fought over him as well, like two well-intentioned dogs with a bone.

Mikael sighed inwardly but did his best to swallow his resignation. Dahar would feel it. He *was* a sensitive, although not a very strong one. "I can't imagine whom you could ask, then, sir. Perhaps Rachel?"

Kai had two younger sisters, but they moved in very different circles than he did. Rachel, like Kai, lived among the Lucas Family in the fortress below. She was an engineer, though, which meant she spent all her time in the deepest depths of the fortress—Deep Below—and usually slept during the day. She was Mikael's age, and although he didn't know her well, he found her likable. Sera was a different story. Eighteen or so, Sera was difficult and angry and got along so poorly with her father that he'd sent her to a cousin in Halvdan Province to foster.

"I don't think Kai sees Rachel much." Dahar stalked away to the far end of the office, where the windows overlooked the courtyard at the back of the palace.

A knock came at the door, distracting Mikael from the letter in his hands. Glancing at Dahar for permission, Mikael went to the door and opened it. A young girl, a fifteen- or a sixteen-year-old, stood in the hallway, a slip of paper in her hand. Her uniform, similar in cut to his own but brown and without trim, identified her as a child. As she was assigned to runner duty, she was allowed to speak to him, although only in the course of her duties. She peered up at him with a properly expressionless face. "Mr. Lee?"

He nodded, and she handed him the paper. She inclined her head and jogged away to resume her post at the end of the hall, braids bobbing behind her.

The paper had his name on the outside in Deborah's tidy hand. As he'd guessed, a reminder for him to stop by the infirmary to speak with her before she got off duty. She always had him check in with her after one of his dreams. He only hoped she didn't ask too many pointed questions this time. He sighed, tucked the note in his jacket pocket, and headed back to his files.

"You left the door unlocked again," a voice said from behind him. Kai had come in so quietly that Mikael hadn't noticed him.

"Yes, I did," he admitted.

"You're supposed to keep it locked."

With himself and Dahar in the office, as well as a dozen sentries in the hallway, it was unlikely that a stranger could creep into the office unnoticed. "I'll keep that in mind."

"Kai, leave it alone," Dahar snapped.

Kai raised one dark eyebrow. Mikael didn't need to be a sensitive to know another argument was brewing between them. He *hated* getting caught up in the Valarens' fights. They always wanted him to take sides.

As such, it seemed a good time to go down to the mess, get something to eat, and make his requested visit to the infirmary. Mikael asked for Dahar's permission and then headed for the door, under Kai's baleful glare.

Just inside the doorway, Elisabet silently stepped to one side to let him pass. She held her precious rifle in one hand now. Mikael thought a frown fleeted across her cool, perfect features, but she turned her attention back to watching the office as if she'd never seen him at all.

CHAPTER FIVE

Mikael trotted down the wide stairwell that led from the first floor of the palace to the fortress below it. He paused at the halfway point, where the steps changed. At that point the white marble treads set in place by the Anvarrid gave way to the gray stone laid centuries before that by the Founders. He leaned down, touched the ancient stone, then brought his fingers to his lips, his unspoken oath of fealty as he entered the sovereign territory of the Lucas Family.

When he reached the bottom of the grand stair, he stopped at the landing to sign the log at the main doors, large wooden ones ornately carved around the edges with the geometric patterns the Lucas Family favored. In the flickering light of the lamps, Mikael smiled at the two sentries on duty, not wanting to intrude unpleasantly on their emotions. "Good morning to you both."

The younger he didn't know. Probably no older than an eighteen, she regarded him with skepticism, which told him she was the sensitive of the pair. Her pale eyes flickered over his uniform, taking in his trim markings. Then her eyes lifted to gaze at his face as she tried to judge his intentions. Mikael kept his thoughts mild and pleasant, but her nose wrinkled anyway, prompting him to reflect that her lack of control must be the reason she was down here instead of serving on the sentry line. If she couldn't hide her reactions better, she wouldn't ever be allowed aboveground.

"You're Mr. Lee," she said, making no effort to mask her distaste.

No, she definitely wasn't going to be allowed up into the palace anytime soon. Despite his broadcasting, Mikael did have his emotions under control most of the time. He knew better than to push them off onto others. And if this sentry couldn't handle him on a good day, she would find the disordered minds beyond the fortress walls unbearable. He didn't comment on that, though. He turned to the other sentry, Tobias, a man who saw him often enough not to question his existence. "I'm going to the mess."

With gray hair showing in his braids, Tobias might be the younger sentry's grandfather. He opened the main door and stepped aside. "Don't forget to check in with Elder Deborah."

Mikael shook his head as he passed. Everyone knew Deborah expected him. As the door closed behind him, he heard Tobias admonishing the young sentry to control herself.

After walking down a long hallway with bare stone walls, Mikael stopped at the inner door and laid one hand on the archway, this time assuring the fortress itself of his good intentions. Already warned by his first touch on the stair that he was coming, the fortress didn't react to him, not in any way that he could tell. Sensitives could *feel* the fortress welcoming them, but the onset of his dreams when he was a thirteen had erased whatever nascent sensitivity he'd once possessed. To him this was merely a stone archway. He walked through the arch to where the hallway emptied out into the commons under the glow of the fortress' unnatural light.

Here the walls and floors were worn smooth by the passage of thousands of feet and the touch of as many hands. It was a place of grayness—the walls, the floors. This far underground there was no sky, no stars at night. There was no weather to trouble them, and even in the coldest winter, the temperatures inside the fortress were bearable. That was, after all, the reason the Founders had built this place. When Father Winter returned to take back these lands, and glaciers scoured away all those living on the surface, the Six Families would be safe underground.

But Mikael missed the brighter colors, the blues and reds he'd known as a child in the Lee fortress. Here murals of geometric patterns were painted only in grays and black and white. The patterns were meant solely to calm, giving unruly minds a focus on which to concentrate. They told the viewer nothing of the purpose of any space, nor the direction to go to find anything. It was a tactic intended to confuse intruders. Family children memorized the layout early so that even if the fortress chose to let its lights go dark—as it did periodically—they would be able to make their way to a safe spot. Chevrons set at waist height on all the hallway walls directed them which way to go, even in complete darkness.

The commons was easy to find, though, not far past the entry. One of the great rooms of One Down, the commons was larger than most squares in the city of Noikinos and served a similar function. The mess operated out of the side farthest from the entry archway, the smells of bread and soup carrying on the air today. Groups scattered about the commons ate together and conversed in quiet voices. A yeargroup of twenty or so children in brown uniforms—eights or nines, Mikael guessed—turned to watch him walk along the wall. Their sponsor snapped his fingers, and they all turned away, although one child turned back to peek furtively at Mikael again.

As Mikael headed toward the mess, a pair of young women walked in the opposite direction, heading toward the main hallway to go downstairs to the residential levels. Judging by their sweat-dampened shirts and unbuttoned vests, they'd recently come up from the sparring floor on Six Down. Once sentries were off duty, full uniform wasn't required inside the fortress. Unfortunately, the same wasn't true for Mikael, since he lived in the palace above.

One of the young women smiled at him and appraised him with heavy-lidded eyes, while the other tsked under her breath. Mikael smiled back at the first, who sidled closer and stopped him with a hand on his arm.

Jannika was exactly the person he needed at the moment. They'd parted ways amicably enough, but she'd been avoiding him for months, likely because she'd dropped him for one of the men in the twenty-fives—Elisabet's yeargroup. That relationship must have ended, though, if she'd stopped to make conversation with him.

"Mikael, I haven't seen you in a long time," she observed, a winsome smile on her full lips.

Her friend stopped a few feet away, one tapping foot signaling her impatience. Iselin, Mikael recalled, Jannika's yearmate and closest friend. Iselin was one of the strong sensitives and thus inclined to dislike him, especially on the day after one of his dreams. He nodded politely to her and turned back to the woman before him. He looked down to meet her eyes—one of Jannika's many attractions was that she was actually shorter than him.

"Would you have time to chat this evening?" Mikael asked.

Jannika was a weak sensitive and thus found him interesting. He was easy for her to sense. The sensitives with very little talent were always the ones who tolerated him best. "I'm heading to bed," she told him, fingering the First trim on his sleeve. "But maybe tomorrow? I've got early duty on Three Above, so after that?"

For the Six Families, the world was defined by where they were in the palace . . . or the fortress below it, often simply called Above and Below. Certainly, Mikael could wait until after Jannika's duty shift to ask what he wanted about Kai. "I'll see you then."

Jannika walked away with only one glance over her shoulder and rejoined her friend. Mikael watched her swaying hips as they headed on toward the main stairwell, thinking the day suddenly had much more promise. He doubted she wanted anything serious of him—certainly not a contract—but it was pleasant to be chased for a change.

A low whistle sounded nearby, though, a sure sign he'd irritated someone. The Family was taught young to control their emotions, especially in the presence of children. Whistling served as a polite notice that someone's feelings were running questionably high. Mikael heard it more frequently than most.

He breathed in slowly. His reaction to Jannika probably hadn't been inappropriate for the younger children seated across the commons to share. Well, he hoped not. Then again, it wouldn't have been anything they hadn't sensed before. By eight or nine, young sensitives had been exposed to almost every emotion that existed. It was more a matter of controlling the intensity and duration of that exposure. So Mikael concentrated on thinking nothing, feeling nothing.

After a moment he opened his eyes and, ignoring the whispering voices in the commons, went to the mess counter to pick up lunch.

. . .

The infirmary on One Down was near the center of the fortress, so it took a few minutes for Mikael to reach it, as he carefully carried the mess tray along the featureless halls. It was a path he'd memorized long before. A few people spoke to him in passing, but most went by in silence, intent on their own business.

One of the brightest areas in the fortress, the infirmary usually held a few patients, even on the slow days. As he entered with his tray in his hands, Mikael nodded to the infirmarian on duty, Jakob. Wearing informal blacks, Jakob sat next to one of the beds, working with a girl in brown trousers and a baggy sweater. He carefully wrapped the child's ankle under the watchful eyes of one of her yeargroup's sponsors. The sponsor glanced up, nodded once to Mikael, and turned back to his charge.

Mikael walked through the main ward, carefully keeping his thoughts cheerful. Past the neat rows of empty beds, there were a series of narrow hallways where the infirmarians had their offices and rooms for private examinations. Even though she was Head Infirmarian, Deborah's office was a small room with books and periodicals stacked on every horizontal surface. Three sturdy wooden chairs crowded about her battered desk, which, at the moment, would serve as an impromptu mess table as well. Mikael often took his meals in her office, worried that Deborah might forget to eat if he didn't.

Deborah's black uniform jacket hung from the back of her chair, the long-skirted formal one she wore when volunteering down at the City Hospital. She must have gone out first thing in the morning. She always returned from such endeavors exhausted, but Mikael knew it gave her a chance to keep in touch with physicians outside the fortress. Her jacket's presence meant she was somewhere nearby, but there was no telling when she would get back to her office. Mikael checked his watch and, noting the time, started to eat. After consuming about half of the soup he'd brought for himself, he set down his bowl, fingered his right shoulder, and grimaced. His skin still felt tender.

Deborah stepped into the office just then and caught the expression on his face. "Are you all right, dear?"

"I'm fine, ma'am," he lied. She wasn't a sensitive, so she wouldn't know.

She settled across from him and uncovered the bowl of soup he'd brought for her. She wore her blond hair in a single braid, one of the advantages of being past the years of compulsory sentry duty: she didn't have to wear her hair in the required pattern of braids any longer. One of the first things Mikael had done after completing his three years was cut off his hair. Since then he'd worn it in the short crop most Anvarrid men currently favored.

"I was down at the City Hospital this morning and spoke with some of the doctors," she told him, stopping to blow on a spoonful of soup. "None of them heard of any unusual deaths last night."

"It may be days before we hear anything," Mikael said with a shrug. His relationship to the dreams often took weeks, or even months, to become clear. The worst of them he dreamed over and over, nightmares returning sporadically until he found the victim's killer. Even a decade later, he still dreamed of his father's death on occasion.

"How are you feeling?" she asked.

"Tired, and I was short of breath earlier." No harm in admitting that.

She leaned back in her seat, head tilted as she gazed at him. At forty-four, she was old enough to be his mother, although just barely. "There's more to it than that. What happened this time?"

"In the dream? I don't remember much."

"I didn't mean in the dream, Mikael. What happened *after*? Elisabet said I needed to talk to you."

Elisabet wouldn't have told Deborah about the blood that had seeped through his jacket. Instead she'd probably suggested that Deborah pry harder than usual to get information out of him. He couldn't even resent Elisabet's interference. She meant well by it. If Elisabet wanted to get him in trouble, she would have told *Kai*.

But Mikael didn't know what to tell Deborah. If Deborah knew the full extent of his dreams' effects on his body, she would order him kept under her thumb at all times—for his own good. The idea of losing his freedom, though, worried him, and the potential effect on the fortress' sensitives didn't bear thinking on. "I just . . ."

Deborah's brows rose.

"I had some blistering across my chest," he finished weakly.

"Why didn't you come down here straightaway so I could look at it?" she asked. "Or Jakob if I hadn't returned yet?"

"It's gone by now, anyway," Mikael said dismissively, hoping she wouldn't march him into the main infirmary and order him to take off his shirt. "When that happens, it's usually gone within a few hours."

Deborah continued to gaze at him with a narrow line between her brows, so Mikael thought calming thoughts at her. Even though she wasn't a sensitive, she might be influenced. As she wasn't a child, it was merely rude, not forbidden. But someone out in the main infirmary whistled, making him regret his pushiness.

"I think it might be wise," she said, "to have you stay here the next time you feel a dream coming on."

In a fortress full of sensitives? He tamped down his doubtful reaction. They'd tried that a couple of times when he'd first come here four years past. The sensitives had not been happy. What Deborah didn't know was that his dreams were much worse now. "I can't do that, Deborah."

"If we keep you sedated, that should limit your broadcasting as effectively as alcohol."

Should. Mikael swallowed, fighting down the twinge of panic at the back of his mind. They'd discussed that a couple of years ago, but he hadn't tried it because the system he had *worked.* Or it worked in terms of minimizing the exposure of the sensitives in the fortress to his dreams. The alcohol didn't control his dreams in any way, though, nor did it mitigate the toll the deaths took on his body.

If she kept him here, Deborah would learn how close he came to dying each time he dreamed. He felt worse every time now. He recovered, of course, but he worried that one day soon he simply wouldn't wake at all, too closely tied to the victim to escape his or her death.

"Do you think the sensitives here are so weak that they can't handle what you do with every dream?" she asked when he didn't respond.

"No, of course not," he said quickly. "I simply don't want to drag them into my dreams."

She gazed at him a moment longer. "While your current method of handling the issue does limit their exposure, it doesn't help you *understand* your dreams in any way. If you weren't intoxicated, it might be easier for you to recall facets of your dream."

He hadn't done that intentionally in years. It left every emotion in his dream bare, and that would be horrible for the sensitives. "I don't recall that it ever made a difference."

Deborah gazed at him, brow rumpled.

She wanted the best for him, he knew. She was hunting for a way for him to both recall his dreams *and* not bother the sensitives. Mikael wasn't certain the two could ever be balanced. No matter how hard Deborah fought to keep him here in Lucas Province, there were some among the elders of the Lucas Family who disapproved of his presence. So far, the elders had elected to let him stay, but he never took that for granted.

"It might be months, anyway," he tried. "Until the next dream, I mean." The longest he'd gone without a dream was four months, just after he'd moved to Noikinos. He'd actually believed for a time that the dreams might never come back. It had been an appalling disappointment when the first one hit.

"True." Deborah picked up her spoon again.

Mikael ate the remainder of his own meal, trying to decide how he could get himself out of this situation. If he couldn't, things were going to be very unpleasant indeed.

CHAPTER SIX

Mikael rose and dressed earlier than normal the next morning, hoping to get to the office early and catch up on some of the paperwork he'd missed the morning before. He cheated and went down to the palace kitchens to grab a meal—lamb and egg hash this morning—rather than going down the grand stair to the mess in Below. Fortunately, the palace kitchen workers liked him and didn't seem to mind.

Mikael let himself into the office and went still, surprised to find Dahar and Kai already there, both standing on the far side of the office near Dahar's desk. Dahar's arms were crossed over his chest, and his jaw was clenched. Mikael couldn't see Kai's face from where he stood, but he had no doubt he'd walked in on another argument. Whatever they were saying to each other, they kept it low enough that Mikael couldn't hear them.

Elisabet waited near the door, rifle propped against her foot. Mikael glanced at her and raised his eyebrows, but she didn't respond. He would swear she was unhappy about whatever Kai and Dahar were discussing, but her face seemed impassive, as always.

"What is this about?" he asked her softly.

She only shook her head.

Kai abruptly walked away from his father, passed Mikael without speaking, opened the office door, and left, forcing Elisabet to gather her rifle and hurry after him. Dahar still stood by his desk, arms folded and one fist held against his lips—the same gesture Kai made when upset. His eyes were fixed on the windows across from him, but Mikael doubted he saw anything beyond them. "Is there anything I can help with, sir?"

Dahar's head snapped toward him. "Don't get in the middle."

He was *always* in the middle with the Valarens.

Mikael sat at his desk and began sorting through the paperwork left there. There were two new folders from Anna, the chief officer in the back rooms, both concerning the Hedraya issue. He kept his eyes on the papers in front of him, determined to plow through the files he'd not read the day before.

"What do you have on your schedule today?" Dahar asked, surprising him. He'd approached while Mikael had his head down.

Mikael drew out his schedule. Dahar could have picked it up and looked at it himself, but he preferred to be told. "I have a session with Eli at noon," he said, "and I'm supposed to meet a friend at dinnertime."

Eli was his only swordsmanship student, a test from the elders to see whether he could be trusted to control his emotions around children, so Mikael did his best not to miss any appointments with the young man. If he did well with Eli, they might let him work a few more students into his schedule, although at this rate it would take years to earn the status of fight master.

"Who?" Dahar asked.

"Eli," Mikael repeated. "Of the sixteens."

"I meant for dinner," Dahar said, sounding vexed.

That was one of the advantages of being a member of the Royal House—no one expected Dahar to control his emotions, even though he'd been trained by the Family. Mikael opened his mouth to answer Dahar's question, only to stop himself before he blurted out Jannika's name.

When Mikael had first come to Lucas Province as a nineteen, Dahar had come up with the strange idea that Mikael should marry his daughter Sera. The girl had been a thirteen or fourteen then, and quite obnoxious. No agreement had been signed, but Dahar still had the idea in his head that Mikael should be betrothed to his daughter.

"Just a friend," Mikael managed. "I'm trying to get some information. And after that I'm going down into the city to meet with one of the writers."

"Hunting your dead body?" Dahar said dryly.

Mikael didn't think for a moment that Dahar had missed that he'd not answered the first question. "He's got a friend in the police."

"You're duplicating Cerradine's efforts, then," Dahar said.

That wasn't strictly true. Cerradine was looking for a corpse, while Mikael was only looking for a name. "I'll be off duty, sir."

Dahar sighed and strode off, back to his end of the office. Mikael resumed reading, imagining Dahar's glare on his back. When he glanced in that direction, Dahar stood at the windows, staring moodily outside. Mikael forced his attention to stay on the papers before him.

A crash came from the other side of the room. Mikael jumped to his feet, hand reaching for a pistol he didn't have.

Just Dahar, he realized a panicked second later.

The fine porcelain tea set that had been sitting on a tray on Dahar's desk now lay shattered against the far wall. Dahar strode the length of the office, opened the door, and slammed it on the way out.

What was that about? Mikael felt reasonably sure that it wasn't his evasive answer that had triggered it. This had to be about Kai and whatever they had been arguing about so quietly before Mikael had arrived. Poor timing on Kai's part. Dahar was never at his best first thing in the morning, before his tea.

And Kai *had* been avoiding his father. Kai had other commitments. They all did. There was a schedule on Kai's desk that showed his teaching duties, his required sessions with the king, and his time to work on his own yeargroup's schedules and issues. That was why Dahar needed two aides—Kai simply had too many other duties.

Mikael suspected if he asked Kai, he would probably have to listen to a long-winded answer that made perfect sense. Whether it was true or not was another thing altogether.

Sighing, Mikael crossed to the other end of the room, turned over the wooden tray, and began picking up the broken bits of the tea set. It wasn't as if they let maids into the Daujom's offices to clean, not without an appointment. And since he was alone now, that left no doubt whose job it was.

. . .

Shironne woke that morning relieved that she'd had an uninterrupted night's sleep. A message from the colonel told her that they hadn't yet found the body from her dream, so she took her time over breakfast and getting dressed before asking Messine to escort her to Army Square.

Messine helped her down from the family's old coach, and then their driver drove back home so that her mother could take Perrin for a fitting for a new outfit. One of the army's drivers could take them back home later. "So just working in Kassannan's office today?" Messine asked.

She was at her best, her *most useful,* when she had a body or the site of a crime to examine. Although Captain Kassannan and his orderlies came up with much of the same information she did, she always found *more.* But they had actual crimes to work on only infrequently. She sometimes had to remind herself that was a good thing. "Yes. Unless they've found that body in the interim."

She'd begun working for the army three years ago. Her maid's lover had been murdered, and the woman had poured out her distress while braiding Shironne's hair. Shironne had sat befuddled, recognizing in the woman's tale snippets of the nightmare she'd suffered a few nights before. Until that discussion, she'd tried to forget the dream. But after that, she rashly promised her maid she would help find out who'd killed the man, a sergeant in the army. Fortunately, her mother had supported her in her desire to find some way to do so. Without her husband's permission, she'd taken

Shironne to Colonel Cerradine's office, and he had actually listened to her, despite how far-fetched her story seemed.

In the years since, Shironne had worked hard to develop her odd powers into tools that could be used to find killers. She watched her dreams now with a more careful eye. She paid attention to everything she touched, knowing that each item she could label increased her effectiveness. "Yes, I'm sure the captain has things for me to identify," she answered Messine. "He always does."

"I'll stay in the office, then," Messine said. "Help Pamini look over the reports from Andersen."

Ah yes, the man missing out in Andersen Province. Shironne didn't think she'd ever met the absent Paal Endiren, but the others were worried about the length of time he'd been gone. Messine walked her down to the army hospital's basement and left her there with Captain Kassannan.

"The squads the colonel sent out to comb along the river's banks haven't found anything," Kassannan said, getting down to business immediately. "They did, however, retrieve a bunch of soil samples for me."

He was always finding new challenges for her. She'd spent the first few months working with him learning all the proper names for the anatomy and all the things that could go wrong in death. Then she'd moved on to learning minerals and metals, plants and woods and fabrics. Evidently this week's visits would entail the study of soil samples . . . unless they found that body.

Sometime later, she sat on a tall bench before one of the worktables, Kassannan handing her samples and one of the orderlies silently taking notes. She dipped one finger gingerly into the small glass dish, the essences within sparkling into her inner vision on contact with her skin. Sand, hard and cool in her mind, washed by the familiar water of the Laksitya River, tiny bits worn down from granite: quartz, mica, and feldspar. She felt no stain of sewage on the grains, which told her the sample had been taken upstream of the city. Black soil, rich with humus, probably carried off from a farm farther upstream. Fibers from the stems of stiff plants like those used to make baskets. A scale from a fish nestled among the grains and silt, totally different in composition, with a shining durability she could only imagine now. A memory of the iridescent fish swimming in the clear pool in a garden somewhere drifted into her mind, evoking a smile. It had been summer, warm and green, the countryside, and she'd been a little girl.

"Well, Miss Anjir?" The captain's voice intruded on her concentration. "What do you think?"

Shironne took a deep breath. "This sample's from upstream. Probably a place where people fish. There's green matter in it, something tough and fibrous, so I suspect it's close to, or downstream from, that shallow edge of the river with all the reeds."

His approval wrapped around her like a warm smile. "Very good," he said. "But why the people fishing?"

As the orderly's pen scratched on paper, Shironne spun her finger about in the grains again, double-checking her conclusions. "I feel a fish scale in here. Just one, but it's there. It could be from something else, but fishing is the most logical explanation."

"I'll have to look at that sample again," he noted. "It is from upstream, south of the reeds, but I didn't spot the scale. Corporal, make a note of that."

"Yes, sir," the young man said from off to her left.

Shironne felt the glass bowl easing away from her, so she lifted her hand. She laid her hand back in her lap to grasp the crystal lying there and focused her powers on it. "Do you need to stop?" the captain asked, concern welling about him.

Shironne drew a slow breath and retreated from her focus. "No, I'm fine. A bit cold."

"Want your jacket?"

The basement room was always cool, but as the ground grew colder with the onset of winter, so did Kassannan's office. Since the series of rooms he ruled occasionally held the bodies of army personnel who'd died in questionable ways, the chill was a welcome quality. It suppressed smells that could be quite horrid in the warmer seasons.

"No, I'll be fine." She heard the faint scrape of another glass bowl being pushed toward her along the marble surface of the tabletop and shifted on her tall metal stool. They'd been working for more than an hour now, and her rump was getting numb.

"Try this one, then," he said.

One of the good things about Captain Kassannan. He never treated her like a helpless child, the way some adults persisted in doing. Despite being nearly two decades older than her seventeen, the captain treated her like a colleague, even a friend. He had worked with her on enough investigations that they'd developed a solid working relationship.

Shironne lifted her hand from her lap and held it over the small bowl. Even without touching it, she knew the sample contained remnants of living matter. *Blood.* This soil had been drenched in it. She wrapped her other hand—still gloved—around her focus to help mitigate the initial shock. "There's blood in this sample."

"I wasn't aware of that." His alarm jarred her determination. "You can skip this one."

Shironne licked her lip, a nervous gesture that she'd never managed to quell. She tasted smoke from oily house fires on her tongue and humidity from the river on her lips. She cringed, ingesting sooty particles left by the smoke. Someday she would learn not to do that. "No," she told him. "I'll do it."

One of the odder aspects of her powers was that she could tell if blood came from a man or a woman, and if it was someone she knew, she might even recognize whose it was. While that might seem a trivial thing, it had been pivotal in solving the murder of an army lieutenant only a few months past—that of Captain Kassannan's wife, Hanna, one of the office's lieutenants. At first her death had been seen as an accident, the result of an exploding gas line. But Shironne had recognized a puddle of blood some distance away from Hanna's body as hers, which meant her body had been moved.

Her killer had tried to make her death look like an accident when it wasn't.

The difference in the blood from man to woman, or from person to person, was impossible for her to describe, but she always *knew.*

Before he could slide the bowl away, she touched her finger to the soil in it. The feel of the blood welled through her senses, redness creeping up that finger to cover her hand and then crawling up her arm under her sleeves. It became colder in the office, far colder than it truly was, sending shivers through her thin frame despite her wool tunic, undershirt, and layers of petticoats. She clenched her jaw, forcing herself to remain calm, to master her reaction rather than letting it control her. She tried instead to feel the soil and its remnants of river water and plant matter and the leavings of fish. "This came from the very edge of the river. There was blood there, but then it washed away."

"And you can still sense it?"

Even when he couldn't verify it under his magnifying lenses, she could still *feel* things with her powers. Unfortunately, it meant he had only her word for it. Fortunately, he never doubted her. "Yes. The blood is a day or two old. Human. A woman, so it can't be from the man in my dream. It has . . ."

How could she explain the glow the blood had taken on in her mind? It was hot and hostile, angry. Licked up by a hungry river, mostly borne away on its tongue. "It has the feel of magic about it," she finally admitted. "I think she made a blood sacrifice at the river's edge."

She could sense the orderly's disgust as clearly as if he'd spoken it aloud. Shironne pushed the man's reaction to a distance.

Kassannan found the idea of blood magic curious but didn't react otherwise. He had little tolerance for superstition, possibly one of the reasons he was so good at his work, but neither did he judge others for it. The surgeon slid away that bowl, his mind turning in ordered thought that reminded Shironne of the ticking of a clock. "Make a note of that site," he said, and the orderly's pen scratched on paper again. "There's a new cloth in front of you."

The captain kept new cloths on hand just for her, knowing that every time a piece of fabric was laundered, the wash water deposited matter from other items on it. Bits of lint from the machine that wove the cloth and a hint of oil from the surgeon's hand clung to the new fibers anyway, but it was far purer than anything that came from a public laundry. Shironne took the cloth in her gloved hand and began rubbing her finger, scrubbing away the remnants of the blood- and magic-stained soil.

"I wonder if it happened in the same place where the victim in your dream died," Kassannan mused.

"I don't think so. That seemed like a field, and this soil is too sandy to be anywhere but the edge of the river." Shironne shook her head. A stray lock of hair, loosened from her braid, drifted across her forehead, bearing with it the touch of the soap she'd used to wash it the previous night and the lemon water she'd rinsed it in afterward to make it shine. Both familiar to her, so it wasn't troubling. She tucked the strand behind one ear with her gloved hand, the threadbare cotton tickling her skin. Her own possessions rarely bothered her any longer. She was accustomed to the feel of her well-worn clothes. Unfamiliar things—*those* were far harder to deal with. If they were clean, she could accept them easily, but if they'd been handled by others, worn, or even laundered, they would have distracting contaminants on them. She focused her attention on the captain again. "Why can no one talk to me about him?"

Kassannan didn't pretend not to know whom she meant. Not the victim in the dream, but the dreamer himself. "People like him," Kassannan said gently, "can be dangerous. They tend to overpower those who are receptive to their will, so you, especially, shouldn't go near him."

Especially. This was part of the *childhood* thing.

The Lucas Family had strangely strict rules about who could

interact with a child. Many of the colonel's personnel had been raised in the fortress, and they retained those beliefs even now that they lived outside the fortress. The rules were meant to keep young sensitives from being influenced by the thoughts of an adult who might try to take advantage of them. She understood that logic. That didn't mean it didn't irritate her. Even though she was seventeen *now*, they wouldn't consider her seventeen—an adult—until the New Year. They grouped all their children by age at the beginning of the year, apparently to save confusion, but it seemed silly to think she didn't have the strength of will to fight off an intrusive mind today, but *would* after the first day of the year.

"So he's loud," she noted. "Anvarrid always are."

"He's a broadcaster," Kassannan said mildly, his uniform jacket rustling as he shrugged. "Not just loud. That means he can influence others. He pushes his dreams off on you. Does that not bother you?"

Shironne thought for a moment and then realized that her mouth was hanging open. She shut it. "I think he's only desperate for someone to hear him."

She had Kassannan's full attention now. "Is that what it seems like to you?" he asked. "That he wants to be heard?"

Shironne dropped one hand to her lap, where the crystal lay. She chased the captain's question through her mind, trying to reassemble all her impressions of the dreams over the last few years. They'd slowly become easier for her to follow, but much of that ease came from understanding what it was she was experiencing. She'd made an *effort* to recall the dreams, but they were still fuzzy and veiled. It was almost like he was trying to be heard, and trying *not* to be heard. She explained that to the captain, who listened to her verdict with his mind clicking away like clockwork.

"What reason might he have for not wanting to be heard?" Kassannan asked.

"I guess he's trying to protect people." She could hear the orderly writing that down, as if what she said was actually important.

"Wouldn't it be easier, then, not to broadcast his dreams at all?" Kassannan asked.

"I don't think he can help that," she said. "I mean, if you had a choice whether to dream those dreams, would you?"

"Hmm . . ." The captain paused before answering. "I suppose not. Shall we move on?"

The truth was, though, *she might*. If she had those dreams, she probably would try to use them. As overwhelming and awful as her own power had been at first, laying her open to everything around her, she had learned to use it. She didn't know if she would give that up.

Kassannan pushed another bowl in her direction. Shironne took a deep breath and set her finger into the contents, her attention only halfway on the mixture of minerals.

After they finished working through the exercises Kassannan had planned for her, he escorted her back to the main office, where Messine was working, helping Ensign Pamini—one of the office's newest workers—sort through a large folder full of reports that had come in from their agents working in Andersen Province. Before she could collect Messine and leave, though, the colonel asked her to come back to his office.

Shironne walked behind him along the paneled halls, terrain familiar enough that she didn't need anyone to direct her. When she reached the doorway, she stepped inside, felt for the high back of one of the wooden chairs, and sat, tugging her braid out of the way first so she wouldn't sit on it.

She'd always liked the colonel. The very first time he'd met her, he'd listened to her talk about that quick promise made to her maid. He'd listened while she'd discussed her powers and hadn't dismissed her as insane. But what had actually won her over was his reaction to her mother. The colonel had noticed a bruise on her mother's cheek and, rather than asking what she'd done to earn her husband's ire, had been furious. That had raised the colonel to a very lofty position in her mind, and he had yet to disappoint her.

Although it was uncommon for a Larossan widow to remarry, Shironne suspected her mother was considering it. Given her mother's dislike of scandal, it said a great deal that she was willing to face censure for his sake. Of course, neither of them had said anything to her, but Shironne could hardly miss the way the colonel reacted to her mother, or her mother reacted to his presence.

But today, she was sure the colonel wanted to talk about something else.

"I wanted to talk to you about your father," he began, which presaged something unpleasant.

Anything to do with her late father was unpleasant. Her father had been abusive, unkind, and unfaithful to her mother. Only after Shironne had started working for the colonel's office had she learned that her father was using his position as one of the city's aldermen for personal gain. Blackmail seemed to be his preferred source of income, earning him enemies, and although his close ties to the police had always protected him from charges before, evidence had surfaced that beggar children had been disappearing off the street. That had caused the city's religious leaders to pressure the authorities into an investigation. The police had been on the brink of arresting her father when he'd died in an inglorious fashion, stabbed by his young mistress.

"What is it this time?" she asked, resigned to more bad news.

He shifted. It sounded to her like he was sitting on the edge of his desk again. "You recall that we had a man who followed the trail of the child-transportation scheme all the way out to Andersen Province, don't you?"

Child-transportation scheme was a polite way of saying that her father had been selling those children stolen off the streets of Noikinos to Pedraisi clans, either for slave labor or for other purposes that she didn't want to examine too closely. "Endiren," she said. "Kassannan told me about him. He's been missing for a while now, hasn't he?"

"Since shortly before your father died. Endiren was following the trail of a caravan bearing children, possibly the last one that left Noikinos. Since the victim in your most recent dream was likely killed in some form of blood magic, there *might* be a relationship between the two. A very slim chance, but I wanted to ask if your mother has received any correspondence addressed to your father."

As a widow in mourning, her mother should not receive male visitors outside her own family, so the colonel couldn't ask her those questions directly. "I will ask, sir, although I suspect if she had, she would have already forwarded it to you."

"It is . . . a delicate subject," the colonel said, pushing a sense of wanting to be trusted at her.

Shironne smiled. He hadn't had an opportunity to speak with her mother since her father's death, and she suspected that he wanted news of Savelle Anjir more than he wanted any letters. "I understand, sir."

"You always do," he said.

CHAPTER SEVEN

Mikael's sparring session with his student, Eli, helped work out some of his frustrations with his inability to do anything about the death in his dream. Teaching was one of the ways he felt he actually could earn his place in the Lucas Family. If they ever let him have more students, that was.

But he had a couple of leads to pursue, so after he went off duty, Mikael headed down to Below to find Jannika. It was shortly after the shift change, so while she ate, he sat with one leg folded beneath him on the wooden chair, sipping an overly hot cup of tea.

Jannika had chosen a table on the far edge of the mess and sat stirring her soup—a bean soup this time that smelled exceptionally meaty. The mess was crowded with tired sentries, so Mikael's emotions weren't likely to stand out above the ambient in the room. It was currently the overwhelming group feeling of relief and pleasure at having come off a long, chilly shift. The comfort of bootlaces loosened, jackets and overcoats set aside. No one even gave Mikael a second glance at this hour, but he held his thoughts quiet to keep it that way.

Jannika began their conversation by bemoaning the state of her feet. Since she'd just come off duty, Mikael didn't blame her. Every sentry complained, just as he had back in Lee Province. And while he hadn't stood sentry duty since then, the previous year he'd been sent to investigate a violation of the treaty in Jannsen Province. The Jannsen Family had refused to provide guards for the Anvarrid House ruling there, and as part of his intervention, Mikael had served as a guard while the House and Family involved worked out their problems.

Jannika set down her spoon and leaned closer. "So what happened in your office today? Iselin said the prince slipped rather spectacularly. A big explosion of fury, she called it. She was on Two Above directly over the Daujom's offices, so she felt it."

Iselin said. Mikael sighed inwardly, suspecting that Iselin blamed him for that incident. But it did save him time fishing about for a tactful way to insert his desired topic into the conversation. "You know I can't discuss that with you."

Jannika sat back in her chair and actually smiled at him. "And?"

Lucas girls didn't smile much. It was one of the things he missed from Lee; people there smiled more. The Lucas Family took itself far too seriously, even when not on duty.

As if to belie that thought, the occupants of the long table nearest them broke up in sudden laughter, the volume about them rising sharply before it settled again to normal.

"Well, it wasn't my fault," Mikael said to Jannika with relative surety. "I can tell you that much."

There was a limit to what he could say about Dahar without feeling disloyal. He didn't have many sources of information among the Lucas Family, though. Deborah wouldn't discuss her nephew with him. Mikael wouldn't go to Elisabet, either. Asking her to share what she knew might put her in an uncomfortable spot since she was both Kai's guard *and* under Deborah's sponsorship. Eli was far too straightlaced to gossip. No, Jannika was his best bet for rooting out what he wanted to know.

So when she continued to smile at him, he added, "He had an argument with Kai, and that set him off."

The sentries in the hallways would have noticed Dahar's stalking out of the office shortly after Kai's exit, so Mikael wasn't giving away anything that wasn't common knowledge.

Jannika shook her head and picked up her spoon again. "The chaplains should lock them up."

Mikael choked on his tea. It was an old tactic, to take a pair of complainants and lock them in a room together until they worked out their differences. He could only imagine how poorly that would work out. Dahar would not take well to being told what to do and would rant about the elders overstepping the bounds of their authority. Kai would sit down in a corner and furiously ignore his father. "That's an interesting image," Mikael managed after a moment. "I *do* think Kai's upset about something."

Now, *that* was walking the line.

Jannika took a bite of her soup. "Kai's difficult. That's what I heard from Demas."

Ah yes, Demas was the man in the twenty-fives for whom she'd broken off *their* relationship. And while Mikael didn't care about Demas' opinion one way or another, Demas was in Elisabet's yeargroup. Elisabet was Kai's primary guard and would never gossip, but Tova and Peder filled in for her when she had other commitments. Surely one of them let something slip. "Did he ever stand in for Elisabet?"

Jannika shook her head. "No. The others just talked about Kai a great deal. I would have tea with them in the evenings back then. You should come visit the twenty-twos."

Mikael nearly dropped his teacup, but ruthlessly tamped down his surprise at that offer. He'd believed that Jannika wasn't after a contract, but he might have to change that assessment. An invitation to join a yeargroup for an evening was tantamount to courtship. Each yeargroup had a delicate balance of *togetherness*, their own particular way of acting that kept the yeargroup comfortable and happy—the sensitives in particular. Introducing a new person into the group was a delicate proposition, rarely undertaken lightly.

"I didn't mean it *that* way," she said quickly, which let him know she hadn't missed his reaction. "I only think you should socialize with the yeargroups more, get to know some of us."

He'd never been asked. Never, not even when he'd been involved with Jannika the year before. The twenty-threes, who were his own age, had never made any friendly overtures, and the twenty-fours were Kai's group. Kai was *definitely* not welcoming. "I don't know how the elders would feel about that."

Jannika shrugged, her braids slipping back over her black-clad shoulder. "If I took off my boot, would you rub my foot?"

How can I say no to that? "Of course."

She pried off one boot with her other foot, revealing a grayed sock—everything eventually turned gray in the laundry—and set the foot on the edge of his chair. Mikael obligingly rubbed the arch of her foot, provoking another smile from her.

"You're not serious about this, are you?" she asked, her head tilting slightly.

She meant a potential relationship, he decided. He stopped rubbing, startled, until her eyebrows rose. "I don't know," he finally admitted.

Jannika was simple, one of the things he liked about her. She was easy to talk with. She had siblings and parents who were on good terms, pleasant friends—save for Iselin—and she didn't have grand designs for her life. Or *his,* for that matter. He wasn't sure whether she even knew about the Anvarrid side of his parentage and all the complications that came with that. They certainly hadn't discussed his father. Or, more to the point, his grandfather.

There were reasons he'd never worried about finding a wife. He was only twenty-three. Plenty of Family men his age weren't married. There was the niggling issue of Dahar's wanting him to marry his daughter too. But most of all, Mikael wasn't entirely certain he would live through his next dream. That would be a miserable thing to wish on any woman. Until his dreams were under control, he couldn't see himself taking a wife.

He rubbed her foot with one hand and lifted his teacup with the other. "I'm not averse."

She leaned farther back in her chair and set her foot on his thigh, allowing him to rub her ankle. The familiarity, which would have caused rebuke at any other time of day, was permissible at this hour in the mess, since there wouldn't be any children around. This was a time slot reserved for adults.

He could feel an anklet under her sock, a fine chain. Sentries weren't allowed any jewelry that would show, but if they could hide it under their uniforms, it was permitted. He'd have to remember that if he decided to buy her a present. Had the one she wore now come from Demas?

"This wasn't an advance," she said, "so why *are* we having dinner? Or tea, in your case."

Another thing he liked about Jannika—her directness. She'd assumed his asking to join her had been a prelude to courtship on *his* part. "I was hoping to find out if you've heard any rumors."

"About?"

"Kai."

"Most of them are common knowledge," she said with half a shrug. "He's obsessed with Elisabet but he's not bedding her, or rather she doesn't let him. On the other hand, Tova is more than willing to take Elisabet's place, although she's not as good as Elisabet."

Jannika meant, he suspected, that Elisabet was a better choice as *guard*, not a reference to any romantic advantages Tova—Elisabet's Second among the female contingent of the twenty-fives—might or might not have. Mikael had heard all of that before, although never stated as bluntly. "That's old news."

"True." She contemplated as she ate a bit more of her soup. "He's been especially short-tempered lately. I *have* heard that."

Again, nothing he didn't know.

"There *was* some nasty gossip about him that came out a few weeks ago, but I don't know what it was. The twenty-fives all shushed the person who hinted at it, like they'd spoken of poison."

Mikael rubbed the tendon at the back of her ankle and rolled her foot around. *A few weeks ago—that might be around the right time.*

"That's what you're after, right?" Jannika asked before he had to ask.

"I wouldn't know until I heard it."

"And what do you intend to do with it?"

"Again, I won't know until I know what it is."

"Hmm." She regarded him, eyes narrowed. "I could ask around."

"Without getting into trouble?"

She shrugged. "Would you make it worth my time?"

"That depends on how much of your time I'm repaying you."

"Never a straight answer from you," she complained halfheartedly.

He gave her his brightest smile, wishing very delicately for her to trust him. Her brows rose again, but he suspected he'd won. He unfolded his legs so he could get a better grasp on her foot.

"Now, that I do remember," she said, eyes closing with pleasure. "Strong hands. Can't you come down this evening?"

He sighed, actually regretting that he couldn't. He probably could have talked her into rubbing his feet in return, and while his feet didn't hurt, he hadn't been this close to a woman in months. Not in any capacity other than professional. He missed simple exchanges like this. "I'm sorry. I have to meet a writer for dinner to pry out some information."

Her eyes opened halfway. "A woman writer?"

Was she going to be jealous over him? That would be a novel experience, one he might enjoy. "A writer for one of the Larossan newspapers, so no."

"Ah. That's fine, then," she said. "Do you have time to do the other foot, at least?"

CHAPTER EIGHT

Mama's room smelled of vanilla and sandalwood. Shironne breathed it in as her mother brushed out her hair, her mother's bracelet tinkling with every movement. The little bells were soothing. Her mother brushed out her hair every night, and the ritual gave structure to their evening, a chance to talk privately while the governess made certain her two younger sisters bathed adequately.

Unlike her mother's smooth hair, Shironne's curled wildly and cracked with static in the winter as the house grew drier from the fires. Her hair picked up things from the air, touches of smoke and pollen and dust carried on the wind. Ash and soot from the fireplaces. Her mother brushed it out nightly, rubbing it with a damp towel first to remove some of the impurities and tame the curls.

Her mother's sleeve grazed the side of Shironne's neck, a startling touch. Even her nightdress was of undyed cotton, another sign of mourning. Her mother insisted on strictly following the mourning customs, so she hadn't been out to any gathering since her husband's death, nor had she gone to the temple. Honestly, Shironne suspected it was an excuse to stay at home. Her mother had always hated attention, a trait grown out of weathering the scandals that surrounded her own mother. The death of Shironne's father in disreputable circumstances had only fed her mother's determination to behave the way the most stringent members of Larossan society expected.

Savelle Anjir had other options. Shironne knew that, even if her younger sisters didn't.

Her mother had been born of an affair with the previous king, making the current king her half brother. He and his younger brother had secretly corresponded with her in the past, offering to acknowledge her as their sister and a member of their House. Even though the former king had never admitted fathering Savelle Anjir, Anvarrid Houses apparently allowed for members to be *adopted*, given that a large enough percentage of the House agreed.

It sounded almost like an election to Shironne, probably carried out in some dark hall where the members of that House wore robes covered with at least a year's worth of embroidery work and grumbled about the cold. Colonel Cerradine had once joked that all Anvarrid were required to complain about the cold winters, even though they'd lived in Larossa for centuries now. Shironne laughed softly at that thought.

"What is it, sweetheart?" her mother asked.

Her mother was prickly about the subject of adoption. Instead of accepting her brothers' offer, Mama preferred to hide the scandal that surrounded her birth. If that became common knowledge, it might hurt Perrin's chance of finding a proper Larossan husband. Shironne had tried to keep her own work with the army quiet for the same reason, knowing that such an unconventional choice for a young woman could reflect badly on her younger sisters, although being blind meant she was given some leeway. Most families with a blind daughter would simply ship her off to some relative in the countryside or to an asylum. Shironne was grateful that her mother loved her enough to keep her close despite the potential for outrage should it get out what she actually did for the army.

But Perrin dreamed of finding a wealthy suitor, a goal that Shironne had always found perplexing, given the example of their own father. When he'd asked for her mother's hand, he'd appeared wealthy and charming. It hadn't taken long for those perceptions to prove false. Among his other sins, he had been a terrible spendthrift, going through Mama's dowry and then selling off most of the properties she'd inherited. Perrin was convinced that she would choose the *perfect* husband, despite her young age, and Mama was determined to give Perrin that opportunity. Shironne hoped that when it came time to accept an offer, Mama carefully vetted Perrin's choices. She wasn't convinced that Perrin would pick wisely on her own.

The fact that the Royal House was wealthy simply made the choice more difficult for her mother. Adoption might ease all their financial woes. But her mother had been raised with very Larossan sensibilities, and therefore the idea of becoming an Anvarrid citizen and stepping into the ruling class seemed wrong to her.

Knowing her mother wouldn't want to talk about *that* topic, Shironne said, "The colonel was asking after you today."

The brush paused in its motion. "Was he? What did he want?"

"I suspect he wanted to know how you're faring, but he actually *asked* if you'd received any letters sent to my father after his death." Hearing the first part of that sentence had made her mother feel warm, as if she'd flushed. The second part of that sentence left her cold.

Her mother sighed. "I will write to our business manager," she said. "He's not brought anything to my attention, but he likely doesn't wish to disturb my mourning with something that I cannot change."

The business manager had been hired recently, after Shironne's father's death, in an effort to retrieve any funds possible from her father's *legal* business ventures, and to sever ties to any ventures that weren't legal. Fortunately, Cerradine had recommended the man, which meant they could trust him. The man's wife accompanied him on his visits for propriety's sake, so he'd been able to speak with her mother directly about the situation. His findings had not been favorable so far, though, and coming up with the money to present Perrin to society was stretching the family's already limited budget.

"The colonel thinks that there might be some relationship between Father's past business ventures and the dream I had." After giving the request some thought, Shironne had mentally dismissed that as a pretext on the colonel's part, but she did her best to make her words sound sincere.

Her mother laughed softly. "Well, it won't hurt me to ask, will it?"

"No, Mama. And when you do hear back, I could take a note to the colonel from you."

"I shall consider that," she replied, still amused.

Having carried out the colonel's request, Shironne's mind turned back to the conversation she'd had with Kassannan. "Mama, when the angel dreams, do you feel like he's talking to you?"

Her mother didn't seem surprised by the change of topic. "If he is," she said in her velvety voice, "he's not doing a particularly good job."

"I feel like he is," Shironne said, and went on to relate most of what she and Kassannan had discussed that morning.

"I see." Her mother tucked that away in her mind, perhaps to worry over later. Her mother did that, stewing over things for days before she acted. It was one of the ways they were different—Shironne simply lacked her patience. There were times when Shironne regretted her rashness, but her mother's lack of impulsiveness sometimes irritated her as well.

Then again, she hadn't had her mother's life. Her mother had *secrets*, things that she never wanted to come to light. Shironne need only touch her mother's skin to access her thoughts, fluttering around like butterflies. If she waited long enough, she could find all her mother's secrets, but she didn't want to do that. She wanted to keep her mother's trust, so she didn't pry. Instead they talked about her mother's upcoming trip to the countryside to begin the process of selling the fine country estate where Savelle Anjir had lived as a child. Her mother hoped the excursion would produce enough funds that they wouldn't be forced to let any of the servants go.

The sound of feet in the hallway and the tinkle of a differently pitched bracelet warned Shironne that Melanna had finally escaped her bath. She suspected her youngest sister would forgo baths altogether if allowed. A moment later, Melanna, smelling of soap and damp skin, bounded into the bedroom and pounced onto Mama's bed.

Perrin followed more sedately, her slippered feet nearly silent. She'd worked hard to attain a graceful walk, but her bracelet gave her away.

Shironne gave over her position on her mother's bed so that her mother could comb out Perrin's less troublesome hair, and the conversation naturally turned to Perrin's new clothing and jewelry and music lessons. Unlike the rest of them, Perrin had no powers, and thus never could sense any undercurrent of emotion in the room. While Shironne sat on the bench near the wall, braiding her own hair for the night, Melanna curled up next to her and thought aggravated thoughts about what she perceived as their sister's silly obsessions.

Shironne ignored Perrin's chatter, her thoughts turning back to the Angel of Death. She wished she knew who he was so she could have a better sense of him. She wanted to understand why he did this, why it seemed like he singled her out. Was it because she was such a strong sensitive? Or just because he felt like no one else was listening to him?

She might still be a child by their standards, but in a few months, she was going to be an adult. Despite Kassannan's concerns, she didn't think that the angel would overpower her. Once the New Year came, she was going to pester the colonel until he did introduce her to the man.

. . .

Joio Dimani was a young man of clear Larossan descent, his skin a medium brown and his eyes so dark they seemed black. He'd proven willing to work with the Daujom, providing information for a small stipend and an occasional story lead. So far it had been a mutually beneficial arrangement, as Dimani knew Larossan society far better than Mikael ever would.

Mikael enjoyed the times he could get out and try new foods.

The chicken curry he ate wasn't particularly strong, just enough to be thoroughly enjoyable. The restaurant, with its fine red-draped tables and efficient waiters, was a hint of what his life would be like if he left the Family and lived in the Anvarrid world his father had occupied. His grandfather's world.

He usually ignored that traitorous impulse. He *was* Family. He belonged in the Family. But at times, especially after a dream that made the sensitives despise him, it seemed a seductive possibility.

His grandfather, Lord Vandriyen, was the Master of Lee Province. Mikael's father, Valerion, had been the favored son, the chosen heir. But Valerion had been missing for almost a decade now, and Mikael's grandfather stubbornly refused to name a new heir, claiming that Valerion would return. Should Lord Vandriyen die without doing so, Mikael would become the new Lord Vandriyen by default.

Mikael knew his father was dead. He'd dreamed it, many times.

"Do you have any idea how many people disappear every day in a city this size?" Dimani was saying. His dark brows raised, he pushed a sheet of paper across the red tablecloth to Mikael. "These are only the ones who were reported to the police. I've crossed off the ones who disappeared *before* that night. That should help a bit."

Noikinos was the capital and currently held almost two hundred thousand lives spilling down the sides of the hills and onto the plain on the other side of the Laksitya River, the vast majority of them Larossan. Dozens of people disappeared daily, although many did so by choice, fleeing creditors, abusers, or responsibilities. Or looking for a new life. The police generally waited a few days before beginning any investigation, believing that such a gap would decrease their workload.

"I do appreciate that," Mikael said, glancing down at the list.

Joio sat back. "I certainly hope so. That fat ass Faralis asked why I was asking for that, and I had to make up a story about a cousin who'd . . ."

He went on to describe his run-in with Police Commissioner Faralis, who was rampantly unpopular these days, given the man's well-known corruption. Mikael had stopped paying attention, though. He was staring down at the list the writer had given him.

One of those names was *his*.

Not his in the sense that it said *Mikael Lee* there, but he'd worn the name for a brief time in his sleep. His mind had made contact with the victim's. He'd known what the victim knew, only it was buried deep in his brain. Bits and hints would float to the surface of his mind, the victim's fleeting memories. Sometimes that helped him find the killer. Sometimes it didn't.

Liran Prifata. He'd *been* Liran Prifata for a time. He'd shared the man's death.

His breath came short, and he tried to crush down the fear he didn't quite recall. A sudden headache dug its talons into his brain, sending twinges of nausea through his gut. He turned the list back toward Dimani and pointed. "This is the one, Liran Prifata. He's dead."

Mouth hanging open, Dimani didn't say anything.

I interrupted him while he was speaking. He probably thinks I'm crazed now.

"I'm sorry," Mikael managed, rubbing his temple with his free hand. "I recognized his name. But if you start asking questions, I think you'll find he's dead. In a manner sensational enough to sell newspapers, I'm afraid."

Dimani had taken out a notepad and was taking notes. "How do you know that? Does his death fall under the purview of your office?"

Mikael knew nothing about the man in question, but given the Larossan name, it was unlikely. Then again, if he dreamed the man's death, somehow it *would* become his concern eventually. That was a self-fulfilling prophecy for the most part, since once he dreamed of a death, he felt obligated to pursue the killer. "I don't know," he admitted. "Does his name mean anything to you?"

"No," Dimani said.

Mikael mentally cursed at his aching head. When he had flashes of memory from one of his dreams, the associated pain usually faded after a moment. It was lingering this time. "I feel certain it's important to the Daujom, somehow. I don't know the link yet."

"This is one of those things, isn't it?" Dimani asked warily. "Because you're a witch?"

Mikael bit down his irritation. That was Larossan terminology, calling *any* talent witchcraft. Dimani hadn't meant to be offensive. He simply didn't see any distinction. Mikael pinched the bridge of his nose, feeling the urge to abandon this meeting. "Yes."

Dimani gazed at him, perturbed. Larossans had a strange relationship with their witches. They were respected, but given that the majority entered the priesthood, most Larossans wouldn't wish it for their children unless they were poor. The loss of autonomy upon entering the priesthood was accepted as necessary for the greater good of the people, but was periodically called into question, almost as if it were a form of *slavery* rather than duty. Most Family—raised from infancy to *serve*—found that protest inexplicable.

He *would* choose the restricted life of the Family over his father's life any day. Unfortunately, he would probably always be caught between the two worlds.

"Do you have any idea what time this happened?" Dimani asked.

"Between midnight and one." That was what he'd heard from Deborah. The sensitives who were awake often felt just a touch of his dream and could report the time, even if *he* slept through the whole affair.

He sat back, his thoughts clarifying. He had a headache, not simply left over from the memory of the dream. It was one of *those*, a harbinger of death. *Can the dream be repeating?*

There were some dreams that repeated, over and over, until he solved the crime, but to have only one night passing between dreams was unusual. There must be something particularly urgent about this man's murder.

Then Mikael laughed softly. For tonight he'd escaped Deborah's well-meaning orders. He *should* return to the fortress and let

Deborah keep watch over his dreams in the infirmary, using some soporific to keep him from inflicting his dreams on the sensitives. He should.

But he wasn't going to. Not tonight. He was outside the fortress and thus beyond Deborah's reach.

"I need to head down into the Old Town," he told Dimani. After cleaning his hands on a damp towel, Mikael took thirty royals out of his wallet, more than enough to pay the restaurant's bill, and handed it to Dimani. "If you could pay, I would greatly appreciate it."

Dimani regarded him with suspicious eyes but agreed, and a few minutes later Mikael was walking down the narrow, stone-walled streets of the Old Town toward the Hermlin Black. He walked through the tavern's back courtyard, past the stables, where the number of horses told him the tavern was crowded. He let himself into the tavern's back entrance, through the kitchen.

Synen's son didn't look surprised to see him. "There's a creepy moon tonight," he said as he gathered two fistfuls of mugs to carry out into the common room of the tavern. "Looks orange. Good night for killing someone."

Mikael didn't tell the young man there wouldn't be a fresh death, merely a repeat of his earlier dream. The smells from the massive stove made him consider a second dinner, but he wanted a bottle more.

"I'll ask Father to set up a room for you," the young man said as he headed out the kitchen door.

It's nice to have an arrangement. Mikael took off his overcoat and hung it among the others on hooks near the kitchen door. One of the waitresses came back into the kitchen and smiled winsomely at Mikael, her gold earrings flashing with a toss of her head. "Hello again, Mikael."

Oh, Father Winter, what's her name? He was supposed to know, since she'd come up and sat with him one night the previous year when he'd reportedly started screaming in his sleep. Apparently Synen's customers had found it disturbing; Synen had ordered the girl to hold a pillow over Mikael's mouth to stifle the sound. He was lucky the girl hadn't suffocated him.

She was pretty, with thick, dark hair, brown eyes that glittered with merriment, and the ready smile that he liked so much about Larossan girls. Even so, he didn't recall ever having a lengthy conversation with her, and had no idea if she was kind or cruel, or somewhere between. At least, he'd never had a conversation with her that he remembered. They might have talked at some point when he was drunk. Given her apparent perception of familiarity, perhaps they had.

Merival, that's it.

"Good evening, Merival," he managed with moderate certainty. "How are you this evening?"

She sidled closer, so he'd gotten the name right, at least. "Better, now that you've come to visit."

"I'm just going upstairs tonight, get some sleep," he said quickly.

"We all know what you think passes for sleep." She ladled curry into a shallow bowl and set it on her tray. "Keep yourself quiet this time."

Mikael hoped he could manage that. Synen, his dark face flushed from rushing about, strode into the kitchen a moment later, a broad smile creasing his features. "Back again already, boy? I've got number four open."

He'd yet to come here and find that Synen didn't have a room open for him. He often wondered if Synen tossed other patrons out to make room for him, since he faithfully paid his bills. "Thank you, sir."

"Why don't you follow me on up, boy?" Synen held the kitchen door open and Mikael trailed him out to the stairwell at the edge of the tavern floor.

The patronage of the tavern was usually exclusively Larossan, but Mikael could see a group of five young men at one table in the corner who could pass for Anvarrid. Or half bloods perhaps, although they certainly weren't ones who'd been raised by the Family, given their boisterous behavior.

"Are they a problem?" Mikael asked, pointing toward them with his chin as he mounted the stairs.

Synen glanced back at him and snorted. "Not worth dragging the palace into it. They come, get drunk, fondle the waitresses, but in the end they leave."

The Daujom wouldn't get involved unless there was a crime committed. Mikael pinched his nose but gazed back at the men, fixing those faces in his memory anyway. "Does the name Liran Prifata mean anything to you?" he asked Synen then.

"Are you courting him too?" Synen asked with a grin.

Mikael paused on the next-to-last step, his stomach sinking again. "Too?"

Chuckling, Synen led him along the mezzanine walkway. "Merival said you didn't remember her."

His host had reached the appropriate room and opened the door to let Mikael inside—the yellow room again.

"Remember what about her, exactly?" Mikael managed in what he hoped sounded like a calm voice.

"That you asked her to marry you," Synen said, a wide grin splitting his face.

He wasn't sure whether that was the truth . . . or an expression of Synen's sense of humor. Mikael stepped inside the shabby bedroom. "Uh . . . when was this?"

"That night you were screaming." Synen laughed jovially. "Months ago. You were pretty drunk, son."

He didn't recall much of that night, but Synen had sent her up to quiet him. That had been her with the pillow, hadn't it? For the first time, Deborah's idea didn't sound like a bad thing.

Mikael sighed. "I didn't mean . . . I'm sort of engaged already."

"Sort of? You don't sound pleased about it."

He hadn't mentioned Sera when he'd talked to Jannika, but

Sera did make a convenient excuse at times. Deborah had told him the elders wouldn't approve the match with Dahar's daughter, so he'd never taken it too seriously, but he needed to get that straightened out with Dahar one of these days. Mikael hated the idea of disappointing him.

"The girl's . . . temperamental," he told Synen, which was the absolute truth.

"You're just lucky Merival knows you Family boys don't have any money. She might have held you to it."

Mikael cringed. People talked to Synen, so Mikael considered it possible that the innkeeper had actually heard of his legal situation. He would inherit a fortune when his father was eventually declared dead.

"I'll send my boy up with a bottle," Synen said, patting his shoulder. "You should lock the door after that, in case Merival changes her mind."

Mikael sat down on the shabby bed, gazed at the wood of the closed door, and rubbed fingers across his aching forehead. The statue of the Larossans' true god seemed to smile at him from its corner. He grinned at a sudden memory of his father talking about how the House gods of the Anvarrid were made up, that none of the Anvarrid actually believed in them but each House felt they *had* to have them if other Houses did. His father had put more trust in Father Winter, who, although distant and incorporeal, seemed to have kept the Six Families safe. The Larossans believed that their true god was simply another face of Father Winter—or the opposite; Mikael had never been certain which way that went—but that smiling icon in the corner never offered him any protection from his dreams.

Why was this dream recurring so quickly? What made Liran Prifata so important? Mikael closed his eyes, trying to dig up any memory of the first dream, but it eluded him, like fog slipping through his fingers.

A tap came at the door, and he pushed himself off the bed. He eased the door open a crack, and Synen's son passed a bottle of oak-aged whiskey through the narrow opening and hurried away. Mikael shut the door and sat on the edge of the bed again.

He gazed down at the bottle and the golden whiskey inside. When had this gone from being a temporary measure to take the edge from his broadcasting to the only thing that kept him from drowning others in his dreams? Who had suggested alcohol in the first place? It hadn't been long after he'd arrived in Lucas Province, back when his dreams hadn't been nearly so urgent.

Perhaps the reason they were so bad was the alcohol itself. He frowned down at the bottle, wondering if he shouldn't go back up to the fortress and put himself in Deborah's hands after all.

But the bed, while shabby, was comfortable. And he was already here. He considered the bottle a moment longer, then lifted it to his lips and drank.

CHAPTER NINE

Shironne had only half dressed when she heard footsteps coming up the stairs that led to the kitchen. *Kirya,* she decided, recognizing the bells she wore and the disciplined determination of her mind.

"Ah, Miss Anjir," Kirya's voice said then, confirming her guess. "Messine is down in the kitchen, asking to talk to you."

That saved her time, since she would have had to send for him anyway. She'd had another dream, this one bizarrely similar to the one two nights ago, yet different enough to assure her that the victim hadn't been the same. She wasn't sure how to quantify that for the colonel, what evidence led her to that conclusion, but she felt certain of it anyway.

One thing she never saw in the dream was the victim's face. The colonel guessed that was because the victim couldn't see his own face, and therefore the angel—who was touching that victim's mind—couldn't see the face, either. That also implied that the angel could know only what the victim knew, if he remembered it at all.

"I'm on my way down. Tell him I'll be there in a moment." Shironne walked toward the stairwell, trailing one hand against the plastered wall. Kirya's footsteps clicked back down the steps. Shironne followed as quickly as she could, coming down into a kitchen full of busy minds.

Melanna was already there, irritated and itching to know what was happening, with Cook bidding her to sit down again and *eat.* Perrin was trying to look pretty. At least that was what Shironne called it to herself. Whenever an attractive male showed up—in this case Filip Messine—Perrin did her best to be *pleasing*. Perrin had told her more than once that Messine was handsome. Shironne hadn't told her sister that the lieutenant returned her admiration, primarily because it was Messine's business to do so, not hers. But somehow she doubted he *would* do so, given that Perrin was even younger than Shironne herself.

"Miss Anjir," Messine said quickly. "Captain Kassannan is out in the mews, wanting to know if your mother would let you go to view . . . a *person* with him."

A body, he meant. Shironne didn't need any more clarification than that. Messine didn't want to talk about a dead body in the kitchen. Not in front of Perrin or Melanna, even though they knew what manner of work their elder sister did for the army. "I'll go ask my mother."

"Would you like me to go up, miss?" Kirya inserted. "Kassannan's in a hurry."

And she could get up and down the stairs faster. When Shironne agreed, Kirya's feet fled back up the stairs, along with her determination. Shironne went to sit in her usual chair but kept her face turned toward Messine. "Did Kassannan say why he's in a hurry?"

"Not in his office," Messine answered, not making sense. "He's wanting to take you down to the city's morgue. On the sly, I think."

The *city* morgue? That *was* odd. "He thinks they have one of the people I dreamed about?"

It was the only explanation she had for Kassannan wanting to take her down there, where he had no authority.

"*One* of them?" Messine asked, mind clicking away now. "Did you dream again last night? That would be why the brown's so cranky."

The brown was his way of referring to a child. A rude noise came from where Melanna sat. Shironne smiled. She would bet that interchange involved Melanna sticking her tongue out at Messine. While Perrin worked hard to be a perfectly behaved young lady,

Melanna had a very long way to go. Verinne, her sisters' elderly governess, claimed that Melanna would drive her to her death.

Cook brought her a plate then that smelled of flatbread, potatoes, and onions. Shironne removed her gloves and set them in her lap before carefully touching the plate with a finger to locate the flatbread. Cook had filled the bread for her, making it simpler to handle.

This was the hardest part of her day, facing food. She picked up the stuffed flatbread and took a large bite, chewing and swallowing before too much information from her overly sensitive tongue reached her mind. The water the potatoes and onions had been cooked in was clean, though, and she was accustomed now to the spices Cook used.

It hadn't been that way at first, when she'd abruptly become sensitive to everything that touched her skin. She hadn't been able to eat, since her tongue and lips had been even more sensitive than her hands. Fortunately, Cook had thought to boil milk for her. That helped tremendously, eliminating many of the impurities she'd sensed in it. In time she'd learned to stomach foods again, although she still balked at most meats.

She'd managed to consume four bites when she heard her mother coming down the stairs. Shironne laid down the flatbread and found the warm, damp cloth Cook had laid next to her plate. Her mother's hand touched her shoulder. "Is this something you want to do, sweetheart?"

Her mother's concern was held tight around her, like a shawl. Shironne thought she must have a headache, given her unusual agitation. "I think it would be best, Mama. Kassannan wouldn't ask if he didn't think it was important."

"I've asked Kirya to bring your coat and your leather slippers." Her mother touched Shironne's braid, her bracelet tinkling. "You'll be especially careful down there, won't you?"

"Of course, Mama." Her mother had always insisted on her remaining independent. That didn't mean her mother didn't want to protect her. "Kassannan will look after me."

"The colonel asked that I accompany them as well, Madam Anjir," Messine said, provoking a flash of jealousy from Perrin. "We'll keep her safe."

Feet descending into the kitchen heralded Kirya's return, and she carried with her the familiar smell of Shironne's coat. After a moment of wrangling with her garments, Shironne was ready to go. She tugged on the leather gloves that she'd left in one of the coat's pockets.

Messine helped her up into the coach that waited in the house's back courtyard. Shironne thanked him absently and arranged her petticoats and coat about her on the seat while she exchanged greetings with Captain Kassannan. The carriage shifted and creaked as Messine climbed inside, choosing the opposite corner from her, next to Kassannan. She reached up and found a hand strap, and the carriage lurched into motion. "Are we actually going to the city morgue?" she asked.

"Yes," Kassannan assured her. "My friend there says a body was brought in during the early hours, dragged out of the river by some fishermen. He says we should hurry, though."

"Why?" She could feel Kassannan's puzzlement, so she didn't think he knew the answer.

"He didn't say—or rather, the beggar boy he sent with the message didn't—but the boy did tell me the police were disturbed."

"He didn't die in the river," she said. "Not in the dream. I'm sure of that."

Kassannan made a humming sound that meant he was thinking.

"And I had another dream last night. It was very similar, so it had to be the same killers."

Kassannan's concern rose. "Why didn't you tell me that?"

"I just did," she pointed out, asperity in her voice.

Filip Messine's mind laughed, but he quickly tucked that emotion away, returning to listening to the traffic. Shironne clutched the hand strap as the driver took a curve more quickly than she'd expected. The carriage slowed, though, as they headed into traffic.

The sounds of horses and pedestrian bustle assailed her, all the noise of the morning rush into the Old Town. The streets smelled of manure and mud, and the buildings of moldering stone. The air reached damp and chill fingers into the carriage, brushing her sensitive skin.

Eventually, they came to a halt somewhere not far from the low rush of the river. She could smell the green dirtiness of downstream, the river's water fouled with sewage. The Lower Town, Shironne reckoned, or the edge of it, where the poorest citizens of Noikinos lived. That was surely the reason the morgue was down here; no one would notice another building with a foul odor.

Messine leaned past her to open the door, his sleeve brushing her coat. He stepped down, helped her from her seat, and then set her hand on his arm and led her inside. Even though she was blind and needed some guidance, touching an unrelated man in public was still forbidden, but since Messine dressed as a servant, it would be ignored. Kassannan walked behind them, his mind already occupied with whatever waited for them inside.

The outer door closed, leaving them in some manner of anteroom where an officious-minded man surveyed Shironne with disdain. "Are you here to claim a body?"

"To identify one," Kassannan answered. "Can I see Officer Harinen?"

The man reflected an irritation that Shironne suspected was accompanied by a rolling of his eyes. A wooden chair scraped across softer wood—tired floorboards. Then his footsteps moved toward their right. Another door swung on its hinges, and the man hollered Harinen's name down along an echoing hallway.

The movement of the door had carried with it a draft of air from farther back in the building. The scents of decay and ammonia and death billowed into the room about them. This morgue lacked the cleanliness the army insisted upon in theirs, Shironne decided, or possibly the ventilation.

She heard another man's approach, his heels ringing on a stone floor, coming up along that long hallway. A mind worrying, furtive. The door swung open again, and something caught Kassannan's attention. "Come with me," he said.

She could feel Messine's resignation. "You could stay here," she offered. "I'll be fine with the captain."

Messine's relief was palpable. Dead bodies turned his stomach. "I'll wait right here, then."

With that settled, Kassannan lifted her hand onto his sleeve and led her after the other man, holding open the door so she wouldn't have to touch it. The floor under her feet changed from wood to stone, and the smells grew stronger as he escorted her down the echoing hallway. He opened a well-oiled door, and they came to a halt in a larger room. Harinen reflected worry. "Should she be in here?"

"She's my assistant," Kassannan lied. "Don't worry, she's done this sort of thing before."

"Isn't she a bit young?"

"I'm seventeen," Shironne answered him. "But I've been . . ."

A warning blared through Kassannan's mind, almost taking the form of words, and she stopped speaking.

"It's better you forget she was here," Kassannan said softly.

Officer Harinen contemplated that for a moment, mind spinning amid a sea of worries. This situation must be terribly uncomfortable for him, and Shironne suspected it wasn't merely due to her presence. "Yes, that's best," the officer said. "The faster you're out of here, the better. Come look at him."

"Do you have an identity yet?" Kassannan asked.

The man moved about, pulling back the sheets that covered a nearby body. Smells roiled into the room with the motion. Shironne breathed through her mouth, forcing herself to ignore the stench. The corpse had to be two days dead, but she wasn't smelling the body nearly as much as she was smelling the scent of downstream, the area where sewage emptied into the river.

"We don't have a name, and he came out of the river only wearing trousers," the officer said, "but those were dove gray."

Shironne pressed her lips together. That wasn't actually a comment on the color of the man's trousers. The officer meant instead that the man's trousers were part of a police uniform. The distinctive color had earned the police the nickname of *pigeons*.

They were looking at the body of a police officer.

"Oh *Hel*," Kassannan swore softly.

Kassannan had stepped away from her when the officer uncovered the body, but she carefully stepped closer to the spot from which he'd spoken. He apologized, took her gloved hand, and laid it on the edge of a table. "Give me a moment," he told her, agitated now. "Stay here."

He was concerned about something. It was more than just that their victim was a police officer, so she did her best to be patient. Kassannan opened up his bag and a second later Shironne smelled ink. For a short time, she heard the nib of Kassannan's pen scratching across paper. Then it stopped.

"I've got it," he said. "Now let's see what you can tell me."

Ah, now it's my turn. "May I touch him?"

That brought another flare of worry from Officer Harinen. It was bad enough that she was facing what must be a nude body, but now she wanted to touch it. "Should she be doing this?"

"She's perfectly fine," Kassannan said. "Go ahead."

Shironne reached out her hand and touched a familiar surface. Recognizing the rubbery texture of a corpse's skin, she took off her right glove, tucked it into a coat pocket, and laid her hand on the body. The feel of river water reached her first through the light contact. She pressed her hand more firmly against the side of the man's chest. His skin shifted slightly under her fingers, already losing its fragile hold on muscles and bone. The impulses of his dead mind flooded through the contact, though, immediately overriding the physical impressions. Faint memories lingered in this body: of whom he'd been in life, of how he had died.

"His name was Liran Prifata and he *was* a police officer," she said.

"How does she know that?" Officer Harinen whispered, not quietly enough.

"She's simply does," Kassannan replied.

"The body still holds traces of memory, even though the spirit is gone. The memories are like leaves fallen off a tree. They don't know they're dead yet. So this told me," she said, laying her bare hand against the man's torn chest. She concentrated, sifting through the disordered fragments of memory. "Three nights ago. He didn't know why they took him, I think. He asked over and over *why*, but they never answered him."

That reinforced her impressions from her dream.

"They? More than one?" the officer asked.

She'd been sure about that beforehand, given what she recalled of the dreams. "Yes, but I'm not sure how many. They pulled him into a coach and took him somewhere near the river. The memories that still exist are hazy, though, much more so than normal for a body this long gone. I don't know why."

She stood there for a time, considering those dead leaves of memory, trying to determine what from among them she needed to know. Their dry whispers echoed in her mind, reflecting fear and protesting the senseless death. A blasphemous death.

One leaf told her of a sense of protection, though. At the end, the police officer had felt a presence with him. Shironne smiled, recognizing the angel's presence. Every time she touched a body from one of his dreams, she found that sense of protection in the fragments of the victim's mind.

Shironne set that leaf aside, sifting again through the dead man's thoughts. Other memories vied for her attention: falling dazed in the street, the sound of his wife's voice, the scent of spiced tea on a chilly morning, the sharp sting of a late mosquito, a strange numbness in his lips. All were clear images, imprinted on the fading fragments of the man's mind, which made her curious about the vagueness of his last memories.

There were no mosquitoes this time of year, she realized, not after the early frost they'd had. "Is there a mark on him? Like, um . . . a pinprick, or a dart?"

"Good eye," Harinen answered. "There's a small puncture wound on the side of his neck."

The muddiness of the memories near to death suddenly made sense. "That's how they captured him. They drugged him."

She slid her hand toward the man's neck and heard the wet sound of the body shifting as the officer turned it to allow her access to the sting. Her fingers found the spot. A ghostly memory surfaced of the officer brushing his neck before falling down in the street.

Shironne pressed her fingers against the mark, sensing an odd, venomous presence there, collected in the tissues of the skin. It was one she hadn't encountered before, but powerful in its virility. "I can't tell you what they used on him. I don't recognize it, but it reminds me of snake venom—fast and strong. He didn't live long enough for it to dissipate."

Putting names to things she'd never encountered before often confounded her. She had some idea as to their properties, but that wasn't the same as naming them. It was the reason she spent so much time identifying things in Kassannan's office—so that she'd know all the names.

"I wasn't certain whether it was a sting or a puncture," the officer admitted. "No noticeable smell or color to it."

Shironne slid her hand back down to the man's, touching one of the breaks in the skin, forcing herself to listen for the substance, the body, rather than the impulses of the mind. Silt, algae, and other matter fouled the torn flesh, along with the tiny living creatures that dwelt in dirt. "This came from the bottom of the river," she said. "The current pulled him along, and these injuries must have come from branches or rocks or . . . um, something else on the river's bottom. There are probably other cuts on his face and feet, I think. Those happened after he died."

"There are marks," the officer said, curiosity beginning to replace his worry. He'd clearly moved past his concerns over propriety. "What else, miss?"

Shironne laid her fingers on the man's bloated abdomen and slid them upward until she found the gaping mouth of a slash crossing the man's chest. She ran her fingers along the edge of it, leaning over the table to do so. "He bled from this wound. He watched his life bleeding out of him."

"And what of the carvings?" The officer awaited her answer, apprehensive about that part.

Shironne remembered the strange mutilations from vague snatches of her dream. A word ran from one shoulder to the other across the man's chest; letters carefully carved into his flesh to announce *something.* What, she couldn't tell. She reached up to touch the marks. "The cuts were made by a knife with a short blade, but I can't read them."

"Pedraisi," Kassannan said softly. "You wouldn't recognize it if you could see it."

"You'd rather not see him at all, miss," Officer Harinen added.

On rare occasions, being blind had its advantages. Shironne supposed the man's body must look ghastly, having lain in the grip of the river for two days. On the other hand, Harinen likely had no idea of the depth of the changes the river and its denizens had wrought upon the body, changes far beneath the skin. Its spirit stolen away, the corpse had begun the swift progress from man to meat.

Shironne had encountered a good number of corpses in her time working for Colonel Cerradine. There were nameless things she didn't want to contemplate at work in the bodies, especially because she knew they existed in her *own* body as well. She tried not to think about that.

A door banged loudly in the hallway outside, followed by the sound of footsteps pounding on the stone floor. Harinen abruptly began to worry, and Shironne could sense Kassannan thinking fast. He buckled his bag. She lifted her hand from the body and turned halfway toward him, wondering who had set them both off.

She opened her mouth to ask, but the door to the room opened, slamming back against a wall.

"I gave orders that no one was to view this body," the newcomer snapped, agitation spreading around him. "Who are these people?"

Shironne felt it coming a split second in advance, but there was no way for her to get away, not with the table on one side and the man on the other. A fleshy hand locked about her jaw, turning her chin this way and that. The improper contact brought with it a lust that shocked her, the man's thoughts tumbling in a disordered manner into her consciousness.

She gasped and stumbled back, then tripped over an uneven spot in the tiles. She tumbled toward the floor, slamming her cheek against a wall in the process.

"Shironne!" The captain's hands grasped her arms, and he lifted her to her feet amid a cloud of anger and worry. "Are you hurt?"

Shironne tried to catch her breath, her head spinning. Not only from hitting it against the wall; that hurt enough to make her eyes water. No, even worse, she still felt that man's hand against her skin, his right hand, carrying with it traces that said he hadn't washed his hands since he last ate. She could still feel the oily sense of his lust at the edges of her mind too. His touch had left a clear impression of the man's psyche, a connection she didn't want. She felt dirty just having had his fingers on her skin. "I'm fine," she whispered anyway, holding the hand that had touched the body away from her clothing. "Cloth?"

Standing between her and the newcomer, Kassannan placed a cloth into her still-gloved hand. She used that to wipe first her face, and then the hand she'd used to touch the dead man. That wasn't truly clean, but it was the best she could do without water.

"Well," the oily man said, "if it isn't Tornin Anjir's pretty little daughter."

CHAPTER TEN

"And who are you?" the unknown man asked, the irritation that crowded around him belying his genial tone.

"Kassannan," the captain replied, leaving out his rank. "We were just leaving." He took a firm grasp of Shironne's sleeve and hauled her close to him. Shironne didn't argue. She wanted to get away from any man who spoke of her father by his given name.

"You are not to discuss this with anyone else, Miss Anjir," the unknown man barked.

"With whom would I discuss it, sir?" Shironne asked, trying to sound small and intimidated.

The man flared with annoyance, but his attention quickly turned from her to Officer Harinen. "I want this room sealed until I've decided how to handle this. No word of this to anyone. If it gets out, people will panic."

Shironne wondered *why* the man believed that. She couldn't take the thought from him at a distance, though, and she never intended to let that man touch her bare skin again.

"And you," the man went on. "You're one of Cerradine's lackeys, aren't you? Tell your keeper that this is police business. The army can stay out of it. If word of this gets out, I'll know who to blame."

Shironne expected the captain to fight back, but he didn't. He was intent instead on getting *her* out of the room. She went willingly. She wouldn't say that Kassannan was spooked. It was more like he was uncomfortable at having been caught in that place. Or causing her to be caught there. She followed him along the hallway, back down the steps of the building, and onto the cobbles.

She breathed in the dank breeze, relieved to be out of that place. Even the rankness of the river seemed preferable to the fetid air in that morgue. She could hear and smell the horses now, so the carriage stood close by, and she waited until the captain helped her up onto the bench before tugging her glove out of her pocket.

Shironne wished she could wash her hand thoroughly. Kassannan was usually more aware of her needs, so he must be perturbed indeed to drag her out here so abruptly. Shivering, she pulled her glove back on, sensing tiny bits of dead flesh digging into the leather. She would never be able to clean the glove well enough to be comfortable wearing it again. The distance back to the house—that long she could bear having her hand so contaminated.

The carriage moved as Kassannan settled next to her, and then Messine. The lieutenant's mind swarmed with angry bees, all wanting to know the reason for their precipitous departure from the building. He waited until the carriage got under way, though. "What happened in there? You came out like you were being chased by fire imps."

Imps were creatures of Family legend, although Shironne suspected that was simply another name for demons.

"Faralis showed up," Kassannan said, "and demanded that we keep our mouths shut."

She recognized that name. Faralis was one of her father's cronies, and currently the commissioner of the police of Noikinos. Her own surprise was overshadowed by Messine's, though. "I thought the man never got out of his bed until half past three," Messine said. "What in Hel's name was *he* doing there? At this hour?"

Kassannan tamped down his frustration. "The dead man *was* a policeman."

"So it's their jurisdiction. I can't imagine that the commissioner actually cares."

"There's something else," Kassannan said. "Let me run this by the colonel first, Lieutenant. It's the manner of death that's problematic."

"Any manner of death is problematic," Shironne said dryly. "Do you mean the letters?"

Kassannan had laughed at her observation, but answered, concern welling around him again. "Yes, that inscription worries me."

"Was it blood magic?" Messine asked before Shironne could.

"Yes," the captain said softly. "I need you to tell me everything about this second dream of yours, Shironne."

Something was bothering him, but he was holding it close. She could touch him and see what wandered through his mind, but he clearly didn't want to share whatever it was yet. She didn't want to abuse the captain's trust, either, so she spent the remainder of the journey recounting every tiny detail that she recalled. Once she'd spun out everything she could, her jaw ached and she stopped to rub it.

"What happened to you?" Messine asked, apparently just then noticing her cheek.

"She was trying to get away from Faralis and tripped," Kassannan said. "I wasn't fast enough to catch her, and she hit the wall face-first." Anguish wrapped around him as he admitted that.

"You were on the wrong side of me to do anything, Captain," Shironne pointed out. Now that they were *both* worrying over her sore cheek, it hurt more than it had before. She set her hand in her lap, though, not wanting them to worry.

"I'm most concerned," Kassannan said, "that he recognized Shironne."

"Faralis recognized her?" Messine asked. "That can't be good."

"No," Kassannan agreed. "Has he ever been inside your house, Shironne? Would he have met you before there?"

Now that she knew who he was, she could put together her sense of him with his name. Her mother despised the man, a man whom she blamed for encouraging her husband in his criminal activities. "My mother wouldn't let my father's friends into the house," she said. "Especially not him."

There was a complicated secret behind that, one that Shironne always tried not to look at in her mother's mind.

"He *did* recognize you, though," Kassannan said.

Shironne shook her head. "My father took me around to a lot of doctors when I first went blind. Perhaps Faralis saw me there. That's the only time I've been out of my mother's or the army's control. Otherwise my father never bothered with me."

She'd always been glad of that. Her father had never favored her, preferring Perrin in everything. Perrin was *normal.* When Shironne had shown signs of being a sensitive like her mother, his ambivalence toward her had turned to active dislike, as if he could no longer trust her. She hadn't done anything to earn his reaction, other than to be different from him. At least not anything she'd ever known. That made it hard for her to like her own father.

"It's definitely something the colonel needs to know," Messine said.

Shironne didn't know enough about Faralis to know why Messine felt so strongly about that. She raised her hand to rub her cheek again, but jerked it back down.

"I will tell him," Kassannan said in an angry tone, "have no doubt."

Messine seemed satisfied with that promise, so he let the matter drop. Fortunately, they'd reached the familiar back court of her house, distinguishable by its rustling trees and the smell of the kitchen. After the carriage stopped, Messine helped her down and, after a quick farewell to Captain Kassannan, led her back to the house's kitchen door.

Shironne walked into the kitchen and sat down at the servants' table. Cook came into the room a moment later, a smell of flour and garlic floating with her. She caught sight of Shironne's swollen cheek, and Shironne had to sit through the flurry of Cook's exclamations and summons. Her mother hastened down the stairs, a combination of the drifting scent of vanilla and concern. She brushed Shironne's cheek with gentle fingers, shocked by the bruise blossoming there. Her hand lifted Shironne's chin to inspect her face. "What happened?"

"A man came in while we were in the morgue. He touched my face, so I tried to get away from him. I tripped and I hit the wall, of all things. Captain Kassannan tried to catch me, but he wasn't close enough."

Her mother's mind flared with irritation.

Cook brought her a cup of honeyed tea and a towel-wrapped chunk of ice chipped from the block in the cellar to hold to her swelling cheek.

Her sisters dashed into the kitchen a moment later, eager to find the cause of the disturbance. Perrin said that Shironne shouldn't be so clumsy, but Melanna's anger flared through Shironne's senses. She wanted to blame *someone* for hurting her sister. Shironne dropped her clean hand atop Melanna's coarse hair and ruffled it, uncertain whether to applaud her hot temper or reprove her for it. In the end, she chose to accept it as her sister's love, and said nothing, but the attention made her cheek hurt worse and set her eyes tearing.

Her mother, of course, asked for all the details, and Shironne decided it would be best to admit that the police commissioner was the one who'd caught them in the morgue. As she'd expected, her mother's mind went guarded at the news that Faralis had recognized her. But her mother said nothing more about the matter, packing her worry away carefully in a corner of her mind.

. . .

Mikael woke when a fist pounded on the door of the small room. His head ached, his lungs weren't much better, and he'd managed to spill his bottle onto the bed. He smelled like a vendor's stall, a combination of last night's curry and whiskey. "Oh Hel," he croaked.

This time is worse.

He coughed wetly. He raised a hand to his face as the pounding on the door went on, and touched his mouth. Then he held up the hand and squinted at it. It was splattered red from a torn lip. The victim had put up a fight before dying.

"Move whatever you have in front of the damned door," Kai yelled at him through the wood.

Mikael turned his head, seeing for the first time the chair propped under the door latch. He didn't remember doing that. He must have been pretty drunk by then. He forced himself into a sitting position, head still spinning, then hooked the chair away from the door with one foot.

The door pushed inward, Kai predictably following. He shoved the door hard enough to force the chair into a corner and then came and loomed over Mikael where he sat on the edge of the bed. "What is wrong with you?"

Mikael closed his eyes. He didn't want to look at Kai's accusing face. His head was still spinning, although he couldn't be sure that wasn't just the alcohol. His pulse pounded behind his ears, but he still heard the sound of footsteps as Elisabet entered the room, Kai moving aside. "This is ridiculous," Kai muttered under his breath. "He's trying to get out of work."

Mikael swallowed down a dry laugh.

"Let me look at your face, Mikael," Deborah ordered.

Oh no. It hadn't been Elisabet he'd heard. He opened his eyes to find Deborah standing before him instead.

Her fingers tilted his chin so she could peer at his face. "Open your mouth."

There was no point in fighting this. It had been inevitable for months now. He opened his mouth and let her peer at his teeth.

"Where's the blood coming from?" she asked.

"I don't know." Now he could taste the blood. He wanted to rinse out his mouth.

"Did someone hit you?"

No, he had no memory of anything like that, not in his waking life, anyway. "In the dream, I think."

He closed his eyes again, not wanting to look at her face. His life as he knew it was over.

"There's too much blood on your shirt to be from your mouth. Can you take off your vest?" she asked.

No jacket, he recalled. He'd taken off his uniform jacket and laid it over the bed's footboard, not wanting to get it bloody like the last time. But the vest's neckline dipped down to reveal a vee of white shirt, and he would have bled there.

"Do I need to do it for you?" Deborah asked.

That was not a complaint about his slow response, he could tell. Just concern. Mikael started to unbutton his vest, fumbling with the hidden placket since his fingers were still numb. After a moment, he'd gotten all the buttons and slipped the vest off his shoulders.

"What in Hel's name happened to you?" Kai asked.

Mikael couldn't see directly under his chin, but the front of his shirt was discolored from one side to the other, drying to brown about the outer edges of the stain.

"And the shirt," Deborah said.

Mikael unbuttoned his cuffs and collar before pulling the shirt over his head. Gooseflesh prickled along his arms as the cold hit his bare skin. Better than heat, at least, which might have turned his stomach. He held the shirt in his lap, strangely unwilling to let it go, even if it was ruined.

Deborah's eyes went bleak. "Kai, go down to the kitchen and ask the owner for a pitcher of water and a basin."

"What is wrong with him?" Kai asked instead.

"Now, Kai," Deborah said more firmly, a tone she rarely took with her nephew. "Take Elisabet with you."

Kai shifted, and Mikael saw Elisabet waiting outside the door. No expression crossed her features, but she looked paler than usual. He wouldn't have thought her one to shrink from injuries.

Elisabet was responsible for Deborah's presence, he realized dully. She'd told Deborah something after his previous dream, and that had brought Deborah down here this morning.

For a moment, Mikael thought Kai might refuse Deborah's order, but he turned away abruptly and gestured for Elisabet to precede him down the hallway.

Deborah retrieved the displaced chair and sat down in front of Mikael. "How long has this been going on?"

She didn't ask what was happening. She didn't ask why he had letters carved in weeping bruises across his chest. She already *knew* where it was coming from—his dreams.

Mikael sighed, sensing the end of his freedom. "About two years ago I started seeing the bruises. It's been getting worse, especially when I was away in Jannsen Province. It was terrible there. I don't know why. Although it has always happened when I dream about my father's death."

"You bleed like *this* when you dream about your father?"

"No, just one spot on the chest, but I also cough up blood." He knew exactly how his father had died: a single gunshot to the chest. Valerion hadn't died immediately, though. His lungs had filled with blood, echoed by the blood Mikael coughed up every time he repeated that dream.

Deborah sat back, her lips pressed into a thin line. Footsteps along the mezzanine warned them of Kai's return. He bore a white basin and pink pitcher, and had a towel over one arm, like one of the waiters at the restaurant. *Kai serving me.* Mikael would have laughed at the idea if he wasn't so exhausted.

No, Kai was doing this for Deborah, not for him. "What's wrong with him?" Kai asked again

Deborah reached up for the basin and set it carefully next to Mikael on the bed. Then she took the pitcher, poured a small amount of water into the basin, and set the pitcher on the floor. Lastly, she took the towel from Kai. "Demonstrating that he's still a sensitive, even if only in his sleep," she said. "He's *sharing* the victim's wounds.

Kai, get my pad out of my satchel and copy down that mess across his chest."

As Kai complied, she dampened the towel in the water and began to gently pat Mikael's chest clean. He said a quick prayer of thanks that the water was warm, a sign that Father Winter—or Synen—was looking after him. "They're not cuts," Deborah observed. "Just bruises. Where does the blood come from?"

"It just seeps through the skin," Mikael admitted. "There's never an actual break unless I bump one of the bruises."

Deborah set the towel on the edge of the basin. "I'm not certain *bruise* is the right word for this." She gently touched one of the lines on his right shoulder. "It's raised just a bit."

"That'll go down in a couple of hours."

"What about these scabs?" she said, pointing to the cluster where Kai had shoved his boots into his chest two mornings before.

"I got hit before they faded," Mikael said, not glancing Kai's way. "They break and then scab over."

"What am I not seeing?" Deborah asked. "What other symptoms?"

"I'll be short of breath for a few hours; this victim couldn't breathe. I'm tired. And my head hurts."

"The aching head is called a hangover, Mikael. That part you did to yourself."

"I know," he said wearily, shaking his head and then flinching from the stab of pain in his neck. "And my neck hurts. Right here." He laid a hand on the sore spot.

"Did you have this last time?" She rose and leaned over him to inspect his neck.

"Yes."

"I don't see any wound there," she said, fingers cool on his neck.

"It feels like a stab wound. Small and deep."

Deborah sat again, nodded. "Kai, do you have that sketch done?"

"Yes, ma'am." Kai handed her the notebook, then busied himself closing up the ink and returning her supplies to her satchel.

The marks on the paper resembled the drawing Mikael had made himself a few days before. There wasn't much more detail. It certainly wasn't legible, although he could still swear it was Pedraisi. "Is this like the last dream?" Deborah asked, gesturing toward Kai's work with her chin.

"It's the same," he said. "It has to have been blood magic."

She rose from the chair and pushed it back against the wall. "I suppose you'll have to put that shirt back on," she said. "It's chilly out."

No point in arguing. Mikael shook out the ruined shirt and drew it back on over his head, grimacing when it slipped across the tender spot on his neck. The front of the shirt was cold and sticky against his clean skin. He didn't bother to button it, just drew the vest on over it. He retrieved his uniform jacket and put that on over everything else. Once he buttoned up the jacket and hooked the collar, no one would see it anyway. Then he cast about for his boots.

"Here," Kai said, holding them out with one hand.

Mumbling his thanks, Mikael took the boots and worked them onto his feet, then laced them with shaking fingers. It was slow, but he did them himself, feeling Kai's eyes on him the whole time. He pushed himself up off the bed and managed not to sway.

"Let's get you back home," Deborah said, one hand on his arm.

Mikael wasn't sure how much longer it would be his home. Deborah would insist on keeping him in the fortress the next time he dreamed, and the sensitives would be the ones hurt. The elders would have ample cause to send him away to one of the enclaves once that happened. That they'd let him stay so long when he was an irritant to the sensitives was a testament to Deborah's interference. She was determined to find a way to fix him.

But the next time he dreamed would likely be the breaking point, and he very much feared he would find himself without a home.

• • •

Cerradine stared at the sketch Kassannan presented him, a series of letters in the Pedraisi language. An uneasy feeling settled in his stomach. "I think I recognize this."

Kassannan had returned from his foray to the city's morgue brimming with news about the police commissioner's actions, and guilt that he'd allowed Shironne to be hurt. He was still dressed in civilian clothes since he hadn't had time yet to don his uniform. "Yes, it's clearly blood magic," he said, "although what this particular inscription is meant to do, I've no idea."

Cerradine shook his head. "That's not what I meant. I think I've seen this *specific* inscription before." He sat down on the edge of his desk. Surely the Daujom would have a record of the inscription. "I'll need to take this up to the palace. I need to be sure."

"What does it remind you of?"

"I was out in Andersen Province in the cleanup after the Farunas massacres."

Kassannan's mouth pursed. "No. The victims are wrong. This can't be the same thing."

"No, it's not," Cerradine agreed. The Farunas massacres had seen entire families butchered, sacrificed in blood magic. Plucking a single police officer off the street wasn't the same at all. "I want to check the writing anyway. It looks very close to what I remember."

Few people this far away from the border with Pedrossa would have much familiarity with a series of deaths fourteen years past. Kassannan would have been young then, probably still at the medical college, and most of the workers in the office were even younger. Shironne wouldn't recognize the killings, nor would Mikael Lee, Cerradine suspected. He would.

The Larossan army had been called in only afterward, to deal with the bodies and restore security along that section of the Larossa-Pedrossa border. The army had counted seventy-two dead from twelve different households along a thirty-mile stretch of border, all sacrificed over about a month. That was, however, only the ones they'd actually accounted for. Homesteads along that border were spread out, and very often a family's nearest neighbor wouldn't see them for months. Added to that, many of the bodies had been dumped in the Sorianas River, which grew more turbulent as it flowed south toward Kithria. It was impossible to know exactly how many lives had been lost in that incident.

It had ended without their interference. The Andersens, the Family associated with that border province, claimed that vigilantes shot and killed several of the priests involved, and the remaining perpetrators had fled back across the river into Pedrossa. The territory into which they'd fled housed many of the most violent clans in the country, those most determined to cling to the old ways.

The Pedraisi government hadn't been willing to help, and neither the Andersens nor the army had been able to do much more than gather information about the killers. They'd never learned much, though, merely that they had to have come from one of a handful of clans that followed the ancient god Farunas. Only those clans knew what Farunas promised his followers. And since they had no treaty with Larossa that guaranteed extradition, the pursuit of justice for all those families murdered in the name of a foreign god had simply died out. Fourteen years had passed, but that time was still vivid in Cerradine's memory.

"Faralis may have made the connection," he said. "He may not have. But if a *second* body turns up with the same markings, his reaction will probably be even worse." Having one of their own officers fall victim to practitioners of blood magic made the Larossan authorities here look weak. That was likely the reason why Faralis had reacted the way he had, calling for the body to be sequestered and demanding secrecy. "Go talk to Officer Harinen again after he gets off his duty shift," he told Kassannan. "I'm willing to take him on if Faralis fires him over this."

Kassannan nodded. "I'll need to write a letter of apology to Madam Anjir first, but after that, I'll go find him."

"Good." Cerradine pushed himself to his feet. "And I will talk to Aldassa."

He found David Aldassa in the front of the office. After carefully laying out every detail about the second dream that Shironne had shared, he charged the lieutenant with locating that second body before the police did. If these murders did have something to do with the Farunas massacres, he was far more likely to recognize it than the police were. And far more likely to do something about it instead of pretending it hadn't happened. He only hoped that the second body hadn't been dumped in the river after death as the first had. When it came to evidence, water played havoc with timing and details.

Aldassa sent an ensign off to retrieve a map of the river's course along the edge of the city and turned his attention back to the colonel. "The first body was pulled out of the river south of the sewage outlet, is that right? So it could have gone in anywhere north of there."

Cerradine nodded. "I don't know how much it would help to have the site where he died, so the priority has to be on finding that second body."

Aldassa peered down at the list Kassannan had written of all the small details Shironne had gleaned from the previous night's dream. "Eliminate any heavily populated area. That takes us to the edge of the city. Not too far out, because a coach would need roads. Don't want to be dragging a victim very far. We can eliminate some of the farms we've already searched as well."

The ensign returned with a large map, and Aldassa hung it carefully on the chalkboard that he kept near his desk. Then he fetched a straightedge and, after peering at the map a moment longer, drew a line that roughly followed the river before it turned in the middle of the city, creating a grid of parallel and perpendicular lines that followed along the edge of the river. "Ideally, sir, I'd like a squad to search each square I've drawn here. And I think it would be easier to run a search from the tavern up on Lana's Road. Shorter distance to report in before going back out."

"I'll talk to the general before I leave for the palace," Cerradine told him. "I'll get you as many squads as you need."

"If I can have eight, sir, I think that would work. I'll pair them with some of *our* people." He went on to list off most of the office's workers.

"Isn't Pamini working on the Endiren case?"

Aldassa shook his head. "She can step away for a while. And there is a slim possibility they're related."

Cerradine *had* put forward that possibility himself. Asking Shironne to query her mother about it had mainly been a formality, though, and also an excuse to communicate with her. Endiren had gone to the border to pursue news of children being sold into Pedrossa, not religious fanatics. Cerradine rose and picked up his hat. "Then I'll go get you your eight squads."

CHAPTER ELEVEN

Shironne woke to her mother's touch on her forehead. The pillow underneath her was damp, which confused her until she remembered the piece of ice she'd held to her cheek before falling asleep. She sat up, and her mother slid the sodden pillow away.

"I'll get you a dry one," Mama said. "How do you feel?"

Her mother's fingers tilted her face to get a better look at her eyes, worry in her mind.

"Passable." Her head hurt, the cheek throbbed, but her mouth ached the most, which surprised her.

Her mother's concern washed about her, flooding back at the hesitant sound of her reply. "It always gets worse before it gets better. You'll feel better tomorrow."

Before Shironne had lost her sight, she'd never been the sort to trip or fall. Now she walked into things on a regular basis, too eager to be cautious.

"I received a letter from the captain." Irritation flared briefly across her mother's mind, quickly tamped down. "Apologizing for what happened."

"Don't be angry with him," Shironne said. "He couldn't have prevented it."

Her mother sighed. "He seems like a nice man, so I'll try not to be too vexed with him."

But Shironne could still feel that hint of ire in her mother's words. "Not Messine either. Or the colonel."

Her mother's fingers brushed her cheek, her bracelet tinkling. "Sweetheart, I know very well that you will do what you want, so I will not blame your colonel when going there was your choice."

Her mother's thoughts spun away. When Mama contemplated a new idea, her mind turned in a whispering tumble, unformed concepts not yet made into words. Shironne waited in silence while her mother chased her ideas to their ends, wrapping words around them so she could hold them.

"What is it?" Shironne finally asked.

"All I've ever wanted for the three of you was that you each be able to make your own decisions," her mother said. "I didn't have any choice. I *had* to marry your father. I didn't know why at the time, but I learned later that he had evidence of one of my mother's affairs—a packet of letters. My father agreed to give me to your father in exchange for hiding yet another of my mother's indiscretions."

Her mother had been married off at fifteen to Tornin Anjir, a man with neither family ties nor money, but ample ambition. Shironne *had* wondered why her grandfather, a man of means and social standing, had agreed to that, another thing in her mother's mind she'd avoided touching.

"Some children grow up," her mother went on, "and never face any repercussions for their parents' actions, but my mother's sins have haunted me my entire life. That's why I've always done my best to protect the three of you. I don't want you suffering for mistakes *I've* made."

They never spoke of Shironne's wanton grandmother, as if that would prevent her pernicious influence from touching their lives. Shironne knew very little about the woman. "Mama, you're not like your mother," she protested anyway.

Her mother's amusement swelled around her. "I see her whenever I look in the mirror, sweetheart. And when I look at you, lately. We both resemble her."

Shironne didn't think about her appearance often. Not *very* often. She knew her grandmother had been considered a great beauty. Her mother had a serene loveliness that made men adore her and want to help her—especially Colonel Cerradine. *But her?* The last time she'd seen her face, at thirteen years old, she'd had chubby cheeks and hair that curled enough to make it horribly unruly, unlike her mother's sleek fall of dark hair. And she would never be tall and elegant like her mother. "Was Grandmother short?"

"Actually, she was," her mother said, laughter in her voice now. "I get my height from the other side."

Shironne had never heard her mother *laugh* about her own mother. "Did you like Grandmother at all?"

Her mother took her hand, as if wanting Shironne to be clear about her meaning. "Your grandmother treated me like a toy. She had the nursemaid bring me out whenever she wanted to show me off, and sent me away as soon as I didn't entertain her or her friends any longer. As I started growing taller, my value as a source of entertainment lessened, so I saw her only rarely. I don't know that I ever had much of a chance to like or dislike her. My nursemaid was more of a mother to me than my mother ever was."

That was absolute truth. A touch of anger lurked behind those words, combined with regret. Verinne was still with her, and no matter how tight the family's funds became, Shironne knew her mother would never turn the old woman out.

"My father loved me," her mother added, "even if he hadn't fathered me. He later told me he regretted the marriage contract he signed with your father."

"Far too late to change the fact," Shironne said.

"True," her mother allowed. "But it made me feel better to know. I've tried to make the best choices for you. You do know that, don't you?"

"Of course you have."

Her mother shook her head, a faint whisper of her hair moving. "There are times that I regret allowing you to involve yourself with the army, times like this when you come home with a bruise on your cheek or a hank of your hair torn out. I don't want you to someday regret it as well."

"I'm seventeen now, Mama," Shironne reminded her. "If I didn't want to work for the colonel, I would tell you so."

"Oh, I've little doubt of that," her mother said with a laugh. She rose from the bed, her hand pulling away from Shironne's. "Cook kept some lentil soup warm for you. After you eat, will you feel well enough to help your sister with her reading?"

Now that her mother had distracted her from her aching cheek, Shironne felt ready to take on anything. Even Melanna's terrible reading.

. . .

After he bathed, changed into a fresh uniform, and took a nap, Mikael felt better. Physically, at least. His head still ached, and his mind wasn't at its best. On occasion he heard a whistle in the hall, warning him that he'd allowed himself to grow agitated again and was bothering one of the sensitives. So he clamped down on his anxiety and reminded himself to be calm. To be *happy*.

He didn't relish the idea of reporting to Dahar, though. While Deborah handled everything with the least amount of fuss possible, Dahar would do the opposite. There would be yelling, guilt, and possibly broken porcelain. He could only hope that Deborah got to Dahar and smoothed his feathers first.

When he reached the office near noontime, he was rather shocked to find he had it to himself again. Dahar wasn't pacing around the room, and Kai had to be off on another of the mysterious missions that kept him beyond his father's reach. Mikael settled there and started in on his pile of papers.

He'd been there nearly half an hour before a knock sounded at the office door. When he went to answer it, he found Eli standing outside. The younger man looked as if he'd just stepped from his barracks, a handful of blond braids trailing smoothly over his shoulder and not a wrinkle on his brown uniform. Mikael doubted that Eli ever sat down while on duty.

"I'm to ask you to come with me to Dahar's quarters. Colonel Cerradine is with him." Eli served runner duty in the portion of the palace where the king's household lived.

And that explained where Dahar was. Mikael checked to make certain nothing sensitive was open on his desk, joined Eli in the hallway, and locked the office door behind him. Eli could have gone back to his post, but Mikael was grateful he'd stayed to escort him. "I wanted to apologize for missing our appointment this morning."

Eli pulled a stray hair off his otherwise immaculate woolen jacket and favored it with an offended look as they walked down the hallway toward the stairs. "Half my yeargroup had dreams last night, so I knew you weren't going to make it today. I used the hour to study instead."

"We can make it up later, then?"

"Tomorrow, same time?" Eli asked as he headed up the first set of steps.

Mikael took a deep breath and started the climb, grateful he wasn't climbing up out of the fortress instead. "That's fine. I'll alter my schedule."

"You look tired today," Eli said, stopping on the landing and waiting for Mikael to catch up.

"I feel like hell." Mikael could afford to be honest with him, a rare luxury. Despite his age, Eli was the closest thing to a friend he had in the fortress . . . other than Jannika, of course. "Did I wake any of your yeargroup?"

Eli's yeargroup had more than its share of sensitives, so Mikael figured Eli heard plenty of gripes about him. "Just a couple," Eli said. "They'll live."

The sentries who stood duty in the royal household were quarterguards, a special service. *All* the quarterguards were sensitives, and they watched Mikael as if he were a particularly noxious form of insect crawling up into their territory. He wished apology at them and tried to keep his thoughts pleasant, hoping not to disturb them further.

Mikael and Eli passed down a side hall to Dahar's apartment. Eli rapped on the heavy door and opened it when they heard Dahar's summons from within.

Dahar and the colonel sat dining at the graceful mahogany table in Dahar's sitting room, possibly the most austerely furnished room in all the king's household. Compared to the rest of Above, it was plain. Even so, the trappings of the room hinted at wealth: the massive, finely crafted desk; floorcloths figured in Valaren burgundy and brown rather than the thick carpets used elsewhere in the king's household; and heavy window hangings of black silk exactly like those in the office. Mikael always wondered if Dahar had intended to mimic his office.

The room's only adornment, a portrait, hung above the marble hearth. Nearly two hundred years old, it depicted an Anvarrid woman both Mikael and Dahar could name in their lineages. Rumor claimed that Dahar had ordered everything in his rooms burned when his wife was executed a decade before—everything except that painting.

Colonel Cerradine rose when he spotted Mikael. He shook Mikael's hand, towering over him for a second before returning to the table. "Just the man I wanted to see," he said. "Have you eaten?"

Mikael suppressed a smile at Cerradine's proprietary air. He suspected the colonel did it just to irritate Dahar, who sat frowning at his table. "No, sir. I don't have the stomach for it right now."

"Come and sit down, Mikael," Dahar snapped, likely tired of being upstaged. "Cerradine needs to talk with you about your dreams."

Mikael settled uncomfortably on one of the stark wooden chairs. Had Deborah not talked to Dahar yet? Surely if Dahar knew about the blood, he would have said more.

"Will you need me any longer, sir?" Eli asked from where he waited inside the doorway.

"Why don't you return to your post, Eli? If we do, we'll send for you." Dahar waved him away, and the young man slipped out, closing the door behind him.

"Tell me about your dreams, Mikael," Cerradine commanded.

Surely Cerradine's sensitive had already told him about the dreams. Otherwise the colonel wouldn't be asking. "I've had the same dream twice in the last three nights. The victim is grabbed on the street at night. They cut him up and leave him to bleed to death."

Cerradine ran a hand through his white hair, disarranging it. His dark eyes gave him a hawklike appearance as he leaned forward, placing his elbows on the table to observe Mikael more closely. "Anything else?"

"The men who did the killing. Their actions were . . . ritualistic. They made cuts across the victim's upper chest that must have been writing, but I'm not sure what it said."

"Why not?" Cerradine asked.

Mikael mimicked looking at his own shoulders. "Couldn't see, sir. Not in the dream. And when I looked down, I couldn't breathe."

"You couldn't breathe?"

"Yes, sir. My lungs and throat felt numb. I couldn't move, as if I was paralyzed."

Cerradine leaned back again and folded his hands together, his eyes closed. Dahar got up and stalked around the room, unable to sit still any longer. He picked up a letter opener from the desk in one corner and flipped it in his hand as he paced before the fireplace. Mikael decided to wait them out.

"You can't be sure," Dahar said.

"I never said I was," Cerradine answered mildly. "But given the markings, we need to investigate this as if it was."

Mikael sat up. "They found the body, then?"

Cerradine gazed at Mikael over the tips of his steepled fingers. "One of them. Aldassa has teams out looking for the second."

A chill settled in Mikael's stomach. It had been so obvious, but he'd missed it. That blow to the face . . . that hadn't happened in the first dream. The slight differences that he'd put down to faulty memory and alcohol hadn't been figments of his imagination after all. "Are you certain?"

Cerradine nodded. "My sensitive told me there were two *different* victims. The first was taken to the city's morgue. Unfortunately, Faralis walked in on her when she was viewing the body and therefore he knows that she knows about it."

"The city's morgue? Why would she have gone there?"

"Kassannan has a friend who works there. The man sent word he had a body we needed to look at, so Kassannan took her with him. Unfortunately, Faralis arrived and found them there. He ordered the officer in charge not to let anyone see the body."

"He'll damn well let the Daujom in," Dahar snapped.

It was notable that the police were trying to conceal the first death, but Mikael was more curious about why Cerradine would take a sensitive to view a body. After all, bodies didn't have emotions for a sensitive to pick up.

"You're welcome to try." Cerradine reached into a jacket pocket, withdrew a piece of paper, and unfolded it. "In Andersen Province, fourteen years ago, I was with the army detail assigned to investigate the Farunas massacres. This slash across the lower chest immediately made me think about that, though, which is why I came to you. I'm not certain about the lettering, but they used that same method to bleed them dry."

The Farunas massacres? Mikael vaguely remembered his mother citing the gruesome murders as the sort of thing that happened to boys caught outside the fortress after dark. He'd been only nine when the massacres took place, out on the eastern border between Larossa and Pedrossa. Dozens of homesteaders were murdered, making it one of the more horrific series of crimes in Larossan history. "I thought the Andersens investigated that incident, not the army."

"They did," Cerradine said. "But most of the victims were Larossan, so the Larossan authorities in Aldranos asked the army to investigate as well. They didn't trust the Andersen Family to show as much concern as was warranted, since the victims were Larossan."

"Not too surprising," Mikael said with a shrug. He'd never been to Andersen Province, much less to the provincial capital of Aldranos, but he'd heard enough about the Andersen Family to believe that claim. While the Lucas and Lee Families rarely had problems working with their local governments, the Andersens seemed to thrive on discord, much as the Jannsen did. And whenever an investigation required interaction between the different races, there always seemed to be suspicion of cutting corners. But while the Larossan authorities controlled the cities, issues in the countryside or on the borders usually fell to the national government—the Anvarrid government—to handle. That was why the Andersens and the army had been there rather than any local police force.

"We arrived on the border a few days after the Andersens," the colonel continued. "It was over by then. We just helped bury the bodies." Cerradine pinched the bridge of his nose as if his head ached. Then he shoved the paper over to Mikael. "Does this look familiar?"

The sketch was a near-complete version of the one Kai had drawn earlier that morning when looking at Mikael's false injuries. Of the one that Mikael himself had made two days before. Mikael recognized it, almost as if he'd felt every stroke of that word cut across his own shoulders. He swallowed. "Yes. This is it."

"I think this is the same thing that appeared on the bodies in the Farunas massacres. I just need to look at the Daujom's records to be sure."

Ah, that explains this visit to Dahar. It was usually Deborah whom Cerradine came to see when he showed up at the palace, but Cerradine wanted Dahar's *professional* help.

"Weren't most of the foreign priests killed?" Mikael asked. "Why would they come back? And why here? There's no reason for a priest looking for a warm body to sacrifice to make his way—what? almost three hundred miles?—across the country to Noikinos."

"We've asked the same questions, Mikael." Cerradine whistled at Dahar to get his attention. "I'd like to see any files the Andersens turned over on this, Dahar. I'm asking as a friend. I'm aware your files are confidential, but it would take time to get an answer back from the Andersen Family, if they bothered to answer at all."

"I'll consider it," Dahar said after a moment, looking peeved.

"If you don't mind, then," Cerradine said, "I'll head back to the headquarters to see if my people have located that second body."

The colonel retrieved his blue jacket from the back of a nearby chair. He pulled it on and buttoned it, and then wrapped the brown sash about his waist. The uniform seemed almost garish next to Mikael and Dahar's unrelieved black.

Dahar frowned, his face worried. "Give me a day or so to get our files together. I'll turn them over."

Once the colonel had left, Dahar stalked around his sitting room, picking up items and then putting them down. After a moment, Dahar stopped his pacing and gazed out of one of the windows that overlooked the courtyard. "The Andersens may have made some questionable decisions. My uncle had charge of the Daujom then and chose not to question their reports."

Mikael searched his memory, trying to recall anything he'd heard about the Andersen Family at the time of the massacres. Andersen Province lay to the south of Lee—far enough away that to a nine-year-old boy, events there had seemed a distant fable. "What did they do?" he asked, unable to rummage any specific memory out of his mind.

"I don't know that they *did* anything, but I had my suspicions. They found nine of the so-called priests dead, rifle shot. The Andersens claimed that *vigilantes* killed the nine priests and drove the others away. I believed then that the Andersens did it themselves, deciding to forgo the expense of a trial." Dahar sighed. "I suppose I still do."

That would be a violation of the treaty. If true, it could trigger a very unpleasant incident between the Daujom and the Andersens. "Is that why you don't want to turn their files over to Cerradine?"

"Yes." Dahar ran a hand through his short hair. "I don't mind your going down to the morgue to check, but be discreet. I don't want to offend the local Larossan authorities by interfering with their police investigation. They complain enough about us 'Warbirds' meddling in their petty politics."

The term *Warbirds* for the Anvarrid dated back to the invasion, when the invaders painted their faces with hawk or falcon motifs to show their allegiance to various Anvarrid Houses. The name wasn't meant any more fondly now than it had been then.

Dahar glanced back at Mikael. "I don't want to drag us into this. I don't want my brother forced to ask questions about what happened then."

Mikael understood Dahar's reluctance. Back then, an uncle of Dahar's had run the Daujom, and he apparently hadn't revealed any concerns about the Andersens' actions to the king. But should the issue be raised now, if they found evidence now that the Andersens had acted outside the law, Dahar *would* feel bound to pursue it to the point of prosecution.

"I'll keep that in mind, sir," Mikael promised, rising to take his leave.

"Well, if you're going to help out the colonel, you'd better go."

Mikael didn't argue.

CHAPTER TWELVE

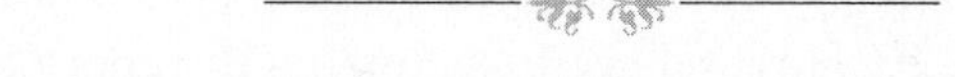

Cerradine trotted down the grand stair toward Below. All the sentries on duty knew him, but he signed his name on the log as an outsider. Whether the fortress acknowledged him when he reached the entryway arch, he never knew.

Clutching his hat in his fingers, he made his way through the cavernous mess hall, which was empty at the moment save for a few workers in the far back toward the service area. He went out one side and then along a secondary hall in the direction of the infirmary wing, his heels clicking on the hard stone. It always took him a few minutes to become accustomed to the odd lighting and faint tang in the air. He ignored the difference, intent on reaching his destination. His blue coat drew a quick glance from the few people he passed, but he was a familiar enough figure in these halls that no one actually stopped his progress.

He found Deborah in her office in the back of the infirmary, brooding over one of her notebooks. She held up her hand to forestall interruption and continued writing without even glancing at him.

He smiled at that gesture. When his mother died and his father—or rather, his father's secretary—dumped him on the Lucas Family like a sack of onions, he'd been given as a foster child to Deborah's parents. He and Deborah had both been six and had immediately become fast friends. Some people misunderstood their relationship, but they remained like brother and sister to this day. When he needed to talk, Deborah was the one he usually sought out, even if he had to come down into Below to find her.

Her office could have fit in Dahar's water closet. Space was limited in Below, so she crammed all her medical books and journals into the tiny room, stacks upon stacks resting on every level surface. She needed more shelves, Cerradine thought. He spotted her formal jacket hanging over her chair and decided she must have been out at the City Hospital again, reminding the poor of Noikinos that the Six Families might be *required* the serve the Anvarrid, but they were willing to help Larossans as well.

"Oh, Jon. I didn't realize it was you." She finished her notations and set the book aside to dry. "I'm glad you came to see me."

She edged around the small desk, and he hugged her, placing a brotherly kiss on her cheek. She looked tired, the fine lines around her eyes more marked today. Every time Mikael had a dream, Deborah ended up losing sleep.

Cerradine gently nudged a pile of books aside so he could sit on the edge of the desk, dropped his hat on his knee, and picked up a leather-bound journal to flip through its handwritten pages. It looked very old, the ink sketchy and the pages yellowed. "What are you researching now, Deb?"

"The writings of Lucasedrion. I thought they might be pertinent."

He stared at the worn journal. He doubted anyone outside the Family had ever seen it. "May I borrow it?"

"No, give it back. That's irreplaceable, Jon." She took it away from him and returned it to its stack. "These are his *private* journals."

He gave the leather-bound book a second glance. The first Anvarrid to marry into the Lucas Family, Lucasedrion had masterminded the Six Families' evolution from pacifist victims of the Anvarrid invasion to the military protectors of their former conquerors. The private journals of the man who'd orchestrated *that* would be fascinating. "Can I read it when you're done?"

Deborah gave him a wry look. "Them. There are twenty-seven

volumes, Jon, and I don't seem to recall your ever completing an entire book as a child."

He shrugged. She was right about that. "Just curious."

"As always. The elders wouldn't let you anyway."

Not too surprising, Cerradine decided. He might have been raised by the Lucas Family, but once he'd chosen to leave Below to see the outside world, he'd ceased to be one of theirs. "How are they pertinent?"

"Historical precedent. If you'll recall, Lucasedrion's wife was a touch-sensitive, and *bound* to him."

"Ah, of course." *Bound* in that sense meant more than their marriage ties. Their minds had become linked. "Like Mikael and Shironne."

"We don't *know* that they're *bound,* Jon."

He gave her a dry glance. Deborah hated to jump to conclusions, but they'd been discussing this possibility since Mikael returned from Jannsen Province and confirmed that he'd suffered dreams that matched Shironne's . . . because he'd been the source of hers. "You said that's an Anvarrid thing, and they both have Anvarrid blood."

The Six Families hadn't known of *binding* before the Anvarrid came to their lands, making that one anomaly—Jon didn't see any way it could be called a *power*—that could definitively be traced to the invaders. Anvarrid actually cut their hands during their wedding ceremonies; the exchange of blood was supposed to promote a closer bond between the two parties involved. In rare cases, though, it provoked a bond so close that the two parties involved eventually lost any sense of individuality. They shared one mind, if he understood legend correctly.

Deborah just shook her head, refusing to discuss the topic further. "Did your girl pick up on Mikael's dream last night? I assume that's what you came to tell me."

"Yes, she did," he said. "But I actually came to tell you she went with Kassannan down to the morgue in the city this morning." He had the satisfaction of seeing Deborah's mouth hang open for a split second. He repeated most of what he'd told Dahar.

She frowned. "Could it be the real thing? The massacres starting over again?"

"Perhaps, but here? Why come *here*? To a city crowded with police and military?"

Deborah looked withdrawn for a moment. "It's a possibility that should be considered, Jon."

"I know," he said. "I want to bring Shironne here. She needs to meet Mikael. Working together they can give us more information." He held up a hand before she could protest. "I know you don't want me interfering with your boy, Deb. I just think that . . ."

Deborah sighed. "I don't think I can, in good conscience, let him go on the way he is any longer. Elisabet told me after the previous dream that Mikael was in far worse shape than he'd been letting on. She wasn't any more specific than that, but I accompanied Kai when he went to find Mikael this morning. We found him covered in blood."

"What?"

"Mikael's bleeding," she said. "A reflected injury incurred during his dreams. The blood seeps through the skin. He also mimics other symptoms: shortness of breath, pain, even bruising. Reflection of injuries is rare but not unheard of. Something only the strongest sensitives do."

Cerradine gazed at her, baffled. He was familiar enough with Mikael's history that he knew the young man had been a sensitive once, but that had been before his ability to broadcast became evident. "Mikael's not a sensitive, is he?"

Deborah shook her head. "The only time he connects with others is in their moment of death, via his dreams. I think his injuries may be a result of his inability to let go of the victim, an effort to record the death by writing the evidence on his own body. What he needs is someone to interpret his dreams, to remember them for him so that he doesn't have to do that to himself. And to . . . anchor him, to keep him from following the victim down into death."

That was a great deal of responsibility to lay on Shironne's shoulders. When he said so to Deborah, she just shook her head.

"This is all conjecture on my part," she added. "I have little to go on, but I think she's the only one who can do that. She's his complement."

He sat back. Apparently Deborah thought this was part of the *binding* between them. "Complement? How is that possible? He doesn't even know her."

She opened her mouth to say something, caught herself, and closed it. A faint scowl crossed her features.

"You can trust me, Deb," he reminded her.

"It's not a matter of trusting you, Jon," she said. "It's a matter of not violating my oaths to the other elders. There are things I can't say."

As one of the Lucas Family elders, she knew of things that would never be revealed to an outsider. That included things that he needed to know, particularly when it came to Shironne, or to Mikael, but she couldn't tell him. She ended up withholding things from him at times, and he did his best to understand her dilemma. It sounded, though, as if she was trying to think of a way around her oaths in this case, so he waited. It had to be important if she was willing to do that.

"What do you know about oysters, Jon?" she finally asked.

This *had* to be going somewhere. "They're slimy."

She gave him another wry smile. "But they make pearls. Do you know how that happens?"

"If I recall this correctly, it's something about sand getting inside their shells."

"Yes, a grain of sand becomes an irritant," she said. "The oysters develop a pearl around it, to protect themselves, I guess."

She folded her hands and waited, a clear sign that he was supposed to figure out the rest himself.

If this has something to do with Shironne and Mikael . . .

He glanced out into the hallway to see if any of the other infirmarians were nearby before asking, "Are you saying that Mikael Lee is the irritant? That he *created* Shironne's powers? Or created some form of *binding* between them? Or that she did it to protect herself from him?"

She continued to gaze at him helplessly.

If she couldn't discuss it, that meant it was a subject the elders were currently discussing. That, in turn, gave it some validity in his mind. Apparently the elders—or the chaplains, who were the experts on sensitives—thought Mikael Lee's mere presence had caused Shironne to become a touch-sensitive. "That's why they're willing to put up with him," he guessed. "He's annoying because of his broadcasting, but that creates touch-sensitives. Or stronger sensitives."

"I can't comment on that," she said. "I can, however, comment on the curious fact that the *percentage* of sensitives in the yeargroups from the elevens to the sixteens is much higher than the comparable groups five years ago."

"And five years ago was before Mikael Lee was sent here to live." Cerradine had been raised in this fortress and had sat in all the same Family history classes Deborah had. Touch-sensitives had once been vital to many functions in the Six Families. Currently the elders worked around those functions without them, to some extent. That was why the Lucas Family was curious about Shironne Anjir, why Deborah had come out several times to observe Shironne working. Shironne had spontaneously developed a power they could put to use . . . or rather, Mikael had somehow prompted her to develop that power. "The Lee elders can't possibly know that," he said, "or they wouldn't have sent Mikael here."

"I can only speculate on what the Lee elders know or don't know, Jon," Deborah said. "I will, however, say that the Lucas Family doesn't *know* what causes a sensitive to turn into a touch-sensitive. They have to have inherited some potential for it, but beyond that factor, we have only speculation. How can we possibly study them when there aren't any to study?"

Speculation. Deborah had long held ideas about Shironne's powers, and Mikael's. She simply couldn't discuss most of them with him, parceling out only dribs and drabs, which forced him to figure out what he could on his own.

Deborah sighed then. "If we force them together, physical proximity alone will hasten the process. Miss Anjir would be locking herself into the *binding.* They should be kept apart in order to preserve some option for her."

Originally they'd kept Mikael away from the army's offices because of his loudness, but lately it had been due to their suspicions of a *binding* between them. They'd wanted to give Shironne time to mature. Due to the intimacy of sharing thoughts, relationships that involved *binding* usually became intimate in a physical sense as well as the mental. And while it was clear that touch-sensitives usually learned to tolerate physical contact in time, he didn't know *how much* physical contact Shironne could bear. She could touch her family and the servants. She seemed to tolerate Messine and Kassannan guiding her about. She touched dead bodies and dirt and all other manner of disgusting things with equanimity now. She'd learned all that in the years she'd worked for him.

But eating still troubled her. There were people whose touch made her cringe, although he suspected that was a reaction more to their undisciplined thoughts than to a lack of cleanliness. Even so, Shironne *was* the sort to go looking for trouble. She seemed to thrive on challenges.

For years, Deborah had struggled with balancing the expectations of the Lucas elders against Mikael's well-being. Adding Shironne and their concerns about her had simply made Deborah's predicament more complicated. Cerradine was sure she would love to tell Mikael that Shironne might hold the key to controlling his dreams, but she was trapped by the expectations of the Family. He shook his head. "Deb, if these deaths turn out to be the real thing, we'll have to stop it quickly. That means using anything at hand, even a child. It's only four months until she's an adult. Surely the elders will grant some leeway if they understand the severity of his problems."

Deborah didn't argue. That meant she was resigned to the idea. That alone told him she truly feared for Mikael's life. There were few things Deborah would value above a child's autonomy and safety, but Mikael's life was one of them.

"The things you say she does," she said finally. "They don't all fit with what we know of touch-sensitives."

That had bothered Deborah from the beginning—Shironne's ability to "read" corpses. Touch-sensitives were supposedly able to read what passed through another's mind through touch, one of the reasons they'd so often served as interpreters in the past. Early on, Deborah had pointed out to him that corpses didn't have *anything* passing through their minds. How, then, did Shironne catch those thoughts? "She hasn't found her limits yet."

Deborah shook her head slowly. "I prefer her to be a known quantity before we expose Mikael to her."

While Shironne might be slightly disaster prone, she would never harm anyone. "She's not contagious, Deborah."

Deborah stretched her shoulders wearily. "Dahar will be angry."

Cerradine stood, deciding Deborah must be exhausted if she used the "Dahar will be angry" argument. Dahar was always angry with her about *something*. "If he comes up harsh with you, tell him I swore you to secrecy."

"It won't matter. He'll still blame me." She sighed and rubbed at her temples.

"I'll walk with you to your quarters," he said.

"I have more work to do, Jon."

"It can wait. Come along, Deb; you need sleep. What time did you get up?" When she admitted that she'd risen at two in the morning, he reached across the desk and plucked her jacket off the back of her chair. "This thing has dragged all over the ground."

Deborah took the jacket from him, dusted off the skirt, and draped it over her arm. He linked his arm with hers and led her through the doorway out into the hallway. They didn't have far to go; the infirmarians all had their quarters near the infirmary wing. Cerradine left Deborah at her door only after extracting her promise *not* to return to her office as soon as he'd gone.

Once out of the fortress and down in the city, he stopped at his own office before heading to his house in the Seychas District. The ensign waiting there had no news for him, so Cerradine scribbled off a note and headed down to the tavern where Aldassa had set up his search.

. . .

The cool evening breeze felt good against Mikael's skin as he walked down Hermlin Street into the Old Town. His afternoon excursion down to the city's morgue had been useless. The police insisted that there wasn't a body, that there never had been a body.

Even the threat of the Daujom's ire didn't shake the officer at the morgue's front desk. Mikael *could* go to the Family's legal counsel in the morning and start the paperwork necessary to force the police to let him in, but that might take a full day to process. By then, the body would be long gone. Mikael had the feeling that the officer who'd been daring enough to send for Kassannan that morning wasn't with the police any longer either.

However, in her rush to get him back to the palace that morning, Deborah hadn't bothered to retrieve his overcoat, so Mikael decided to visit Synen. He wasn't as surprised that Deborah had forgotten his overcoat as he was that *Kai* had. Kai always made sure he retrieved every last uniform piece, as if Synen couldn't be trusted not to sell a forgotten glove on the nearest street corner. Kai disliked loose ends.

People cleared out of Mikael's way at the sight of his black uniform, probably surprised by the presence of a Family boy there at this hour, even though Mikael had walked this street many times before. The Six Families generally stayed close to their fortresses.

He walked through the front doors, slipped through the crowded common room, and stepped into the kitchen.

The tavern might smell dank and tired in the mornings, but in the evening it was a symphony of wonderful scents. It was joked that Larossans would sell their own mothers for spices. Mikael had carefully never inquired as to whether there was any truth behind that saying. Fresh flatbread cooled on the table near where Synen's wife cubed chicken and vegetables for a curry, her red tunic a bright spot against the large oven. She wore no petticoats over her trousers, a concession to the heat in the kitchen, and probably so as not to set herself afire.

She absently waved one bracelet-laden arm at Mikael, so he sat down out of her way. Pennants hung sullenly in the hot air rising from the large oven, the sigil on them one that Mikael didn't recognize. It looked suspiciously like Pedraisi lettering, although any self-respecting Larossan would vehemently deny that. They would insist that it was an ancient sigil that their priests had used for centuries.

"Your coat's on the wall over there, lad," Synen said as he walked past with four clean mugs. He handed them off to a *new* waitress, one wearing more than enough jewelry to show she was of marriageable age, and that girl dashed back out to the common room. Mikael located his hooded overcoat and pulled it down from among the mass of coats on hooks on the wall. He sniffed it discreetly and found that the scent of the kitchen had permeated the wool, not an entirely bad thing. Deciding that he should have it cleaned anyway, he went and settled into his chair to wait until Synen had a chance to talk to him.

A quarter hour passed before the rush died down enough that Synen could come and join him. He brought a couple of bowls of curry over with him.

"What's the sigil on those pennants?" Mikael asked.

"Warmth, of course," Synen said, as if that was the only prayer a Larossan might have for his kitchen.

"Ah, I see."

Synen rolled his eyes and sat at the table. "What's happening out there?"

Mikael blew on the curry in his spoon to cool it. Or was this stew? He'd never quite understood what made something curry rather than soup or stew. The main difference seemed to be the amount of spices used, but he suspected that if he asked Synen, he'd simply be treated to another series of eye rolls. He considered Synen's question instead, a chance to find out whether any rumors about the body had reached the streets of Noikinos yet. "What I've heard is that the police had a body this morning, but now they don't."

Synen's bushy eyebrows rose. "Did it get up and walk away?"

"Good question." He stirred his soup. "My information said the body belonged to a police officer."

Synen gave Mikael a long, knowing look and then waved his finger in Mikael's face. "The pigeons *are* spooked. I wondered why."

Mikael wasn't going to argue his use of that nickname for the police. "I hear that the manner of death was . . . *interesting*."

"Blood magic?" Synen asked.

"What makes you ask that?"

"Officer Gastenin—he patrols this neighborhood—came in and asked if I had any visitors from Pedrossa. Put that together with a dead body the police want to hide, and that says blood magic to me."

So the police are asking about Pedraisi visitors at taverns. That alone would be enough to make innkeepers stop welcoming Pedraisi travelers, the vast majority of whom would be as horrified by the death as anyone local. News of that would get around the city quickly. "Would Faralis be able to keep something like that hidden?"

Synen shrugged. "Who knows? But when he can lock up anyone who talks, it will slow the gossip."

Mikael had never understood why the police commissioner had so much power. "Lock people up just to keep them silent?"

Synen laughed. "You clearly underestimate his desire to hang on to power. There's an election coming at year's end, and a blood magic scandal wouldn't look good for those currently in power."

Mikael finished his curry, contemplating the wisdom of *electing* one's officials, something neither the Family nor the Anvarrid did. "I'm going to head back to the fortress, Synen. Thank your wife for me."

Synen followed him to the alley door. "If they were daring enough to use a police officer in blood magic, the killer might not balk at grabbing someone like you, lad. Be careful."

"Thanks for the warning, Synen."

"You're a paying customer. I don't want to lose you." Synen strolled back toward the kitchen, laughing to himself.

Mikael headed uphill to the fortress, donning his fragrant overcoat as he walked. Synen had a point. Assuming that it hadn't been random, the killers had chosen a figure of authority for their first victim. That served to alert the police, which would only make it harder for the killers to remain hidden. It had been a risky choice, one surely meant to get attention.

He had to wonder why, and whether the second victim would be equally significant.

CHAPTER THIRTEEN

A note came for Shironne in the morning, just after the clock struck ten.

"The second . . ." Sitting on the bed next to her, Melanna struggled with the word but eventually sounded it out, having heard it before. *". . . corpse was found near the river this morning. I would . . ."*

"Spell the word for me," Shironne suggested.

Melanna complied, spelling slowly.

"Appreciate," Shironne supplied.

"Oh, all right. *I would appreciate your assistance as soon as possible.* That's it," she finished brightly.

Shironne sensed her sister's pride in her accomplishment and said, "Good work. Could you find Mama and show it to her?"

Melanna bounced off the edge of the bed, and her feet pattered out of the room.

Shironne deduced from the sound that her sister was running about the house barefooted again. She almost jumped off the bed herself. She went to the armoire in her dressing room and dug out her sturdiest leather slippers to replace the ones she wore about the house. Her mother came into her room as Shironne sat slipping on the second.

"Do you mind if I go?" Even from across the room, Shironne could sense her mother's agitation. She must have heard Melanna read the note.

"I need to have a word with the colonel," Mama said from the doorway. "I'll go with you, although I'll leave it to him to bring you back home."

The very fact that she was leaving the house while in mourning hinted at her urgency. Her mother might have said she wasn't upset about the bruise, but Shironne suspected she wanted to give the colonel a piece of her mind before she left anyway. "When will you have time to go?" Shironne asked.

"I need to accompany Perrin to the clothier's in about two hours," her mother said. "Verinne can stay with your sisters, so I think it would be best to go now. I've already sent for the driver to ready the carriage."

Poor Melanna, trapped here with Verinne. "Let me finish with my slippers, and I'll be ready."

"I'll meet you at the kitchen door," her mother said. "Just give me a few minutes."

As the sound of her mother's bracelet faded away, Shironne crossed to the hooks by her door to get her coat. The gloves in the pockets were her last decent pair of leather gloves. She hated to ask her mother to purchase more, since she was unsure about their financial future, so Shironne ground her teeth together and put on the old pair, still soiled after her trip to the morgue. It took a moment to control the reaction that shuddered through her, but she managed, wrapping one hand about the focus that rested in her tunic pocket. Then she headed down to the kitchen, and together she and her mother walked down to the back courtyard of the house.

When he saw that her mother intended to accompany them, Messine let out a flash of surprise before tucking away the reaction. He dutifully helped both of them into the carriage and then joined the driver on the box.

Their old carriage rolled into the streets, heading in the direction of the noise and traffic. Her mother sat silent, mind uneasy, leaving Shironne curious about what Mama intended to tell Colonel Cerradine. She probably wouldn't decide that until confronted by the colonel himself.

They stopped at Army Square, and, once on the walkway, Shironne placed her hand on her mother's arm. They walked down the familiar path to the colonel's office.

A soldier at the top of the steps opened the door of the administration building for them and they passed inside. Another soldier greeted Shironne as he passed on some mission, but his "Hello, miss" was too quick for her to identify the voice. Finally locating the door of the office, Shironne opened it and stepped inside, her mother close behind.

She couldn't hear anyone moving in the anteroom. Aldassa wasn't at his desk. None of them were. She and her mother went to the small room off the hallway where the colonel usually had them wait.

"I wonder where they all are," her mother said.

"The colonel's in his office. I think some of the others are there with him," Shironne told her after a moment of concentration. She knew the colonel well enough to be able to sense his presence. She recognized Captain Kassannan and a couple of the ensigns past the unseen wall as well.

Shironne located the bench near the door. She sat down, resigned to waiting. "The colonel asked me to come as soon as possible," Shironne said. "He won't leave us out here for long."

"I've never seen all of them gone like this." Worry snuck past her mother's guard, making Shironne's spine tingle.

"Something important must be going on, then."

Fortunately, the meeting in the colonel's office ended not long after they arrived. Shironne heard the door open and the sound of feet coming and going. Chairs scraped against the floor. Varied reactions came from different members of the colonel's staff as they spotted her sitting in the waiting area, some concerned by the bruise on her face. Most greeted her and her mother as they passed, although Shironne couldn't identify all of them by voice.

The sound of familiar brisk steps on the wood floor warned her of Lieutenant Aldassa's approach. "Madam Anjir, Miss Anjir," he said, "Colonel's been expecting you."

Shironne detected some surprise on Aldassa's part, so that wasn't exactly true. She didn't catch any concern in Aldassa's words, though, other than his underlying preoccupation. Aldassa *always* seemed as if a thousand tasks awaited him.

"Actually, I'd like to speak to the colonel for a moment," her mother said. "Alone."

. . .

Cerradine was surprised she'd come to into his office unaccompanied *and* dressed in colors. It stopped him in his tracks for a moment.

She'd been so adamant about her mourning. Savelle Anjir generally tried not to put herself into any situation that could be misconstrued—a habit for her, born of years of avoiding censure. Had she decided to abandon her mourning after all?

Then he saw the truth. *She's disguised as one of her maids.* She still wore no jewelry other than her bracelet with its tiny silver bells. A sheer veil in a bronzy color covered her face, and she wore a dark orange tunic over black trousers—the trousers a servant would wear. If she'd walked through Army Square garbed in mourning white, it would have been remarked, but this allowed her to seem like Shironne's escort. And Messine had surely been with them all along, keeping them safe.

"Madam Anjir," he said softly, waving Aldassa away. "Please sit down."

She settled gracefully into a chair after Aldassa left, tugging loose the scarf that had obscured her lovely face. She balled the scarf in her hands as if nervous, setting the bracelet on her wrist tinkling. Her brown eyes fixed on the side of his desk. She wore her dark hair swept up into a simple chignon at the nape of her neck. Of all the ways he'd seen her wear her hair, this was his favorite. He wondered, as always, if she knew that.

Almost four years before, she'd brought her daughter to him to help with an investigation. She'd worn a light dusting of cosmetics and kept her face turned away from him but hadn't been entirely successful in hiding the bruising on her cheek.

That had begun his relationship with the woman's husband. He considered a man beating his wife unacceptable, no matter what Larossan custom permitted. He'd had Anjir investigated and learned that among his other sins, Anjir practiced blackmail and larceny. Fortunately, Cerradine had possessed an excellent threat of his own to hold over Anjir—not that he'd ruin Anjir himself, but that he would inform *Dahar* of how his half sister had been treated. Anjir had immediately grasped the seriousness of that threat and moved out of the family home and into the house in the Old Town he kept for his mistress. Cerradine had never asked if Savelle Anjir suspected why her husband had left, but he did know from Shironne that their lives had been far better since.

Savelle Anjir was a very proper woman, almost obsessively so, and therefore Cerradine had never even touched her. Despite working with Shironne for more than three years, he'd been inside the Anjir house only a few times, and those times he'd gone in the servants' entrance in back. He'd never gone beyond the kitchen. Even so, he vividly recalled every conversation he'd had with this woman, and had some hope that she returned his regard for her.

Her continued silence warned him she'd come to say something she didn't want to. Cerradine sat down in the chair next to her, keeping his thoughts calm. He suspected she was about to take him to task for exposing Shironne to Faralis, and he was going to take it without argument or demur. He'd failed to protect Shironne and, ultimately, there was no excuse.

"Before you ask," Savelle began, "I haven't dropped my mourning. No matter what you thought of him, he was my husband, and I will do as the world expects. It's not a question of his worth, Colonel, but of *my* correctness."

"I understand," he said, even if he didn't agree. "You came here in disguise, a wise decision."

She nodded, twisting the scarf tighter. "I have to leave town tomorrow. A matter regarding my father's estate. Shironne and her sisters will be in their governess' care. Lieutenant Messine will stay behind at the house, although Lieutenant Aldrine insists on accompanying me."

Yes, the lieutenants had warned him that the trip was coming, Savelle's effort to salvage what she could of her family's monies. It wasn't necessary. Dahar would forward to her any funds that she needed without question, but she apparently didn't want to take the Royal House's money. "How long will you be gone?"

"Three days at best, but it could be a few longer than that. The girls should be fine with Messine to watch over them."

"I'd like to send Pamini over anyway, if you'd allow it. That way if Shironne needs to come to the headquarters and Messine with her, there will still be someone at the house."

Her jaw flexed, and he thought she was about to argue. Then she capitulated. "I am concerned that Faralis recognized my daughter, Colonel, so if you can spare someone, I won't turn them away."

"Thank you. I will sleep better knowing there's someone there. And that Aldrine is with you."

"She was *very* insistent." Savelle shook her head. "I was rather hoping that Shironne wouldn't be needed while I was gone. That no one would die."

"Would you prefer that we not involve her while you're away?"

"And keep her at the house like a bird in a cage? It would drive her to distraction to do nothing."

He couldn't help laughing at her vexed tone. Savelle had pushed her daughter to be independent, to know her own mind and do as she wished. That didn't mean she always liked what Shironne chose.

"That's not why I'm here, though," she said. "You asked if there had been any correspondence sent to my husband after his death regarding his various . . . businesses. No, there hasn't."

"Thank you. We've since decided that these murders likely aren't related to him, but we prefer not to dismiss any lead."

One corner of Savelle's mouth twisted upward. "And I thought it was an excuse to talk to me."

Her tone was almost playful, so he said, "I admit, I've been curious about your plans for your future, and for your daughters as well. Have you considered your brothers' offer?"

Savelle took a deep breath and launched into what sounded like a practiced speech. "I was married at fifteen to a man I didn't know and quickly came to fear. But I am a widow now, no longer under my father's control . . . or Tornin's. Why would I give myself over to a new family who may turn around and force me to marry someone else I don't want? I prefer my independence, both for myself and my daughters."

Cerradine shook his head. It had never once occurred to him that she would fear that. *Never once.* "I apologize for not grasping that concern, Madam Anjir, but your brothers would never try to force you into marriage. Or your daughters."

Her expression was guarded, as if she didn't quite believe him.

"I swear to you," he said. "They would not dare."

"And if I chose to remarry? Perhaps to someone they don't favor? A Larossan?"

Cerradine did his best to smother the stab of jealousy that question brought forth. There was no possibility that she didn't sense it anyway. Just as there was no possibility that she didn't know of his interest in her. "Anvarrid women may do as they please. Their families may cajole and plead, but no law says they must obey."

Most Larossans had little concept of how the Anvarrid Houses ran, so he understood her doubts. She'd been raised Larossan and must think all peoples treated their women the same.

"I see. If I wished to marry a Larossan man," she said, "then I would prefer not to complicate things unnecessarily. I want to bring as spotless a reputation as possible into any new marriage, and the only way I can do that is to observe a proper period of mourning. And then, should a man wish it, he could properly court me."

It was surprising that she was considering remarriage, but it sounded more like a foregone conclusion, her marriage to this unknown Larossan man. He felt his jaw clench and made an effort to calm his thoughts. "I do understand that, Madam Anjir."

She reached across the short distance between them and laid her hand lightly on his, surprising him. "Do you? Do you understand why I've come?"

He turned his hand and took hers in his own, and she allowed the familiarity, unable to withdraw her hand gracefully now. He regretted that he'd asked. He would rather not have learned that she had plans to marry. "I had no business asking into your choices, madam, other than my friendship with Dahar. I apologize."

For a moment she gazed at him as if surprised by his answer.

Yes, he'd answered incorrectly again. It seemed unfair that she was a sensitive and thus could sense what he felt, while he couldn't grasp what she sought at all. "What did you *want* me to say?"

She licked her lips, as if nervous. "Perhaps," she said, her voice trembling, "that if you were the sort of man who wished to court a woman in mourning, *you* would be willing to wait that long."

The weight that had seemed to crouch on his chest abruptly fled. Cerradine felt a smile creeping across his face. Savelle Anjir had, in a strictly hypothetical sense, asked him to court her once she'd completed her year of mourning. He set his other hand over hers. "I would be willing to wait that long."

Her eyes flitted down to his hands holding hers, and she blushed. It had likely taken all her nerve to pose that question. And since her relationships with men had been limited to Tornin Anjir, that made her leap of faith even more courageous.

"I want to be clear about one thing," he said, peering at her lowered face. "If I were courting a woman, I wouldn't let any quibbles about a year of mourning deter me, particularly not when he was not a man worth her time."

Her lips pressed together in a vexed line. "You're an officer," she said firmly. "You'll probably be a general one day. You need to consider how a wife's reputation would reflect on you."

He didn't argue. Reputation would *always* matter to Savelle. "I understand."

"But you don't agree," she said.

He shook his head. "You know how I felt about him."

"Please . . . let me do this my way. The proper way."

"Whatever you want," he said.

She smiled ruefully then. "You almost mean that."

The hazard of speaking with a sensitive who knew him well—he couldn't easily fool her. And rehashing this topic wouldn't help. "Thank you."

"I must return home now," she said then. "I must take Perrin to visit a seamstress, and need time to change clothes first."

He let her hand slip away, and she busied herself wrapping the sheer scarf about her head. He rose to accompany her, but she stopped with one hand on the door latch. "Why did you not think I was speaking of you?"

He chased that question around in his mind for a moment and then grasped what she meant. "When you suggested you might marry a Larossan man? Because I'm not Larossan."

Her head tilted, expression now obscured by her veil. "But you are."

"Those of us raised by the Family, we *are* Family, no matter how we appear on the outside. Just as you are Larossan, rather than Anvarrid."

Her mouth opened, as if that explained something that had long puzzled her. "That's why you use your Family name, isn't it?"

Very few people addressed him by that name. "Yes."

"Until the next time, then, Jon."

It surprised him how much he enjoyed hearing her say his name, and the tacit permission to use her name it conveyed. "I'll hold that hope close, Savelle."

She slipped out of his office, drawing the scarf over her face as she went. Cerradine watched her go, mesmerized, as he had been since the first time he saw her.

• • •

Messine had left to talk to Aldassa about the case at hand, so Shironne sat abandoned on the bench next to Aldassa's empty desk, waiting until the colonel was ready to speak with her. Her mother had already returned home, pleased with herself over something. It surprised Shironne that the colonel left her waiting so long, but he finally sent one of the ensigns out to fetch her back to his office.

The ensign, a young girl with a deep voice, took Shironne's hand and put it on her sleeve. Evidently she'd seen Aldassa or Messine do that before, and although Shironne didn't need the help, she wasn't going to turn it away. If nothing else, it would be rude.

"What is your name?" Shironne asked as she walked at the young woman's side.

The question caught her escort off guard. "Uh . . . Ensign Pamini."

The ensign must have looked at her as she said that. That took her off course, forcing Shironne slightly to the right, and Shironne's knee collided with wood—a bench in the hallway.

Shironne drew in a pained breath as the young woman apologized. "It's fine," she managed. "I do that all the time."

Despite her assurances, the girl radiated guilt and worry. "I'm very sorry."

Shironne knew the benches were there, and if not for the ensign guiding her, she would never have hit one unless it had been moved. She shook her leg, trying to mitigate her knee's anger. "It takes practice, Ensign. How old are you?"

"I'm a twenty," the young woman said.

That was the age when they could leave the Family. "So you're new here?"

"Only a month," she said. "I worked for the Daujom after yearchange but had to leave."

And thus still said things like *yearchange* when the rest of the world called it the New Year. "The Daujom?"

"Shironne? Why don't you come in here?" the colonel asked from not far away.

Ensign Pamini set Shironne's gloved hand on the doorframe. Shironne found the back of one of the chairs and sat, flipping her braid over her shoulder as she did so. She heard the colonel sit nearby. She could still smell him, wool and gun oil and a cologne she'd always liked. Her father had favored musk. "So, uh . . . there's a body you want me to look at?"

The colonel accepted her change of subject without demur. "We found the second corpse up near Miller's Point early this morning. As it turns out, it was a good thing Captain Kassannan took you to examine that first body, as the police refused to let him look at it a second time. Word leaked out the body was cremated this morning."

Had she heard him wrong? "Can they do that? Um, I mean, burn the body before they find out who killed him?"

The colonel laughed. "They're denying the body ever existed, and since the army had no business being there, we can hardly use as leverage the fact that Kassannan—and you—saw it."

No, a court would never believe that she'd seen anything. "Why would they hide it?"

"A police officer killed in blood magic makes the police seem weak. And given that some people suspect that Faralis had something to do with the children sold into Pedraisi slavery, anything that reminds the public of the Pedraisi brings up the subject of his possible involvement in that."

The colonel had, tactfully, not mentioned that Shironne's own father had been suspected of selling children. "Well, surely someone else saw the body, sir. What about the police officers, or the fishermen who pulled the body out of the river? Wouldn't they say something?"

He sighed, letting her sense the edge of his annoyance. "The fishermen who discovered the body can't be found. Rumor says Faralis arrested them."

"Can you . . . um, get them out?"

"Well, we'll have to see," he said, and she heard him rise. "I suggest we walk over to the hospital and look at our body. Perhaps I can tell you more then."

Shironne followed the colonel out of the office. He took her gloved hand, placed it on his arm, and led her out of the building into the sunshine. She could feel the sun on her face. "Why is this one in *your* morgue rather than the city's?" she asked as they crossed the lawn in the square.

"One, because we found him first. Two, we've identified him as army."

The killers had taken a police officer as their sacrifice first, and now a soldier? That seemed especially brazen to her. It could be a coincidence, but she doubted that.

The colonel opened a door and Shironne smelled the morgue as they headed down the stairwell into the basement. The colonel opened the inner door and the familiar scent roiled forth, not nearly as pungent as the smell of the city's morgue, thankfully. She pressed one gloved finger under her nose, trying to minimize the odor.

Cerradine always insisted that the more information they collected about a death, the faster they could catch the killer. She hoped there was *some* insight she could offer.

CHAPTER FOURTEEN

Mikael had spent the better part of an hour searching through wooden boxes that held files from years past. The Daujom generated a phenomenal amount of paper, all of which had to be stored away somewhere. An old box in one of the narrow storage rooms farther down the hall from the office divulged the files Mikael sought.

The papers smelled old and musty, and he suspected mice had been in them. A tiny desiccated skeleton and a few tufts of moldering fur in the corner of the box confirmed that guess. It would be more prudent to store old files in the fortress below, where vermin never intruded. He made a mental note to suggest that to Dahar, although he couldn't be the first person to have thought of that.

Mikael sneezed, dust from the files getting up his nose. He patted more out of his hair and followed Dahar back to the main office with their prize. Somehow, despite looking through several boxes himself, Dahar had managed to stay completely clean, not a speck on his uniform or in his dark hair. Mikael suspected that he, on the other hand, looked like a reversed version of a chimney sweep. Swathes of white dust marked his black trousers and vest. He would have to sponge them off later. At least he'd removed his uniform jacket before digging among the files.

Dahar still hadn't found out about the aftereffects of Mikael's last dream.

That meant Kai hadn't told his father. Deborah hadn't mentioned it either. When Mikael had been Below for his sparring practice with Eli, the young man hadn't said anything. That told Mikael that Deborah was keeping the information close for now, probably waiting until after she discussed it with the elders. He was living on borrowed time, then, waiting for the news to spread through the fortress like wildfire.

Everything seemed to be at a standstill. He hoped they could find some evidence in these files that would definitively link the deaths in his dreams to the massacres. Or perhaps it would be better to find evidence that *didn't*.

As if in answer to his worries, when they got back to the main office of the Daujom, an ensign waited for them with a message from the colonel. Mikael set down the heavy file box on Kai's desk, dusted off his vest and trousers, and donned his uniform jacket, grateful for the warmth.

The note was terse to the point of being useless, asking that Mikael come down to the army headquarters *later*, but the ensign who carried it imparted more information. The army had found the second body that morning and identified the victim as one of their own.

"Wait until after lunch to see Cerradine," Dahar said. "Khader should be done with Kai by then, and he can go with you."

Mikael always found it amusing to hear the king being spoken of by his short name—Khader—rather than Khaderion. He supposed that as the king's brother, Dahar had the right to do so. Some Anvarrid were prickly about that, though, as if not giving them their full title name was an insult. On the other hand, Dahar hated being called Daharion, and Mikael didn't think that Kai would ever be comfortable being called Khandrasion.

"I'll wait for Kai, then," Mikael said, unable to keep the resignation from his voice. He hated viewing his corpses, despite the fact that he'd dreamed those same deaths. It was too *personal.* He usually lost whatever meal he'd most recently eaten. There were buckets in the cold rooms in Below that Mikael suspected had never been needed there before he came along.

Dahar clapped him on the shoulder as he walked by. He must have sensed Mikael's trepidation. "I don't like it either."

It's different for me, Mikael thought. Dahar didn't identify with the dead in the personal way he did. But there was a purpose to doing it. When he looked down at those bodies, memories he couldn't recall before shook loose, giving him his first real clues about the killer. And if this *was* a case of murder by blood magic, particularly an instance that imitated the massacres, then they needed every bit of information that he had stored away from his dream.

"I suppose the colonel will want me to bring these files," Mikael said.

Dahar folded his arms over his chest, scowling at the file box. "We need to go through them before turning them over. I trust Jon, but the Andersens might have put information in here that we don't want the army to see."

The idea of hiding information from Cerradine rubbed Mikael the wrong way, but protecting the treaty between the Families and the Anvarrid was the Daujom's *primary* function. "What exactly are we trying to find in here?"

"Anything regarding the deaths of the murdered priests." Dahar started dividing the papers into piles. "I don't want these reviewed by anyone other than the three of us before we turn them over."

That meant he and Dahar would have to do the bulk of it since Kai was spending so much time with the king, if that was where he actually was. Mikael picked the tallest stack and carried it over to his own desk. Sighing, he sat down and began thumbing through the top file. He saw no point in eating lunch.

. . .

As Captain Kassannan pulled back the sheets from the table, he recounted for Shironne his failed attempt to get back in to see the corpse at the city morgue. This time he'd been blocked every step of the way. He managed to make the experience of being dragged from the morgue sound like an adventure, even though it had more likely been frustrating and time-consuming. "They think they can just deny it and that'll make these killers go away?" she asked.

"Hmm," Cerradine said. "Sometimes that tactic works."

Shironne heard Kassannan settle somewhere away from them, probably to take notes again. The colonel led her to the table where the body lay. She removed one of her gloves and touched the dead man's skin. He'd been dead only about a day and a half, she decided, definitely the victim in the last dream. "Nalyan Moradine," Shironne told the colonel without hesitation, "but you already knew his name."

"Yes," the colonel said.

"How did you find the body?" she asked.

"I borrowed several squads of soldiers and Aldassa had them search the riverside. Took all night, but a while before dawn, one of them tripped over the body."

Shironne grimaced. "That must have been an unpleasant experience."

"Yes. Fortunately, we identified the man easily enough. Moradine, that is, not the soldier who fell over him. Still had on his uniform trousers. That prevents the police taking him from us."

"Did you know the man?" she asked.

"No," the colonel said softly, sounding regretful anyway.

Shironne touched the edge of a gaping wound in the chest, all blood from it washed carefully away. Kassannan would have done that. "Has someone come to identify him?"

"His wife," Kassannan said tightly.

Shironne closed her mouth, reminding herself not to say anything insensitive. Several months before, it had been Captain Kassannan who'd stood there to identify his wife's body. The colonel, however, had moved on. He stood directly behind her now, presumably looking over her shoulder. "Is this the same as the first?"

She concentrated on that cut across the man's chest. "Yes. The same type of blade made this cut, although I can't assure you it was the same blade. Did you find a mark on his neck?" she asked Kassannan.

Kassannan's voice drifted toward her from several feet to her left. "Definitely poison, perhaps to keep the victim compliant."

Shironne caught a flash of surprise from the colonel, but he said nothing. She slid her fingers to the markings across the shoulders. "What does this word mean, do you think?"

"Blood magic is often written in an older dialect," the colonel said, "no longer a spoken language. Because of that, we don't have anyone who can translate it precisely."

He might not know what the word meant, but it still carried a great significance to him. They weren't telling her what that was, though, probably to keep from biasing her answers. She turned toward where she thought he was standing, hoping to get a more direct impression of his reactions. "This word. This is why everyone's in such a . . . bother over this, isn't it? I don't mean to sound like two murders isn't a bother, sir, but this is different. Is that because it's blood magic?"

"Yes," the colonel answered, without further explanation.

Shironne kept her hand above the cuts, sorting out her impressions of blood and body to determine if there was anything distinctive about this body when compared to the last. There was dirt in the cuts, she realized and, after brief contemplation, asked, "Was the body found north of the reeds?"

Kassannan's attention sharpened.

The colonel asked, "How did you know that?"

"The dirt," she said. "There's dirt in some of the wounds, and the composition is very similar to a sample the captain had me study."

That surprised the colonel, who likely thought that her study of dirt had been time wasted. "I see. We know from the blood that he was killed there, near Miller's Point. Did you sense that with the first victim?"

She shook her head. "After a couple of days in the river, no.

There was some silt from the bottom of the river, but any dirt from where he was killed was long gone."

"Aldassa's still trying to figure out where the police officer was killed," the colonel said with a breath. "And trying to figure out why the first one ended up in the river, but this one didn't."

"The killers didn't put him in the river," she said, feeling sure of that.

"The theory that Aldassa's following," the colonel said, "is that someone came across the body, realized they were dealing with blood magic, and dumped the body into the river to protect against recrimination . . . or a curse."

That made sense. Shironne held her hand on the body awhile longer, pushing her perception past the stiffness lingering in the muscles. She dug through the fading memories, asking the same things the young lieutenant had at the end: why he had died, why they took him and not some other, and why this way. He'd been afraid, confused. He'd had no chance, not with so many of them. And what of the man forced to watch? He hadn't understood that. As she often did, Shironne found a sense of comfort at the end, the dead man's realization that he wasn't alone, that the Angel of Death was with him. She turned her attention back to the colonel and Kassannan. "He didn't know why he died, sir, just like the other. Nor why he was chosen."

"I expected not."

"It's a problem, isn't it? That they took a police officer and now a soldier?"

The colonel didn't answer, but Shironne could tell she'd gotten that correct. There were far easier men to target than young and healthy ones.

"In the first dream, I got a sense of someone watching. I think that someone—a man—was forced to witness this man's murder. One of the things that Moradine didn't understand."

"A witness?" the colonel repeated, perplexed.

"Why would the killers bring a witness along?" Kassannan asked.

Shironne chased that reflection for a time but couldn't find any answer inscribed on the leaves of the soldier's memories. "Moradine was drugged," Shironne said, "so the memory was vague."

"Well, we've learned all we can just now," the colonel said then. "Let Aldassa write down everything you can recall. That will give us something to go by. He may ask some questions as well."

"He always does." She sighed.

After a thorough washing of her hands, Shironne said her goodbyes to the captain and headed back to the colonel's office with him. The air was fresher outside, and she took a deep breath. She didn't hear any men or horses nearby, just the colonel's shortened stride sounding along with hers. She waited until they were halfway across the square before she asked her question. "You've seen something like this before, haven't you, sir?"

"Years ago," he said, his reaction indicating resignation. "You would have been just a child then, so you won't remember."

"What happened?" she asked.

"I'll not say, so you won't have to hide it from your mother."

Shironne paused midstride, almost falling over when the colonel kept going. "She *would* remember it, then?"

"Yes. I don't want her to worry," he said firmly, "so don't tell her."

The colonel never actually lied to her mother about anything he involved Shironne in, but she knew he hated for her mother to worry. She started walking again and the colonel resumed his measured steps. "Tell her what?"

"Exactly," he replied.

"Did she take you to task about the police commissioner? I told her that wasn't Kassannan's fault."

Amusement fled through his mind, as it often did when she tried to pry. But whatever he'd discussed with her mother, it had left him pleased with himself. "Don't concern yourself about it for now, Shironne. She wanted to talk about her plans. To visit the countryside, I mean."

"Oh," she said, pausing as a breeze across her face startled her. "Anything else?"

But the colonel refused to explain further about his conversation with her mother as they made their way back to the office, vexing her. Before he left her in Aldassa's hands, though, he handed her a slim box. "A birthday present."

Through her gloves, the box told her very little. "My birthday was a month ago, sir."

"We're late. Consider this a present from all of us."

Shironne found the opening of the box and pulled it apart, hoping nothing would slither out. She reached inside and grasped what felt like heavy fabric. She pulled off one of her worn gloves and fingered fine leather, feeling tanner's chemicals, the tang of dye, and the touch of the hands of the maker.

It took a moment to accustom herself to the feel of them. Very few hands had touched the gloves so far, making them easier for her skin to bear, but even new clothes had been touched by others, leaving behind bits of skin and dirt and oils. Clothes that had been worn by someone else took even more time to adapt to. She could always feel the other person about her, almost as if they touched her themselves.

"What color are they?" She stripped off her old glove and held up one of the new ones, deciding it fit the left hand.

"One pair is black, the other plain tan," Aldassa answered.

Two pairs? Shironne loosened the paper in the box and located a second pair that had no feel of dye about it. Those would be the tan ones. She grinned and slid the black glove onto her hand. She knew that dye well enough that she could quickly dismiss the feel of it from her senses. The glove fit perfectly, on which she commented.

"Thank Aldassa's wife for that," the colonel said. "Liana suggested taking in an old pair you left behind a couple of months ago. The glover used them as a pattern."

Shironne sensed the colonel's pleasure that they'd managed to surprise her. "Thank you so much," she said. "And please tell everyone in the office I appreciate it." She slid on the second black glove. "These are wonderful."

"I'm glad you like them. Kassannan mentioned that you didn't have a chance to wash your hands before you put on your old pair." She opened her mouth to comment, but the colonel continued, "I'll leave you with Aldassa, then. He'll see to it that you get home." He swept out before she could thank him again.

"Here, put this other pair in your pocket before we forget about them," Aldassa suggested.

"Will you thank your wife for me?" she begged, and Aldassa agreed, settling down across the desk from her. As a clothier's assistant, his wife knew more about articles of clothing than Shironne could ever hope to understand. She folded the second pair of gloves carefully and placed them in her coat pocket.

Aldassa questioned her for almost an hour, taking down everything she could recall about the body missing from the city's morgue. She was probably feeding him much of the same information they'd gotten from Kassannan, but different people always picked up different things. When Aldassa had exhausted all the logical avenues of questioning, he ordered a closed carriage brought around. Since Messine had accompanied Shironne's mother back to the house, Ensign Pamini accompanied her again, settling across from her in the carriage and explaining that she was going to be coming to the house the next day to help Messine watch over them in Kirya Aldrine's absence. The driver set them down in the back courtyard, away from the curious eyes of their neighbors. After Pamini made certain Shironne got up the back stairs to the kitchen, the carriage drove slowly away.

Her mother and Perrin had gone on to the clothier's, but Shironne found Melanna hiding in the kitchen. In the warmth of the flour-scented room, Melanna admired the new gloves dutifully, not sharing Shironne's attachment to such items of apparel. She declared that they'd be very good for riding should they ever have riding horses again, a rare attempt at diplomacy on Melanna's part.

"I'll bear that in mind, little brat," Shironne said with a laugh. She hadn't ridden a horse since she'd gone blind and doubted she would *ever* have that opportunity. "Now, go find that book we're reading."

Melanna slipped away and returned a few minutes later with her lurid novel. She sat next to Shironne at the servants' table, reading aloud, with Shironne supplying the occasional pronunciation or definition. They spent the next hour there, amusing Cook and the kitchen maids with the exploits of the handsome young Larossan hero and his heroine, who wailed with alarming frequency, much to Melanna's disgust.

CHAPTER FIFTEEN

Mikael decided he must have the nonincriminating stack of files on the Farunas incident. He'd skimmed through a handful and seen nothing so far that hinted the Andersens had done anything worth lying about. Dahar left to eat lunch, so Mikael dragged one of the wooden chairs from its normal position over by the hearth and propped his feet up on it. He passed the noon hour that way, winnowing through a few more files.

Kai strode into the office just after one, giving Mikael only a cursory glance. He shrugged off his overcoat, tossed it over his chair, and frowned down at the pile on his desk. He had the same flair for the dramatic entry that his father had. Mikael slipped his feet off the chair.

Elisabet gazed at Mikael, a faint line between her arching brows. But she merely nodded to him and assumed her regular post, setting her long rifle by her foot and easing into a resting stance next to the entry door. She would stand there watching until Kai left, or until evening, when one of her Seconds—Peder or Tova—came to relieve her.

Kai glanced up from the pile of folders on his desk and fixed Mikael with a dark stare. "What is this?"

"Don't complain," Mikael warned. "You got the smaller stack. *I* had to fish out the dead mouse."

That almost got a smile out of Elisabet, but she controlled herself before she let it slip.

Kai regarded him with one raised brow but turned his attention to the folders on his desk. When he moved to sit, Mikael forestalled him. "Have you talked to your father today?"

"I missed him this morning," Kai answered shortly, his tone verifying that the feud with his father continued.

While Dahar's temper was mercurial, Kai's irritable spells lasted weeks at a time. Mikael reminded himself to go down to Below and talk to Jannika later; perhaps she'd discovered the source of Kai's recent foul mood. "Well, Cerradine's searchers turned up a body," Mikael told him. "They want us to come down and look at it."

Kai fixed him with an annoyed gaze, dark eyes flat. "They want *you* to come and look at it, Mikael. I didn't even know Cerradine had searchers out."

Mikael ignored the faintly accusing tone. This was all part of the battle of wills between Dahar and his son. Dahar had ordered Kai to babysit Mikael, and Kai wasn't entirely in the wrong for being annoyed with his father. Mikael didn't actually need Kai's escort, and Kai had other things to do, especially since he hadn't come in that morning. "If you'd prefer not to, I can go by myself, but your father told me to wait for you."

Kai fingered the files, picked one up to peer at it, and then dropped it on his desk. "I'll go."

Mikael stepped past Elisabet out to the hall and waved for a runner. A young man in browns—probably one of Eli's sixteens, judging by his size—started up from where he crouched next to one of the sentries. He listened to Mikael's instructions and ran off toward the courtyard.

Meanwhile, Kai migrated away from his own desk to Mikael's, inspecting the labels set into the file folders Mikael had already scanned. "What is all of this?"

"Someone pulled a body from the river yesterday and now the police are hiding it. Cerradine's sensitive claimed it was the victim from my first dream. The colonel came to have lunch with your father yesterday and wanted to check with me." Too late, it occurred to Mikael that Kai might take offense; they'd asked *him* to join them but not Kai.

Kai frowned at the chair next to Mikael's desk as if he'd just spotted it, and then carried it back over to its usual position by the hearth. "How would she know that?"

Mikael shook his head. "Captain Kassannan spirited her into the morgue to view the body."

Kai paused on the rug in front of the hearth. His dark brows drew together and his eyes went distant.

A knock on the door was the runner returned to tell them the coach was approaching, so Mikael put on his jacket. He tied his sash around his waist, the uniform jacket bunching under it. *At least I can keep up with Kai today,* he thought, relieved that he'd had an uninterrupted night's sleep.

The day had warmed considerably after the frigid morning. Standing in the courtyard behind the palace, Elisabet glanced into the waiting coach and then ushered Kai inside. Mikael entered last, ending up facing backward. Kai and Elisabet shared the other bench, Elisabet holding her rifle awkwardly between them, the butt resting on the coach floor.

She was spooked, Mikael realized. She wouldn't have brought her rifle with her into this coach otherwise. She'd carried this same one since he first met her, a weapon from one of the eastern foundries, he thought. Decorative etchings on the barrels had been worn down by years of use. The wood of the butt had grayed with age but looked clean. A good weapon, but in the coach it was merely in the way.

With Kai brooding, Mikael resigned himself to a quiet ride. Despite the fact that they both had Deborah as sponsor, he rarely spoke with Elisabet. She was simply too reticent. She pushed the shade aside to peer out at the afternoon traffic. The light flickered across her pale face, highlighting the blond braids that trailed over the shoulders of her black uniform.

He hadn't been sent to the Lucas Family until he was an adult.

He hadn't actually needed a sponsor when he'd arrived, but Deborah had volunteered to watch over him anyway. Elisabet, on the other hand, had to have been adopted into the Lucas Family at an early age, although close to eight, since she'd been given a widow as a sponsor. Most childern adopted into the Six Families were placed within a family so they would have two parents to look after them, but as soon as they became eights, they went to live in their yeargroup quarters. Elisabet wouldn't need a sponsor as much then; thus they'd given her to Deborah, a single adult, to watch over.

As if sensing he thought of her, Elisabet turned her light eyes on Mikael, her face unreadable in the gloom of the coach.

They rolled to a stop in front of the army's administrative offices. Elisabet handed her rifle to Mikael while she stepped down, one hand on her pistol. He passed the rifle down to her when she gestured for it and then followed Kai out of the coach.

The administrative building stood on one side of Army Square. A squad practiced a loading drill on the wide green, and Kai stopped to watch. The Family inherited the army's old munitions when the government purchased new ones, and the army was more than due. The weapons they used now were years out of date, but steel was expensive, and replacing the army's weapons every time a new design came along impractical.

Elisabet touched Kai's back, a silent reminder not to stand on the steps of the building. Kai glanced at her and proceeded up the granite steps into the headquarters building. They walked along the wood-paneled hallways until they reached the first-floor office marked INTELLIGENCE AND INVESTIGATION. Four large desks crowded the anteroom of the office, but only David Aldassa sat there today, scowling down at some paperwork.

Aldassa rose and nodded to Elisabet first. He and Elisabet came from the same yeargroup, a year ahead of Kai and two ahead of Mikael. The members of a yeargroup often stayed in touch, even when they left the Family. With the constant interaction between this office and the Daujom, Aldassa saw Elisabet frequently.

"Good afternoon, David," she said in her cool voice. "Have you heard from Paal Endiren?"

Aldassa shook his head. "No word. The Andersens haven't located him."

Mikael recalled then that Endiren was from the same yeargroup as Elisabet and Aldassa, explaining why the man came up as the first topic of conversation. Mikael knew Lieutenant Endiren only in passing but held out little hope for the man's return. The lieutenant had evidently pursued a rumor across the border and vanished into Pedraisi territory. Most people who did that never returned. While the other four pentarchies that made up the country of Pedrossa had predominantly peaceful dealings with Larossa, the pentarchy that bordered Andersen Province—simply named the Southwestern Pentarchy—had long had hostile relations with Larossa, fueled by differences over culture and religion.

The Andersens would never be permitted to cross the border to search for Endiren. From her slumped shoulders, Mikael guessed Elisabet knew that.

"Will the colonel have time to see us?" Kai asked, sounding annoyed again. Mikael suspected that had something to do with the easy way Elisabet talked to Aldassa.

"I'll tell him you're here." Aldassa left them for a moment. When he returned, he gestured for them to go on to the colonel's office.

"Why don't you wait here with Aldassa?" Kai said.

For a confused second, Mikael thought Kai meant *him*.

Then he realized Kai had spoken to Elisabet. Her eyes flicked toward Mikael, as if to ask Mikael to keep an eye on Kai. Mikael nodded. He didn't think there was much threat to Kai there in the colonel's office anyway.

They left Elisabet behind with Aldassa and walked down the short hallway to the colonel's office. With no windows, the wood-paneled walls seemed like a stark cage, reinforced by the monochromatic effect of the wooden desk and chairs. The blue of the colonel's uniform jacket provided a bright spot in the room. He rose and greeted them both with his usual avuncular air, then asked Kai about the king's well-being.

A map of Larossa hung on one wall, neatly framed. While Kai spoke with the colonel about the king's dilemma regarding one Anvarrid House or another, Mikael crossed the room to gaze at the map. With a finger, he traced one of the lakes he remembered swimming in as a boy.

The colonel's voice drummed through Mikael's reverie. "I may have a prior involvement in this case," Cerradine admitted, "so Aldassa's running this investigation. Can you tell us when they'll strike again? If they're following a pattern, someone will die tonight."

Ah, that was a question for *him*. Mikael had already worked out that since there had been one night between the first two killings, tonight might mean another murder if the killers were on a schedule. Unfortunately, he couldn't be sure. He often had a headache before one of his dreams, but they sometimes came on very suddenly. He didn't have one at the moment. "No, sir," he said. "I can't answer that."

Cerradine frowned, glancing over at Kai. "Have you had a chance to catch up on this yet?"

"No, sir, I haven't," Kai said. "I've been . . . occupied."

The colonel grabbed his hat from the corner of his desk and gestured for them to precede him out the door of the office. On the way over to the hospital, Cerradine talked with Kai, a hand on his shoulder. Mikael trailed in Elisabet's silent company. She kept her eyes on Kai but allowed the colonel's familiarity, a measure of her trust in the man. Although her face didn't show it, Mikael had the feeling Kai's earlier interference had annoyed her.

The drilling company of soldiers had left the green, and for the moment there was silence, the sound of carriage horses clopping around the square about the only thing that broke the early afternoon calm. The air had warmed, making Mikael appreciate the fact that he wasn't wearing a plated coat like Elisabet's. They crossed the stone-paved road, walked into the side entrance of the hospital, and headed down the steps into the basement.

They reached the morgue in the basement of the hospital and had to wait until Captain Kassannan came trotting down with the keys. He led them back to the large workroom where the body waited. High windows allowed ample light in from the ground level. The tile floors appeared perfectly clean, and the white plastered walls gave a crisp look to the place, but the faint odor of death left no doubt as to the room's function. Mikael wrinkled his nose at the smell and then did his best to ignore it.

Kai followed Cerradine and Kassannan into the room, but Mikael stopped just inside the door. He dreaded doing this. Kai had an iron stomach and never flinched. Mikael had lived through the death with the victim, though, and that made the experience very personal.

It was always strange, doing this. Cerradine had Kassannan and his orderlies to study the body and make their determinations as to how the man had died. He had his sensitive, who provided him with some other form of information. What Cerradine deigned to tell Mikael about the woman's conclusions was sometimes strangely detailed, although Cerradine said her impressions were limited by her distance from the palace.

But Mikael was the one who actually touched the dead man's mind. Sometimes staring down at the body jarred loose memories, not always of the murder. Sometimes it was a simple fact that the victim had wanted remembered. Often it seemed random, as if the mind had simply plucked out a memory and wove it into Mikael's consciousness. It was his calling to remember all of those things. To know what needed to be avenged. To know what needed to be said.

Kassannan pulled back the sheet. The corpse under it seemed startled to be there, a surprised expression frozen on the young man's face.

"Stay by the door," Kai said to Elisabet.

Standing next to her, Mikael caught the brief tightening of Elisabet's lips but couldn't tell whether she was offended or relieved. Kai walked around to the other side of the table as the captain folded the sheet down to the man's waist. He leaned over to read the writing on the man's chest. Reaching into a pocket, he withdrew a pristine handkerchief and held it up to his nose as he continued to survey the man's injuries.

"The massacres," Kai murmured to the colonel, just loud enough for Mikael to hear. "How accurate a replication of those deaths is this?"

"From what I recall," Cerradine said, "quite accurate." They stood together for a moment, discussing the investigation in lowered voices.

Mikael decided he had his stomach sufficiently under control and walked over to the table. He looked down at the young man's face. The dark eyes had clouded over slightly, and his skin, a medium brown, had paled with his death. The young officer couldn't be more than a year or two older than Mikael himself.

"He had a wife," Mikael said, interrupting Kai's quiet voice.

"She's identified the body." Cerradine didn't ask how Mikael knew about the wife. They'd been through this experience before and both knew the pattern of it. "We're withholding the body for now," the colonel said. "We'll need to turn it over soon. The mortuary service wants to go ahead and prepare him for burial."

"Did she see what they did to him?"

"No. She only saw his face."

"Good," Mikael said, recalling the woman's fragility. He wrapped his arms about his chest. "She shouldn't see this. It would break her heart."

"I'll make certain of it," Cerradine said.

Mikael gazed down at the body laid out before him. The horrible carvings, the anonymous death—none of it made any sense. He felt warm suddenly and broke into a cold sweat. His breath went shallow as he saw *himself* lying there dead on the table. He stumbled back and ended up on his knees on the floor. His stomach turned. He retched up his breakfast and then retched again until nothing remained but bile.

Captain Kassannan placed a damp towel on Mikael's neck, forcing Mikael to sit with his head on his knees. "Just stay put."

Mikael sat on the chilly tile floor while shudders chased themselves along his body. His skin felt clammy. He breathed slowly, trying to reestablish calm. At least he'd managed not to dirty his uniform this time.

Kassannan came back with another towel, a metal basin, and a cup of water. Mikael rinsed out his mouth and wiped his overwarm face. Kassannan directed him to lay the towel over the mess for the moment and helped him to his feet. Mikael apologized, but Kai merely gave him a level stare. Mikael suspected Kai would like nothing better than never to have to deal with him again.

Cerradine shook his head. "Don't worry about it, Mikael."

Stepping back to the table, Mikael did his best to hold himself aloof, trying to see only a corpse in front of him, not his own death. "What do you make of the writing, Colonel? *Is* the word the same?"

"Did you not find it in your files?"

"Not yet," Mikael said. "I'm beginning to suspect the Andersens omitted it intentionally. What about everything else?"

"The victims of the original massacres weren't drugged. They bound them instead. This man was drugged, but *not* tied." Cerradine glanced over at Kassannan for confirmation.

"Country, city, I figure." Kassannan gestured toward the corpse's unmarked wrist. "In the city, they'd have to be certain not to draw attention. The massacres happened in the country along the river, the homesteads separated by miles. Once they rounded up the members of a household, who would hear them screaming? Look here." He turned the dead man's head slightly and pointed out a spot on the neck.

Mikael glanced at it. "What kind of drug is it?"

"We don't know. No idea about the symptoms."

Mikael turned to surveying the letters painstakingly cut into the skin, completing the marks he'd seen before on his own shoulders. "What did the Andersens think it meant, Colonel?"

Cerradine tapped a finger against his cheek. "I never heard."

"*Willing sacrifice.*" Elisabet's voice startled them. They all turned to look at her where she waited just inside the door. Kai shot her an angry look, as if to reprimand her for speaking.

"What makes you say that?" Cerradine asked.

"That's what they said. I'm from the border," she said, volunteering a rare fact about herself.

The border? He'd assumed she came from one of the enclaves in Lucas Province. Mikael was from the Larossan-Pedraisi border himself, but he'd been only nine when the massacres happened. Elisabet would have been an eleven then and might have heard more. But no, she would have come to Lucas years before that, wouldn't she?

"Did it get about, what had been written on the bodies?" Mikael asked, glancing at her face.

The colonel nodded. "There were reports all over the province. Varying things. I wouldn't swear to any of them. I was hoping to look at the Daujom's files soon. If we can match the current inscriptions to the old, then we'll know for certain what we're dealing with."

"We'll get them to you first thing tomorrow," Kai promised.

Mikael suppressed a groan. They had a long night of reviewing musty old files ahead of them, then. "Has your sensitive come by to see him?"

Cerradine gave Mikael a secretive smile. "She was here this morning."

"You said she knew the other man, the one the city had, was the one from my dream. How?"

"A body like that doesn't turn up every day, so she knew it was your victim. Besides, she claims she senses your presence in the bodies."

Mikael gaped at him, the sour feeling in his stomach rising again. "My presence?"

"She always can," Cerradine said with a shrug.

The colonel had never before told him he left a touch of himself behind in the victims, almost as if he left a part of his soul with each dream. He swallowed. "We should head back to the fortress. I have paperwork to finish."

"Deborah and I have discussed letting the two of you work together."

Surprise made Mikael's breath go short. The idea of meeting someone who'd been running across abandoned bits of his soul quashed any desire he'd had to know more about this woman.

"There are two dead already, Mikael. In your mind somewhere, you have evidence we need. She could get at it."

"How?" he asked, his stomach roiling again. "I don't even know how to find what's buried in my mind." What could a sensitive do?

"Trust me, she can," Cerradine said in a placating tone. "If she looked into your dreams, she could find more. I only want you to consider it."

Look into his dreams? How did he mean for the woman to do that? Was Cerradine suggesting that he allow her to be present while he dreamed? Mikael didn't know what to say.

Kai made all the proper responses, his diplomatic training showing, and they left the morgue. Mikael forced himself not to look back at the colonel or the body he'd left behind. Once inside the coach and headed back to the palace, Kai turned to him.

"You're afraid to do what he wants." No accusation colored Kai's tone this time, merely observation.

Of course I am. Mikael leaned against the wall of the coach and closed his eyes. "He doesn't understand what he's asking."

"I would prefer to reach a quick conclusion to this case," Kai told him sternly. "If you can help this way, you should be willing to consider it."

That was an odd stance for Kai to take, the first time Mikael recalled Kai *wanting* him to dream. He lifted the blind and gazed outside, just wanting to escape Kai at the moment.

Kai opened his mouth to make another argument, but Elisabet's hand settled on his sleeve. "Leave it," she told him. "No one should have to live through that. He doesn't want to force another."

Kai gazed at her, an offended expression on his face, as if she'd betrayed him by coming down on Mikael's side. Then his eyes fixed on Mikael again. The only one of Dahar's children not to have inherited his green eyes, Kai had eyes of dark brown, excellent for glaring. None of them spoke for the remainder of the trip.

Dahar had left by the time they returned, so they spent the afternoon reviewing files for Cerradine, hunting for anything incriminating the Andersens might have left behind. Mikael suspected the other Family had been too thorough for that. He skimmed through the remaining files in the stack he'd chosen. On the other hand, it appeared that Kai intended to read every word in his. They both continued past sunset. "I have an appointment on the sparring floor," Mikael lied when the clock on the mantel struck seven.

"Fine," Kai snapped, not even looking up. "I'll finish."

Once Kai began something, he usually stayed with it until the end. Mikael left Kai there, reading in the wan glow of the gaslights. "He's going to be here all night," he said quietly to Elisabet as he passed her at the door.

"I don't doubt it," she replied.

Deborah was in yet another meeting with the other elders, so Mikael decided this would be an excellent time to hunt for Jannika.

CHAPTER SIXTEEN

The twenty-twos were gathered in their common room, drinking tea and laughing. Like most common rooms, it was filled with a haphazard collection of furniture—couches and chairs and settees most likely cast off from some household, or purchased with Family credits and then used until it *looked* cast-off.

Although some had their backs to him, Mikael counted ten women gathered there, along with a half dozen children too young for yeargroups, and two young men. All wore casual garb—loose pants probably retired from the sparring floor, shirts old enough to be gray, some with their sleeves cut out. Sweaters and socks for some of them, the colder-natured among the yeargroup. A long, low table was cluttered with teacups, and one of the toddlers tried to grab one kept just out of reach. A large urn safely set aside on a tall stand kept the hot tea safe from grasping little hands. One of the young women brushed out another's hair, preparatory to braiding it. That girl eyed Mikael for a moment.

He stood at the end of their hallway, waiting for someone to give him permission to step over the guideline that divided the main corridor from the individual hall. He could walk in there, claiming that it was a matter pertinent to the Daujom, but he didn't see Jannika among that group, and he didn't want to annoy them by being high-handed. And it wasn't legitimately Daujom business anyway. He just wanted information on Kai.

One of the young women prodded another with a bare foot. "Isn't that Jannika's current?"

Mikael felt a dull flash of surprise, followed by a brief surge of panic. He did his best to quash his reaction but had no doubt it was felt since a handful of the group's members began to laugh. He might have initiated this renewed friendship with Jannika, but he'd done so to gather information. He hadn't expected her to try to court him. And he wasn't sure he wanted to be her current, however that was meant.

The woman doing the braiding swiveled about so she could see him, and Mikael recognized Iselin. After muttering something indistinct to the other young woman, Iselin rose and wended her way through the ragtag furniture, while he counted in his head to get his emotions under control.

When she stood a few feet away, Iselin acknowledged him with a mere lift of her chin. "What do you want?"

"I wanted to talk to Jannika."

Iselin shook her head. She didn't look displeased to see him, but she didn't look pleased either. "Duty. She switched with one of the twenty-fives, took evening in Three Above."

That translated into going back up two flights of stairs, up the grand stair to the palace, and then up another two flights to the third floor of the palace. And then he had to find her on that third floor. "Quarterguard duty?"

Iselin folded her arms over her chest. "Yes."

"Thank you, then," he said from the other side of the line. "That's all I needed."

Iselin nodded once and walked away, rejoining the cozy group in their evening's sit-down. Jannika might have invited him to come have tea with her yeargroup, but Iselin wasn't going to extend the same invitation. So Mikael made his way from Three Down all the way back up, contemplating what it meant that they apparently considered him Jannika's current. Since she was on quarterguard duty, Jannika would be near the king's quarters, or his consort's—

on the other end of the palace. Unfortunately, *all* the quarterguards were sensitives, so he had to work even harder to keep his reactions under control there.

He paused in the stairwell to catch his breath. When he stepped out onto the third floor, the quarterguard there looked down his long nose at Mikael but didn't question his presence—the Daujom had access to all parts of the palace at any time. Mikael just walked on, thinking calm thoughts at each sentry as he passed. He finally spotted Jannika near the turn to the king's quarters, staring stonily off at the far wall.

When he stopped a few feet away, she glanced both ways, possibly to discern whether the other quarterguards were ones likely to report her speaking to him while on duty, and only then did she look at him. On duty, her face was impassive, so he had no idea whether she was pleased to see him or not. "What are you doing up here?" she whispered.

"Still hunting information," he admitted.

He saw a hint of a frown that quickly passed. "About Kai?" she asked.

"I'm afraid so."

The quarterguard stationed on the other side of the turn into the king's quarters watched them now, although surely he couldn't overhear them.

Jannika sighed. "There was a rumor that he's not Dahar's son. That was the gossip that went around."

Mikael felt his brows rise, even as he tried to quell his disbelief. Kai looked too much like Dahar to be anything other than his son, even if his eye color was different.

"Yes, I know," Jannika said as if he'd spoken aloud. "You asked; I dug up the rumor. That doesn't mean it's true. All it means is that someone said it, and it got back to Kai's ears."

And what was important was whether Kai believed it, and whether it bothered him enough to have set off his most recent spell of ill temper. Mikael took a deep breath, tucking away that information so he could contemplate it later, where there weren't sentries standing about with nothing better to do than eavesdrop on his reactions. "Thank you, then. I owe you."

She didn't move from her post, but leaned closer. "I could come by your quarters after my shift and we could discuss my payment."

His flash of surprise provoked that nearest quarterguard to click his tongue at him. He hadn't been fast enough to quash it. There was no misconstruing Jannika's offer this time, though. She would go off duty in the early hours of the morning, when he planned to be sound asleep and, he hoped, not dreaming. "Perhaps tomorrow evening," he said instead. "If you're not on duty."

Her lips twisted—disappointment, he decided—and then her face went still again. "Dinner, then?"

At this point, he *was* free for dinner tomorrow. "As long as my work doesn't interfere."

She completely broke her impassiveness by rolling her eyes. "Always work. Good night, Mikael."

And so he was dismissed. Mikael wished her an uneventful shift and headed back the way he'd come, counting his steps to keep his mind clear of emotion.

It wasn't until he was in his quarters one level lower—and on the opposite side of the palace—that he allowed himself to contemplate that brief discussion. He changed out of his uniform, wondering why Jannika had suddenly developed such a strong interest in him.

They had been involved before, but it had been, from the beginning, a casual relationship. They had agreed on that explicitly. When she'd decided to drop him, he hadn't been heartbroken. Given the amount of time she'd been spending with the twenty-fives, he'd guessed it was coming. Now it seemed she'd decided she wanted to renew that arrangement, and possibly more. Apparently others in her yeargroup knew that too, although his sitting with her in the mess a few days before might have been enough to inform them.

While it was pleasing to know she fancied him enough to defy her closest friend's aversion to him, he wasn't sure *why* Jannika was doing so. That was enough to make him question the wisdom of pursuing a relationship with her. He wished for a moment that Deborah wasn't tied up in elders' meetings. He would appreciate her advice. Wasn't that what sponsors were for?

He pulled on an old pair of sparring trousers, tied the drawstring, and lay down on his narrow bed, mind still chasing the conundrum that Jannika presented. As problems went, it wasn't that bad. But now he owed Jannika *something*, and he had no idea how he was going to pay, not without raising hopes he wasn't willing to fulfill.

CHAPTER SEVENTEEN

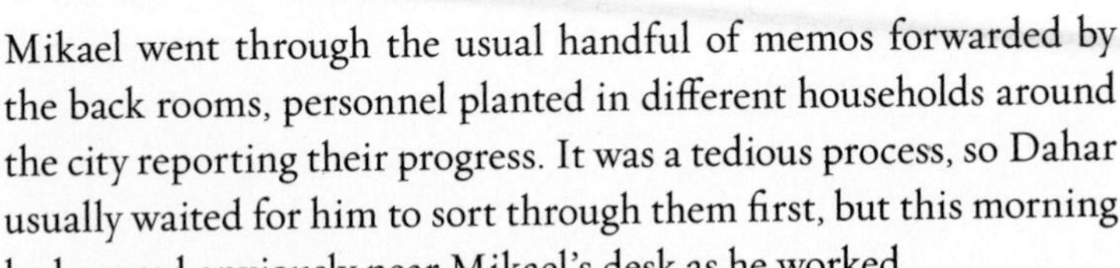

Mikael went through the usual handful of memos forwarded by the back rooms, personnel planted in different households around the city reporting their progress. It was a tedious process, so Dahar usually waited for him to sort through them first, but this morning he hovered anxiously near Mikael's desk as he worked.

Colonel Cerradine came in as Mikael read through one of the notes.

"Dahar, Mikael can read without your help," Cerradine said in an amused tone. He laid his hat on Kai's desk.

Dahar glanced up but otherwise ignored the statement.

"Are there files I can review?" Cerradine hinted.

"Did you get the dead mouse out of the file box?" Dahar asked. He picked up one of Mikael's paperweights—a large river rock—and began to toss it from hand to hand.

Mikael belatedly realized that Dahar had addressed *him*. "Oh. Yes, no more dead mouse."

He began packing the last files, having organized his and Dahar's earlier that morning. He grabbed up the stack left behind atop Kai's desk and slid them into the back of the box. "I hope these will be of some help."

Cerradine watched the rock move back and forth. "I do too."

"How is the case going, sir?"

Cerradine tore his eyes away from Dahar. "We're searching for eighty different things, Mikael. Aldassa finally located where the first body went into the river. The killers didn't do that, by the way. The farmer who owns the land found the body the next morning and realized what he was dealing with. He was afraid that if word got out, buyers would believe his crops were cursed, so he got one of his field hands to help him drag the body to the river and dump it in."

Well, that solves that discrepancy between the two deaths.

"I doubt the general populace has made the connection to the massacres," Cerradine added. "The rumors are only of blood magic so far." He grabbed the paperweight midflight and set it firmly back on Mikael's desk, glaring at Dahar.

Looking offended, Dahar perched on the edge of Mikael's desk and crossed his arms over his chest.

Mikael stifled a laugh. "I can go talk to a couple of writers if you think it would help, Colonel. See what they've found out." Dimani would have heard something, surely.

"I'd appreciate that, Mikael." Cerradine picked up the box of files and, carrying it carefully by its leather straps, walked out of the office.

"I assume you didn't find anything in your papers," Dahar said, "that we need to take up with the Andersens."

Mikael shook his head. If the Andersens *had* broken the law and blamed it on nonexistent vigilantes, he hadn't seen any evidence of it.

. . .

Cerradine handed the file box over to his driver to stow in his carriage and, after checking his pocket watch, headed upstairs to the king's household, hunting Deborah. She often checked on the king's consort, Amdiria, in the mornings. He ran her down there, talking quietly with that white-haired lady. Almost old enough to be Dahar's mother, Amdiria had always treated Dahar more like a son than a brother-in-law. As Dahar's closest friend growing up, Cerradine had often been included in her motherly affection.

Amdiria stretched out a hand when she saw him lingering in her doorway. Cerradine went and kissed her cheek. Amdiria spent most days in her wheeled chair in her rooms, so she enjoyed visitors. While a patterned burgundy throw covered her withered legs, her warm smile and teasing voice countered her frail appearance. Cerradine chatted with her for a while before stealing Deborah away.

Deborah looked more rested than she had the last time he'd seen her, and very professional in her formal black uniform, high collar tightly hooked. He linked arms with her and drew her down the ornate hallway toward the stairs.

"Thank you for staying a bit, Jon," Deborah said. "She doesn't have visitors as often as I'd like."

Cerradine grinned. "She rather likes me, you know."

Deborah shook her head in mock despair. "No accounting for it. Why *are* you here bothering me?"

The exasperation in Deborah's voice was only half-joking, he knew. She was always busy. He tugged her into the alcove beside the stairs, still in sight but not within earshot of the nearest sentry. "I ran the idea past Mikael yesterday, of working with Shironne. Did he mention that to you?"

"No. I've been busy trying to convince the elders to allow it. Yesterday's incident changes things."

He'd hoped she would have a definite answer from them. Apparently not yet. "So what do we do?"

"I will hold Mikael in the infirmary the next time he dreams. I'll try drugging him, as per the elders' instructions. Since he managed to slip off the palace grounds last time, I've asked a few people to keep an eye on him. If I don't make any progress with the other elders, we'll talk about . . . finding some other way."

"Thank you, Deb." He dropped a kiss on her forehead and they went on to discuss more personal matters as he walked with her down to the grand stair.

. . .

Mama took Shironne's hands in her own, knowing full well that meant that Shironne would catch everything she thought, not just what she said aloud. "I want you to do your best to obey Verinne."

Shironne held in a groan. "I will try, Mama."

When she'd been a toddler, Verinne had already been old and fragile. She'd been terrified of Shironne's father but had even stood up to him on a couple of occasions for the sake of Shironne's mother. He hadn't been above striking an old woman who got in his way, though, so her mother had begged Verinne to stay out of their altercations. Over the last sixteen years, Verinne had become more and more brittle, like crazed glass about to break.

"It's only for a few days, sweetheart." Her mother's mind swirled with regret and resignation. It was frustrating that she must go to such lengths to preserve her family's income. She didn't want to sell the estate in the countryside, but they were running out of funds, and she had few options left.

And while her late father had a brother there whose presence would lend her mother respectability, the man wasn't overly fond of Savelle Anjir. He hadn't agreed to his brother's taking in his wife's bastard.

The horses moved restlessly, a hoof striking the stone of the courtyard. One of them snorted, and the wheels of the old carriage creaked as it shifted.

"If the colonel sends for you," her mother went on, "try to keep . . ."

Thoughts whirled in her mother's mind, not quite formed into words, worry that Shironne would be hurt again, that she'd end up entangled in something too big for her to handle, as had happened a few times before.

"I'm not going to forbid your going," her mother said, rather than finishing her earlier effort. "Just try to exercise caution."

"I'll be cautious," Shironne promised rashly.

Her mother recognized the chances of her keeping that promise and laughed softly. "I'm certain you will."

After a few final words to a restive Melanna and a sulking Perrin, her mother touched Shironne's cheek one last time and then climbed into the carriage. Kirya Aldrine stepped up behind her, and a moment later, the carriage rolled away.

Shironne resigned herself to a few very frustrating days. Verinne was a stickler for propriety and believed that Shironne truly should have entered the priesthood, although she never said so aloud any longer out of respect for Shironne's mother. She had, however, commented a few times that it wasn't too late to train Melanna for that life. *What a disaster that would be.*

On the other hand, Verinne doted on Perrin and was doing an excellent job of preparing her for a life as a rich man's wife. As Perrin seemed perfectly content with that path, Shironne didn't try to dissuade her.

Shironne sighed and grasped Melanna's syrup-sticky hand. She cringed but let her little sister lead her back to the house.

. . .

Mikael spent an hour sparring with Eli that afternoon, a good way to work off some of the frustrations of the day. He'd spent several hours talking to various writers down in the city about the two deaths. He hadn't turned up anything more than rumors. Given that two men were dead, it was concerning.

Distracted as he half watched one of the fight masters instruct two sentries on a nearby square, Mikael ended up on the floor when Eli landed a particularly hard blow. Blunted swords, even rapiers, still left livid bruises. That spot would be tender for days, Mikael expected. He deserved as much for allowing his attention to wander.

"I've got a headache," he admitted, rubbing at his side. "I can hardly wait to shower."

"Lucky you," Eli commented under his breath.

"No shower?" Mikael asked.

Eli stopped, one foot on the stairs. "There's a run on tonight, sir."

Mikael's headache flared. Orange flashed behind his eyes.

A midnight run, where nearly a hundred children of the Family would chase through the dark streets of Noikinos. Originally intended to teach the children the layout of the city, the runs had evolved over decades into a public way to impress the citizens of

Noikinos, much like the melee. Young Larossans would creep out of their homes in the darkness to watch the silent Family children run by.

Eli came back to where Mikael stood. "Are you all right, sir?"

Mikael closed his eyes, trying to banish the anxiety that flared through him. "I don't know. Keep your yeargroup out of it."

Eli's voice penetrated the fog in his head. "Why?"

"I have a headache," Mikael said. He wanted to get away by himself where he wouldn't bother anyone. "What time is it?"

Eli dug his pocket watch out of the brown jacket folded neatly over his arm. "Just after five."

Mikael turned and headed back up the stair, debating.

"No, you don't." Eli grabbed his arm. "You made a promise to Elder Deborah, Mikael. Remember?"

Mikael clenched his jaw. "What?"

"She asked several of us to keep an eye on you," Eli said. "She said you gave her your word."

Mikael could hear the disapproval in Eli's voice. He *could* get away from Eli and get out of the fortress. Despite Eli's larger size, Mikael could still easily outfight him. Eli would just call on the others on the sparring ground for help, though, and Mikael couldn't escape from that many. He gave in—and Eli marched him up five flights of stairs to the infirmary.

Jakob, the infirmarian on duty, left them there while he went off to hunt for Deborah. Mikael sank down on one of the beds that lined each side of the main infirmary room and continued around the corner to the private rooms. He stared at the neat beds, shelves, and screens, Deborah's tidy and efficient domain. He was about to ruin her night again. "This is a terrible idea, Eli."

Eli folded his arms over his chest and watched Mikael as if daring him to bolt. "Why did you give your word, then?"

"Have you ever tried to say no to Deborah?" Mikael asked.

"If I chose to do so, I would." Eli glowered down at him, supremely certain of himself.

Did I have such self-assurance at sixteen? "It's harder than it sounds."

"Stop trying to please everyone, Mikael." Eli shook his head, glancing back across the infirmary as Jakob came in with Deborah, who'd evidently been rousted from her room. She wore loose black pants and an old gray sweater thrown over her shirt for warmth. She braided her hair as she approached.

After surveying the two young men waiting for her, still dressed in their sparring clothes, she guessed the source of the problem. "Mikael, are you about to start dreaming on us?"

"I believe so, ma'am," he admitted, shifting on the edge of the bed. "I would truly like to leave now."

"Thank you, Eli." She came and sat on a bed across from him, folding one leg underneath her. "You're not leaving, Mikael. You gave your word. I'll keep an eye on you, I promise."

"Ma'am?" Eli began.

Deborah laid a cool hand against Mikael's brow. "Yes, Eli?"

"I'd like to go talk to my uncle about canceling the run for tonight. Mikael advised me not to take my yeargroup." Eli's uncle, Simeon, was one of several fight masters in charge of organizing the yeargroups for those rare activities that took children *outside* the fortress. If he listened to Eli's story, he could cancel the run on his authority alone.

Deborah's blue eyes fixed on Mikael's. "*Is* someone in the Family threatened?"

They're going to cancel a midnight run, just because I feel panicky, he thought sourly. "I don't know."

Deborah cast a doubtful look at him and then rose. "Eli, go ahead and talk to your uncle. Tell him that I'm asking for them to keep everyone within the fortress tonight. Advise your yeargroup, and if you would come back afterward, I'd appreciate it. I'll need a runner overnight and I don't think your cousin will be fit for it."

Eli's cousin Gabriel was in the same yeargroup but served runner duty in Below since he was a sensitive. Given that Mikael was going to dream at some point tonight, Gabriel would likely be among those affected if the sedatives didn't mute Mikael's dream in the same way as alcohol did.

Eli left the infirmary, and Mikael drew a heavy breath. He was resigned to this now. He'd already defied Deborah once by escaping the fortress before his last dream, although he'd not intended to do so at first. He'd happened to be out of the fortress when he'd figured out he was going to dream. Deborah came and laid one cool hand across his forehead.

"You're warm, Mikael, but that may be that you came from the sparring floor." She left for a moment to talk to Jakob and then returned. "We're going to put you in one of the back rooms."

The back rooms afforded some measure of privacy, rooms used for births or for long stays in the infirmary wing. They were rooms where people died.

"I was supposed to meet Jannika tonight for dinner."

Deborah cast a dry look at him. "I'll send her a note. You're not getting out of my sight."

Mikael followed her to the back rooms, counting to smother the tension singing through his head. He had to remain calm.

The room had a single bed, a small table, and a chair. He sat down on the edge of the bed, the gray wool blanket scratchy under his fingers.

Deborah handed him a glass and said, "Drink this."

"This could be ugly, ma'am." He drank the draft she'd given him, grimacing at the bitter taste.

She took away the glass and brought her hand to his cheek. "I know, dear. But it also might work."

Mikael sighed. *She'll probably stay up all night herself.*

Deborah settled on the chair. "I'll send for dinner here. Do you have any idea when you'll start dreaming?"

The last two dreams had come in the middle of the night. If he assumed that the dream matched the same pattern, he had several hours to sit here in the infirmary. Then again, he couldn't assume that. If he didn't fall asleep first, he would simply drop to the floor wherever he was, even if that was halfway down a stairwell. It was safer to find a bed. "I don't have any way to be sure."

"Then we wait," Deborah said, and added, "So . . . Jannika again?"

Mikael cringed inwardly. It was going to be a long night.

. . .

Shironne woke late into the night with a familiar dread tickling down her spine. She sat up and dragged a pillow into her arms. She breathed slowly, four counts in and four counts out, trying to think of the fear as a thing rather than feeling it. She held it at a distance.

He's afraid. His mind screamed panic into the night, terrified death would drag him down along with the victim. He knew death waited just around the corner, its victim already chosen.

It was him—her Angel of Death. She had no doubt of that. He seemed to call her by name, almost as if he knew her.

His terror rattled on and on, a drone in the back of her mind. How long that continued she didn't know. When he finally slipped into a dream, she let out a sigh of relief, thinking she'd finally reached something familiar, but it was unlike any they'd shared before.

CHAPTER EIGHTEEN

The victim panicked when she realized she was bound, her heart straining. Her head ached fiercely. She'd been hit from behind.

She sensed the others' triumph, their worry, their fear and anger, a jumble of discordant emotions. Panic rushed through her. She tried to call for help but couldn't. Hands rolled her over. A dark face came near, studying her—a man. He touched her cheek.

The dark man rifled through her memories, reading the journal of her mind, an intensely personal survey. The man searched for something, only to be denied. He spoke words, but nothing reached her ears. A sense of frustration flooded through the contact, and the hand fell away.

She stared up into starless blackness, the inside of a coach. Others moved around her, all indistinct in her mind save that one man who still watched her but no longer touched. Another leaned close, and something jabbed into the side of her neck. Her heart beat faster, the inside of the coach spinning. The men ignored her as if she were no threat.

For a long time the coach swayed until her stomach rebelled, vomit choking her. One of the men grabbed her head and turned it to one side so that the vomit ran free of her mouth and onto the straw covering the coach's floor. The motion made her dizzier and she retched again, smelling the sour odor.

They stopped, a sudden lurch. The men began to climb down from the coach. They untied the ropes about her arms, which fell limp at her sides. Then two men dragged her out, one on each side—annoyed, hurried, worried. The others followed.

Her heart struggled to keep up with her fear. She couldn't get a good breath. She smelled the river.

They pushed her to her knees. She felt the jar of hitting the ground in her gut. She couldn't feel her legs now. She willed her arms and her legs to move—to show them she was prepared to fight—but nothing answered her call. One of the men stripped her jacket from her unresisting arms. Her head fell forward and suddenly she couldn't breathe at all. She looked at the stony ground before her, the moon visible on the river's surface. Shame flushed through her then that she would die without putting up a fight.

One of them grabbed her braids and yanked her head back. Her lungs drew in air, reprieved. They removed her vest and shirt. The dark face watched her as if waiting for something.

Another man stood at the dark man's side, the bait who'd drawn her in. He looked regretful, eyes turned away, as if he would stop the others if he could.

She was going to die. They would not do all this and not *kill her. She closed her eyes and began to pray, thinking that Father Winter, at least, would not abandon her. She felt pressure on her skin, smelled the scent of blood.*

Deep in her mind, she felt the presence of another, watching and waiting with her in the last moments. His familiar presence reassured her.

Her lungs wouldn't draw breath any longer, simply stopping in their motion. She let go, and the darkness and confusion around her faded away.

. . .

Mikael sputtered when the icy water hit him. Air rushed into his lungs. The room was lit, blindingly bright after the darkness of his dream. He tried to wipe water from his face but his arms didn't move.

Someone bent over him, features obscured in contrast, mopping at the water puddled on his shoulders and neck.

"Mikael?" Deborah's voice betrayed her anxiety.

Mikael tried to reply, but his throat seemed frozen.

"Can you talk at all?"

He found he could move an arm and grasped her sleeve.

Deborah sat down on the edge of his bed, concern plain on her face now that his eyes had adjusted. She touched his bare chest, and Mikael discovered he had the ability to flinch now. They'd removed his shirt, he recalled, to get a better view of any fresh welts that bloomed across his chest.

"Water," he finally managed to croak.

She got up, went away, and then loomed over him again, cup in hand. "Let's see if we can get you sitting up."

Eli had returned to help her. Between the two of them, they propped Mikael up like a rag doll on the bed. Deborah sat next to him again, holding the water to his numb lips so he could drink. He gagged but managed to swallow at the last moment.

"There'll be trouble over this," she said, shaking her head.

"I know," Mikael whispered. His neck responded to instructions now, and he looked downward to see the marks on his chest. He couldn't see directly below his chin, but he thought that the letters ended halfway across. He raised a hand to check and found no tender streak running across his lower ribs. In the earlier dreams, he'd had a slash crossing his chest, the largest of the echoed wounds. He remembered his lungs failing. "The victim died. *Before* they killed her, ma'am."

Her eyes narrowed. "Are you sure of that?"

He pointed at his chest. "This is how far they got."

She stood up and frowned down at him. "Dahar needs to be aware of what's happening to you. If nothing else, to take you off duty the day after one of these . . ."

"No." He didn't want to be removed from duty as if he were aged and infirm. "Please."

She folded her arms across her chest, her jaw clenched. She looked away, gazing out the open door for a moment, and then turned back to him. "I won't request that, then, but if Dahar insists, you'll have to abide by his ruling."

Mikael knew better than to argue. "Have you heard from any of the sensitives yet?"

Deborah glanced over at Eli. His serious face drew up in a mocking smile. "Hel reigned in our quarters, sir. There was *actual* screaming and gnashing of teeth. Very interesting."

How like Eli to see the plight of his sensitives as an amusing curiosity. He probably viewed it as a weakness. Of the twenty-eight in his yeargroup, seventeen were sensitives, an unprecedented proportion. Most yeargroups had no more than one out of four with the talent. Mikael hoped Eli learned to have more patience.

"Echoes," Deborah offered. "The sensitives were repeating everything among themselves and it got out of hand."

Eli nodded. "Once Gabriel woke up and I got *him* calmed down, the others followed suit, so I came back to check on you, sir."

Deborah leaned forward again to touch his bare chest. "I'm curious to see how many of them echo your . . . lettering."

Mikael dreaded that. In the past, his drunken stupor had muted his broadcasting enough that the sensitives had only vague impressions of his dreams. This time they apparently hadn't been spared. There would be angry and frightened sensitives all over the fortress, each correctly blaming him.

This had been a terrible mistake. He could see from Deborah's face that she knew it, too. No point in saying it aloud.

"Why am I wet?" he asked then, throat hoarse.

"I dumped a basin on you. You stopped breathing, and I couldn't get you to wake."

"Oh, I thought my pillow felt soggy," he commented. Drowsiness stole over him, making everything less urgent. Even so, something nagged at him. He caught her sleeve as she moved away. "This one was Lucas. A sensitive."

She stared down at him. "Are you certain?"

Mikael remembered the pressure of a hand tangled in his braids—braids he hadn't worn since he became a nineteen. "Yes, ma'am."

"They canceled the run. Everyone should be Below except the sentries." Deborah sounded alarmed, but Mikael couldn't summon the will to move.

He slid to the left, leaning up against the cool stone corner of the two walls. He didn't notice if she replied to him, her voice trailing away as the room grew dim.

. . .

Shironne sat at her table, the hot tea before her long since gone cold. The clock had told her it was morning now, but she felt exhausted. She ignored the tray Cook sent up for breakfast, her stomach too knotted to deal with food.

"Someone died last night," Shironne said when Melanna came into the room and sat nearby. Her sister seemed unusually subdued this morning. No bouncing on the bed.

"You all right?" Melanna asked hesitantly. Her sister took her hand, and Shironne caught the sense of what Melanna had dreamed, similar to her own terrors. Fortunately, Melanna had dreamed of only unformed fear, shame, and captivity—the emotions of the dream.

"Yes, we'll be fine," Shironne insisted.

This time, though, *had* been different. She just didn't know why.

CHAPTER NINETEEN

Mikael didn't want to leave the infirmary. He lay under the blanket, staring at the gray walls of his tiny room. He'd called up the lights, but they didn't let off any heat. While it might be cool in the infirmary, the reception awaiting him outside would be far chillier. Even so, he would have to leave this room if he ever hoped to shower again.

The door opened and Deborah came inside, a cup of tea in her hand. She pulled the wooden chair nearer to the bed and sat for a moment contemplating him.

"Good morning, ma'am," Mikael said. He didn't know where to begin. "Did you get any sleep?"

"I haven't had the chance yet, dear. I've been talking to Dahar." She handed him the cup.

"Not angry words, I hope."

"He has a headache, Mikael, which makes him unreasonable. Well, slightly more unreasonable than usual. How do you feel?" She went on to ask him the same questions she'd asked before. He didn't have better answers to give this time.

"Is there anything else you haven't told me?" Deborah asked. When he shook his head, she stood up and briskly brushed off her trousers. "I want you to return to your quarters and get cleaned up. I should warn you that a couple dozen of the stronger sensitives imitated your response to the dream."

He felt sick to his stomach. "You mean . . . ?"

"Fainter markings than yours, but still tender, most with some shortness of breath. The elders are understandably concerned."

Mikael cringed. *The elders.* He was probably going to be dragged into an elders' meeting, and it would all be aired out there. "Is anyone missing?"

"The elders have requested that the Firsts take stock. Not all have reported in yet." She leaned down and checked his forehead for warmth again, like his mother had done during his childhood. "I want to see you again later today," she ordered.

"Yes, ma'am." Mikael didn't bother to suggest she get some sleep. Once she left, he got up and dressed. Then he sat down again in a cold sweat from that effort.

An hour later, bathed and wearing a fresh uniform, Mikael made his way to the office. He'd been stopped this morning in the halls by six different sentries—two frightened, but four alarmingly thankful because their children had not gone out with the midnight run. The reaction embarrassed him.

He had no idea how word had spread so quickly. He told them they should thank Deborah, who'd gotten it called off. Even so, Mikael found gratitude a pleasant, if confusing, change.

All of the Firsts had reported in, save one. One of the twenty-twos was missing—Iselin. After he dismissed the runner who'd brought the news, Mikael wanted to sit in a corner and cry. Even if she hadn't liked him, he would never have wished this on her. Someone from the Daujom would have to question the twenty-twos to find out where Iselin had gone the night before.

He could ask someone from the back rooms to go. Anna could handle the questions with appropriate tact and composure.

But it has to be me.

He'd known that from the moment the runner came from Below with the message. Since Dahar hadn't come to the office yet—he was probably still out of sorts from bad dreams—Mikael sent the runner on her way, locked up the office, and began the long trek back down into the fortress.

Eventually he stood at the guideline of the twenty-twos' hallway, although today there was no laughter. There were only a handful of the twenty-twos there, and no children. They spoke together in low voices, heads bowed over the central table. Mikael waited, unsure he wanted to approach them, but there wasn't much choice.

One of the men finally deigned to acknowledge his presence and rose from the couches. Taller than Mikael, with a distinctive reddish tint to his braids, he stopped just on the other side of the line, much as Iselin had when Mikael had spoken to her. "What do you need?" he asked bluntly.

He has to know why I'm here. "Daujom business. Is there anyone who can tell me where Iselin went last night, and what time?"

The younger man's lip twisted. He gazed at Mikael a moment longer. "I suppose you want to talk to Jannika," he finally said.

He'd suspected it would be Jannika. She would be the most likely of the group to know Iselin's plans. "Yes."

The younger man simply walked away, heading down the long hall toward the individual quarters. He stopped at one of the closed doors and knocked softly, then spoke to someone within. After a moment, Jannika emerged from the room, another woman with loose, curling hair accompanying her. That woman walked with Jannika as far as the common room, then stopped to wait. Jannika walked to the line and, after a moment of indecision, finally glanced up at Mikael.

She looked worse than he felt, her eyes bloodshot and her nose reddened. She wore an aged shirt over sparring trousers, her feet bare. "What do you need to know?"

Her tone didn't invite any pleasantries, and he had no idea what to say to her anyway. He tried to keep his demeanor professional. "Do you know why Iselin was out of the fortress last night? I need to know where she would have gone."

Jannika wrapped her arms over her chest. "She went to meet her boyfriend, Savrin Nisimi. He's a musician." She shook her head, no longer looking at him. "He was playing for the king and she met him there. She was going to marry him, leave the Family."

Mikael tucked that name away in his memory—a Larossan name. That information should make it easy enough for him to find the young man. The king's seneschal had to pay the musicians somehow. "Do you know what time she left the fortress?"

"She had night shift the night before," Jannika said, sounding weary now. "She napped and then left before dinner, about four?"

That gave him a rough time to work with. The sentries at the back gate to the palace grounds could narrow down what time she'd gone out. Finding her trail from there would take time, and he wondered if the colonel's people would be willing to take that on, since they were more likely to get answers out of any Larossans they spoke with. "I assume she's done this before. Was there anything different about yesterday?"

Jannika's eyes lifted, tears glistening in them. For a moment he wished he could step over the line to comfort her, but he was very aware she hadn't invited him to do so. From the common area, the man who'd spoken to him before rose and began approaching, apparently picking up on Jannika's distress.

"You made me live through my best friend's death," she said tightly. Her jaw clenched. "I don't want to talk to you anymore. Not ever. Do you understand that?"

Mikael pressed his lips together, breathing in through his nose and counting his breaths to control his pained reaction. Jannika simply turned away from him and walked back toward her quarters. She paused briefly to embrace the young man and then went on to where her friend waited.

The young man with reddish hair came and joined Mikael outside the line. He wasn't in uniform, but Mikael guessed this was Jannika's First—the leader of her yeargroup. "She's upset," he told Mikael, eyeing him speculatively. "Last night we felt your dream, far more clearly than ever before. I have . . . marks. On my chest. Is it like that for you every time?"

He'd expected a far more accusing tone. "Yes."

"I assume it's actually *worse* for you."

Was he being given a chance to explain himself? "Yes."

"You leave the fortress when you're about to dream." He touched his chest with two fingers. "This is why, isn't it?"

Mikael nodded. "Distance helps. I'm sorry that you . . . had to share that. That anyone did."

The younger man crossed his arms over his chest. "Jannika's upset. Worse when we realized Iselin was the only one missing. If you have any further questions, can you run them through me instead?"

"You're the First?"

"I am," the young man said. "Tomas."

Mikael nodded once. "Thank you. I know it's a bad time."

"Find out what happened," Tomas said. "That will make all the twenty-twos a lot happier."

"I will," Mikael promised. He turned to leave, but Tomas grabbed his sleeve to stop him.

"We all know Jannika's been chasing you lately," Tomas said. "Perhaps unwisely so."

Mikael didn't have any response for that.

"She's upset because Iselin planned to leave the Family. She just doesn't want to be alone. You were easier than nothing." And with that pronouncement, Tomas let go his grasp on Mikael's sleeve and headed back toward the common area. Mikael glanced down that long gray hallway, but Jannika had already disappeared into her quarters. Given that, he decided it would be best to get out of the fortress before he thought over that parting shot. So he turned onto the main corridor and headed for the main stairwell that would take him back up.

Once he'd reached One Down, he made for the grand stair, thinking he could get back to the office and stew over Tomas' pronouncement there. It hadn't been meant to reassure him. No, Tomas meant that Jannika had started chasing him out of desperation. She'd seen him as an easy choice, since they'd had a relationship before.

It hadn't *quite* been an insult. But close.

Hadn't he asked himself more than once why she'd seemed so eager to renew their relationship? Perhaps Tomas was doing him a favor, letting him know Jannika's logic before their relationship went too far. Or perhaps Tomas was simply wrong. Given that the yeargroup appeared close, Mikael doubted it.

It made what had already been a terrible day seem worse.

Mikael went through the main archway and, after signing out, faced the grand stair with tired eyes. His lungs ached just contemplating it. Either way, he took as deep a breath as he could manage and began the trek upstairs, concentrating on being happy, being contented. He had to keep his mind clear, or he would make the day worse for the sentries than it already was.

By the time he reached the ground level, he'd broken out in a cold sweat again. Not wanting to walk into the office that way, instead he took the side hallway that led out to the courtyard behind the palace. Breath steaming in the chilly morning air, he made his way across the wide flagstone drive and into the gardens. He walked the paths there to calm his mind. The garden was tired with fall, the leaves on many of the plants turning in response to the shorter days, and flowers drooping following the early cold snap they'd had.

He rarely walked here. He usually maintained his calm better. He hadn't actually wanted to pursue Jannika, so her reaction shouldn't sting so much, but he'd thought they were friends. Talking to Tomas had served to remind him what a disruption he would be to the togetherness of any yeargroup.

He'd become too much of a problem in his own yeargroup, one of the main reasons the Lee elders had sent him away. He missed it. He missed the comfort of being part of a group. This stung so much because it was a reminder that he was never going to have that again.

Mikael let out a heavy sigh and did his best to order his thoughts. There was no point in dwelling on this. He had a killer to find. Iselin's murder meant that this case now fell under the Daujom's jurisdiction, and that meant it was *his* case now.

. . .

On entering the office he learned that Cerradine *had* mobilized a squad of men to walk the banks of the river. Dahar had sent a message as soon as he'd woken, sparing Mikael the need to do so. Not being a strong sensitive, Dahar probably hadn't recognized that the victim was Lucas Family, so Mikael needed to convey that information to Aldassa. It might help him to know where she'd gone before being killed. Not so much for locating the body, but it might help find the *killers* if he knew how they were finding their victims.

With the death of a Lucas, the jurisdiction of the case had changed. Justice for Iselin's death fell beyond the purview of the army and into the Daujom's hands. Even so, the army already had personnel working on the case, and Mikael was inclined to work with them. And when he discussed the identity of the victim with Dahar and Kai, Dahar quickly reached the same conclusion. The army simply had more bodies available to them, while most of the Daujom's field personnel were hidden in households throughout the province. Bringing them in to search for the killers would be wasteful, given that most had worked hard to establish themselves under fake identities.

Mikael rubbed his hands across his face, trying to banish the lingering exhaustion. Out of the corner of his eye, he glimpsed Elisabet. She didn't have her overcoat on, a sign she must be exhausted as well. She had likely been awake at all hours soothing frayed nerves and playing nursemaid for her own yeargroup, an odd image.

He cast a sympathetic smile her way and got to work. He drafted a note for Aldassa and sent it off via a runner, who would hand it over to a courier to take down to the army's office. Then he turned to the paperwork waiting on his desk.

Deborah came to the office not much later, earning an aggrieved look from Dahar. "Haven't you gone to bed yet?" he asked as soon as Mikael let her in the door.

"I don't have time." She turned to Mikael. "Have you told him?"

Mikael flushed. There was no graceful way out of this. "No, ma'am."

"Should I, then?"

She looked worn, and older than her forty-four years. Mikael hated that he'd caused her so much trouble. "You'll explain it better than I can, I think."

Deborah crossed her arms, appearing ready for a fight. "Do you recall, Dahar, that we had a discussion about two years ago regarding Mikael's ties to his victims in his dreams? That I thought he was getting too close to the victim, or hanging on too long?" Dahar had come close to her in his peregrinations, and Deborah grabbed his sleeve to stop him. "Mikael, would you take off your shirt, please?"

"Ma'am, this really isn't necessary," he said.

She turned and gave him a level glance. "Were you going to tell him? At all?"

Shaking his head, Mikael stood and unbuttoned his vest, and then his shirt. He pulled them loose enough that Dahar could see the purplish welts left across his skin. The letters had partially faded, leaving an unformed word from his right shoulder to the end of his collarbone.

Dahar came closer to gaze at Mikael's nascent injuries. "Is this painful?" he asked.

"Yes." Mikael buttoned his shirt again and tucked it into his trousers, grateful his employer had seen only this limited manifestation. Fortunately, Dahar was too weak a sensitive to have reflected the injuries.

"Does it match . . . ?" Dahar asked.

"Usually, yes." Mikael straightened his braces and buttoned his vest, not wanting to look at any of them. "She died before they could finish what they were writing. That's why the inscription isn't complete this time."

"That's the only explanation that makes sense." Deborah folded her arms again, looking at Dahar. "In other words, whatever drug they used to immobilize the first two victims proved fatal to a member of the Family."

"Is that possible?" Dahar asked.

"They must be using one that doesn't always kill, or kills slowly, only they chose someone whose body couldn't deal with it this time. The poison killed her first, before she bled out. Merciful, actually. Family *are* far more susceptible to most drugs than Larossans or Anvarrid."

Mikael felt his eyebrows rise. He didn't recall having heard that before, but if Deborah believed it, there must be ample evidence. If it was true, it wasn't something the elders would want to become common knowledge.

Dahar walked to the windows that overlooked the courtyard. "Some of the sentries complained that they couldn't breathe."

"Yes," Deborah said softly. "Given Mikael's description of the dream and what the other sensitives reported, I suspect that the drug involved paralyzed her lungs. Mikael, you actually stopped breathing for a few minutes."

Dahar turned from the windows to glare at Mikael. "Your elders sent you here for us to find a way to deal with this. From now on, you're under Deborah's control, sunset to dawn, until we can find a way to keep this from happening again. Whatever she tells you, you do it."

"It's for your own good," Kai said from across the room. "You lack self-control when you're drunk."

At that moment, Mikael wanted nothing more than to put a fist in Kai's face.

Deborah knew them both well enough to intervene. "Dahar, may I take Mikael down to the infirmary to ask him some more questions?"

"Provided that you get some sleep after that," Dahar said.

Having had enough humiliation, Mikael grabbed up his jacket and followed Deborah from the office.

Deborah stopped at the doorway and turned back. "I'm going to send for Jon, Dahar. The three of us need to have a talk. There's something—someone—you need to know about."

Dahar scowled, but Mikael noted that he didn't argue.

CHAPTER TWENTY

They hadn't gotten far when a commotion at the outside entry to the grand stair made Mikael turn back. David Aldassa stood talking to the sentries there. Mikael met Deborah's weary eyes. She nodded at him. "Fine. Go deal with Aldassa. I'll send word for the mortuary officers to expect her."

She headed on down the grand stair, shoulders slumped in exhaustion. Mikael went back up. He drew Aldassa away from the sentries. "You found her?"

Aldassa didn't ask how he knew. "Yes. Near the Iron Bridge. Body was simply abandoned on the river walk, sometime before dawn. They meant for her to be found quickly."

"If it was there, they meant as many people as possible to see the body." Something in his dreams made him think that the killer wanted the attention. Wanted to be seen. *Where did that idea come from?*

"Looks so," Aldassa said. "Newspapers aren't printing this, police aren't talking about it, so they're making sure it gets out by word of mouth. You look like shit."

"It's been a lousy morning," Mikael agreed, unoffended. "Did you bring the body here?"

"Yes." Aldassa tilted his dark head toward the courtyard. "I think the sentries knew what we were bringing in. They all wanted to touch. Come see?"

Mikael followed Aldassa back out into the cool air of the courtyard.

The army's cart was likely made for transporting supplies, but today it held a single blanket-wrapped form.

Mikael glanced up at the rooftops of the palace and saw several of the sentries there watching the scene in the courtyard below. Aldassa nodded to the two soldiers who held the horses' reins, and they averted their faces. He gently drew back the blanket, exposing the body to midchest.

Mikael stared down at the pale face of Iselin Lucas. Whoever had laid her in the cart had carefully straightened her braids, leaving them to lie over her shoulder as if she lay sleeping, but the sheen of blood that covered her chest and abdomen and the terrible carvings in her skin were still clear to see.

"Did you know her?" Aldassa asked.

"Yes. One of the twenty-twos." He didn't want to explain that he'd talked to her only the night before last. "Her name is Iselin. They missed her this morning."

Aldassa raised his eyebrows, an unspoken question.

"I was told she had a boyfriend in the city," Mikael explained. "Evidently, she went out early yesterday evening to meet him and never returned. I sent that message to your office, but they probably missed you." Then he realized what seemed wrong about this body. "They kept writing."

Aldassa's brows drew together. "Meaning?"

Mikael took a deep breath and then cringed when his aching lungs protested. "She died *before* they finished," he said. "I know that from my dream. But for blood magic to work, the victim has to be alive, doesn't she? So why finish the inscription *after* she died?"

Mikael's stomach abruptly turned, but he held the nausea at bay, quickly looking away from Iselin's face.

Aldassa covered Iselin's body again, obscuring the marks from curious eyes, but then he lifted the side of the blanket to show Mikael the dead woman's wrist, ringed with bruising and scrapes. "Ligature marks," Aldassa said. "She was bound."

"Any marks on the first two?" Mikael asked.

"No."

Mikael felt his neck, fingering that tender spot that told him Iselin had been drugged like the others. "Why bind her and drug her?"

"More for *you* to answer," Aldassa said. "Will I have access to the body? We did find her."

Dahar hadn't yet discussed with the colonel the issue of jurisdiction, so Mikael didn't tell Aldassa that they wanted to use his people to continue the investigation. "I can see to it that you and Kassannan are given access, under the Daujom's name. Cerradine, too, of course."

The three of them had been raised in the fortress, so it was a simpler matter to get them past the sentries than it would be to allow outsiders in. Aldassa nodded, accepting those conditions. He glanced toward the palace walls, and Mikael turned back to see that a pair of sentries now stood at the door that led to the grand stair, waiting on them.

"Can they take her?" Mikael asked.

Aldassa gestured for the sentries to come over. The four of them lifted the body from the cart, still wrapped in its blue army blanket, and carried it directly to the grand stair into Below. Mikael's aching lungs began to protest, his breath coming short again. The cold rooms were on Seven Down, a long way to go.

But halfway down the grand stair, two more sentries came away from their duty posts, not asking what the blanket held. They helped carry the body down the stairs. More joined the first two as they reached One Down, sparing Mikael the burden. He let one take his place and followed.

Some came merely to touch the blanket-wrapped burden, a silent contact, then moved away. They became a somber processional in black, slowly moving down each level into the depths of Below.

• • •

The first housemaid, ostensibly needing to build up the fire in Shironne's bedroom, came to tell her that Verinne had left the colonel standing on the steps outside the front door.

Infuriated, Shironne dashed down to the door and opened it herself.

Verinne tottered up behind her, exuding a mixture of terror and fury. "You mustn't let him in!"

The colonel didn't seem daunted by the old woman's protest. "I need to borrow Shironne for a time. Things have taken a bad turn."

"No," Verinne said quickly.

"Of course I'll come," Shironne said over her. "Verinne, this is important."

"I can wait here on the steps, madam," the colonel said in a placating voice. "I won't enter the household."

"There's been another death," Shironne told him. "I had terrible dreams. Or perhaps I wasn't dreaming. I wasn't sure this time."

That sparked the colonel's interest. "They found the body a couple of hours ago, and it's been taken to the palace. I need to take you *there,* so I felt I should come myself to take you."

A thrill of exhilaration spun through Shironne. He meant to take her to the *palace*. "I'll go get my coat."

"No, you'll stay here," Verinne insisted, her agitation spreading. "This household is in mourning. Your mother wouldn't want . . ."

Shironne wanted to yell at the old woman but shook her head to get that idea out of it. She was reflecting Verinne's frustration. She drew a deep breath and interrupted the woman's nascent tirade. "My mother would want me to help. I have her permission to work with the colonel. I'm going, and I won't change my mind."

She didn't wait for an answer. Instead she made her way back up to her room, located her coat, and returned to the front door, where the colonel was still trying to smooth Verinne's ruffled feathers. Shironne didn't give the governess a chance to protest again. She walked out the door and held out one hand for the colonel to take.

Fortunately, her bravado wasn't in vain, because the colonel set her hand on his arm and led her down the steps and to the waiting carriage. Once he'd gotten her settled and stepped up himself, she grabbed the hand strap and held on. The carriage immediately began to roll away.

"Did you notice anything unusual about the dream?" he asked.

Shironne shifted against the seat as the coach took a turn. "It was odd, in many ways. It was clearer, to begin with."

"Anything else?"

She tilted her head. "Before the dream, sir. It seemed almost like the Angel of Death was . . . I don't know, *calling* me. Like he was afraid I might not hear. I don't know how to explain that."

He found that interesting but didn't respond.

"And . . ." She hesitated. "I felt like there was someone *else* there, watching everything. Someone evil. I know that sounds melodramatic, sir. I've sensed that before, but not as clearly."

"The young woman who died was a Lucas, Shironne," he informed her.

"They killed someone from the Family? That's legally . . . um, bad, isn't it?"

"Yes, legally bad," the colonel said, letting her feel his amusement over her flawed terminology. "Among other things, it changes who's in control of investigating the deaths. Now the Daujom's in charge."

"What does that mean for us?"

"It means the prince would be within his rights to demand that I turn over everything concerning the investigation, including you."

"What?"

"As a witness," the colonel clarified. "You viewed the first body, and since he doesn't have that body to look at, you and Kassannan could be required to supply that information."

Judging by his tone and her sense of him, Shironne didn't think that would happen. But it was interesting how much this third death changed his sense of urgency about the whole thing. "I'm willing to do whatever is needed."

"I'm hoping Dahar—the prince—will leave the case in my hands, or at least offer to coordinate with our investigation. I don't know how he'll react to involving you. You are his niece, after all."

Shironne had known that the palace's investigators, the Daujom, were overseen by the king's brother. For some reason, she hadn't ever thought of him as her *uncle*. It was a strange thought. "Does he know I work for you?"

"Whenever I've mentioned you," Cerradine said, "I haven't used your name. But he has numerous investigators who work for his office, so I wouldn't be surprised if he knows your identity. On the other hand, we've worked hard to keep your actual duties secret, so I don't think he knows that you're anything other than a regular sensitive like your mother."

"Will that make a difference?"

"Yes," Cerradine said. "You see, it means that I've been keeping a secret from him. That I'm acquainted with your family and he's not. Dahar hates being left out, whether or not there's a good reason. I always felt that if your mother wasn't ready to meet him, then she shouldn't."

"It's not that she didn't want to meet him," Shironne corrected. "Mama's actually curious about her half brothers. She's seen the king on a number of occasions, but not his brother, so she took us to a melee when we were children in the hope of catching a glimpse of him. She'd heard he was a judge there, or something like that."

That set off the wheels of thought in the colonel's mind. He didn't speak for a moment, so Shironne turned her attention to the sounds outside the carriage. Traffic seemed quieter than usual, as if people were in mourning. No, they were frightened, she decided, the worry almost a taste in the air.

"When was this?" Cerradine asked.

Called back to attention, Shironne smiled ruefully. It wasn't as if she could forget that fair. She'd made an idiot out of herself. "I was eleven," she said. "The summer fair."

The fair took up a great deal of the king's public park, an area that had once been on the outskirts of Noikinos but had since been subsumed by the city.

"Interesting. *Did* she see Dahar?"

"I . . . um, fell and we had to go home," Shironne admitted, rubbing the scar that crossed her palm. *Fell* was the kindest way she could put what had happened. She'd actually tumbled over the rail into the arena itself, forcing the martial competition to come to a halt. Her mother had been mortified and whisked her away before anyone recognized them. "Mama didn't have the chance."

"Too bad. Dahar would have noticed the resemblance immediately. He sees himself in a mirror often enough."

Shironne grinned. The comment was tinged with affection, though. "You like him, don't you?"

"Yes, I do. Sometimes he irritates me. I'm certain I annoy him. But we've been good friends for many, many years."

The carriage came to a stop then, and the door opened from without. They were at the palace, Shironne realized. Whoever stood at the door managed to combine curiosity with control, a reaction that fit what she knew about the Lucas Family. This had to be the sentry line at the fence. She'd seen it when she was a child, of course, the wrought-iron fence defended by a line of stern Family all in black, pale hair in sleek braids, all alike. They had seemed mystical, but she'd been young and had used only her eyes. The minds around her now seemed little different from those of the colonel's people, only more *uniformly* controlled.

The person standing at the carriage door stepped up onto the frame, causing the carriage to sway a bit. "Colonel Cerradine, who is your companion?"

Ah . . . the sentry's a woman. Shironne smiled at her.

"Miss Anjir," the colonel said coolly.

A hint of curiosity snaked out around the person in the carriage's doorway, with a touch of disdain. Shironne swallowed. In the dim light in the carriage, she must look rumpled and ill dressed.

She'd braided her hair hurriedly that morning. If she'd known she would be making her first visit to the palace, she would have checked to be sure her garments matched. She surreptitiously fingered the hem of her long tunic. Even with her gloves on, she recognized the embroidery and beading. This was her bright pink tunic, one that seemed to go with most of her petticoats. At least her mother had always told her so. She let out a relieved breath.

The sentry still considered her. "Are you willing to vouch for her intentions, sir?"

"I will vouch for her intentions and her actions," the colonel answered.

The sentry's mind stilled as she weighed the emotions behind his words. "Very well. They're expecting you, sir."

She stepped down from the carriage and shut the door. The carriage rolled slowly forward.

"They don't always do that," the colonel explained, "but they're upset."

They came to a halt. Cerradine opened the door, stepped down, and then helped Shironne to the ground. The carriage clattered away across flagstones, Cerradine's driver likely heading to the companionship of the stables and a quick game of tiles.

The colonel led Shironne up a flight of stairs. "We're in the courtyard behind the palace," he explained, knowing she liked to have some idea of where she was. "There's a double stair leading up to the back entry of the first floor of the palace. When we go in the doors, we'll turn to the left and walk down the hall to Dahar's office. The sentries know me, so we'll not be stopped."

She followed him along the hallways, not as far as she'd expected. She could feel people watching her, curious about her presence but not overly so. That had to be the sentries. They were supposedly posted everywhere in the palace.

The colonel drew her to a stop and rapped on a door. "Are you ready?"

Shironne shrugged. "I suppose it's too late if I'm not."

CHAPTER TWENTY-ONE

When they entered the quiet room, Shironne felt someone's sharp mind focus on her immediately.

"What is this, Jon?" a man asked. That had to be her uncle Dahar. She couldn't imagine anyone else having the nerve to address the colonel so informally. She'd certainly never heard anyone do so before.

Shironne could sense his anger, curiosity, and frustration, all in rapid succession. Then the emotion was locked away, held at bay for a moment, only to burst forth in seething curiosity again. The prince was, she decided, one of those people who took things apart to see how they worked and then neglected to put them back together, endlessly curious but always moving on to something else.

A second person stood not far away, mind tinged with curiosity but rigidly controlled. Another sentry? Shironne suspected this one was a woman, although she wasn't certain why. She turned her face in that direction. The woman's response turned to caution then, almost as if she feared Shironne might attack her.

A third person waited in the room, a sullen mind, carefully *not* thinking in her direction. He resented her—not personally, of course, just a mild resentment like that reserved for a class of people.

She hesitated in the doorway, one hand clenched on the colonel's sleeve, not knowing what to do with herself. She didn't know where anything in this room was. How big was it? Were there steps? Where were all the things she would trip over? The prince's agitation and the unknown man's resentment tore at her nerves, making her more anxious than she would normally have been in the colonel's presence.

She reached into her pocket and wrapped a gloved hand around her focus, throwing herself into contemplation of its smooth lines to drive out the foreign emotions.

"Kai, would you give us a few minutes in private?" the colonel asked.

The resentful man left the room, the woman fading away with him as if she had no identity other than his.

"I'm not leaving," Shironne whispered to the colonel before he could ask the same thing of her. She had little desire to sit in the hallway of an unknown building surrounded by unknown people.

"Of course not," the colonel told her. "Come with me." He walked with her across the room, warned her of a step up, and then placed her hand on the arm of an upholstered chair. "Why don't you sit down?"

She stroked the unfamiliar chair before sitting. It proved to be overstuffed and smelled of leather. She sank into it more deeply than she'd expected, feeling hopelessly small.

"I don't think you've met Miss Anjir," the colonel began.

"You shouldn't have brought her here," the prince said quickly. "She's a child."

"I'm not a child," she insisted. "I'm seventeen years old."

Surprise ran through him. Shironne wasn't sure whether her age provoked that reaction, or the fact that she'd spoken. "You *are* still a child, Miss Anjir," the prince told her firmly. "Why did you bring her here, Jon?"

"I want to stay in control of this investigation," the colonel continued. "I have more people to put on this than you. You can pull in all of your planted servants and shopkeepers and I'll still have more."

Shironne sensed the colonel's urgency.

Dahar reflected irritation at him. "You didn't answer my question."

"I would like her to work *with* Mikael on this. Deborah and I . . ."

Shironne sat up straighter. *Who is Mikael?* She opened her mouth to ask that.

Agitation swelled out of the prince, though. "Would you be willing to wait outside just for a few minutes, Miss Anjir? I'd like to speak with the colonel privately."

No, it's not a good time to ask for an explanation. The colonel wanted her to cooperate. For his sake, she agreed. He hauled her out of the enveloping chair and led her back across the office toward the door. He took her outside, placing her hand on the back of a straight wooden chair.

"Who is Mikael?" she asked him in a whisper.

"I suspect you'll find out in a few minutes. I'll try to make this quick," he promised and then disappeared back behind the door.

. . .

Cerradine hoped this wouldn't get ugly.

Dahar returned to the windows and stood peering through the small panes at the courtyard. "Does she know?"

"Know what, exactly?"

Dahar turned to glare at him, folding his arms over his chest. "Of her mother's relationship to my father?"

"Yes, she does," Cerradine assured him, "although the two younger sisters don't. I assume since *you* didn't know that, Deborah hasn't had a chance to discuss this with you yet."

Dahar, rather predictably, grimaced. "Discuss what?"

Being the head of the Daujom, Dahar could force his way in on every Lucas Family elders' meeting, but he chose not to do so. That was meant to show trust in both their judgment and their commitment to upholding the treaty. Unfortunately, it meant that Dahar often learned things later than he liked. "Shironne's powers," Cerradine told him. "The elders know, but I think they decided you weren't to be told. She's a touch-sensitive."

Dahar made a scoffing sound. "Is that even possible?"

He'd expected that reaction. "Yes. You're likely to see her demonstrate it, soon. When she touches someone, she can get at their actual thoughts, not just their emotions. Even a short time after that person's death."

Dahar continued to gaze at him, his lean face, for once, expressionless.

"Deborah thinks that she developed her powers in response to Mikael's need."

"Need for what?" Dahar said.

"Someone to listen to him. Deborah thinks that his broadcasting and his . . . new symptoms are all part of an effort to draw in a touch-sensitive to see his dreams. There's a possibility that she's *bound* to him." Cerradine shook his head. "Until last week, Deborah has advised me not to bring her up here. She's concerned that Shironne is too young to work with him, among other things, but you know that no one can get to his dreams like a touch-sensitive could."

"And how long have you known all this?" Dahar snapped. "And what about Deborah?"

"I asked her to come out to observe Shironne working not long after she first came to work for the army. To determine whether she truly is a touch-sensitive." He wasn't going to go into Deborah's reservations about Shironne's powers. Not now. "It wasn't until much later that we began to suspect a tie to Mikael. She's always picked up on his dreams, but when he was sent to Jannsen Province, she still did. No sensitive, no matter how strong, should be able to sense someone that far away. Not without being *bound*."

Dahar gazed at him, scowling. Cerradine hadn't thought Dahar would take that last bit well, particularly not when he had hoped that Mikael would marry Sera eventually. For Mikael to marry Dahar's daughter when he was *bound* to someone else would be unkind to all parties involved.

"And no one thought to tell me?" Dahar finally asked.

"Did you ever ask Deborah? No, of course not, because you don't talk to her." He sighed. "Yes, she knew Shironne might be *bound* to Mikael. And yes, Deb knew that Shironne is your niece. The fact that she's been working for the army has been kept quiet because Savelle didn't want anyone to know, not while her husband was alive. Anjir's only interest in his daughters was whether they could make a politically or financially advantageous marriage. Shironne's unconventional choice of work might reflect poorly on her sister, Perrin. He might have locked Shironne up to keep her from the public eye."

"Because she was working for the army?"

"Yes," Cerradine said. "You forget, it's not accepted among Larossans, Dahar, for someone with powers to refuse the priesthood. Madam Anjir didn't want anyone to know. Not even you."

"So why now?"

"I didn't want you to subpoena her, and . . ."

"Subpoena?" Dahar frowned at the window. "She's a child. I did think to *ask* you to bring her. I need to know what she knows, Jon."

"Let the army work this case, Dahar. My people can handle it more discreetly."

"We've had three deaths now. Exactly how discreet do you intend to be?" Dahar snapped. "I want to know why the police hid the first death. If I have to pull in the police commissioner to discover that, I will. There's a meeting of the city's council today, and . . ."

"Don't, Dahar. It's not going to tell you anything about the deaths, and Madam Anjir will never forgive you if her daughter is dragged into a court proceeding. Faralis *would* do that. If you press him based on their testimony, he will drag Shironne and Kassannan into court and call them liars."

Dahar stewed over that for a moment and then turned away from the window to glare at him. "There's a bruise on that girl's face. Who hit her?"

"She tripped, fell, and hit a wall. Easy to do when you've no idea where the wall is."

"Oh, I see." Dahar stared out over the cobbles of the courtyard. "Is it true that her husband used to beat her?"

That wasn't a question about Shironne. "Yes."

"Is that why you broke his hand?"

"You heard about that?" That had been his very first discussion with Anjir. "I wanted to make a point."

Dahar turned and glared at him. "Why did she go to you for help? Not us?"

He'd known that would be a sticking point for Dahar. "Chance—that's all. Shironne was trying to find out who'd killed her maid's lover. He was a sergeant, so they came to my office. That was when I first met your sister."

"Did Anjir leave her alone after that?"

"Yes. I've had a couple of people working in her house since then. They made sure he didn't bother her." And all in all, it was probably better that Savelle Anjir *hadn't* gone to her brothers for help. Although Dahar no longer took students, he was still a fight master, a fact evidenced by the black chevron trim across the chest of his uniform jacket. He could have killed Anjir with his bare hands and, since he was a member of the Royal House, probably would never have been charged. "So, will you leave this in the army's hands for now? Let us run the investigation?"

"I had planned to. Keep me informed, and I'll let Mikael coordinate with Aldassa." Dahar stopped pacing and perched on the edge of his desk, brow furrowed in concentration. Once he had something to plot over, he usually calmed down. "This meeting with Mikael and Miss Anjir. What exactly are you trying to accomplish?"

"Deborah thinks that once he has made a *connection*, for lack of a better term, with Shironne, he might stop exhibiting the symptoms that worry her so much."

"Do you know how many times you've said *Deborah thinks* in this conversation?" Dahar snapped. "Do you actually believe she knows what she's talking about? This is Mikael we're discussing, not some dusty character out of a history book."

"What will it hurt, Dahar?" Cerradine asked. "To try?"

. . .

After returning from the depths of the fortress, Mikael went back up to his quarters and tied the single white ribbon that marked mourning in the Lucas Family on his sleeve. As he walked back down to the office, he saw that the sentries in the hallways already wore them. It was amazing how quickly news traveled in Above and Below.

He carried his knife with him now, sheath secured to the back of his sash. As upset as the sentries were, they shouldn't take offense at his going armed within their purview. Fortunately, they still seemed favorably disposed toward him.

As he turned onto the hall that housed the Daujom, he spotted a lone figure sitting on a chair outside the main office like an abandoned pile of laundry. Mikael stared at the Larossan girl, wondering what she could be doing there. The hall held only the offices of the Daujom and shouldn't attract the presence of a child.

From her size, Mikael judged her to be about thirteen. Her feet swung above the runner. She wore a pink tunic that had seen too much wear, along with orange petticoats of equal age. Her shining brown hair fell in an untidy braid to her waist, tied off with a bright green ribbon. Larossan, certainly, judging by the color of her skin. She wasn't wearing any jewelry, so not of marriageable age. She must be one of the servants' daughters, lost in the palace.

"Are you . . . ?" he began.

"No, I'm not lost." She spoke as if in answer to his unuttered question, sounding irritated. "Also, I can't help it if my clothes are old, and I'm seventeen."

Mikael gaped. In his experience, particularly strong sensitives could guess the gist of his thoughts by reading his emotional reactions, but she had answered his internal queries as if she'd heard the words running through his mind.

"I'm told that I'm, um"—she paused, appearing to search for the proper word—"unusual, but you're *loud.* Do the others not hear you talking to yourself?"

This has to be the colonel's sensitive. He'd known she had to be a strong sensitive to pick up his dreams, but this was amazing. She was far younger than he'd expected. No wonder the colonel had been so adamant about his not visiting the army's offices while she was there. "You hear me *talking*?"

"Sometimes I hear other people mumbling in their heads. It's as if everyone else is facing the other direction from me, but you . . . you're facing me. And I do work for Colonel Cerradine."

Mikael stared into her pretty brown eyes, trying to place what struck him as odd about her, and then he stepped to one side. Her head turned with the movement, but not far enough. "You're blind," he said, fascinated.

"Yes, I am. Most people don't find that interesting. They feel sorry for me instead." She folded her gloved hands in her lap, an intrigued expression on her face.

"Should I feel sorry for you?" Mikael asked, unable to help the grin he felt creeping across his face. This was one of the most interesting conversations he'd had in weeks.

"I'd rather you didn't," she said. "I'm Shironne Anjir." She removed one of her gloves and held out her hand for him to grasp.

Mikael touched his fingers to her palm. He felt the faint ridge of a scar and then her slender fingers curled around his own. Only then did it occur to him that allowing him to touch her wasn't proper for a Larossan girl of good breeding.

"And you're the Angel of Death."

Mikael almost snatched his hand away, but she rattled on. "I don't mean that badly. I've felt your presence before in the bodies. You were with them when they died. Some of them find that comforting, you know."

Had Iselin felt that? Or only been disgusted with his presence, as always? He crouched down. Miss Anjir's face followed the sound of his movement, and at that angle, he could see a suspicious bruise on one cheek.

"I thought you were Anvarrid, but you use Lee, don't you? That sounds right, although I don't know why."

"My name is Mikael Lee," he said aloud.

She shook her head slightly. "People just call you that because it's simpler than your real name. Mikoletrion?"

There was no possibility she'd heard that before. "No one calls me *that*," he admitted. "It's my Anvarrid name."

"I wondered if you were part Anvarrid," she said. "Because you're loud, I mean."

"My father was a Vandriyen," he said. "My mother was a Lee."

"And Mikael is easier than Mikoletrion? No, that's not really why you use that name. It's because you don't want to seem like an Anvarrid."

He tilted his head to gaze at her face. "How is that any different?"

"You're hiding," she said. "You're hiding that you're part of the Van . . . Vandriyen House. It's not a secret; you just don't want people to think about it."

Very few within the Lucas Family knew his actual position in the House of Vandriyen. Deborah knew, of course, and Dahar did. Although he was next in line to become the Master of Lee Province, it was more of a technicality than anything else. But the very mention of his Anvarrid name sent that circling through his head, along with the worries that accompanied the issue, and he suddenly realized she could have picked up every last thought.

She's a touch-sensitive, he realized with a rising sense of amazement.

That was why she'd offered him her hand. He let her hand go, suddenly aware that he held far too many secrets that she wasn't supposed to share.

She sighed and started tugging her glove back on. "I know when not to tell people's secrets, Mr. Lee. Don't worry."

"Secrets?"

"Some just shouldn't be told. Everyone has secrets, even my mother, and she's the most proper person I know."

That seemed like a heavy burden. "How do you know? Which ones not to tell, I mean?"

She tilted her head to one side. "I suppose if you can't do any good by telling it, you shouldn't."

A remarkably mature attitude for someone so young.

"I'm seventeen," she said, scowling. "I'm not a child."

He fought hard not to think any reply to that. He began counting to force his mind away from the topic but was distracted when she laughed.

"Five?" she said.

"What?"

"You started counting but you got stuck on five and just kept repeating that over and over. Five five five five five."

He felt his cheeks flushing. "You're not touching me now. How clearly *do* you hear me thinking?"

"Like you're inside my head, even if I'm not touching you. You're not what I expected either. I used to think you would be wise and ancient, which is probably why Lieutenant Aldassa smirked inside whenever I said so."

Mikael laughed, unable to help himself. He shouldn't be laughing on a day when a member of the Lucas Family had died, but he could easily visualize that expression on Aldassa's face.

The girl smiled ruefully. "I didn't mean any offense. Sometimes I say things without thinking first."

"No doubt." Mikael stood up. "How old were you when you lost your sight?"

"Thirteen," she said. "It was an accident."

"Accident?"

"The bruise on my cheek. I fell into a wall." When he didn't respond, she added, "And no, I'm not lying to protect anyone. I did fall."

A member of his yeargroup had lost his sight in an accident when they were twelves. It had taken Samuel Lee a few years to learn to compensate for his blindness. The whole yeargroup had worked to keep things in fixed locations so Samuel wouldn't trip over random objects. Despite their efforts, odd things *would* trip him up, even years later. Miss Anjir apparently had learning still to do. Her braid resembled the work of a five-year-old, and her hair ribbon didn't match her clothes at all.

"I was in a rush this morning," she said tartly. "I usually take more time, but the colonel came for me unexpectedly."

Mikael shook his head, thinking goodwill at her. "I didn't mean to be critical."

"I was *clarifying*," she said. "Not defending myself. I merely wanted to say I'm not usually so haphazard. Not with the braid, I mean. You spend a lot of your time concentrating on being happy, don't you?"

Startled, Mikael rose. "It's best for everyone."

Her head tilted again, turning as if following his movement. "Is it for *you*?"

No. That was why he liked to go out into the city, why he fled the sensitives—because sometimes he was just too tired to control his mood.

When he didn't respond aloud, she said, "That seems unfair."

She rose as well, barely as tall as his shoulder, and he wasn't tall. No wonder he'd mistaken her for a child. She turned her head as if looking around then. "The other man is coming back, the resentful one."

Mikael turned to look in the direction she'd indicated. Kai emerged from the stairwell a second later, Elisabet a couple of steps behind him. They came toward the office. "Ah, that would be Kai Lucas."

"Kai? Is that the prince's son?" she whispered.

"Yes." It wasn't too surprising that she knew his name, given that there was occasional speculation in the newspapers about Kai one day assuming the throne.

"That would make him my cousin," she said then. "Hmm."

Of course. Mikael had known that Dahar had a half sister down in the city, but she didn't want to be acknowledged. Mikael just hadn't made the connection when Miss Anjir told him her name. He glanced down at the girl's face; while her coloring was Larossan, her heart-shaped face rather resembled that of Rachel, the elder of Kai's two sisters. She was *definitely* prettier than Sera.

The girl flushed. With her dark skin it wasn't nearly as obvious as his own rather embarrassing blush. He was not supposed to think of a child in those terms.

"I'm seventeen," she whispered. "I'm not a child."

Having reached them, Kai glanced between Mikael and the girl, his expression displeased. Elisabet stayed back several feet as Mikael attempted to smooth Kai's ruffled feathers. "Have you met Miss Anjir yet, Kai?"

The look Kai gave him could have frozen the river. "We weren't introduced, but yes."

"I'm not sure why you're angry with me," she said.

Kai's nostrils flared white around the edges. "I'm not angry with *you*. There are things I should have been told long ago."

Mikael grimaced. Like Dahar, Kai hated to be left out of anything. Mikael could only wonder how long Kai had known he had cousins. He was not going to ask that.

"Which isn't my fault," she said in an irritated voice.

Mikael glanced at her, surprised at her tone, and then realized she'd *reflected* Kai's anger. The Lucas Family trained their children not to do so, but it was, in Mikael's opinion, simply human nature.

The girl paused with her glove halfway pulled on and then stuck her hand in a pocket and wrapped her fingers around something within, as if for reassurance. "I'm sorry."

Kai said nothing. Mikael thought calm at the girl, like wishing the waters of a lake to be still.

She hid a yawn behind the other gloved hand. "If you do that much more, Mr. Lee, I'm going to fall asleep."

Mikael stopped, appalled. She was extremely susceptible to

him. He would have to remember to guard his thoughts around this girl. She said nothing, but an apologetic smile touched her lips.

"Why exactly did the colonel bring you here?" Kai asked her. "We have work to do."

Kai had evidently made up his mind to dislike Miss Anjir, even if she was his cousin.

"The colonel has not chosen to enlighten me as to his intention," she replied, lifting her chin and turning her face away from Kai as she answered. "I suggest you ask him."

Don't antagonize Kai. Mikael formed the words in his mind, saying it in his head clearly and slowly. He hoped the girl would pick up something of it.

Her head turned in his direction. "I—would—not—if—he—didn't—me," she said with exaggerated slowness.

Kai folded his arms across his chest, looking annoyed.

Try to think nice thoughts. Smile, Mikael thought at her. He'd somehow gotten off on the wrong foot with Kai, and four years had *not* improved their working relationship. He hoped she might do better.

She sighed and turned a forced smile toward Kai. "I don't know what I could do that you can't, but the colonel has an idea he wants me to try. That's all I know, sir."

The door opened inward, and Cerradine stepped into the hallway. He took in the group standing there, his eyebrows raised. "Mikael, I'm glad you're here. Saves me sending runners after you." He reached out, took the girl's hand, and placed it on his sleeve. "Why don't we all go inside?"

Kai scowled at Mikael, who figured he shouldn't comment.

The girl followed the colonel back into the office. He settled her in Mikael's favorite chair, so Mikael took the other leather one, leaving the wooden chairs for Kai. Kai always chose those anyway. Elisabet assumed her regular post at the door.

"First things first," Dahar said as he perched on the edge of his desk, addressing Mikael and Kai. "I suppose you both met Miss Anjir out in the hallway. Miss Anjir's mother is my half sister. That makes Madam Anjir your aunt and Miss Anjir your cousin, Kai, although that's never been made public because Madam Anjir doesn't want it to be."

Kai glowered. "May I tell my sisters? Or my aunt?"

"Your sisters don't have any need to know, Kai," Dahar said. "It appears that Deborah, however, has known for some time."

The girl folded her gloved hands in her lap, looking regretful. She had very expressive features, Mikael noted, something Lucas girls learned to quell very young. "You mean the doctor who comes to watch me sometimes?" she asked softly.

"Infirmarian," Kai corrected.

Dahar rolled his eyes.

"They're called infirmarians in the Lucas Family," Mikael explained for her.

Her head turned in his direction. "Why?"

"Because they work in the infirmary," Kai said.

"Then why aren't doctors called hospitalians?"

Mikael pressed his lips together to hold in a laugh.

"Will the three of you be quiet?" Dahar interjected.

Now you've gotten us in trouble, Mikael thought at her.

Her lips turned up at the corners, and Dahar scowled at them both.

Mikael knew better than to think Dahar sensed what he *thought*, but apparently Dahar had picked up something. Mikael resolved to behave himself. The girl took the end of her braid and flipped it in his direction, which he took to signify her doubt that he could accomplish such a feat.

"Stop that," Dahar said, his scowl unabated. "Jon has a strange idea, entailing a blending of your talents. Dreamers *have* worked with touch-sensitives in the past."

Mikael sat up straighter. The House of Vandriyen did have a history of working with touch-sensitives to understand their dreams, running all the way back to their first encounters with the Six Families. It had never occurred to him to think such an option might work for him, primarily because he hadn't thought any touch-sensitives existed.

The girl seemed fascinated. "You mean there have been people with dreams like his before?"

"Well, it runs in Mr. Lee's bloodlines, but he's an aberration. Dreamers usually don't broadcast their dreams, and they almost never dream about what he does," Dahar explained.

"Our idea," Cerradine said, "is for Mikael to recall his last dream. Miss Anjir might be able to pull out more detail, something that will help us stop the killers."

Kai folded his arms over his chest, his expression sour. Mikael glanced over at the girl and then back to the colonel. "I never pick up specifics, Colonel. I get emotions and sensations and a few memories, but not much else."

"Our belief is that you're serving as a bridge to the victim at the time and place of the murder. What happened *must* be in your dream somewhere. Otherwise you wouldn't be able to recall things when you see their bodies."

Our belief had to mean his and Deborah's. "But I can't voluntarily access whatever's there, Colonel. I've never been able to. Do you think she can?"

Miss Anjir didn't seem to have heard this plan before either.

"Possibly. We need to know what these men look like, how many there are, how they're choosing their victims. You're our only *witness*, Mikael, and she's interrogated witnesses before."

Mikael knew Cerradine had used her for that, but he'd always assumed she was much older. It left a bad taste in his mouth to think of a girl this young exposed to such things.

"It's *my* choice," she said. "And I am not a child."

How many times a day does she say that? By Larossan standards, she *was* old enough to make such decisions for herself. "She's already dreamed this dream," Mikael said to the colonel. "Why would it help to go through it again?"

Cerradine ran a hand through his white hair. "She dreams only what you broadcast. She doesn't *see* what you dream. If she was touching you, she might get at something more definite."

Mikael swallowed. It was one thing for her to touch his hand. It was something else entirely to invite her to go wandering through his thoughts.

"I'm very good at keeping secrets," she reminded him.

He wondered vaguely how many people she touched in the course of a day. Larossans weren't overly prone to touching, but she surely touched her own family and the colonel's people. She had to hold in what she knew about each of them, or no one would ever come near her. "Very well, what do I do?"

"If you tried to remember your last dream, she could try to see that," Cerradine suggested.

"Whenever I do try to recall a dream," he admitted, "I just fall asleep."

"She might be able to follow you, Mikael."

"I see in my dreams." The girl stood and, without direction, came to wait in front of him. "Well, most of them."

How does she know where I am?

"It's like knowing where a crow is when it's cawing," she said with a touch of exasperation in her voice. "And I figured you would have reacted if I was about to trip over anything."

She was using his mind like a spare set of eyes. *What a handy trick.*

"You're loud. If I was trying to find *her*," Miss Anjir said with a tilt of her head toward where Elisabet stood by the door, "I would probably fall flat on my face because she's so quiet."

Kai got up and briskly walked to the other side of the room, waiting near Elisabet as if he had secrets to hide. Mikael watched him go, briefly thinking perhaps he too should run.

The girl pulled off her gloves, carefully tucked them in the pocket hidden on a seam of her pink tunic, and reached out to touch his face. Mikael could feel the heat of her skin before her fingers made contact. He flinched back, unable to quell the instinctive response.

Miss Anjir's brows drew together.

"I'm sorry." He doubted that Cerradine had any idea how personal this was. His dreams were his own private dance with death. To take someone else there seemed almost voyeuristic. Since the very first one, he'd struggled *not* to expose others to them.

She frowned, the line between her brows deepening. "This might be easier if we had some . . . um, space," she hinted to the two older men. "You're worrying very noisily."

Are they? Mikael forced down his surprise.

Dahar and Cerradine removed themselves to the far side of the office, leaving her alone with him. She stood only inches away from Mikael, her hands poised on either side of his face. Her eyes, he noticed, were a cool brown, exactly the same color as her hair.

"That's what my mother says," she whispered. "You should concentrate. Trust me."

He'd asked her to trust him, so it only seemed fair. He closed his eyes. He felt the warmth of her hands touching his cheeks, his jaw. She must be uncomfortable leaning over him like this for so long. This would be much easier if she just sat in his lap, he decided, thinking that he would much rather have her in his lap than Merival.

Mikael panicked, grabbing her wrists to pull her hands away from his face. "I don't think this is a good idea," he said in a tight voice.

For a second, she didn't respond. "I'm not offended," she whispered back.

"That was . . . inappropriate. I'm sorry." He knew he was blushing.

"People think what they think, Mr. Lee," she said as if it were of no import. "I can't see you blushing, so it doesn't matter. Who is Merival?"

He was *not* going to explain that. He felt grateful the colonel and Dahar were on the other side of the office, unable to hear this conversation. He drew a deep breath and marshaled his thoughts, trying to focus on last night's dream. As if sensing his renewed resolve, she laid her hands against his face.

He put himself into the memory of his dream. He felt her hands on him. His heart beat faster, trying to answer the fear that surged through his veins.

CHAPTER TWENTY-TWO

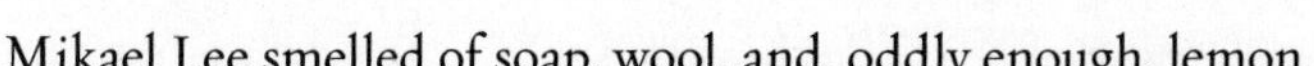

Mikael Lee smelled of soap, wool, and, oddly enough, lemon.

He was afraid—always afraid he'd slip away and die, with everything forgotten and no purpose served. The fear beat through his mind like the frantic wings of a bird trapped inside the house. He wanted to live, but it was hard to let go when they died.

Shironne tried to tear away, shocked at the strength of the pull he exerted on her, unlike any mind she'd ever felt before. Mikael Lee's thoughts wrapped themselves around her, pulling her down with him into sleep.

He *was* the woman. Suddenly his terror became very clear to her. He *became* the victim, tangled into the woman's feelings and fear. The colonel had told Shironne that, but she'd never truly understood until now. Together they shared the woman's confusion and fear. They felt her numbness and utter helplessness.

Mikael's memories of the dream flowed around her, blurry and tattered. The faces of the woman's killers were flesh-colored smears, holes already stretching into the fabric of them, doorways into nothingness. The memory had begun to rot away, like moldering leaves found under a hedge in spring.

Someone watched it all, familiar but unformed, another of those tattered faces, but apart from them.

One of the attackers reached out a crumbling hand then, touching the woman's face, a violation that felt worse than the helplessness.

She couldn't understand why that one touch should be so terrible among all the others, but to Shironne it seemed as if that hand reached into *her* mind as well as the victim's.

Shironne felt the woman's decision to give herself up to death, to escape the fear and humiliation. Suddenly calm, she knew she wasn't alone. She was going to die, but Mikael would remember it all for her. He would avenge her.

I have to escape; we'll all three die together, even in this tattered memory.

Shironne screamed at Mikael to wake, but he stayed with the woman, refusing to give up on this chance to understand, to preserve something of her. The third presence in the dream hung on as well, trying to reach *them*—almost as if he could extend his touch through the victim and, in doing so, reach Mikael himself.

"Wake up!" Shironne yelled at him, determined not to let that other presence have him.

Her lungs failed, forgetting how to breathe. Her time had run out.

Shironne reached into her pocket and wrapped her hand around her focus. She forced herself into the crystal, seeking its calm to escape the horror of the dream. Anchored, she tore Mikael away from the dying woman.

Shironne woke, drawing a deep breath into lungs that felt broken and aged. Disoriented, she discovered she'd sat down. Then, realizing she'd sat down in Mikael's lap, she tried to jerk free. The top of her head cracked against his jaw. He yelped and pushed her away.

She tumbled onto the floor, one slipper catching in the other trouser leg and keeping her from rising.

"I bit my tongue," Mikael mumbled. "I'm sorry."

He helped her stand, placing one hand under her elbow and pulling her up with his other hand. She could sense his embarrassment, too overwhelming to be shaped into words.

"You deserve worse, stupid," Shironne snapped, uncaring of the audience. "What did you think you were doing?"

"I tried to remember everything that happened." *Why are you angry?* his thoughts asked.

"The next time I tell you to wake up, *wake up,* you idiot. I don't need to know what it feels like to die. You don't either, for that matter." She wanted to shake him, like her father used to do to her when he was angry.

"I'm sorry," Mikael said again. His mind coiled and twisted, aghast at the danger in which he'd placed her. It repeated that apology over and over in half-formed words.

Shironne stepped back. He must have to apologize to every person like herself every time he dreamed—atoning for actions done without effort or intention. He'd not intended to place her in danger. He'd simply done what he did. This was what he'd been created to do, and he had no idea how to protect himself from it.

He needs to anchor himself in the world of the living. He needed something to prevent him from slipping away in tandem with one of the people about whom he dreamed, and he didn't have a focus, did he?

"I don't think we made much progress," he said over her head. That last wasn't for her.

Shironne removed her hand from his, deciding the colonel and Dahar had come near. "All I saw was the copy, and it's faded," Shironne told them. "But I'm sure about a couple of things I wasn't before."

"What did you see?" the colonel asked.

"There *was* someone there, just watching everything. A man, I think."

"Do you mean Mikael?" Dahar asked, a touch of condescension in his tone.

She shook her head. "No. Mr. Lee became the victim. It was *another* witness, and I don't think he was one of the killers either."

"Forced to watch?" Cerradine asked from somewhere nearer.

"I don't know," Shironne said. "There was someone else who seemed to be . . . trying to reach Mikael. Like he was trying to reach through the victim to touch him."

Shock ran through Mikael, generating a shudder down Shironne's spine.

"How can someone touch me in a dream?" he asked.

"I don't know," she whispered. "The dream's too faded."

"What do you mean by faded?" Dahar asked.

"Memories are like leaves," she said in Dahar's direction. "They rot away after time. His memory of the dream is only hours old and already it's beginning to fade, maybe because he was drugged."

"So you don't think this will work?" the colonel asked.

Shironne tried to get a sense of what Mikael thought, but his mind had gone closed, mulling over some idea. "Mr. Lee just showed me what he showed me last night. I think . . . um, I think I need to see what *he* sees, not what he shows people."

Mikael focused abruptly on her words. He didn't like it, but he didn't disagree. He must have reasoned out the same thing.

"Do you understand what you're suggesting?" he asked aloud.

The colonel touched her shoulder. "What exactly are you saying?"

"I need to see into the original dream, not a memory."

The colonel responded after a moment of furious calculation. "That *can* be arranged. Take him off the palace grounds to keep him away from all the sensitives this time. I might be able to get you there. What is the name of that place where Kai always finds him in the middle of the night?" he asked the room in general.

"The Hermlin Black," Kai's voice floated from across the room, sounding self-satisfied now.

"I'll see what I can arrange," Dahar said.

Shironne opened her mouth to protest—Verinne would never allow that—but the colonel spoke first. "If you can get word to me in time, I might be able to bring Miss Anjir there."

Mind reeling, Shironne felt for the chair she'd sat in before. There was no point in joining the argument since the two older men were already arranging everything between them.

About a foot to the left.

She moved over in that direction and her fingers collided with the arm of the leather chair. Bare fingered still, she sensed that Mikael often sat in this chair. The leather bore the feel of his hands, oils from his skin—recognizable to her now since she'd touched him. She sank into the chair and drew her gloves back on, leaving only her face exposed. This sense of his skin lingered on her hands. Not unpleasant, but not yet familiar.

Mikael had settled back in the other chair, seeming amused and resigned at the same time. *Between them, they think they run the world,* he thought at her. *Well, them and Deborah.*

"Deborah needs to be involved with this," the colonel said then.

Shironne clapped a hand over her mouth to hold in the laughter, but it leaked out as a strangled cough.

"Are you all right?" the colonel asked, worried. He came nearer and said, "You look flushed."

"I'm fine," she gasped. "I just need to sit here and rest."

Mikael projected innocence, as if he thought he could affect the colonel. *Perhaps he can.* He was *that* loud. Kassannan had been correct about that.

Dahar's irritation flared again, but he said, "If she's willing, we can set it up. But she's supposed to be getting some sleep now, so don't go down and wake her."

"You're assuming there's going to be another dream," Mikael said, all amusement fading from his thoughts.

"I have no doubt there will be," the colonel said. "I hope the two of you can tell us why this is happening then."

Shironne bit her lip. She wasn't sure she could, even if she walked into Mikael's dreams. She wasn't sure *how* she was supposed to do that. If she met the killers in the colonel's office, she could touch them and know what they thought. She doubted she could do so in a dream.

". . . I thought they could take her down with them while I'm gone. She's very good in that sort of situation."

What? Shironne wished she'd been listening. "Where are you going, sir?"

"The city council is meeting this afternoon. It's best I go," the colonel said. "Will you be all right if I leave you in your uncle's hands? His aides can take you to view the body, and I should be back by the time you return."

The colonel was leaving her here alone, Shironne realized. He'd left her with Aldassa before, but never with strangers. Then again, she really couldn't consider Mikael a stranger anymore, could she? "I'll be fine, sir."

. . .

"I need to make some arrangements first," Kai pronounced. "We can meet in the cold rooms on the hour."

Mikael had almost forgotten about Kai and Elisabet over near the door. Kai simply walked out of the office without waiting for any answer, leaving Dahar looking vexed again.

Mikael was annoyed for Miss Anjir's sake. Why couldn't Kai make an effort to be friendly?

The girl sat with her gloved hands meekly folded, a posture that Mikael suspected now was not a true representation of her demeanor. If he understood the expectations of Larossan society, she'd violated about half their rules already today. Sitting on the lap of a man to whom she wasn't married was more something a barmaid would do. But for her powers to be useful, she had to touch people. That must have taken some determination on her part.

Her head turned his way and she shrugged with one shoulder.

Dahar walked to the chair where Miss Anjir sat, looking distinctly uncomfortable. "Miss Anjir, I hope your mother won't be upset when she finds out Cerradine left you in our charge."

Miss Anjir shook her head. "I don't often work with the colonel anyway, sir. I usually work with Captain Kassannan or Lieutenant Aldassa."

Dahar cast a helpless glance at Mikael, as if to beg for his assistance. He was clearly in a foul mood, and Mikael suspected he'd prefer not to deal with a child while he was in a temper.

Mikael's stomach reminded him then that he'd never had lunch. "Have you eaten, Miss Anjir?" he asked.

"Ever? Or in the last hour?"

Dahar rolled his eyes.

"You knew what I meant," Mikael said, amused.

Taking advantage of his interference, Dahar drifted away from the chairs to pace the entry floorcloth.

The girl's head followed Dahar's motion almost as if she could see him, but then she turned back to Mikael. "You meant that you're hungry and want to eat something before we go downstairs, having successfully kept down your breakfast this long. Do you really do that?"

"Do what?" Mikael knew but wanted to hear Miss Anjir say it.

She looked uncomfortable, amazingly easy to read with her expressive face. It seemed almost as if he could sense her emotions as he had when he'd been a normal sensitive.

"Vomit," she said, and flushed. "You were like me once?"

"Yes, I do. All sensitives start out the same, but for some reason a few of us change. Yes, I'm hungry." Mikael decided he'd answered all her questions. "If you'll give me your arm, I'll walk you down to the kitchens and I, at least, can get something to eat."

The girl hesitated.

"If you want, I'll let you hold the end of my sash."

"Like a dog?" Her expression was dubious.

"I've never had a dog. It might be an interesting experience," he joked.

She rose and regally held out her hand. "Are you always so annoying?"

"I'm afraid so." Mikael placed her hand on his arm. "You seem to bring out the sharp side of my tongue. Although it's nice to talk to someone who doesn't seem to mind my joking. The Lucases are very serious."

Dahar stepped out of their way as Mikael led Miss Anjir to the office door. Mikael nodded to him as he passed, and then led the girl down the hall to the back of the palace, where the kitchens occupied the ground level.

What did the sentries think of him walking the halls with an unfamiliar Larossan girl on his arm? Word of this would be all over Above and Below within an hour, especially since he was going to take her down into the fortress. He'd opened himself up to all manner of gossip.

"They seem too serious to gossip," the girl said in a pensive tone. "Does the woman ever talk?"

The woman? "Oh, Elisabet. Not much. She's a guard. Her job is to watch, not converse."

"I'll bet she's good at it. The former, not the latter. She seems very . . . um, controlled."

"She is." *Controlled* was an excellent word to describe Elisabet, Mikael reflected. "Stair. She's been contracted to Kai as his guard for three years now, so she's had time to perfect her silence."

The girl walked down the steps with him, slowing when he did.

"Do you count?" he asked. "I had a friend who used a cane on the stairs because he said he never knew how many there were." He started to take a step forward, but the girl had stopped on the landing, a perplexed expression on her face. "Miss Anjir?"

"I think I'm still trying to look at them," she replied after a moment. "It's like my mind still thinks I should see things but nothing's there. Does that make sense?"

"Yes. I'm never going to get any food at this rate. Second stair." The girl slid out a foot and found the steps. Mikael started down. "One of my friends was blinded when we were twelves. It took him a while to stop looking for things."

Her head tilted. "What happened to him?"

"He's a quartermaster now. In the Lee Family, of course, not the Lucas."

"Oh." Judging by her expression, she found that intriguing. "How was he blinded?"

"He hit his head against the floor during training."

"And he couldn't see ever again?"

"No." He caught sight of her furrowed brow and wondered if she might see again someday. Deborah should be able to tell. Did she want that?

They stepped out into the main kitchen, a perpetual flurry of motion. Voices sounded from all over the cavernous space as the cooks began early preparations for dinner. The girl's hand tightened on his arm, confirming the anxiety he sensed from her. Mikael gave her a brief description of the kitchen so she could orient herself, recalling that large spaces confused people without sight.

The cloths on the reserved tables were red, and pennants hung in bunches over the ovens and around the walls, making it look like a Larossan place. Most of the palace's servants were Larossan. Even so, the smell of the spices was wrong, a traditional Anvarrid meal in preparation for the evening in the king's household, no doubt.

One of the cooks directed them to the cold repast area, where bread and meat remained from the servants' lunch. The servants of the fortress had a long history of interaction with the Lucas Family and accepted them as fellow servants, a misconception the Family permitted. The Family provided their service as a part of their treaty with the Anvarrid government and not solely for pay. As long as both groups fulfilled their duties, they got along reasonably well.

Mikael led the girl to the broad wooden counter and placed her gloved hand on it while he took a piece of bread and stuffed some meat inside. "Do you want anything?" he asked. "This is the time if you do."

"What is there?"

She sniffed, but the smell of baking flatbread overlaid everything else, so he doubted she could tell. He perused the selection for her. "Meat: lamb, and I believe this is chicken. Some more bread, no cheese, a few apples."

"Apples, this time of year? Could I have one . . . and perhaps a piece of bread?"

"Hothouse fruit." He looked through the apples, picked the best of the remaining ones, and pocketed a second for himself. He turned her gloved hand over and placed the first apple in it. "I have a piece of bread for you as well."

"Is there somewhere to sit?"

"In the kitchens? No, not for us." He tried to think of an appropriate spot to sit and eat, but not one where they would be directly under the eyes of the sentries. "We can sit on the steps outside for a few minutes."

She placed the apple in her tunic pocket and took the flatbread he handed to her. He led her back up the stairs, out the main hallway, and onto the steps leading down into the back courtyard of the palace, describing it as they walked.

"We're standing on the first-floor landing behind the palace," he said, and went on to tell her about the granite stairs and railings, the flagstone courtyard, and the neat and symmetrical gardens beyond that. He led the girl to the half landing, staying to one side so they could eat out of the way of any traffic. He sat next to her on the steps. Here the Rifles on duty on the rooftops could still see, but not overhear, them.

It was sunny now, the flagstones dry, with the wind blowing the scent of the stables in the other direction for a change. A marvelous day, Mikael reflected, save that one of their own had died in the early hours of it. It was strange that he'd had to remind himself of that.

"It *is* much nicer than this morning," the girl said, holding the piece of bread in her gloved hand. She lifted it and brushed it against her cheek. Then she tore off a small piece and touched it with the tip of her tongue.

Mikael watched the process curiously, thinking it perhaps a bizarre new ritual popular in Larossan society.

"You know, I don't stare at people when they eat," she said in a waspish tone.

"I'm sure you would if you could. What are you doing?"

She flushed, putting both her hands in her lap. "I'm not hungry."

"I'm only curious, Miss Anjir. I didn't mean to offend."

She shifted the bread between her gloved hands, dropping the spare bit on the ground. "Cook has to be careful with my food. She knows what I can tolerate. On the other hand, I can always tell her if food has begun to go bad."

He gazed at her lowered face. "Is your *mouth* sensitive?"

"My skin is sensitive," she whispered.

"What, *all* of it?" Had he ever heard that about touch-sensitives?

"My fingers the most, but my feet too. My lips and my tongue—I think my tongue is the worst—but all of it."

"Your face?"

She nodded. "People always want to make me look at them, so they try to lift my chin, because I'm short, you know. I think Dahar meant to. Isn't there something I could call him that would sound *proper*?"

"You're accustomed to Larossan names. Dahar only has the one name. He hates being called by his title name, so you'll have to call him Dahar."

She tore off a little piece of the bread, hesitantly put it in her mouth, and then swallowed.

"Kai," he continued around a bite of his sandwich, "you can call Mr. Lucas or Master Kai, if you wish. He's the king's heir, if you haven't figured that out yet, but the Senate won't confirm him until next year, once he's a twenty-five. Don't bother to address Elisabet at all. She'll ignore you. It's Master Elisabet if you do, since she's a First."

"First?"

"Head of a yeargroup—all the children born in the same year. Elisabet headed her yeargroup. Kai headed his. It's an honor, but also a great deal of work." He ran through a primer of how to address different people in the Lucas Family, and Anvarrid, and then people like himself who had two names, one Family name and one Anvarrid name—an impressively complex set of rules. During his recitation, she choked down half her bread.

He glanced at it, wondering if she intended to finish it or feed it to the pigeons. She simply handed it to him instead. She fished the apple out of her pocket then, and held it in her gloved hand. "It's coated with paraffin."

"You can feel that through your gloves?"

She shrugged. "They . . . um, mask the impressions I get. I have to concentrate to read *through* them, but I can."

"Mine was bitter," he said in consolation. He ate the remainder of her bread as he gave that last revelation some thought.

"I like bitter apples." She sighed and took a careful bite. "I didn't mean to worry you."

Mikael took his knife from its sheath and plucked the apple out of her hand. He cut a sliver and sliced off the peel. "Take your glove off."

Considering how loudly he apparently thought, he wasn't sure the glove would block his thoughts from her anyway.

She yanked at the fingers of her right glove and dropped it in her lap. She took the sliver of apple from him and quickly placed it in her mouth. "*This* is why I don't go out anymore," she said after she swallowed it. "In society, I mean. It's not just that I'm blind."

He could understand. At this rate, she'd never make it through the first course at a formal dinner. She could still carry on a conversation, sing or dance even, but she couldn't eat in public. He'd seen enough of Anvarrid social circles to know how cruel people could be. The Larossans, for all that they had different rules, wouldn't be any kinder to someone who was unusual.

"The colonel told me it's supposed to get easier as I age," she offered. "I'll become . . . um, habituated to things. I don't sing that well anyway."

Mikael wondered where he could dig up more information on touch-sensitives. Deborah would know. He continued handing her thin slices of the apple, and she dutifully ate them. When she'd finished the last piece, she tugged a small cloth from a coat pocket and began scrubbing at her fingers with it.

"I don't know if I want to see again," she said.

He hadn't asked her that, not aloud, but he'd wondered . . . back in the stairwell, before they'd entered the kitchens. "What, you're just answering that *now*?"

"I needed to think about it. It makes some things easier not to see."

Not to see? "Such as?"

"Well, I touch a lot of things, but I don't have to see them. Like the man the police pulled out of the river. To me his body was a thing, not a person. He was a collection of facts, and his memories were like . . . a bunch of old letters I'd found abandoned in a desk. I think if I *saw* him, I would think of him as alive, like you do."

He hadn't given it much thought, but perhaps that was why he reacted to the bodies the way he did. Because he thought of them as alive, and seeing them dead was a horrible shock.

"You need to learn to let go," she added. "You hang on to them too tightly. You think of them as you."

She'd said that back in the office. He needed to give that some serious consideration, but later. "Well, are you ready to look at a body now?"

She tucked the cloth into her tunic pocket. "I suppose so. Does the palace have its own morgue?"

"No," Mikael said, "but the fortress does."

CHAPTER TWENTY-THREE

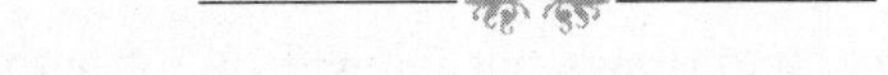

The fortress. For a moment, Shironne forgot to breathe.

She wasn't just getting to visit the palace. Mikael intended to take her down where most Larossans never would go, into the heart of the Lucas Family's sovereign territory. *Melanna will be so jealous.*

He rose and helped her up. "We'll go down to the courtyard," he explained, "and around to the side entrance. Saves going up the steps and back down again."

The fortress was supposed to be deep underground, so she supposed it would be a long way. He was worried about stairs.

"I can do stairs," she reminded him quickly.

"I don't doubt that. The question is, *How fast?* We're running a bit late, and Kai isn't patient."

"I noticed," she said dryly. "I'll go as fast as I can."

Mikael led her down another flight of stairs and to the right. A door opened, and they came off the hard flagstones into a dry-feeling hallway with carpet underfoot. They must be back inside the palace again.

"We're going to go down the grand stair that connects the fortress to the palace," he said. "There are two landings, one at each third. I've never counted the number of steps in this fortress. Fifty-one in Lee."

There were people watching them—the sentries again, surely, thinking curious thoughts about her. They kept flickering in and out of her awareness, their minds too quiet to be clear, almost like they were ghosts.

Using Mikael's reactions to judge her placement, Shironne slid her foot up to the edge of the first step. He counted in his head, very loudly, as they walked downward, making it unnecessary for her to count herself. At one point the stone under her slippered feet changed slightly. Mikael paused there, knelt down, and rose again. He was paying his respects to the fortress, she realized, as if it were an elder or a grandparent. Then he put her hand on his arm again and they resumed their trek down the endless steps.

Forty-eight, his thoughts said as they reached the bottom.

"Somehow I've always pictured it being hundreds of feet below-ground." She sensed the curiosity of someone nearby—yet another sentry, she supposed.

"Daujom business," Mikael informed someone, and she heard the distinct sound of writing, as if he was recording that. After a moment, Mikael led her down another hallway, the sound of it far harder than that of the hallways of the palace above. "You're going to need to put your hand on a wall," he told her. "Bare hand, I mean. Right side."

She cringed, unable to help herself. "Do I have to? Touch it, I mean."

Before she finished her question, she knew from his thoughts that this ritual was necessary. She hadn't had to do what he did on the steps, but this was *required* if she wanted to go a step farther. So she tugged off her right glove and held out her hand, sticking the left hand in her pocket and wrapping it around her focus. He took her sleeve and moved her to the right a few inches. Her hand lightly touched a stone surface—no, it *wasn't* stone—and she laid her hand flat against it.

Words bloomed into her mind, accompanied with a shock like static, startling her into stepping away. *Was that normal?*

From a couple of feet away, Mikael thought reassurance at

her, apparently alarmed by her reaction. No, apparently that *wasn't* normal.

Shironne swallowed and clenched her fingers tighter about her focus. She hadn't recognized those words. They'd been in an unfamiliar language, *not* Pedraisi from the sound of it. But she'd understood what the words meant. The fortress had spoken to her, welcoming her home.

"Are you all right?" Mikael asked as she collected her thoughts.

"It spoke to me," she whispered. "Does it always do that?"

That fascinated him. "What did it say?"

"It spoke in some other language, but it said something like *Welcome home, Lucas.*"

That surprised him. "That's amazing. It recognized you as a Lucas. I think that proves you're a Valaren beyond any doubt."

"Why would it say Lucas, then, not Valaren?"

"The Valarens and the Lucases have intermarried so many times that all the Valarens have a good amount of Lucas blood. That started with the son of the very first Anvarrid governor, Lucasedrion, the first to marry into the Lucas Family. In fact, Lucas isn't their original name, but they took Lucas to honor him."

"Lucasedrion?"

"That's a history lesson for another day," he said, hinting there might be another day on which to discuss it. "We need to keep moving."

She wanted to stay and talk about the wall talking to her. Or perhaps she could just talk with the wall. It wasn't truly stone, although at first touch she'd mistaken it for that. It felt more like charcoal, only that wasn't right at all, because charcoal was soft, not hard. The wall had seemed almost to be woven of the stuff, which made no sense at all. Walls couldn't be woven.

When they'd walked some distance away, Mikael paused, giving her a moment to contemplate their *new* location. They stood in a vast chamber. Echoes chased themselves past her. There were people in this room, dozens of them, close and far—curious, but trained not to ask about her. A faint breeze brushed her face, startling in this place. If not for the echoes, she could be in Army Square.

"It smells," she noted. The air in the fortress had an odd tang to it. It wasn't unpleasant, but not like the outside air either.

"No, it doesn't," he said. "The engineers assure us it doesn't smell. What we think we perceive is a *lack* of smell." His mind said that the engineers smelled—clearly for her benefit—and then reflected wryly that they sometimes did. "You won't notice after a couple of minutes."

"How is there air moving down here? We're underground, aren't we?"

"It's magic," he said, as casually as if discussing the wind aboveground. "Imps carry in air from outside and travel through the walls, blowing it about to keep the temperature the same."

"Imps? Like demons?"

"Not demons," he said firmly. "Imps. That's the only word we have for it. When the Anvarrid came, they forbade us to speak our own languages. They replaced our word with *imp*, so that's what we have to describe them."

His mind considered that an obvious thing, like the mysterious Lucasedrion whom she didn't know about either. The Lucas Family truly lived in a different world.

"Are you impressed?" he asked after a silent moment.

By this place? In her mind, it was just a shapeless open field that echoed slightly. "Am I supposed to be?"

"We're in the main commons, the mess hall. You should be impressed by the size."

He meant that as a joke, she suddenly grasped. He *knew* she couldn't see the room and only had an impression that it was endless. He'd had a blind friend who must have explained how different this place was without sight. "I am suitably amazed, Mr. Lee."

"It's what outsiders always comment on when they first see it," he said with a shrug that she felt through her hand on his arm. "I thought I would give you a chance."

"Oh. How many people live down here?"

He chuckled. "I don't know the answer to that. The elders keep track, mostly so that they can ensure there are enough sentries and quarterguards to fulfill the treaty, but they don't make the number public."

But she could tell he had a guess in his head, somewhere close to two thousand, a staggering number. She wasn't sure how much space that many people needed. How did that compare with all the soldiers living in Army Square? She added that to a mental list of things she needed to ask the colonel someday. Then again, many soldiers didn't live in the barracks there but were dispersed throughout the city with their families. So if she added all those houses to the contents of Army Square, it would be huge.

"You won't leave me alone here, will you?" she asked, her voice sounding more timid than she liked.

"Not if I can help it," he promised. "Here, I'll show you something that will help."

He thought reassurance at her again. Then he placed a hand over hers on his sleeve and led her to a closed-in space, a hallway heading away from the place they'd entered. To her the hall seemed eerily like the one they'd left before. The floor was smooth underfoot without seam or break. It would be terrifyingly easy to get lost in a place like this. Her heart was beating a little harder than normal, but he kept wishing calm on her.

"I guess I always thought it would be a cave," she confessed nervously. "You know, wet and dripping and, I don't know, bats? Don't caves have bats?"

"This isn't a cave. It's a city, only built underground. Here." He took her now-gloved hand and pressed it against the wall. Under her fingers, two round moldings protruded from the smooth wall at waist height. The upper one had chevrons cut into it, angled away from the direction they'd walked. The chevrons on the lower one pointed in the opposite direction. "On *every* floor, in *every* hallway," he said, "the upper one points the direction back to the stairs that lead up or, if you're on this level—One Down—they lead to the main door, the way we came in. If you get separated from me, stick to the wall and follow that. Up is always out."

She ran gloved fingers along the upper molding. "What about the lower one?"

"Those point to the refuge on each level. That's the place you go if there's trouble."

"Trouble?"

"An invasion, for example, or . . . a fire."

He didn't think either of those was likely, but history proved that an invasion *could* happen. Everything about this place had been reinvented after the Anvarrid invasion. They wanted to confuse intruders, so there were no labels or symbols. There were armories at regular intervals. If she pushed harder at his mind, she was sure she could figure out where the nearest was—although what she might do in an armory eluded her. She shook her head to clear away those thoughts. "They made those for someone who couldn't see?" she asked instead.

"Actually, it was done in case all the lights fail," he said, leading her on along the hallway. They walked straight ahead for a long time.

Shironne kept one hand on the comforting moldings on the not-stone wall and the other on his arm. "Is it . . . pretty?"

"You aren't missing anything here," he said wryly, directing her to the left. "Gray walls. Gray floor. There aren't any tapestries allowed on the walls, although there are designs painted along their upper third. Here in Lucas, it's all geometric patterns, black and white and gray."

That didn't sound promising. "Gray ceiling?"

"Actually not," he said. "That's where the light is."

"You mean . . . like gaslights?" She didn't hear any hissing from them.

He paused and puzzled over how to explain it. "No, the whole ceiling is lights. Imps again. They glow, however much you tell them to. I'm sorry, I don't have the words." *An engineer could explain it to her far better,* he thought absently. She caught that without even trying.

"Oh." Nearby, she heard the clatter of voices, too distantly to tell what they said, and feet. The walls seemed closer, the sounds more confined here.

"We're coming up on the main stairwells. They're the primary way down," he said. "It's like that in all the fortresses."

A sudden idea occurred to her. *He's been in more than one.* "You've seen the others?"

"Four—here, Lee, Halvdan, and Jannsen. They're all laid out alike, although Jannsen is smaller in scale. I'm very disappointed you aren't being more effusive in your praise."

Shironne decided she liked his sense of humor. "Well, the floor is very smooth. Nothing to trip over, I guess."

"Much better," Mikael said. "Oh, wait. I'm going to take you past the stairwell to show you something and then we'll come back."

Something else meant to reassure her, she could tell. They walked past an area where warm air rose, combined with more echoes. Shironne nearly stumbled when the direction of the chevrons under her fingers changed, but Mikael led her past that point to a spot where her fingers came to a corner and the wall veered off to her left. She *did* stop then. "Where does it go?"

"There are a lot of hallways that come off the main hallways," he explained. "This one, to the left and just past the main stair, leads to the infirmary wing. Try walking toward it."

She could tell from his mind that it was safe, so she took a step that way. Her slipper came down on rough floor, almost like small pebbles under her foot.

"Guideline," Mikael offered. "You can use that to find . . ."

"The wall on the far side of the hallway," she finished for him. It must be another modification for when there was no light, to keep Family from wandering off course accidentally.

"And if it helps to know," he added, "hallways, stairs, and aisles are always kept clear. Less to worry about for you. Now we're going to tackle more stairwells, twelve of them to be exact."

He guided her back in the direction of the stairwell. Shironne heard people coming toward them. She felt an occasional twinge of interest as someone passed silently. The minds in the fortress were carefully controlled, a strangely comfortable dampening of emotion.

"First stair," Mikael announced, and placed her hand on a rail.

She thanked the true god for the rails, which made everything easier. She felt for the step with her toes and started down. They reversed on the very wide landing and headed down a second set of steps. It went on forever, one well after another, until he announced they'd reached Seven Down. When they reached the bottom she wanted to sit and rest for a time, but Kai waited nearby.

"I was getting ready to come find you. What took so long?" Kai asked with absolute sincerity, as if Shironne could have jogged blithely down a thousand stairs. It was evidently a rhetorical question anyway, since Kai moved away without giving them the chance to answer.

"Are you all right?" Mikael asked. A wave of his concern washed over her.

"I'm just not accustomed to that many stairs," she admitted.

Mikael wrapped up his concern and hid it away, making himself quiet. He led her in the direction Kai had gone, leaning down to whisper next to her ear, "Wait until we go back up."

"God help me." She sighed. "So, where are we?"

"Seven Down, main hallway. Most of this floor belongs to the engineers. They keep the fortress running properly. The cold rooms are near the end of this hall, so it's another long walk, I'm afraid."

Walking the square on Antrija Street didn't compare to this. It was a good thing she'd worn her sturdiest pair of slippers today. "What are the cold rooms?"

He began to slow his pace, and she decided they'd neared their destination. "The Six Families aren't known for imaginative names, Miss Anjir."

"You mean they're . . . cold?"

"Very clever," he said, his voice amused.

"Thank you. I'm not generally this witty," she admitted, "so you must be rubbing off on me."

The arm under her fingers stiffened. His hand, which had rested over her gloved one, slipped away. Her sense of him faded, taking his humor with it and leaving her feeling as if someone had scrubbed off a layer of her skin.

Shironne stopped where she stood, in the middle of nowhere far below the ground. "What did I say?"

"I didn't mean to push you." His voice, without her perception of emotional response, seemed flat. It was still a nice tenor voice, with a faint northern accent—pleasant to listen to, but devoid of any undertone.

She hated being shut away. "I don't understand."

"Who are you," he asked in that odd voice, "when you're alone?"

CHAPTER TWENTY-FOUR

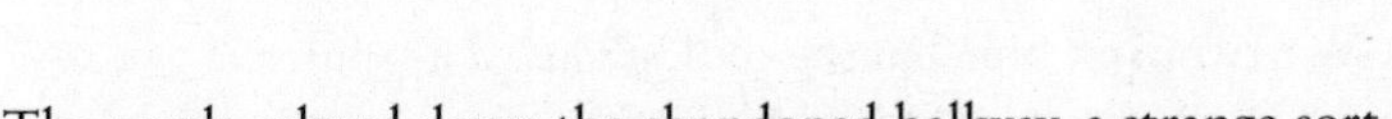

The words echoed down the abandoned hallway, a strange sort of accusation. "Who are you when you're alone?"

The question rattled around in Shironne's mind. Who was she? She was Savelle Anjir's daughter, and Melanna's big sister. Perrin's sister, although that didn't matter nearly as much. She worked for the army. But those all defined her relative to others. Who was she without that? When she sat in her room in the early morning hours? "I'm waiting for something to happen, I guess, for some reason to be . . . useful."

Mikael took a half step away from her. Shironne thought he might be looking at her, but she couldn't tell. His mind hid his response to her words. Then, slowly, she felt him relax. Her sense of him came creeping back like fog, and she held it around herself, a warm feeling of belonging to someone in this huge unknown place. He wasn't angry, but worry still lurked in his mind.

"What did I say to upset you?" she asked again.

"I don't mean to influence you." His voice sounded warmer, with an undertone of apology in it.

The way he said it, *influence* meant *coercion*. "You didn't do anything to me."

"Are you certain of that?" His hand took hers again and laid it on his arm, not waiting for an answer. He wanted her to think about it, not respond.

"Do you intend to take all day?" Kai's voice echoed down the hallway, annoyed and not too distant.

Mikael led her to the voice. She could feel cold pouring from the open doorway in which Kai stood, his warm anger and pain silhouetted in her mind by the emotionless tinge of frost around him. Kai backed into the room, allowing them inside.

Shironne let the cold run through her. She could smell the woman's body, but only just. "How cold is it in here?"

"Cold enough," Kai answered.

Worry ran off him, but she couldn't judge its source.

"Where's Elisabet?" Mikael asked.

Kai's quiet shadow was missing. Shironne hadn't noticed, since the woman seemed no more than a reflection of him.

"I've sent her to my quarters to wait for me," Kai said. "I don't need a guard in Below, and she doesn't need to see this. We both trained Iselin."

Kai's tone discouraged further questions. Mikael had misgivings, thinking loudly that Elisabet didn't need to be protected from the sight of death, that Kai overreacted and that he forgot again who guarded whom.

"Where is the body?" Shironne asked, hoping to head off strife between the two.

"On the table," Kai said. "Deborah will come down to examine the body later, although Jakob has already rendered his judgment."

Jakob must be another doctor, Shironne decided. Kai was going to be weighing her conclusions against his.

Mikael led her to the table. He placed her gloved fingers on the edge and told her how the body had been laid out. He'd maintained a careful distance until that moment, but the sight of the woman's mutilated form sent a wave of nausea through him.

Shironne felt it echo through her own body. Her breath suddenly went short. She found herself sitting inexplicably on the icy floor, sweat trickling down her back. The sensation began to ease as Mikael fought to bring himself under control.

"I'm sorry," he said, "I'm sorry."

He hadn't known he would transfer those sensations to her: his instinctive visceral response over finding himself dead, because he wasn't ready to die yet—not quite yet. Someday it would be him on that table, and they would all be relieved that Mikael had finally gone away, but not today. There were things he still had to do, things he had to figure out, someone he had to find.

Shironne shook her head, trying to sort his thoughts from her own. She could hear his mind's voice rattling on. She wrapped her hand around her focus and used it to force his thoughts away. She held his thoughts at bay, confining them to one small corner of her mind where they howled away like a dog chained in a fenced garden.

"Stop it," she hissed at Mikael. "That isn't *you*."

Mikael heard her and began repeating her words over and over in his head like a mantra. After a moment, he had himself under control again.

Kai kept his distance, radiating annoyance tempered with a touch of curiosity. Shironne blocked him away with ease. Generally someone related by blood was harder for her to shut out, but the strength of Mikael's hold on her had surprised her, clouding her thoughts despite her efforts. He'd *influenced* her, just as he'd feared.

This is why they've been keeping me from meeting him. Shironne struggled to her feet, using the edge of the table to pull herself up. Determined to behave normally—despite him—she tugged off her left glove and laid her hand on the body, her fingers coming to rest on the woman's stomach. The victim's skin felt cold, blood turning to an icy slush inside. Everything had stalled in its creep toward decay. "She's *frozen*."

"Of course she is." Kai's tone indicated she must be stupid not to have expected that.

She'd never encountered a frozen body before. She'd worked for the colonel for years and had never dealt with this. "It's not that cold outside," she said. "How did she freeze?"

"The mortuary service puts bodies in a . . . very cold place," Mikael said. "That's why this room is cold. Because we're close to *that* room."

There was a room colder than this one? Shuddering, Shironne raised her hand to the woman's chest and laid it on her right shoulder. She waited, hand pressed there, until a faint impression reached her, the body thawing enough to give up bits of information. "There's grit in the wounds, a great deal of it, like the gravel on the river walk."

"They dumped her facedown there," Mikael confirmed.

From the sound of his voice, he'd risen and now stood a few feet away.

"The same knife as before made these cuts, but there's so much more blood in her. She didn't bleed away like the other two." Shironne tried to sense the frozen body beneath her hand, attempting to reach through the slush for more, to tell how the woman had died. The static nature of the ice in the body frustrated her, holding everything she needed to know in minute crystallized packets, each a tiny wall she had to batter down.

She tugged off her other glove and dropped it while trying to put it with the other in her pocket. She reached across the body to lay her other hand on the woman's left shoulder, leaning over her to do so.

"What's wrong?" Mikael asked.

He knew something had gone amiss; it probably showed on her face. "I'm hardly sensing anything," she said, embarrassed that her voice came out sounding so plaintive in front of her disdainful cousin. "I've never touched a frozen body before. It's all dead. Like wood, kind of. Oh, I know that doesn't make sense," she said in answer to Mikael's unspoken confusion.

"Then forget it," he urged her. "I think we know everything we need to know."

"This is a waste of time," Kai snapped.

Through the skin Shironne could feel the cuts on that shoulder warming under her hand. They'd been made after death, blood oozing but not flowing. A faint trace of iron rested in one of the cuts, catching her attention—barely a sliver. A connection raced between her palms, as if lighting the body for her from within. The woman's lungs had clenched, simply forgetting to move in their rhythm. She'd ceased breathing long before they'd finished with her.

"That's why the dream ended so abruptly," she said. "She died. Her lungs stopped working." She kept her hands where they were. If she could only thaw a spot or two, she might be able to get a clearer impression.

The woman's mind had frozen along with her flesh. The memories left behind were brittle snowflakes, crumbling when she attempted to touch them, hardly preserved at all. Her name still resided in the fragments—Iselin Lucas: sentry, lover, and daughter. She'd had dreams and intentions, Shironne could tell, all shattered now. She sorted through the memories, trying to find what had been different about Iselin's course that day.

Pain. There had been a burst of pain, and then darkness.

Shironne grasped that one memory—an insult to the body far more violent than the pinprick the others had felt, a surprise blow that rendered Iselin Lucas unconscious. "Someone hit her with something, from behind. More like a stick at the base of the skull. It was daylight."

"She wasn't killed until past midnight," Mikael protested.

"I know that," she answered.

"But that would explain why her wrists were bound," Mikael said.

"Yes, I remember that from my dreams. They drugged her and then cut the bindings."

"You shouldn't do that," he said. "It's bothering Kai."

"Do . . . what?"

He huffed out a breath. "Answering what I'm *thinking*."

Shironne heard the difference then. He wasn't speaking aloud, meaning that Kai had been hearing only half of the conversation. That explained her cousin's rising irritation.

She swallowed, took another deep breath of the icy air, and turned her attention back to the body. She focused on that last memory, that moment before Iselin lost consciousness.

She'd stopped to talk to a man. No, he'd stopped her.

Shironne dug deeper through the fragile memories, trying to find out why Iselin Lucas had stopped, why she hadn't fought. She could have. Shironne sensed that in Iselin's toned muscles—*fighter*. She was probably one of those fighters Shironne had seen at the summer fair years ago.

A memory surfaced of a Larossan face, trustworthy because he was police and she recognized him. She drew her hands away from the body, the chill seeping through her. "She was stopped by a police officer, and that was when someone else hit her from behind."

"A police officer stopped her?" Kai asked doubtfully.

"It's not that simple," Shironne told him. She'd learned from questioning witnesses for the army that reality was often subjective. "She perceived him as a police officer. That doesn't mean he was."

"No," Mikael said—clearly aloud this time. "We know the killers have had an opportunity to collect at least one uniform jacket from a police officer. And that of an army lieutenant as well."

And it was nearly impossible to tell the difference between a Pedraisi and a Larossan. "He looked familiar to her," Shironne added. "I think he was there when she died too, but I can't seem to find that memory."

"Find it?"

"The memories closer to death are broken, I think because of the drug."

"Nothing you could see?" Mikael asked this time.

She shook her head, frustrated by the lack of further information, the lack of answers. And her hands were dirtied now. Tiny bits of blood, grit, and flesh clung to her hands, warmed by the heat of her skin. While she'd been trying to search Iselin's mind, before it unfroze, she'd been distracted by thoughts. With her attention no longer on those, the contamination on her skin took precedence. Suddenly it was all she could sense. She stood there, helpless for a moment, breath coming fast. Nausea rose in her belly. She couldn't reach into her pocket to touch her focus, not with her hands so soiled. There wouldn't be a basin in this room, or if there was, any water in it would surely be frozen.

I'm coming. A towel enveloped her right hand, the sense of Mikael's concern wrapping around her at the same time. "I have your gloves. Be still, there's some frozen blood on your tunic."

He wiped both of her hands with a moderately clean towel, determined to rub some life back into them. He brushed vigorously at her right sleeve afterward, the one she'd dragged across the dead woman's chest.

"How did you know?" she whispered. "That I was about to be sick."

"I felt it," he returned, tightly controlling his worry. Just as his earlier sickened reaction had affected her, she could apparently make *him* ill.

"The towel's not enough," she said.

"I didn't think so, but it's the best I can do on this floor." He threw the towel somewhere away from her. Shironne heard it land in a bowl or basin and felt his bizarre flash of pride that he'd hit his target.

"Is there somewhere I can wash my hands?" she asked.

"Yes." He turned his attention away from her. "I'm going to take her back to the office, Kai. I expect it will take a bit, so please ask the colonel to be patient if he's already back."

Kai flared with annoyance and then controlled the impulse. "Very well, sir," he replied, irony crackling in his tone.

The impulse to kick him surfaced in Shironne's mind. If Melanna had been here, *she* would have, and then some.

Mikael wrapped a calloused hand around her wrist and yanked her out of the icy room. He hauled her a good distance down the echoing hallway before he slowed, allowing her to regain her dignity.

"Sorry. I thought for a moment you were going to kick him," he said, amusement returning to his voice.

"I was thinking that if my sister were here, she would have. Please," she begged, "is there *any*place I can wash my hands?" She shivered, the warmer hall triggering the response, but she didn't dare rub her contaminated hands against her sleeves to warm herself.

"I don't know where anything *is* on this floor save the cold rooms. I can find a water closet on Six Down, if you don't mind the noise."

"What noise?" Shironne asked, shaking her hands. She could put up with anything if it meant she could clean her hands. If she could touch her focus, it would help her distance herself, but if she did that now, she would simply transfer the contaminants to the stone and the inside of her coat pocket.

"Calm down," he said quietly, willing that at her.

It helped, his concern swaddling her like a warm blanket. She took a deep breath, the edge of her panic gone. "So, what noise?" she repeated.

"Six Down is where the sparring floor and the shooting rooms are. During the day it's very loud, although I expect it'll be quieter than usual today." *Mourning,* his mind said, and something about white ribbons.

"I think it would be a good idea to stop there, please."

He led her back to the stairs and then up to the next floor. Once away from the stairwell he proved to be correct in his concerns about the noise. They entered another vast room, where perhaps a hundred people moved about, many of them yelling. The air felt different here—humid and warm. She tightened her hold on his arm, confused amidst the chaos.

A wave of emotion struck her then; joy, elation, exhilaration, anticipation, all sweeping past her, like a river grabbing her in its current. Shironne gasped, the feeling overwhelming her as if it might drown her. Goose pimples fled along her skin.

"Don't listen to it," Mikael advised. "Just push it to the back of your mind and ignore it." He thought calm at her, and the drumming in her heart slowed. A vivid memory reached her of the first time Mikael had felt it, the flow of many minds gathered together, willing the same thing and feeling the same emotion. The grip of the emotions in the cavernous room loosened, and she pushed it away.

She recognized it now. She'd felt this before on New Year's Day when the priests led processionals along the streets. Or when she'd gone with her mother to the summer fair, and the excitement around the melee had drawn her to the railing to watch. "What is this?"

"Ambient," he said. "It's what a group can create together, but it can take almost any form. Enough anger, and they'll turn on each other. It's very seductive to become one of the mob, to be no one. I forget about it sometimes because I don't sense it anymore. It's often stronger in the fortress because it's enclosed."

Of course they have a name for it. Shironne squared her shoulders, determined not to let this ambient business get the better of her. "Like a mob?"

"Exactly," he said. "People get carried away at times."

In an enclosed place with a lot of people like her, she could see it becoming dangerous quickly, offering a new logic behind the Lucas Family's usual expressionless demeanor. They had to control their emotions just to get by. Shironne stood there a moment longer, pushing down the external feelings swirling about, and then recalled their reason for coming here. "Water closet?"

He took her there. He quickly described the layout for her, where to find soap and the tap, and then placed her hand on the door.

Shironne oriented herself in the small room. Although he'd described the room for her with words, his mind had also carried in it a mental sense of where everything was, almost a map, much like her memory of her own bedroom at home. Had he *intended* to give her that memory? Or had she stolen it? Either way, it held true. With one hand she easily found the tap, and water flowed over her fingers. *Clean water,* she noticed—like that from a very deep well, but not as cold.

Deciding she shouldn't keep Mikael waiting, she briskly scrubbed at her hands. She discovered that the plumbing worked in the same manner as that in her home. She emerged a few minutes later, hands thoroughly cleansed and her gloves on.

Mikael led her around the edge of the giant noisy room, far larger than the "mess hall" he'd taken her through earlier. He kept her calm, suppressing her emotions by thinking quiet at her. It would have offended her in any other situation, but at the moment she felt willing to let herself be controlled.

She didn't mind it from him. He wasn't trying to affect her so much as offering a calm refuge, as if she could hide inside his mind. She could almost do that with her mother, but she'd known her mother her entire life.

"This is a different stairwell," he said, drawing her attention back to the physical world, "not as wide, but it's laid out the same."

They began the long trek upward, and Shironne learned she'd been correct in her expectations. It truly *was* awful.

She clung to the rails on the wide stairs. Mikael came up slowly behind her, sounding short of breath himself. By the time they'd climbed up to the palace, she felt like a wet rag. "I don't think I ever want to do that again."

"We do it all the time. One becomes accustomed."

"What if you're hurt?" she asked. "How do you get up and down?"

She could actually tell he was looking at her, deciding whether to tell her something. If she was touching him, she could take that from him, but she wasn't going to do so.

"Well, most would move out of the fortress to one of the enclaves. Many of the elderly do."

The Six Families *did* have enclaves outside their fortresses. She'd heard that before, although she hadn't ever wondered *why*. "So they have to leave?"

"No," he said, the sound of a chuckle in his voice. "They may choose to, though. There are also . . . do you know what an elevator is?"

"Like at the army hospital? The colonel told me it's essentially a very large dumbwaiter. Do you mean there's one of those here?"

"Several, actually, although no one's allowed to use them. They belong to the engineers and they're very, very old. If you get caught trying to use one, you spend hours running the stairs."

As punishment, she guessed from his tone. "Did you try it once?"

"No. I find the idea a little unnerving. I don't care how much my lungs ache. I'd rather trust my feet."

He didn't like the possibility of being trapped in a box, Shironne realized. "Well, I still think it might be better," she told him. "Thank you for going slowly enough for me."

"I'm just glad I didn't go up with Kai, because my lungs aren't working well today. He always runs." A myriad of joking addendums ran through Mikael's mind, some made into words clear enough for her to pick them out.

She laughed, having heard what he'd considered saying. She felt, rather than saw, him flush when he realized she'd gleaned his thought about Kai's eternal quest to impress Elisabet.

"We'd better get back to the office," he said in an exasperated voice, placing her hand back on his arm.

CHAPTER TWENTY-FIVE

Mikael watched from the office windows as Cerradine handed the girl up into his carriage. She turned her head and waved up at him, nearly taking off Cerradine's hat. Mikael grinned, marveling that she knew where he was standing.

It worried him, what had happened in the cold room. She'd fallen to the floor, evidently sickened by the same impulse that usually made him retch. He'd forced himself back under control, but the fact that he could trigger what appeared to be a physical reaction in her concerned him. He'd never before made another sensitive physically ill—not when awake.

Then again, a few times he thought he'd been able to sense her. His own stomach had turned when she'd noticed her hands were contaminated. He'd felt it—*sensed it*—when the ambient seized her on the sparring floor. Not only her shock, but the ambient itself. He'd been deaf to it for so long he couldn't be certain, but it had felt real.

He might just be interpreting her expression. *She does have a delightfully animated face.*

She is a child, he reminded himself then, what felt like the thousandth time that day. As with any other interaction with a child, his behavior would be under strict observation by the elders. In fact, if Deborah had woken in time, she might have refused to go along with the colonel's plans.

And Deborah might be correct in her concern. He had *not* been on his best behavior. True, it was frightening how she read his thoughts like a book, but he'd found himself talking to Miss Anjir like he'd known her for years.

To be honest, he wasn't sure that her attempt to see into his dreams had revealed anything new. He wasn't sure the colonel's idea of having her there when he actually dreamed would produce anything either. What she had done, though, was yank him out of his memories before he felt himself dying. If she could do that when he was actually dreaming . . .

"Why sacrifice Iselin?" Kai asked.

Kai and his father were standing next to Kai's desk talking when Mikael looked away from the windows. Peder, Elisabet's Second, stood in her customary place, his much larger frame nearly blocking the doorway completely. Kai had evidently gotten around Elisabet by taking one of her Seconds with him. Mikael wondered at that for only a split second before dismissing it as Kai's capriciousness.

They'd discussed every bit of information they'd gathered with the colonel before he left, including the fact that Iselin had been struck from behind and tied up. Jakob's conclusions after examining the body had evidently matched Miss Anjir's revelations about Iselin's death. "It wasn't a sacrifice," Mikael said.

Dahar paused midgesture. "What?"

Mikael left the windows and came back toward his desk. "This can't be about sacrifice. If they were making a sacrifice, they would have stopped when Iselin died. From what I read in the Andersens' files, the victim has to bleed out, so Iselin's sacrifice wasn't valid. Yet they kept carving the marks even after she was dead. That has to be the point, then, not the sacrifice itself."

The expression on Kai's face went guarded and still.

The first death, unsubstantiated since the body was missing, could have been seen as a mysterious death. The second killing had alerted the army to the murders, and the third, the Family. On a night when the Family was on alert, the killers had found a Family woman outside the fortress. Mikael would be interested to learn what Aldassa had heard from Iselin's musician paramour—whether she'd arrived at their assignation at all. It might be important to know whether the questionable police officer and his accomplice last night had followed Iselin away from the palace grounds. Given the sudden headache he'd developed the previous evening, Mikael suspected that it coincided with Iselin being knocked unconscious.

"It's a message," he continued. "I don't know to whom it's being sent. We're just in the middle here, between these . . . priests and whoever or whatever they want."

Kai ran a hand through his dark hair, a rare nervous gesture. "The first two bodies were left exposed, even if one of them was later thrown into the river by the landowner. Iselin's body was dumped on the riverside in the middle of the city. They wanted them to be found." He turned away from them for a moment. When he turned back, his face was expressionless. "I'm supposed to be on the sparring floor soon. If you'll excuse me, sir."

Kai left, Peder trailing him. Mikael stared at the door for a moment, wondering what was running through Kai's mind, what had caused him to leave so abruptly.

"He's upset," Dahar observed.

"Kai did train Iselin's yeargroup on rifles at one point, sir. I can understand his feelings. And I think he and Elisabet are having a disagreement," he added with a shrug.

"Don't make excuses for him, Mikael." Dahar strode over to his desk and picked up his teacup. After taking a sip, he turned to throw the porcelain piece into the fireplace, but then stopped himself and set it carefully back on the tray.

"You should go," Dahar told him then, his burst of anger abated. He sounded exhausted. "You've had a long day."

Mikael snatched up his coat from the chair where he'd placed it and left Dahar to brood.

. . .

Shironne felt the colonel's worry as they rode in his carriage toward the house on Antrija Street. He'd queried her about her impressions of the palace and the fortress, and then what she thought of her newfound uncle and cousin. She hadn't interacted much with the prince, and she tried to do her best to be positive about Kai.

"And Mr. Lee?" the colonel asked. "Was he too overpowering?"

She wouldn't have thought to characterize Mikael Lee that way. "No. He's very . . . practiced about when not to feel things."

"He didn't behave in any inappropriate way, did he?"

The colonel dreaded her answer, as if he was responsible for Mikael Lee's actions. She didn't see why he felt that way. It wasn't as if she'd had no choice in the matter. "No, he was fine. He was . . . amusing."

"You would tell me if you don't want to work with him, wouldn't you?" he pressed.

Ah, this was the tiresome *child* thing. "Absolutely. I've wanted to meet him for a couple of years now, sir. You know that."

"And you're sure you've never met him before?"

Now, that was an odd question. "Where would I have met someone from one of the Families?"

The coach came to a halt, and as soon as she sniffed she knew they were in the back courtyard at her house. The colonel opened the door, stepped down, and then helped her down.

"I do wish I could speak to your mother about today's events," he said as he led her toward the back door. "I would feel better if I could keep her abreast of what you were doing."

Shironne sighed. Her mother wasn't likely to be the problem. "She'll be back soon, and I'll tell her everything, I promise."

She felt his resignation wrapped like a cloak around him. "I'd like to speak with her as soon as she returns," he said, "which I realize she's not supposed to do, but I'd prefer not to take you off to some tavern at night without her express permission."

"I *am* an adult, sir."

He chuckled and set her hand on the doorframe. "So you keep telling me."

Shironne shook her head but bid him a good afternoon before going inside. After only a moment, she regretted coming inside. And letting the colonel leave.

Verinne was *not* happy with her.

. . .

Mikael ate a solitary dinner in the mess hall. Most days he sat alone there. If Deborah was unoccupied she would eat with him, but she was meeting with the elders—likely to discuss him again—so he didn't have her to talk with either. He'd almost finished his solitary dinner when he looked up to find Elisabet standing across the table from him. He gestured for her to sit, surprised she'd honored him with her presence. "What do you need?"

She sat as stiffly as if she still wore her overcoat with its steel plates. "Keep an eye on Kai."

"Isn't one of your Seconds with him now?" Mikael asked, confused by the request. *They* were responsible for Kai when she needed to be elsewhere. She should ask them, not him.

"Peder is with him." She paused, her eyes going distant for a moment before she continued. "Kai is having priority problems. He asked me to take myself off duty this afternoon. I'm concerned he might make a poor decision and endanger his safety."

That was the longest speech he'd ever heard Elisabet make, which meant it was important. "I'll try," Mikael said, "but he doesn't listen to me, Elisabet. Are you concerned Peder or Tova might not be able to protect him?"

"Kai is intelligent, Mr. Lee, but foolish at times." Elisabet stood, ending their conversation. She walked out of the mess hall without looking back.

Evidently, Kai had gone too far. Mikael had always considered Elisabet the less fragile of the two, and wondered why Kai didn't see that. Then again, their relationship had always been a mystery to him.

CHAPTER TWENTY-SIX

"Verinne, what if the colonel needs me to come in?"

The old woman blocked the doorway to Shironne's room, her fear clearly evident. "The army can solve their problems without your help. It's not a proper thing for a young lady anyway, to be around young men all day. I've told your mother that a thousand times."

Melanna had crept into Shironne's room the evening before and had listened to Shironne's tales of her visit to the palace and the fortress below it. Then they'd spent an hour working their way through the novel that Shironne had secreted under her pillows. But Verinne had been displeased by this further flouting of her authority in the household and had decided that the only way to keep both of them under control was to lock them in their rooms. Confinement wouldn't bother Melanna too much; she just saved her energy for later. Shironne, on the other hand, wanted to get back into the hunt for the killers.

"Mama will be home tomorrow," she reminded the governess. "It's only one day."

"No," Verinne insisted. "Don't think I don't know what kind of trouble a girl your age can fall into. If you let one man . . ."

Verinne went on, lecturing her on the evils of young men in general. Shironne listened with only half an ear. What had happened to Verinne when she was young to convince her that every man had lecherous intentions toward every girl he met? Perhaps there was a story in her past to justify her vehemence. But Shironne had extra abilities that most girls didn't, and that allowed her to sense a young man's intentions all too well. She was far safer in the company of Cerradine's soldiers—and Mr. Lee—than she was walking along most streets.

So she gave the proper responses when called for, but Verinne wouldn't be deterred, and then dropped her ultimate weapon. She sent the first housemaid into Shironne's room to remove both her coats. The girl radiated embarrassment but said nothing.

Shironne was too surprised to protest—not until she realized that her gloves were in her coats. "You can't take my *gloves*."

"You won't need them in here, will you?" Verinne snapped. "Take all her shoes too. Until your mother returns, Miss Shironne, you will stay here and think about your recent choices."

The maid slipped out into the hallway, leaving Shironne too stunned to do anything other than listen to the door's lock click shut. It was only then that she realized that her focus had still lain in the pocket of one of those coats, so she was without that as well.

She stood there, disbelief warring with outrage. Yes, her mother *had* left Verinne in charge, but that was no excuse for treating her like a criminal. She'd done no more than what her mother had permitted regularly for the last few years. After a moment, she forced her frustration down, determined not to let it rule her. She would just have to work around this setback.

She went to her old desk and opened the drawer. There she touched the rarely used contents until she located a small sheaf of paper, a quill, and ink. She took them back to the table and laid them all out. Shironne felt the top page to be certain the paper was blank. She swirled the ink, gratified to find it hadn't dried out, and then eased out the stopper. Touching the edges of the paper, she tried to fix the bounds of it in her mind. She took the quill and dipped it in the well. Her hand remembered what had come so easily when she could see. She set the pen to the upper corner of the page, hoping she could still make a straight line.

. . .

Services in Below took on the nature of a thunderstorm. When hundreds of the Lucas Family gathered in the chapel, sound reverberated through the chamber, echoing off the impervious walls. Song became thunder, and the ambient in the chapel the wind, the will of hundreds joined in intention sweeping the hearts of even the mildest sensitive along with them.

Mikael sat in the fourth row with Deborah as the Lucas Family sang the memorial for Iselin. He stayed silent, knowing neither the words they used nor the unfamiliar tune. He'd never bothered to learn it, not in four years. His eyes followed the intricate patterns on the vast walls instead, trying to keep his mind calm and out of the ambient.

He was the subject of gossip again. Eli managed to come down the grand stair at the same time as Mikael, and asked him about his trek down to the depths of Seven Below with a Larossan girl on his arm. It was, as he'd expected, the most interesting gossip of the week, especially given that it was believed to be related to Iselin's death. Mikael didn't know how much he was allowed to reveal about the girl, so he chose to say as little as he could, although he did admit that Miss Anjir was Eli's age.

And Deborah had, indeed, been dragged before the other elders to discuss his behavior yet again. As his sponsor, she was nominally responsible for his actions. When Mikael asked her about the meeting, she passed it off as a mere inconvenience, joking that if she'd known beforehand how many meetings the Head Infirmarian had to attend, she would never have accepted the post.

Only after the service did he notice several army uniforms among the Family, the blue glaringly obvious in that sea of brown and black. Cerradine's children had come to pay their respects to the dead woman's family. He spotted David Aldassa talking with Elisabet among the other twenty-fives. As the browns streamed out of the chapel in their yeargroups, Mikael tried to get closer to them.

He stopped suddenly, transfixed by the sight of Aldassa and

Elisabet together, unmoving amidst the flow of black-clad bodies. The image flashed in his mind of a man, a memory from his dream, of a man watching Iselin Lucas die. Not the killer but someone else, a witness, anguish on his dark face. Miss Anjir had seen it too. She'd told the colonel and Dahar about it, only she hadn't ever seen the man's face—not with her own eyes. But Mikael *had*, talking with Elisabet and Aldassa in Cerradine's office.

Hadn't Iselin stopped because the police officer looked familiar to her?

Mikael shouldered his way toward Aldassa, pushing through the mass of bodies and apologizing as he went. Reading his loud urgency, sensitives cleared a path for him. Mikael laid a hand on Aldassa's blue sleeve just as he turned to leave the chapel. Elisabet had already disappeared.

Aldassa looked pleased to see him. "Good. I was going to come up. Talk to you before I went back."

"Paal," Mikael said. "In the dream I saw Paal Endiren."

"Not possible," Aldassa said with a shake of his head. "He wouldn't have come back to the city without reporting in."

Someone nearby whistled, and Aldassa closed his eyes to gather himself and control his disquiet. A displeased look crossed his face. "Paal's most likely dead, Mikael."

"You're wrong. Iselin probably didn't know Paal, but they were only a few yeargroups apart, so she would have seen him regularly enough to *recognize* him years later. He was there when she died."

"He's not a killer," Aldassa protested.

Mikael tried to dredge up that memory from the dream. "No, but he was forced to watch."

. . .

A knock at her window startled Shironne out of her contemplation. The sound came again, and she sensed Melanna standing on her balcony. Fearful that one of the servants might walk past on the path below and report her to Verinne, Shironne ran across the room, threw open the balcony door, and yanked her sister inside.

"How did you get on my balcony?" she asked, amazed.

"I climbed over the railing on mine and jumped to yours," Melanna said, as if that were obvious. A thrill of exhilaration twisted about her.

"What?" Shironne touched her sister's face, worried that she'd been hurt. Melanna felt nothing but pride in her accomplishment, though. Shironne tried to recall how far apart those railings were but couldn't. When she'd been able to see, it had seemed much too far across to jump from one balcony to another. And it was a long way to the ground. "That's dangerous, Lanna. I don't want you to do that again. Promise me."

"But you're in here all alone and I'm bored," Melanna said. "How long is Verinne going to make us stay in our rooms?"

"I don't know. Mama could be back tomorrow." That was an optimistic estimate. Fortunately, the first housemaid, still radiating discomfort over the whole business of taking Shironne's coat and shoes, had brought up a tray from the kitchen with an ample breakfast. Neither of them would starve. "Verinne can't find you in here. How are we going to get you back to your own room?"

"I can climb over the railing and down your tree," Melanna said. "I can go in through the kitchen door. Cook will hide me."

Shironne couldn't figure out any alternative, not without a key, since both of their doors were locked. "Are you sure you can do that?"

Melanna nodded swiftly. "I wish I had a tree. I could climb down all the time."

Shironne drew in a deep breath. Melanna seemed completely certain she could get down from the balcony safely. Mama wasn't going to be happy about it when she found out, but it was good to know that there was some way out. "Very well, if you promise me you'll be very careful. And that you won't jump from your balcony again."

Melanna heaved a heavy sigh but gave her word.

"Good," Shironne said. "Can you give something to Messine for me? You can't let anyone see you giving it to him, though."

"What is it?" Melanna asked.

"I'm not going to tell you, so you won't know if Verinne asks." Shironne ruffled Melanna's coarse hair and laughed. "Will you do it?"

"Yes," Melanna said without hesitation. "It's cold in here."

"Why do you think I have the covers around me, silly?" The fire had died down, and no one had been in to build it back up. It was one chore Shironne didn't feel safe tackling herself. Shironne sat on the edge of the bed and held out her arms for Melanna to come sit next to her. She was relieved to have someone to talk to. The silence had become oppressive. "Now, tell me what you've done today."

Melanna stayed for half an hour, relating that she'd been forced to study the Anvarrid-Cince War until Verinne started snoring and then read her lurid novel until she thought Verinne's sleep sound enough to sneak away.

Unfortunately, Verinne never dozed too long, usually just enough for Melanna to hide herself, so Shironne prodded Melanna forth. She listened anxiously as her sister climbed over the edge of the railing of the balcony, slid down, and jumped into the tree. *Someday Melanna is going to run away and join a circus.*

. . .

Mikael spent the afternoon with David Aldassa, looking over information on Paal Endiren and his disappearance, now almost two months past.

"What was Paal doing out near the border?" Mikael asked.

"Do you recall the caravan of children sold into Pedrossa? He was working on that. Which Pedraisi clans were involved in the purchases, and what names he could pick up about the Larossans selling them." Aldassa snapped his fingers, looking annoyed at himself. "Have to go back up to the fortress to talk to Elisabet again."

To tell her what they'd learned, Mikael expected. "Do you want me to tell her?"

Aldassa sighed. "I should do it myself. She and Paal were friends."

"Good friends?" Mikael asked, an admittedly rude question.

Aldassa smiled, his dark eyes amused. "Ask Elisabet, not me."

"I will, but she's not here just now."

"Good friends. Don't know how close. Never been in her circle. She's Rifle; I was Hand-to-Hand."

Mikael nodded, understanding that oblique statement quite well. Some yeargroups broke down into cliques, usually dividing between the two primary training groups: hand-to-hand combat versus the marksmen.

"With her coming in so late and taking over," Aldassa continued, "not everyone liked her. Paal took to her, though."

"Late?" Mikael asked.

"We must have been twelve, I think. Yes, it was right after the yearchange. She came in, already better at everything than the rest of us. Swept away the hierarchy we'd established, but she was such an emotional null that she hardly affected the *togetherness* at all."

Emotional null was a term for a person whose feelings were kept under strict control at all times. It was a state that the elders likely wished Mikael would achieve. The best he could manage was his perpetual effort to be calm and optimistic. It must be natural for Elisabet, though, if she'd been that way that young.

"Twelve? That's old." The Six Families took in Larossan children up to the age of eight, when children moved from their parents' quarters into yeargroups. Anything later than eight years old required special circumstances, although he wasn't sure of the exact terms. He'd simply *assumed* Elisabet had been eight or younger. Had she actually said she'd lived on the border at the time of the massacres? Mikael couldn't recall her exact words. "Who was First before her?"

"Paal," Aldassa answered. "Before you get any strange ideas, Mikael, he never held it against her. Took Second, and he was fine with that. They got along. Both loners, you know."

Loner was a good word to describe Elisabet, Mikael decided. She never let people get close to her. From what he'd heard, the others in her yeargroup didn't consider her a friend, but their *leader*. Strictly speaking, though, that was a First's function. "Paal was like her?"

"Yes. Workers in this office are all close. Made a sort of Family of our own out here. Paal felt smothered by us, so he spent a lot of time away."

Mikael hadn't really considered before how Cerradine's workers fared in Larossan society after their unusual upbringing. "Do you miss the Family?" Mikael asked.

Aldassa shrugged, a blasé expression on his face. "Why we stay together, I suppose. Not accustomed to being alone."

"Why don't you go back?"

Aldassa sat back in his chair, giving Mikael a searching look. "Lucas Family doesn't encourage their Larossan foster children to stick around."

Mikael tried to think if he'd seen any dark heads among the Lucases that morning in services, and could recall very few.

Customs among the Families differed. Lee was widely considered the most liberal when it came to matters of inclusion, the reason that they had such mixed blood. Jannsen, on the other hand, was frighteningly conservative, almost obsessed with racial purity. Anyone perceived as having mixed blood was forced out of their fortress to one of their enclaves. He would have to talk to Deborah later, Mikael decided, and find out where the Lucas Family came down on that spectrum. "Do none of them stay in the Family?"

"None of us did."

"I'm sorry," he said.

Aldassa shrugged. "Way of the world, isn't it? Larossans don't like half-breeds; the Warbirds won't acknowledge us. At least the Six Families have the decency to raise us."

Mikael didn't have a good response for that. He couldn't imagine not having known his parents at all. "Elisabet is Lucas, though. How did she come to be raised outside?"

"Parents left. Land left to her mother through an Anvarrid grandfather, something like that."

And that explained why she looked like she had a touch of Anvarrid blood. It wasn't unusual for a member of an Anvarrid House to have a child by his or her guard, or one of the quarterguards. Since most guards were sensitives, they were easier to push into a physical relationship.

"She was orphaned later," Aldassa added, "and then came back to Lucas."

"How?" Mikael asked, working over the math in his head.

"Don't know. Never talked about her parents."

"She's from the border. She knew what that inscription supposedly says. I didn't work it out before. I assumed she'd been taken in younger than eight . . ."

Aldassa's eyes narrowed and then went distant, focusing on some thought within. He got up and went into the colonel's office, coming out later with a folder that Mikael recognized. "Meant to ask yesterday. Seemed trivial at the time, so I didn't bother."

He handed over the file. Mikael pulled out the papers inside, a listing of the victims of the massacres fourteen years ago, mostly names of Larossan origin. Some had notations beside them, indicating whether the Andersens had recovered the body. Others were missing, simply presumed dead. Mikael skimmed the list, unsure what Aldassa wanted him to see. "You wanted to ask me about *this*?"

"Look at the last page." When Mikael found the correct one, Aldassa pointed at a notation in one corner. "Page eight of eight."

Mikael counted back only seven pages.

"I figured the Daujom went through the files before we got them," Aldassa said, "looking for anything incriminating about the Andersen Family. Is that why there's a page missing?"

"I didn't remove one," Mikael told Aldassa.

Absolute truth. But the expression on Aldassa's face told Mikael that the lieutenant knew exactly who was to blame.

. . .

Cerradine was out that morning when Filip Messine arrived at his house. The young man had been there for the better part of three hours, sitting at the kitchen table and chatting with the house's elderly caretakers. When Cerradine got home, Messine handed over an ink-blotted sheet of stationery. The lines of writing on the paper were illegible, trailing down the side of the paper and crossing one another. Occasionally the author had run out of ink but hadn't noticed, grooves marking the scratching of a dry nib. "What is this?"

"Miss Anjir gave it to the little one to give to me," Messine said. "They're both locked in their rooms because the governess . . ." Messine considered his words, and then finished, ". . . is old."

Cerradine didn't need that explained. Unfortunately, he could make out only a few words. "She did learn how to write at some time, didn't she?"

Messine shrugged. "Madam Anjir should be back soon, so this is temporary."

True, although Cerradine suspected confinement would drive Shironne to desperate measures. He talked with Messine a moment longer, checking on how Ensign Pamini was doing in her temporary assignment as a stable boy within the Anjir household. Apparently one of the housemaids had decided to pursue her, so her disguise as a young man was clearly effective. Then Messine headed back to the Anjir house. Cerradine decided to take the note to the office. Perhaps Aldassa could make sense of it.

Cerradine was surprised to find Mikael Lee there as well, sitting behind one of the four desks, perusing files as if he worked there. Dahar had agreed to allow Cerradine nominal control over the case so long as Mikael was *included*, but he hadn't expected the young man to take up residence in the army offices.

Shaking his head, he handed the sheet of stationery over to Aldassa. "Can you read this?"

Aldassa just laughed and passed the sheet to Mikael.

Mikael angled the page to catch the light better. "This is truly wretched. I'd swear Miss Anjir wrote this, though. Who else but a blind girl would write this way?"

He sat down and read the note, squinting at a few of the messier words. "Her governess has locked her in her room to keep her from associating with young men," Mikael said when he reached the end of the letter, where she'd run out of ink. "I think it says she doesn't have any clothes. Is that normal?"

Cerradine let out an aggravated sigh. "The governess is a perfectly nice old lady who raised Miss Anjir's mother before her, but she doesn't handle the girls well. Except for the middle one, I suppose."

"What if we need Miss Anjir?" Mikael asked. "What would happen, sir, if we stole her?"

Cerradine laughed. "You're suggesting kidnapping. Stealing a young Larossan girl would reflect poorly on the Lucas Family, and I'm not sure the old woman wouldn't send for the police."

Mikael shook his head. "I didn't think that through, sir."

Cerradine peered at the young man for a moment. How much did Mikael suspect about Shironne's abilities, particularly where they intersected with his own? At least he seemed to get along with her, which boded well for their working relationship, if nothing else.

But getting Shironne out of the Anjir household was a thorny problem. He was not going to force his way into that house to bring out Shironne. Savelle wouldn't forgive that.

"There is something else, sir," Aldassa interjected. He summed up their morning's discussions of Paal Endiren, and his likely presence at the murders.

"Are you sure?" Cerradine asked, shocked.

"Do you remember Miss Anjir saying there was someone watching?" Mikael prompted. "I'm sure that was him."

Cerradine puffed out his cheeks. Paal Endiren was a quiet, principled young man. He couldn't imagine what would turn him in two months into someone who would abet a killer.

CHAPTER TWENTY-SEVEN

Mikael headed back to the fortress, but his feet took him through the neighborhood where the Anjir family lived, an address he'd pulled from the Daujom's records. He was far too conspicuous in his black uniform, so he stayed to the back alley. The Anjir house was a grand one, probably one of the first built in this section of town. It had more land originally, he decided. The house next to it stood closer than he would have thought comfortable. A small walkway ran between the houses and six little balconies opened over the walk, suggesting they had once overlooked a garden rather than just the stone wall of another house.

"How can I help you, sir?" A groom in a worn tunic and black trousers walked out of the stable into the alleyway, wiping his hands on a towel—Filip Messine.

"Which room is hers?" Mikael asked when Messine got close enough. In most houses of this level of society, the family lived on the second floor, and the inside servants on the third.

Messine pointed to the walkway between the houses. "The first balcony, the one with a tree next to it. The one next to it is the little one's, and then the pretty one's."

"The pretty one?" Mikael asked, taken aback. *There's a daughter prettier than Shironne?*

"Middle daughter," Messine said. "Very pretty, *very* immature." He led Mikael to the edge of the stable, from which angle they could see the first two of the balcony doors. Next to the walkway, trees still bearing their leaves arched close to the balconies, making Mikael wonder what fool had designed the courtyard.

"This morning the little one jumped from one balcony railing to the other," Messine said, "to get in to see her sister. I nearly had a heart attack."

Mikael estimated that to be a four-foot leap, twelve or more feet from the ground. *Most impressive for a little girl.* "How old is she?"

"Nine? Or maybe nine next year. She climbed down one of those trees later, and I sneaked her back into the house. She'd make a great fighter, that one," Messine added admiringly.

Since Messine had fought in the melees representing his year-group, just as Mikael had done, he'd be a good judge.

Mikael stared at the closed door to Shironne's room. Curtains obscured any view within. He formed words in his head, asking if she knew he wanted to talk to her. *If you'd come to the door, perhaps I can.*

A moment later, a delicate hand touched the glass, pushing aside the curtain. The other palm spread against the pane. She could *hear* him, even from this distance. He tucked away his amazement and turned to Messine. "Can I get closer without anyone noticing me?"

Messine glanced back in the direction of the stables, then back at the alley. "If you walk along the tree line, you won't draw attention. I'll keep an eye out for the other servants if you like, sir. I doubt anyone would tell, but the second housemaid has a grudge against Kirya."

"Aldrine?"

"Yes, but Aldrine's away with Madam Anjir, so the maid is getting out of her place. A bit of a sneak, if you ask me. She and the governess are the main ones you need to worry about."

Mikael decided to chance it and walked cautiously along the edge of the courtyard, near the balconies.

"Are you crazy?" her voice hissed at him from above. She stood on the balcony's edge, her slippered feet a few feet above his head. She clutched a burgundy coverlet about herself, probably to keep the chill at bay. At least it didn't look like they'd actually taken her clothes away.

He kept his voice low, realizing she didn't actually need to hear him speak. "I don't think you're in a position to ask that. You're the one dressed as a bed."

"If I had something to throw at you, I would, idiot. They took my coats. And shoes and gloves. And they were my *new* gloves, too."

"I read the note." That explained the bedclothes, although he caught a glimpse of house slippers peeking from underneath the coverlet. "Are you all right?"

"I'm fine." She crouched down, using the edges of the blanket to shield her hands from the railing. Her loose hair tumbled about her feet. "Just very bored."

"We'll think of something," he reassured her. Without her gloves and her coat, she would have trouble leaving this house . . . which must have been the governess' plan. She wouldn't have any protection for her sensitive hands or feet, and if she did flee clutching a coverlet, people would think her mad.

"I'm just trying to decide where I can go," Miss Anjir said. "Perhaps I'll join the circus—telling fortunes or some such nonsense."

That was a joke. At least, he hoped it was a joke.

He dug in the pockets of his overcoat and pulled out his leather gloves. "Here. Not your own, but better than nothing. Reach down."

She put one arm down between the rails, reaching as far as she could. If he stretched upward, he could just get them into her fingers. She grasped them and pulled away.

Mikael reckoned that if he had a good jump he might catch the edge of that balcony and pull himself up. Which wouldn't help her at all, but it meant *she* might be able to get down from there. "Give us a chance to think of something," he told her, "before you do anything rash. I hear the circus is hard work."

"Verinne's coming," she hissed. "Hide."

Mikael ducked back into the shadow of the tree, grateful she'd warned him. He didn't have a good explanation for standing under her balcony. He heard her rise to her feet and shut the door.

She's trapped now, he thought.

The sooner he left the premises, the lower the chance he would get caught. He walked back to where Messine waited in the mews and bid him a good evening. "You'll keep an eye on her?"

"From a distance," Messine said. "Pamini's here too, as a stable boy, but she's in the kitchen right now, trying to turn that annoying maid's head. After this long here, most of them suspect I'm in the colonel's pay. Pamini's a new face. She'll see the things I miss."

Mikael was glad that the colonel had the situation well in hand.

. . .

Shironne sensed Verinne waiting outside her door as the second housemaid brought her tray for dinner. The woman felt nervous about being her jailor. That gave her hope she might be able to talk some sense into the governess tomorrow. Luckily, she'd gotten the curtains drawn without anyone noticing that she'd been out on the balcony—which would have quashed *any* chance of getting back to work at the colonel's office tomorrow. So for now she sat docilely on her bed, Mikael's gloves tucked discreetly under her coverlet.

Once the second housemaid swept out of her room, drawing the door closed behind her, Shironne heard it lock again. Verinne apparently wasn't taking any chances that she would sneak out in the middle of the night.

She could smell the food from across the room, one of Cook's vegetable curries. Those were still good when cold. That could wait.

Instead she drew the gloves out from underneath her coverlet. If Verinne had seen them, there was no chance she would have let her keep them.

She ran her fingers over the gloves, picking up the sense that he'd worn them today. He'd touched dirt recently, and horse. The lesser sense of river water came to her. He'd brushed his hands through grasses, something gone to seed. Stone, he'd touched stone.

She doubted Mikael understood how it felt for her to wear someone else's clothes.

She slid her hand into the right glove. It was too large but warm. It felt almost like touching his skin the day before. He'd given them to her with concern. He'd worried over her while walking here, she knew, having heard him at some distance. It was pleasant to have someone worrying about her.

The left glove fit the same—oversized but friendly. Shironne doubted he had any motivation for giving her the gloves other than concern. Even so, the ghostly feel of his hands on hers was far more warming than she would ever have thought.

. . .

By the time Mikael arrived back at the fortress, dinner service in the mess had ended. He stopped in the kitchens and picked up a small pot of tea instead, carrying it down with him to Deborah's office.

"Is that your dinner?" she asked, gesturing for him to sit. She cleared some of the books off her desk and set them on the counter behind her. She pulled down a couple of teacups from a high shelf and let Mikael fill them.

"Bad timing tonight," Mikael said. The tea was jasmine flavored, not one of his favorites.

"You left with Aldassa after the service, didn't you?" she asked then.

She'd heard that from one of the sentries, Mikael decided. "Do you remember Paal Endiren?"

"Very quiet young man, never sick," she replied with a faint smile. She rarely got to meet children who weren't sick. "He's from Elisabet's yeargroup."

Mikael nodded. He described the strange memory of seeing Paal in the dream. She sat back, listening to him with an indecipherable expression on her face.

"Have you told Elisabet?" she asked when he reached the end of his story.

"Not yet. I don't know how she'll react. Were they particularly close?" He hoped Deborah would answer that question for him. Not too surprisingly, she didn't. She merely smiled at his transparent tactic. Just because she sponsored both him and Elisabet, that didn't mean she shared secrets between them.

"Can you tell me how Elisabet's parents died?" he asked instead.

"I've never been told," she said. "I wasn't one of the elders then, so I wasn't given the information."

"But you're her sponsor," Mikael protested.

"The elders didn't tell me."

"Did Elisabet?"

Deborah seemed exasperated. "If she had, I would consider it confidential, Mikael, and I wouldn't tell *you*."

Mikael sipped his tea, pondering her answer. He could ask in his capacity as a member of the Daujom. She might refuse to answer and still be within her rights as an elder. He didn't want to press the issue, though. He could ill afford to alienate his greatest champion in the fortress.

"Perhaps you should ask *her*, Mikael," Deborah suggested gently.

Mikael put down his cup of tea. "I don't want to bring up something that'll upset her."

Deborah leaned back in her chair, shaking her head at him. "You sound just like Kai."

Mikael recalled Elisabet's warning that Kai might do something unwise. He repeated it to Deborah, who laughed shortly. He didn't mention his suspicion that Kai already had done something by removing pages from the files the Daujom turned over to the army. Deborah didn't need to hear that about her nephew.

"I went to check and see how Miss Anjir is faring," he said, changing the subject. "The governess has her locked up in her room."

"Locked up?"

"Something about being corrupted by young men."

Deborah folded her hands together and gave him one of her unnervingly direct stares. "There might be some validity to her concerns, Mikael."

He didn't respond. There was nothing he could say that wouldn't sound defensive.

"You like children, Mikael," Deborah added. "Because you are a broadcaster, you want them to like you, and they respond in kind, particularly children who are sensitives."

If Miss Anjir were here, she would be protesting. She wouldn't like being called a child. But Deborah had chosen that term deliberately.

"Why does the Family separate the children from the adults, Mikael?" Deborah asked.

"Because children are easily influenced," he replied, the catechized answer.

"I only wanted to remind you, dear, she's legally a child."

If she hadn't been resting the previous day when Miss Anjir arrived at the palace, he would have heard this speech then. "She's Larossan. Their laws are different."

As soon as he said that, he knew it sounded defensive.

Deborah held up her hand to stop him from speaking. "That doesn't change the law as it applies to you, dear. You need to be careful in your handling of the girl."

"I'll keep that in mind, ma'am. I've noticed she is very susceptible. Kai can get her biting at him in less than a minute."

"My point exactly."

"I wouldn't hurt her, ma'am."

"You know how they tease you about little girls falling for you, Mikael? The joke wouldn't be so effective if you'd not given it reinforcement from time to time."

"Kai keeps that joke alive." Mikael glanced at the scar crossing his left palm. When he'd been only a seventeen, he'd come out with two others in his yeargroup to participate in the melee at the summer fair. He was thrown against one of the arena walls by a much larger opponent. That hadn't been what ended that day for him, though. A little girl of eight or nine had been gazing at him from over the low railing, lost her balance, and tumbled over the railing into the arena itself. He'd apparently caught the child and handed her back up to a worried female relative, but the field judges had called him dead as a result of the contact. As he'd had a concussion, he remembered very little of the incident himself.

The story had grown and changed in the telling over the years, recited whenever someone wanted to needle him. There had been instances of spectators injured by the fighters in the past, but never before had a fighter been "killed" by a spectator, much less a child. At the time, it had been laughable. By now the humor had worn thin.

"Be careful what you do, Mikael," Deborah said firmly. "From the elders' point of view, you are dealing with a child, whether or not she thinks she is. Or you do. Keep that in mind."

"Yes, ma'am," he mumbled, and left as quickly as possible. Deborah rarely lectured him, but when she did he felt guilty for days.

Mikael made his way to Three Down, searching out the hall where Elisabet's yeargroup lived. He found the proper hallway, confirmed when he located their common room, crowded with far too much furniture. About a dozen of the twenty-fives sat there talking and drinking tea, which they seemed willing enough to share. Mikael didn't know if any of them had known Iselin. None were in uniform, so they didn't wear the white ribbon of mourning, but they did seem subdued.

Since this was Daujom business, he didn't stop at the guideline but walked on toward the common area. He spotted Tova, Elisabet's Second, among the women. Tova sat on a floral-patterned couch, bare feet up on one of the tables and a cup of tea cradled in her hand. She must not have duty scheduled tonight. Her damp hair was unbraided, drying in wheat-colored waves over her shoulders. Mikael worked his way over to her and asked, "Whose furniture did you steal?"

She shook her head ruefully. "Practical joke, Mr. Lee. The thirties acquired a new sofa and gave us one of their old. Now everyone else in this end of the fortress is spontaneously donating old furniture to us. We've decided we rather like it."

Practical jokes ran rampant among the yeargroups. As long as no one got hurt, the elders didn't interfere. "It's an interesting effect. I suppose Elisabet is ignoring it."

"She's above such pettiness, Mr. Lee," Tova told him in a lofty tone. "In truth, it's annoying her terribly, but she's too stubborn to say anything, so it continues. Did you need to talk to her?"

He'd never been down this hall before, so the inference must have come naturally. "Is she down here?"

"Working on schedules in her quarters. I'll go get her for you," Tova offered. She wended her way out of the common room, clambering over a much-patched couch and a chair to do so.

Elisabet returned with her a moment later, appearing to know why he'd come. She edged through the room and sat down at a table in one corner, gesturing for Mikael to join her. He followed, very aware of the watchful eyes of the remainder of her yeargroup.

Out of uniform, Elisabet looked no less stiff than every other time he saw her. She wore an old uniform shirt and trousers, with an unbuttoned vest worn atop that to ward off the chill of Three Down. Her face retained its cool distance.

"Interesting furniture arrangement," he began.

Elisabet frowned. "What do you need, Mr. Lee?"

"I spent the better part of the day with David Aldassa," Mikael began. "As a result, I need to ask you a few questions."

"What did David say?"

"We talked about Paal Endiren," Mikael told her.

A disturbed look crossed her face. "Why?"

"Because I saw him in a dream. I think he's involved in the murders somehow."

Elisabet didn't shift or move, but Mikael thought he'd surprised her.

"Did he know Iselin?"

"No."

"Were you and Paal particularly close?"

"We were friends," she answered without ambiguity.

Friends only, Mikael divined from the ease of her answer. "Did he know how your parents died?"

Her eyes lost focus, suddenly turning within. "Yes."

One of the men from the yeargroup came closer, a sensitive whose name Mikael couldn't recall. He'd upset her, even if she didn't show it outwardly. "I'm not trying to worry you, but I need to know. Were your parents killed in the massacres?"

She raised a hand to keep the man at a distance, not wanting them overheard, Mikael suspected. *Her yeargroup doesn't know.* Paal must have been the exception.

"Yes," she said in a flat, emotionless voice.

"I had to ask because one of the pages of the report filed by the Andersens is missing: it lists the very first victims. Do you have any idea how that could have happened?"

She said nothing, her face blank.

He asked a more direct question. "Did you see Kai remove any of the pages from the files?"

"No," she said quickly.

Kai could have done it when she was off duty, or when her attention lapsed, but that rarely happened. When he asked if *she'd* taken any pages, she responded easily with another *no*.

"Has Kai talked to you about anything in the files?"

"No," she answered again.

She didn't have to turn Kai in and was relieved about it, Mikael decided. It didn't show on her face, but he saw it in the way she sat. Her shoulders had relaxed. He felt sure, as he never had before, that she cared for Kai—even if she never let Kai near her.

"Will you tell me what you and Kai argued about yesterday before he went down to the cold rooms?" He didn't have cause to ask but hoped she might answer anyway.

It took a while for her to decide. "He wanted Peder," she finally said, "not me. I told you."

Kai had asked her to give way to her Second, not because Peder could do a better job but because Kai didn't want Elisabet exposed to any part of their investigation.

"He means well, Elisabet."

She frowned, staring at a point in front of her on the table. The others in the common room had drifted away, deciding Mikael posed no threat.

Mikael glanced about, taking advantage of the relative privacy. "Are you ever going to reconsider? About Kai, I mean?"

They shared the same sponsor, which technically made them foster brother and sister. That made his question almost forgivable.

She blinked, likely taken aback by the personal nature of the question, then shook her head.

"I don't understand why you keep him at a distance."

"He is the king's heir," Elisabet said.

Mikael sat back and stared at her, wondering why she thought she wouldn't do for a king's consort. Nearly half of the kings during the Anvarrid rule had chosen their consorts from the Six Families. It had even been fashionable to have a Family consort at one time, one of the reasons that sensitives now showed up in many Anvarrid Houses. His own mother had been a guard.

"I would be a poor choice for him," Elisabet volunteered, surprising him. "Once he's confirmed, my contract will be annulled. He'll choose someone better suited."

The primary guard contract between Kai and Elisabet was, in essence, a marriage contract—only a few words differed. "I don't think Kai wants to choose another, Elisabet. He wants to keep you."

A line appeared between her brows. "I would not survive the attention."

Mikael considered *survive* an odd word to use. "I doubt there's much you can't handle."

"*He* wouldn't survive it." She stood, her face closed off now, as if she'd reached the end of her words and her willingness. Recognizing that their conversation had ended, Mikael thanked her and left the common room.

CHAPTER TWENTY-EIGHT

Eli sat with Mikael against the wall on the sparring floor, cooling off. "Lucasedrion's treaty between the Anvarrid and the Family specifies that all unclaimed children of mixed Anvarrid birth should be raised by the Family," he lectured. "Such children are to be turned over to the Family between the time of birth and the age of eight years. The only exception occurs when the elders take in a child already trained to a level commensurate with his or her peers."

Eli, as Mikael expected, knew everything about adoption law. Eli's father was the Lucas Family's head legal counsel, a position that Eli aspired to hold one day himself.

Mikael decided he should find a dictionary and check the word *commensurate*, but he didn't intend to tell Eli that. "I spoke to one of Colonel Cerradine's people yesterday. They said Elisabet was adopted into the Family when she was twelve."

"Yes, sir, but she qualified under that exception. Also, she was born Lucas, which I expect further disposed them to take her in."

"Did you know that? About her age?" Mikael asked. *He* hadn't known, but he was an outsider here.

Eli gave him a strange look. "Of course I knew, sir. She's a First."

Meaning that the Firsts know the other Firsts. The girl Eli intended to marry after the yearchange was the First of the seventeens, but he didn't know how familiar Eli was with those years ahead of him. "Do you ever talk to her?"

"Master Elisabet? Hardly, sir. She's one of the highest all-time scorers on her exams and field tests. She made perfect scores on everything but history and hand-to-hand."

"You keep records like that here?" Mikael asked, unable to keep the disbelief out of his voice.

"Your people don't, sir?"

Mikael pictured a dark room somewhere in the lower levels with the elders gathered, analyzing scores, like a betting den before one of the melees. "The Lees are different from the Lucases, Eli. We put less stock in . . . the objective."

Eli's nostrils flared. Mikael suspected he'd offended the younger man. Still, he didn't think a point system was the best method for choosing a leader.

"Were you not the top in your yeargroup, sir?"

"Hand-to-hand? Yes. There were other things at which I wasn't. My job was to keep my yeargroup working together, Eli. The elders chose me because they thought I could do that."

"I would think that with your father being the Vandriyen heir, you would have been the natural choice."

Mikael shook his head, wondering for the first time how many people thought he'd gotten his standing in his yeargroup because his father was Lord Vandriyen's heir. Then again, Eli's father, Master Elias, came from an Anvarrid House as well. "Is that why *you* were chosen?" Mikael asked.

For a split second, Eli appeared to consider that possibility. Then he said, "I'm sorry, sir. I realize that was an offensive supposition to have made."

Or at least to have voiced, Mikael thought dryly. "I think the elders may have considered that a liability in my case," Mikael said. "My father periodically talked of removing me from the Family." He attempted to steer the conversation back around to what he wanted to know. "Who *would* have trained Elisabet, then, do you think?"

"I've no idea, but by twelve . . . basic hand-to-hand combat, marksmanship, basic blade skills, history, grammar, arithmetic . . .

all those skills would have had to be reasonably in line or the elders wouldn't have accepted her."

"One of her yeargroup told me she came in *better* at everything already."

Eli shrugged. "I can beat her final history scores now."

Mikael expected no less. "I don't doubt that, Eli."

. . .

After cleaning up, Mikael walked down to the office. He unlocked the door, stepped inside, and drew the door closed behind him.

Kai's fist crashed into his nose. The force of the blow sent Mikael staggering, and the back of his head banged against the doorframe.

Then Elisabet stood between them, her hands forcing Kai away from him. She spoke to Kai, saying something in her rusty voice not meant for Mikael's ears, which were ringing anyway.

Mikael cursed, catching blood from his nose in his hand. *The file,* he realized. Elisabet would have taken Kai to task over the missing file page out of concern that he'd filched it while Peder was on duty. And Kai liked nothing less than having Elisabet upset with him.

Kai towered over him as if he still wanted to remove a limb or two. "Never go behind my back again."

"You would have lied to me," Mikael mumbled. Kai *would* have, and without remorse if it served to protect Elisabet.

Kai opened a drawer in his desk, pulled out a handful of file folders, and threw them on the floor at Mikael's feet. "I think you wanted these," he snapped before turning to leave the office.

Elisabet shrugged almost sympathetically at Mikael before she followed, closing the door behind them.

At least I've gotten Kai's fit of temper over with, Mikael thought. Elisabet would have to endure it for the remainder of the day.

Mikael sat down on the carpet next to his desk, dug a handkerchief out of his pocket, and leaned his head back against the desk with the handkerchief pressed to his nose. The back of his head throbbed in that position, but he wanted to get the bleeding stopped before it dripped on the entryway floorcloth. After a time he sat back against his desk, not wanting to stand up quite yet. The files lay near him on the floor, so he lifted one and thumbed through the pages.

The file's label proclaimed that it held a listing of bibliographic information about sources used to gather data about Farunas' followers and their high priest—one Anjaya Ramanet—a government official of some status in that Southwestern Pentarchy of Pedrossa. Ramanet had been among the priests killed at the last site, and having lost their leader, the remaining priests fled back across the river into Pedrossa, where they would never be punished. The pages inside all seemed to be dry dates relating to the actions of those remaining priests, all members of the same clan, apparently. It wasn't helpful, since they couldn't know if the same priests had returned, or if others had merely decided to mimic them.

The second file held the Andersens' report about the "mysterious deaths" of the nine priests found shot at later sacrifice sites. He could see why Kai might have wanted to hold that back since the Andersens had probably fabricated that particular bit of massacre lore.

A third file contained an eyewitness account of the raid on the final household attacked—one where two members of the household had escaped, a seven-year-old boy and his five-year-old brother. They told of the priests coming onto their land and capturing the family unawares. The invaders had tied them up and sacrificed them one at a time.

Mikael read the account through twice, feeling sick to his stomach. The graphic narrative seemed too similar to his hazy dreams for coincidence.

The two boys had survived only because something had scared the priests away. They escaped in the ensuing confusion. They recalled hearing gunshots but hadn't seen any of the purported vigilantes. Three of the priests were found dead at that location, and that was the end of the massacres.

Mikael's nose had stopped bleeding. Sighing, he gathered the files, struggled up from the rug, and moved to his desk. A sheet of paper slipped out from *between* two of the files and fluttered to the floor. Mikael bent down and grabbed it, knowing what he held before he read it.

Like most of the other paperwork, this was a copy of an original probably kept in the records office of the Andersen fortress. It listed the date of the first of the attacks, followed by names, and then the second and the third attacks. Mikael scanned the list, his head throbbing virulently now.

As he'd expected, the very first attack had fallen on a household of a family named Lucas. They would never have suspected what the visitors to their farm wanted of them.

The first name had a note next to it. *Henrik Lucas (52?); missing.* Mikael decided he might be a grandparent. The parents, both ages given as thirty-two, were listed as dead, and Joelle, their eleven-year-old daughter, as well. Mikael swallowed. Eleven-year-old Elisabet, missing; Sander and Sondre, both nine, dead; Lea, Maja, and a baby of three months, not named in the list, probably because it hadn't been named yet. Seven children, all marked as dead save for one.

Mikael slipped the paper into one of the files, trying to decide what to do with the information. He'd like to know where Elisabet was when the attack occurred. *Most likely with her grandfather.* The two had escaped somehow, fleeing across the country to reach Noikinos.

She'd told him her parents had died in the massacres but hadn't mentioned any brothers or sisters. To lose so many members of one's family in one day must be a terrible thing.

None of it seemed relevant to her relationship with Paal Endiren, though, save that Endiren had known of it. Mikael wanted to talk to Elisabet again, but getting past Kai would be difficult. While Kai had been pushing Elisabet away from him for the last two days, requesting other guards, now that he knew Mikael wanted to talk to her, he would keep her with him every moment just to be sure Mikael didn't get her alone again. In any case, Mikael wasn't certain what he could ask that would produce answers any different from last night's.

Dahar hadn't shown up to the office yet, so Mikael wrote him a quick note, deciding he wanted to be away from anywhere Kai might appear. He wanted to think about what he'd read in peace.

He decided to take the papers out to Aldassa at the headquarters. He might find a calm place there where he could rest his throbbing head. If nothing else, the walk would help clear his mind. Once there, Mikael handed over the last of the files along with the errant list of names. Aldassa found them disturbing. He claimed he'd never heard Elisabet mention brothers or sisters, much less a good number of them.

Cerradine gave Mikael a startled glance as he walked into the main office. "Has Dahar sent you to take up permanent residence here, Mikael?" he asked. "Might as well join the army."

Mikael shook his head and winced at the flare of pain that sent purple lights spinning behind his eyes. The chunk of ice Aldassa sent an ensign to fetch from the hospital had kept the swelling down, but it still hurt. "I'm avoiding Kai, sir. I'll head back in a few minutes. I suppose you should see this."

He handed the missing page to Cerradine, who read it with a furrowed brow, his dark eyes hard. "Is there a possibility that this is some other Elisabet Lucas?"

"No, sir," Mikael said. "She told me last night that her parents were killed in the massacres. That's her family."

Aldassa took the paper and placed it in the file from which Kai had removed it. "Just read these today, sir," he told the colonel.

Mikael glanced at Aldassa and then away. The statement, while true, implied he'd merely *overlooked* the pages before. While Aldassa might choose not to bring Kai's actions to the colonel's attention, Mikael had no choice but to tell Dahar. He didn't look forward to that.

Cerradine retired to his office, leaving Mikael and Aldassa alone to discuss the other retrieved files. Thinking he'd avoided Dahar long enough, Mikael headed back shortly afterward. He wended his way through the city, avoiding the neighborhood through which he'd walked the previous afternoon. His head continued to throb, and Mikael stopped amid the crowd bustling along Cadij Street to rub at his temples.

Someone touched him lightly on the back of his hand.

His breath stopped in his throat, his heart pounding wildly in his ears, as if all of his dreams had been called back to the surface of his mind at once. The touch, icy and invasive, ended abruptly, leaving him shaken.

Mikael pulled his hands away from his temples. Around him, people walked past on the sidewalk as if nothing had happened. Some spared him a mystified glance before they stepped out of his way. In the direction from which he'd come, others crowded the street, heading into the center of the city, where they could find their noontime meal. In the other direction, Mikael saw people's backs as they walked away. He stepped back against the wall of a hotel, out of the way of the human traffic.

He felt ill, the sort of hollow sickness one experienced after running the stairs for too long. It had seared down to his bones, that touch. *Someone just tampered with my mind and didn't expect to be caught at it.*

. . .

Shironne sensed it from far away, Mikael Lee's bone-deep horror. She didn't know where he was, but she knew it was *him*. She could distinguish him now from everyone else.

She curled up in her familiar coverlet. That morning's fire had already gone cold. She tried to think calm in his direction as he had done before to her, and hoped that her good wishes counted for something.

. . .

"I come in here this morning to find *you* gone out," Dahar snapped. "And then I get a note from my son, claiming that he will be in his rooms or with the king. No mention of how long, merely that he is *unavailable* to me."

Mikael almost laughed, the relief doing him good. Kai had found a way to protect Elisabet by the simple expedient of removing himself from the office and the investigation. If he locked himself in his rooms in the king's household, she would sit and stew with him.

Avoiding his father showed poor judgment, though; Dahar *hated* being ignored.

"I think you need to know, sir," Mikael finally inserted when Dahar finished venting his aggravation, "that Elisabet's family died in the massacres fourteen years ago. Did you know that?"

Dahar went still. "No."

"I think that has some bearing on Kai's recent behavior. Kai . . ." Mikael stopped, uncertain exactly what word to use. "He held back part of the list of victims out of the files we turned over to Cerradine—the page that listed Elisabet's family."

"How many?" Dahar asked quietly.

"They listed a grandfather, I think, and parents and seven children, including a baby. The grandfather and Elisabet were reported as missing."

Dahar sat on the edge of his desk, a frown on his face. He picked up a compass and began swirling it in his hand. "I didn't know. Six children, dead."

"It offers some explanation, sir, of why Kai has been so . . . uncooperative lately. He must have guessed and didn't want it brought up in front of her."

"What he wants doesn't matter," Dahar snapped. "He withheld information, Mikael. He took information he knew you and I needed and put it beyond our reach."

"He left it in his desk drawer, sir," Mikael pointed out. "I wouldn't even have known it was missing, sir, if Lieutenant Aldassa weren't so thorough with his paperwork."

After pacing in silence for a moment, Dahar sighed heavily. "Kai has duties here. I expect him to be at my disposal while my brother doesn't need him. I'll go up and flush him out later."

Mikael rubbed at his temples, the edge of his headache sharpening now that he stood still. "Yes, sir," he said. He changed the subject, hoping to allay Dahar's anger. "Can any of the Valarens pry into someone's mind with a touch?"

Dahar paused and then came back across the office to take a better look at Mikael. "Pry? Like Miss Anjir does? She's the only one of whom I know."

"That's not what I mean. She seems to pick up on what I'm thinking about at that moment. Can someone go in and dig through whatever they want?"

Dahar considered that. "Not from anything I've ever heard. Are you all right?"

"My head hurts." Mikael rubbed his temples again. "I think someone touched me and . . . dug around. It felt like they actually stuck their hands in my head and searched through all the boxes of files."

"And your head still hurts?"

"No, I've had this headache since this morning."

Dahar put a hand on Mikael's shoulder, taking a good look at Mikael's eyes. "Is it one of *those* headaches?"

Mikael didn't want to discuss his early-morning confrontation with Kai. "I hit my head against the wall," he answered truthfully. "And I haven't stopped to eat yet today."

An irritated Dahar sent him down to the mess with an order to get something in his stomach. Mikael did so and then headed straight for the infirmary.

Mikael found Deborah attending to a ten who'd broken an arm, so he waited, watching her set the bone under the nervous eyes of the boy's yeargroup sponsor. Once she'd finished, she joined him where he waited on one of the empty bunks.

Through her research, she'd narrowed down the possible poisons the killers used, coming up with two. "The more common one is always fatal," she said, "which makes me doubt it, because it generally acts too quickly. The other comes from the south but is unpredictable and expensive to obtain as well. A conotoxin."

Mikael had no idea what that word meant but didn't need to. "Would it keep someone quiet?"

"Highly variable in nature," she said, "but paralysis is one of the symptoms, particularly around the mouth and the respiratory system, so it may."

Mikael ran a hand through his hair. "That must be the reason for using it, then."

When he described what he'd felt on the street that morning, she looked troubled. "Touch-sensitives can't do that, dear. They're limited to what passes through a person's mind. That's why we thought the girl should try when you're actually dreaming. That's when your dream is *in* your head."

"I had the distinct impression that the person who touched me sifted through *at will*, ma'am. It felt very . . . invasive. Not like Miss Anjir at all."

"You're right. Touch-sensitives can't do that," she repeated firmly. "I've done a good deal of research on the colonel's behalf, and they do have limits."

"Ma'am, I'm sure about this. Also, I don't think he expected me to catch him at it."

"He?" she asked.

"I don't know why I think that. I guess I had the impression of someone tall." He puzzled over that for a moment. "Oh, because he touched the back of my hand. He had to be tall enough to do that and not be noticed."

"You're not all that tall, Mikael." Deborah had him stand as he had been that morning, and reached out to touch the back of his hand. "About as tall as I am, then?" she asked.

Mikael nodded. She walked back to her office and then came back a moment later with a book. She handed it to him with an apologetic shrug.

"*The Pentarch's Menagerie?*" The title, stamped in gold leaf on the leather spine, reeked of melodrama. The book smelled musty and crackled when he opened it. The lettering inside suggested an older printing machine, supported by a date more than eighty years past on the title page. Larossans told endless silly stories about the more mythical Pedraisi witches—the Desida, as they were properly called—and the rulers who'd long ago collected such people like trophies.

"It attempts to be a historical overview," Deborah told him.

He glanced up at her, startled. "Historical? You mean there actually was a menagerie?"

She gave him a disappointed look, mouth pursed. "You truly didn't pay attention to your history, did you, dear? Most legends have a basis in fact. One of your own ancestors, Vanya Lee, was property of one of the northern pentarchs. Her daughter returned to Larossa and married back into the Lee Family. Some say there are still menageries in Pedrossa, but now they're held by the wealthy rather than the politicians."

"Can any of these witches sift through someone's mind?" Surely she wouldn't ask him to read this if it wasn't pertinent.

"According to this, their talents are so varied that many of them defy classification. However, there is something in there about Mind Thieves."

"You're joking."

"No, dear. Larossans do have a small amount of inherent sensitivity that runs in their bloodlines. As a culture, though, the Larossans don't want to admit they are related to the Pedraisi, and particularly not to the Desida." She gestured toward the book. "Just read through that section. And while you're reading it, I want you to consider one question that I've had."

"Yes, ma'am?"

"What passes through the mind of a corpse?"

Mikael sat back, trying to work out the meaning of that cryptic question. Her evasiveness meant the topic was one of those she wasn't supposed to discuss . . . not with him. What did these Pedraisi witches have to do with corpses and their minds? "I'll do so, ma'am."

He only hoped he was clever enough to figure it out.

CHAPTER TWENTY-NINE

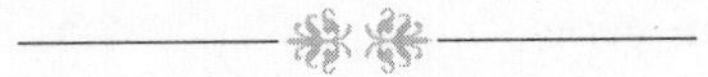

Shironne held Mikael's gloves in her hands, trying to pick up that tenuous thread of connection she'd felt earlier. She could sense him more clearly now, just as she could recognize her mother or her sisters at a distance. That was odd, because usually it took time to develop that familiarity. Everything simply seemed easier with him. Even as far away as the palace, she could feel him. He was agitated, thinking, and she had a strong feeling that his head hurt. But she couldn't grasp *exactly* what was troubling him. She finally took the gloves and stashed them under her pillows, thinking that if Verinne came in she wouldn't want to explain their presence.

Melanna sneaked into Shironne's room just after lunch. Verinne had unlocked Melanna's door so she could go down to the kitchen to eat, and Melanna had, rather predictably, slipped away instead. Unfortunately, she'd unlocked Shironne's door from the hallway and closed it again without once thinking that Shironne might want out. When Shironne went and tried the door, it was locked, leaving both of them trapped.

"Oh, I'll just climb down the tree," Melanna volunteered blithely when Shironne asked how she intended to escape.

Shironne laid one hand against her sister's cheek, trying to see the tree Melanna proposed to clamber down. She could recall what that tree had looked like years ago, before she lost her sight, but Melanna's idea of it was different, overgrown and needing a pruning.

And Melanna had, fortunately, remembered the task Shironne

had set for her. While on the loose, Melanna had gone into Perrin's not-locked room and pilfered a pair of old house slippers. They would be too big for Shironne's feet but were better than nothing. Shironne thanked her sister and, as a reward, drew out the novel from under her pillow.

They spent a long while huddling under the coverlet, hidden behind the bed in case Verinne should peek in. Their heroine continued to fall into trouble every few pages and, too helpless to save herself, relied on her hero to rescue her. The sheer absurdity of it lifted Shironne's spirits.

Shironne listened to the clocks and sent a reluctant Melanna on her way before too long. While Shironne listened, fingers clenched in the curtains, Melanna slipped off the balcony into the tree. She whistled when she reached the ground to reassure her older sister, and Shironne let loose a pent breath. She closed the outside door and drew the curtain shut, glad to know that Melanna's plan had worked again.

. . .

The book proved to be an amusing read. Mikael skimmed through the sections dedicated to Stonebreakers and Movers and something else called a Carrier. The Mind Thief, however—the creature that could glean one's memories and thoughts—was what Deborah had wanted him to see. Mikael doubted she intended for him to take every word of the description seriously, but it sounded worryingly close to what he'd experienced that morning.

Dahar eyed the book with curiosity, asking about it only after stalking by several times. When Mikael explained the source, Dahar plucked the old book out of his hands and began flipping through the pages. "I wouldn't give too much credence to Larossan superstition."

Dahar found the section Mikael had read and started perusing it. Mikael watched, pained, as Dahar paced about, holding the book out at arm's length. He wished Dahar would give in and wear his spectacles. He *did* own a pair.

"Why are you frowning at me, Mikael?" Dahar asked without glancing in his direction.

Mikael sometimes forgot Dahar was a sensitive. "I have a headache, sir."

"From this morning? Or from this afternoon?"

"This morning?"

"While you were off talking to Deborah," Dahar said in a deceptively mild voice, "I sought out my son, who is loitering in grand estate in his rooms like the master of the damned province. He informed me that I should offer his apologies for hitting you this morning."

"Kai was upset," Mikael said, wishing Kai would render his own apologies. "I questioned Elisabet."

"Out of his presence, I take it?"

"I felt he would interfere if he was there."

"He has no right to do so. In fact, he expressed his surprise that you hadn't told me."

Mikael gazed down at the patterned floorcloth in front of his desk, following the traceries of stylized vines. "It was unimportant, sir."

"I would like to know what he thinks he's doing," Dahar snapped, and slapped the book down on Mikael's desk. "I would like to know why he's so bent on protecting that woman, and why you're so bent on protecting him."

Mikael opened his mouth and closed it again, realizing he had absolutely no defense. He *had* been protecting Kai. Kai was protecting Elisabet, of course. And hadn't they just spent a day and a half reading files to protect the Andersens?

"I would like to be kept advised of things that happen in this damned office, Mr. Lee."

Mikael stared at him, surprised. Dahar never called him *Mr. Lee* unless very angry. He never cursed either, but had done so twice in one tirade.

"I would like to know why my son didn't mention to me he

knew how that woman lost her family. I would like to know why Jon and Deborah have been keeping secrets from me. I would like to know why the sister I have always wanted to meet does not want to meet me and would rather deal with Jon Cerradine as a proxy instead." Dahar punctuated that by picking up the book and pitching it against the door of the office. It thumped against the wood and fluttered helplessly to the floor.

"Your headache is bleeding over, Mikael," Dahar said in a tired voice when Mikael merely stared in response. "Why don't you go away for a while?"

I want to leave, Mikael thought suddenly. He wanted to get away from this place, where his moods turned everyone against him and drove them to fury. There was somewhere safe, he knew, if only he could find it.

"I have a headache," Mikael whispered, suddenly recognizing the true source of it. "One of *those* headaches."

Dahar turned slowly. "Is it tonight?"

"Yes," Mikael told him. "I need to get out of here."

Dahar folded his arms over his chest. "You're not leaving my sight, Mikael."

The urge to flee beat along his skin, clearer now that he'd acknowledged it. He slowly reined in his panicked response to the foreknowledge of a dream.

Dahar went to the door and yelled for a runner. A young woman in a brown uniform appeared in the doorway a moment later. "Fetch Deborah for me," Dahar told her.

"Elder Deborah?" she asked with a squeak.

"Who else?" Dahar yelled at her, laying his hands to his temples.

The girl paled and ran, ivory braids flying behind her. Not a sensitive, she couldn't pick up the ambient in the room.

Mikael settled on the edge of his desk, dreading the night. He closed his eyes, wishing it were over.

A few minutes later, Deborah burst into the office, her satchel in hand. Her breath sounded strained. She must have run up the stairs to get to the office so quickly. She glanced back and forth between the two of them. "Could you please attempt to send a clearer message next time, Daharion?"

"Don't call me that," Dahar snapped. "I wanted you up here. How much clearer could I be?"

Deborah laid her satchel on one of the chairs and rubbed her side. "Perhaps you could tell the runner what the nature of the problem might be, Dahar. That would save me a good deal of time and concern."

"I have a headache," Mikael offered.

"Kai hit you," she said, coming over to peer into his eyes. "You should expect that."

"You heard?" He shouldn't be surprised.

"Elisabet told me. She's rather embarrassed, Mikael."

"I doubt she intended to set him on me, ma'am."

"No. She's actually rather fond of you, dear. She wouldn't want Kai to kill you."

Mikael smiled at the notion that Elisabet was fond of him.

"It is one of *those* headaches," Dahar interrupted.

Deborah stood back, giving Mikael a careful once-over. "Are you sure?"

Mikael nodded. "I thought it was from this morning, or this afternoon, but I'm sure now."

"Then I need to contact Jon and see if we can put his plan into action." Deborah picked up her satchel. "Please stay here, Mikael, while I get a few things put together. Then you and I can drive out to see Jon."

She headed for the door. Dahar glared at her from the upper end of the room. "And what part do I play in this?"

Deborah paused and spotted the book on the floor. She picked it up, dusted it off, and handed it to Mikael. She cast a concerned glance in Dahar's direction. "Please don't leave the palace, Dahar. We can do this without your being involved."

Dahar frowned, nostrils flaring. Mikael thought calm at him, and Dahar glared at Mikael as if to rebuke him for his interference.

"Please, Dahar. I don't need to worry about you as well." Deborah slipped out the door.

Mikael sat down, resigned to being pinned in this office until Deborah returned for him. She'd probably order the sentries to keep him confined there. She was nothing if not thorough.

. . .

Aldassa had stayed late in the office, fretting. He'd been reading through the last of the files and some detail must have set off an alarm in his head. Cerradine joined him at his desk in the main anteroom, quiet now that all the other workers had left.

"The Andersens believed the priests were all part of the same clan, acting under the orders of someone with the name Ramanet, their high priest," Aldassa began, turning a single file page over in his hands. "They couldn't identify all the dead priests, but because he was a government official he *was* identified. So we can't be dealing with the same man, but it could easily be one of his surviving followers."

"The question would still be, why would they come here?"

Aldassa settled back behind his desk, putting his booted feet up on it. He laced his fingers over his stomach, puzzling over the question. "Don't know what the motive was the first time."

"Blood magic is generally performed to achieve some purpose," Cerradine said. "A massacre on the scale of what Ramanet attempted had to have some grand purpose, and I doubt that Ramanet *achieved* that purpose. He died instead. If they're trying again, they're going about it completely differently."

"Maybe this is revenge for those nine deaths, and they'll stop when they've gotten nine."

Cerradine shook his head. "I don't want to wait for six more deaths to figure it out."

Aldassa steepled his fingers, unconsciously mimicking one of

Cerradine's gestures. "I've written that name down before. Ramanet, I mean, sir, or something very close to it."

Cerradine tried to dig up any memory of an inquiry where that name had figured. There could be some relative in the city they'd questioned in the course of another investigation. Revelation eluded him, but Aldassa had an excellent memory and would recall it sooner or later.

A young man with sentry braids and wearing Lucas blacks knocked quietly on the doorframe—a courier. He waited for Cerradine's acknowledgment and then came forward, bearing a note. Cerradine glanced at it and then handed it over to Aldassa to read. "Go on back, son," Cerradine told the young man, "and tell her I'm on my way."

The courier nodded and headed out the way he'd come.

"It seems that Mikael is going to be dreaming," Cerradine said. "I only hope we can get Shironne out of her house."

"Will this work, sir?" Aldassa asked.

Cerradine rose and picked up his hat. "I hope so, or I'll feel like a complete fool. I need to oversee this myself, David. If I can find some way to make off with Shironne, I at least owe her mother the assurance of my presence."

"I've some paperwork to review, sir. I'll stay here and wait for word from you."

"No. Go home, David." Cerradine put his coat over his arm. "There's no telling how late we'll be."

He left Aldassa reading through old files, his feet up on his desk. Aldassa would probably be there 'til midnight anyway, Cerradine guessed.

Cerradine's driver took him to the palace, where he found Deborah in Dahar's office. She looked agitated. He couldn't be certain whether worry over Mikael caused it, or having to wait so long in Dahar's presence.

"I need to talk to you," Deborah insisted as soon as he'd stepped through the doorway. She wrapped a hand around his arm and dragged him back out into the hall, closing the door before Dahar had the opportunity to protest.

She glanced at the sentry in each direction down the hallway, both too far to overhear them. "Mikael thinks someone sifted through his head today. He used exactly that word, Jon, *sifted*."

"Shironne would not have done that."

"I don't think she did. Someone *else* did. Someone with that same ability is in the city, and now he knows whatever Mikael knows."

"We can't just assume it was our killer," Cerradine pointed out.

Deborah sighed. "If it was, if this wasn't random, then he had to have followed Mikael from your offices to the hotel where the incident happened. Mikael has been the public face of the Daujom on this investigation."

"What do you mean?"

She shook her head. "They've been very selective about their victims. First a Larossan police officer, then a soldier, then a Lucas sentry. They're working up the ladder of society, and they might be working up to killing an Anvarrid. If the killer sifted through Mikael's mind, then he could know that Mikael is Anvarrid, despite his appearance."

Aldassa had already come out with that theory, and one of the chalkboards in the office had been commandeered to keep track of the betting for the identity of the next victim. Cerradine wasn't going to tell Deborah that, among many others, Mikael's name was already on that board.

"If they *were* looking for an Anvarrid, Dahar or Kai would serve just as well as Mikael." That was what she was actually concerned about, that the killers might take part of *her* family. "We need Mikael to find these people, Deb. Kai won't be involved. There's no reason for him to leave palace grounds at all. And I'll find some excuse to keep Dahar here."

"I don't think so," Dahar said from behind him. He'd opened the door so quietly that neither of them had noticed.

Cerradine turned to face Dahar's wounded expression. "Dahar, we don't need to be worrying about your safety as well."

"I may loan him to you, but Mikael works for me, Jon. You want to do this, I come along."

Cerradine didn't think they had time to negotiate. Darkness would fall soon. So far the killers had struck in the middle of the night, but they'd grabbed Iselin Lucas in the evening and simply held her prisoner. After a brief argument, he gave in to Dahar's plan to meet them at the tavern. He could come out to the Old Town in a well-guarded coach in perfect safety.

For his part, Mikael appeared relieved to be escaping the fortress. He sat in the corner of the carriage as they left the grounds, a rare scowl on his face. Cerradine watched the young man count to himself, lips moving slightly.

He hoped to the heavens that this worked.

. . .

Shironne had eaten dinner alone in her room, her agitation building. She recognized it, now that she knew what to look for. It was that headachy feeling that came over her before one of those dreams. She didn't have a headache, but he did, a constant irritant.

How was she supposed to see into his dream if she was trapped in this room? Verinne would *not* allow her to leave with the colonel.

I have to find some other way.

She'd had a couple of days to consider an escape. She had Mikael's oversized gloves and Perrin's too-large house slippers. She didn't have a coat, but she did have the heavy brocaded house robe. She would look ridiculous. It was an idiotic plan.

But she was out of time. She couldn't wait for her mother to come home and set her free.

After the second housemaid carried away the dinner tray, Shironne guessed she had ample time to pull off her escape. Verinne would be taking care of Perrin and trying to coax Melanna into a bath.

Shironne concentrated, mentally sorting out where each person was in the household. Perrin was down in the drawing room practicing her dancing, mind counting away, no doubt in time to music played by Verinne, who was close by. Melanna was, surprisingly, there also, horribly irritated but unable to escape Verinne's watchful eye. Cook and her helpers were in the kitchen, Messine and Pamini out in the stables. The two maids were also in the kitchen, eating their own dinners, no doubt.

That accounted for everyone.

She plucked Mikael's gloves out from under her pillows. She dressed in her old blue tunic, petticoats, and trousers, and then put a second pair of stockings on over the ones she already wore before donning Perrin's house slippers. She drew on the house robe over her clothes and tightened the belt. The house robe had no pockets, so she took the gloves and stuffed them down the front of her tunic, along with a cloth for her hands. She hoped that the robe's belt held them in place.

She drew aside the curtain, opened her balcony door, and stepped outside. The sun had set, so the air touched her face with cold fingers. She grasped the balcony railing with her bare hand. Familiar iron, and, in one spot, the feel of Melanna's hand. She set her own hand over Melanna's handprint and reached outward with her other hand. For a moment she flailed about, leaning farther and farther over the rail, finding nothing, but then her hand brushed bark. Oak tree, growing up straight and tall, with that one branch that grew toward the house.

She took a deep breath, reminding herself it wasn't that far down. Only a dozen feet or so.

She had plenty of practice falling.

She wrapped one hand around that branch, working through Melanna's memories of the tree again. When she stretched out her other hand, she could feel the second branch, the one Melanna used to lever herself out and onto the first. Shironne said a quick prayer for the true god's protection and pulled herself up into the tree. She had to hold in a nervous giggle when she got her rump settled onto the branch. Her feet dangled into nothingness.

I'm not that much heavier than Melanna. I'm not.

The branch she sat on angled down toward the main trunk. Melanna had shimmied sideways down the branch, and then down the trunk, so with one arm clutching the upper part of the branch, Shironne felt downward. She caught tiny traces of Melanna's touch, verifying the path her sister had taken.

The dry leaves rattled madly around her as she carefully slid her rump downward along the branch. Twigs caught at the sleeves of her house robe as she went, most simply breaking, one snap accompanied by the sound of ripping fabric. The bark she touched bore bits of bird and squirrel dung. She had to tolerate it only until she got to the ground. *Hopefully not by falling.*

She checked the branch with her hand again and this time felt the upward-rising trunk. She shifted the last distance to that, wrapped her arms tightly about it, and tried not to sob in relief. The worst of it was over, surely.

She took a moment to gather her nerve again. For Melanna, this part had been simple. She'd just swung around, wrapped her legs and arms around the trunk, and slid down. But that would mean sliding off the branch that was supporting her, and if she miscalculated, she was going to fall straight to the ground. Shironne patted the trunk with one foot and then groaned when the too-large slipper fell off. It hit the ground below her with a leathery thwack.

That doesn't sound too far, she lied to herself.

But she was here now, and she didn't have too many options. Hoping that no one could see, she parted her house robe, rolled up her tunic and petticoats, and tucked them into the belt so her legs would be free. She stretched out one hand and found another branch, one that bore Melanna's handprint. She grabbed it tightly, pushed off the main branch, and twisted toward the trunk as she slid downward.

The trunk hit her chest hard, but she managed to wrap her legs about it, although not before her elbow protested over taking so much of her weight. She did her best to ignore that and set her arms around the trunk as well.

It had been too long since she'd climbed a tree. Her arms were already getting tired. She was embarrassingly short of breath, as bad as she'd been after climbing all those stairs. If she waited much longer, she would just fall out of the tree. So she started to shimmy down, her trousers catching on the rough bark.

And then her shoeless foot touched something. *Dirt,* her skin told her.

She tried to put the other foot down and let go of the trunk, but her foot came down on the missing house slipper. Her ankle turned and she fell the last bit, landing hard on her bottom in the dirt. She breathed hard for a moment. *Did I make it?*

She concentrated on the denizens of the house, finding them all where they'd been before. No one had noticed she wasn't in her room. No one was outside to see her sitting at the base of a tree like an oversized acorn. Not yet.

But that wasn't going to last forever. She shook her hands, trying to get the traces of tree and dirt and all the accompanying contaminants off her hands. She reached carefully into the neckline of her tunic and drew out the cloth she'd placed there to do a better job of cleaning her hands. It was slightly damp and did a good job. After waving her hands for a moment to dry them, she reached into the top of her tunic again and drew out Mikael's gloves. She tugged them on, immediately feeling better once her hands were covered. She patted around herself gently until she found that fallen house slipper. She managed to get herself up off the ground, slipped the shoe on, and was gratified to find that her ankle seemed to have forgiven her already for twisting it.

She shook her clothes back into their proper place, stepped carefully over to the fence, and followed that back toward the mews.

• • •

They drove down the alley behind the Anjir house so Cerradine might knock at the back door of the house or send Filip through the kitchen with a message.

"Wait here," Mikael said. He opened the carriage door and

jumped down before either of them could protest. "I'll be right back."

Not given much choice, Cerradine called up for the driver to wait for Mikael's return.

In the dim light of the carriage lamp, Deborah shook her head. "Do you remember being that impulsive?"

Cerradine nearly laughed. "Yes. You can't remember it because you never were."

She threw him an offended look. "I've done impulsive things in my life."

"And it's always come back to haunt you, hasn't it?"

She shook her head. "I have my doubts about this, Jon."

Cerradine ran a hand through his hair. "On the way to the palace the other day, I asked Shironne if her mother had ever tried to contact Dahar. She told me Savelle took her to the summer fair a few years ago, hoping to catch a glimpse of Dahar at the melee."

"And did she see him?"

"Shironne told me no. She claimed she fell, and they had to go home before her mother had the chance."

Deborah laughed, covering her face with one hand. "Father Winter, I *am* a fool. I should have thought of that, Jon. Six years ago, Mikael had a child fall out of the stands and land on him." Deborah shook her head again. "The girl cut her hand and he bound it up with her hair ribbon. The mother whisked her away before anyone could get a name."

That sounded exactly like Savelle. "Shironne was eleven, but she would have been small for her age."

"And I'd never met him before that day," Deborah said. "He was just another boy beaten up in the melee. He had . . . I don't recall exactly . . . a broken nose and a split lip, and a couple of cuts on his hand. There would have been plenty of blood on his part. He had a concussion, so he doesn't remember it well, even though Kai periodically drags the story out to embarrass him."

"Have you talked to him about this at all?"

"No," Deborah said with a shake of her head. "He noticed how susceptible she is to him but hasn't made the leap of logic that it's more than that. It's four months until she's an adult, Jon, no matter how mature she actually is. We have rules. We have to . . ."

The carriage door opened and Mikael climbed inside. "You won't believe it. She's not here. We'd better go before anyone in the house notices."

"Wait," Cerradine said, grabbing Mikael's arm. "She's not here?"

"According to Pamini, Miss Anjir climbed over her balcony railing, down one of those trees, and then walked out to the mews and ordered Messine to escort her to the tavern."

Cerradine banged on the roof of the carriage to get the driver on his way. He sat again, pinching the bridge of his nose. "Her mother is going to kill me."

CHAPTER THIRTY

Despite his headache, Mikael felt hopeful, unusual before one of his dreams. The carriage rolled on through the darkness, arriving shortly in the heart of the Old Town. The driver reined in the horses and let them down before the door of the tavern. Cerradine jumped out, leaving Mikael to help Deborah. As soon as Mikael stepped inside, he spotted Synen serving that boisterous group of young Anvarrid men again. Synen caught Mikael's eyes and gestured with one thumb toward the kitchen.

Mikael caught up with Cerradine, who was looking about the common room of the tavern with an angry expression on his face. "Kitchen," Mikael said, and led the colonel and Deborah that way.

When they walked through the doors into the brightly lit kitchen, Mikael almost laughed at Miss Anjir's disheveled appearance. She was swaddled in a golden brocade house robe with a groom's overcoat atop that. She had embroidered house slippers on her feet and wore Mikael's gloves. Her hair, although it looked to have been braided properly this time, had an old dried leaf in it. She looked misplaced again, as if someone had forgotten a young girl in one of the tavern's guest rooms, like a piece of lost luggage. Filip Messine stood protectively nearby, looking extremely relieved to see them.

"Shironne, are you insane?" the colonel asked.

"Sir, I brought her here," Messine began.

"At her behest," the colonel snapped, crossing to tower over her.

"You climbed down a tree, Shironne. You could have broken your neck. What were you thinking?"

She blushed but lifted her chin. "Mr. Lee is going to dream, so I had to get away. I'd heard Melanna climb down that tree, sir, so I knew it could be done."

"Melanna is eight," he said. "You're not a little girl . . ."

"Jon," Deborah interrupted, setting one hand on his arm. "Stop. It's done. Let it go."

He turned a glare on her but quickly controlled it. "Messine, we can take care of her from here. If you would get back to the house and let them know that she's in safe hands."

"I'll do so, sir," Messine said. It took a moment for Miss Anjir to extricate herself from Messine's coat, leaving her in that ridiculous house robe. Once he had his coat, Messine slipped out the tavern's back door, likely grateful to be out of Cerradine's reach.

"Miss Anjir," Deborah said, sitting across from her, "how did you know that Mr. Lee is going to have a dream tonight?"

"I didn't recognize it before," Shironne said, "but I do now. Now that I've met him, I mean. He's so tense that his head hurts. It's like a hum in the back of my mind."

Deborah cast a significant glance at Cerradine, regarding him with raised brows. "Isn't that interesting?"

Cerradine shook his head. "Shironne, you can pick that out all the way from the palace?"

"Well, now that I know what's him and what's not him, it's simple."

Mikael licked his lips, unsure what to make of that. He could barely recognize an oncoming dream himself. How could she?

Synen bustled into the kitchen then, his eyes widening at the sight of the crowd. "What's happening here, lad? Another one of those nights? And you've brought an audience?"

Mikael sighed, not knowing at all where to begin. "Actually, yes. We need a room."

Synen's wife walked in, took one look at Mikael and her husband, wiped her hands on her apron, and headed back out to the common room, shaking her head.

Deborah took charge of the situation. "In addition to the room, we'll need a private sitting area, for myself and the young lady to have a chat. Do we have time for that, Mikael?"

He sometimes miscalculated the timing of one of his dreams, but usually that happened with the old dreams, the ones that repeated. New dreams were clearer, possibly because they were linked to the present—or the future—not the past. "I'm pretty sure I've got time to lie down and get comfortable."

Synen looked dubious about that pronouncement but left to arrange a room.

Mikael cast a concerned glance at Shironne, hoping Deborah wouldn't be too hard on her. Deborah would have a thousand questions. Probably more. Shironne bit her lower lip and nodded—a sign to him that she was willing to go along with Deborah, he decided.

The kitchen door swung open again, narrowly missing Deborah this time. Mikael glanced up, hoping Synen had found a room for him, but instead, Merival strode through the door. He froze as she approached him, a smile on her lips. "Mikael," she said in a teasing voice, "have you come back to see me?"

Words tumbled out of his mouth before he had a chance to think them through. "No, I'm not here to see *you*."

Her smile faded, making him wonder whether she'd been teasing him or not.

His face must be blazing scarlet. "I have other business here tonight."

"Let's go see if he's found a room for you." Cerradine placed a firm hand on Mikael's arm and dragged him from the kitchen before Merival could ask anything else. Mikael went quite willingly.

Fortunately, Synen directed them up to the second floor. The last few rooms on the hall remained unsold, so Synen unlocked one, gesturing for the two of them to precede him inside.

"If he starts screaming," Synen said to the colonel from the doorway, "put a pillow over his face. Shuts him right up."

Cerradine raised his eyebrows and turned back to Mikael after Synen disappeared. "I see you come here often."

"Often enough," Mikael admitted. "Synen is willing to put up with a lot. Mostly he just locks me up until Kai comes to drag me back to the fortress."

"Well, I hope there won't be any screaming tonight."

Cerradine walked around the room, sizing it up. He ran a finger over a wooden chest at the foot of the bed as if checking for dust and eyed the bed cautiously. Mikael suspected that during his years living among the Lucases, the colonel had developed the same distaste for vermin most members of the Six Families shared.

Mikael sat on the neatly made bed, unconcerned about the tavern's cleanliness. He wished the dream would come, but they always happened in their own time. He took off his jacket and boots, lay down, and waited for Cerradine to interrogate him about the waitress downstairs.

Cerradine settled into a chair set under the white-curtained window. "I'm glad to see that young men still do stupid things."

Mikael closed his eyes, pretending not to hear Cerradine's quiet laughter.

. . .

Shironne held a hand over her mouth to keep from laughing aloud at Mikael's poorly hidden panic. The girl in the kitchen must be the Merival who'd sat on Mikael's lap, although he remembered nothing of that event.

Someone else walked into the kitchen just then, and the doctor went to talk with them. Merival took advantage of the doctor's distraction to introduce herself to Shironne as if she owned the tavern. "And you are?"

Shironne knew better than to give her name. She was supposed to be home, locked in her room, and she knew from Mikael's perception of her that she looked ridiculous in her current attire. She needed to get that leaf out of her hair.

"Are you his betrothed?" Merival prompted.

Shironne choked down a cough. "I don't . . ."

"Excuse me," the doctor said sternly to Merival, reflecting annoyance over the waitress' familiarity. "I need to take this young lady up to a private parlor or sitting room. Does this tavern have such a place?"

Shironne was glad she'd been spared the need to answer Merival's questions.

Clearly recognizing authority, the waitress resumed the role of servant. "Yes, ma'am. I can take you up to one if they're not all let."

"Dear," the doctor said, addressing Shironne now, "why don't you come along with me?" She took Shironne's gloved hand and led her across the kitchen in the wake of Merival's rose-oil perfume.

CHAPTER THIRTY-ONE

The doctor instructed Shironne to precede her up the narrow stairwell. Shironne gathered her house robe up in one hand and kept the other on the wall as she felt for each step, the doctor close behind to catch her should she stumble. She warned Shironne when she reached the last step, and they came out into a hallway where the sounds of the tavern's guests crept up into the air, confusing her for a moment. Then she realized that the hall must be open to the tavern on one side like a mezzanine. Merival stopped not far away, and the doctor took Shironne's hand again and led her into a room off that hallway.

The doctor dismissed the serving girl, closing the door firmly behind her. "I hope she didn't upset you, dear."

"Not at all." Shironne stood just inside the doorway, uncertain where anything was once the doctor turned loose her hand. She didn't want to move and trip over something. The doctor walked ahead of her, the faint scent of soap following in her passage. She must be tall, Shironne decided, not as tall as Mama but taller than Mikael.

"Forgive my inquisitiveness, Miss Anjir," the doctor said, "but I've been wanting to talk to you for some time."

The doctor—*infirmarian*, Shironne recalled—kept her curiosity to herself well. She could barely sense it peeping out from behind the woman's control. "You've come to observe me working before. What do you want to know, ma'am?"

"There's a chair to your left, about a foot away. If you reach out your hand, you should be able to touch it."

Shironne followed her instructions and located a wooden-backed chair. She levered herself down into it, grateful that she still had Mikael's gloves. She heard another chair move, wood scraping across a wooden floor, and then the doctor sat.

"You said you knew that Mikael will dream tonight. Is that imminent?"

Shironne considered the question. She reached out to touch Mikael's mind with her own. His thoughts whirled about, a sure sign that he was still awake. She told the doctor that.

"Interesting," the doctor said coolly. "That will give us a few minutes to talk, at a minimum. I wanted to discuss with you why you're here."

"I'm supposed to see what's in his dream, I thought. Like a witness."

The doctor sighed. "Yes, that's the overt intention, but there's a more important reason you're here. The reason that it's you, dear, and not some other sensitive."

"I'm an oddity," Shironne said. "I know that."

"You've done interesting work for the colonel. He's told me you can draw information out of things—or out of people, for that matter."

"Yes, ma'am."

"Would you try something for me?"

The doctor kept her curiosity tightly controlled, but Shironne could sense it like a fish just under the surface of the water. "What do you want me to do?"

"I want you to feel my arm, along one of the bones."

"If I do that, I'll be able to get into your head, ma'am."

"I'm aware of that."

Shironne considered the request and then pulled off her gloves and laid them in her lap. "If you're certain. What am I looking for?"

"I want to see what you tell me." She placed her bared arm under Shironne's fingers.

Shironne felt the woman's intellect stirring, like wind rustling through piles of leaves. Deborah Lucas, who tried very hard to control her thoughts, counting numbers in her head to keep her brain occupied. In the Family, that was how they were trained to control their errant emotions. That revelation made Shironne curious about how she'd come to the same conclusion herself a couple of years ago.

Shironne felt the skin, a woman older than Mama, who'd had a child once. The muscles under her skin spoke of carrying and lifting. Deeper, Shironne sensed strong bones, not gone to brittleness with age. She felt down the length of the arm, up to the elbow, where bone scarred by an old break burned when the weather turned.

Deborah's thoughts winged near her fingers like birds, and Shironne knew she'd found what Deborah wanted her to find, because one of the birds told her. She lifted her fingers from Deborah's arm. "You wanted to see if I could find where your sister broke your arm when you were seven."

Deborah rolled down her sleeve, brisk sounds. "Did you?"

"Yes, but . . . I can't be a doctor, ma'am. I can't see." She'd picked that idea out of Deborah's head as well.

"No. I don't suppose that you could attend the college to study there. There are things you wouldn't be able to do. However, you have the ability to see things that none of the rest of us can. The Family has records of sensitives like you who did an amazing variety of things with their talents—translators, doctors, engineers."

Deborah referred to her powers as *talents*, something she needed to remember. "Truly?"

Deborah laughed, her amusement overriding her self-control. "Certainly, dear. It runs in certain bloodlines, although it's not common."

"Are . . . were they all blind?"

"No, I've only ever read of one being blind, and I have researched this quite a bit. We don't know exactly how the inheritance of these things works." She shifted out of her chair and then stood. "Tone deafness does run among sensitives, though, to varying degrees. Whatever you do, don't ask Dahar to sing."

Shironne sensed humor behind that. Deborah actually regarded him fondly, Shironne decided, despite his lack of vocal ability. "I'll remember that, ma'am. Do other talents run in Families, like Mr. Lee's?"

"His ability is extremely unusual," Deborah qualified. Her voice took on a guarded tone, as if she didn't want to say too much.

"I've never heard anyone else's dreams."

"There have been other dreamers. Mostly among, I must add, the House of Vandriyen. However, I've never before heard of one who combines that with Mikael's ability to broadcast, nor of one who focuses on death as he does. He has what I perceive to be an unprecedented *combination* of talents."

Colonel Cerradine had told her most of that long ago, but without revealing any names. "So his parents didn't have them?"

"Just as yours apparently did not. Sensitives seem to be shaped not only by what they inherit from their parents, but also by what happens to them," Deborah told her. "I have a theory that Mikael's odd dreaming stems from his father's death. I believe that Mikael was on his way to being comparatively normal, but as his father lay dying he reached out to Mikael, trying to tell him something. Perhaps who'd shot him; we don't know for certain. But that experience triggered Mikael's change from normalcy to this unique fixation on others' deaths."

Shironne considered that idea, working out an analogy in her head. "Most of us are like clay balls, then, but a few are a different shape because someone smashed us before we were fired?"

Deborah laughed. "Very impressive, Miss Anjir. Let's say *reshaped* instead of *smashed*."

Reshaped sounds better. "So you think something made me odd as well?"

"Well, I believe you had to inherit the possibility of it, dear, but the correct trigger was required to cause you to become such an extreme sensitive."

"What would have changed me?" Shironne asked.

Deborah's mind tucked itself away from that question, not wanting to divulge that answer. "It's difficult to be certain," she equivocated. "I understand you have a scar on your hand."

"Yes, ma'am. I fell once and cut my hand."

"May I look at it?"

Shironne couldn't guess at the reason behind the request. She tugged off the right glove and held her hand out, thinking that if Deborah took it, she might be able to find the answer.

Two gloved hands took hers, rotating it slightly as if to improve the view. "It seems to have healed well. This happened when you were, what, eleven?"

"Yes, ma'am." Her mother had to have told the colonel about the embarrassing incident. "It seemed infected for a while, and Mama worried about it, but then it healed."

"How interesting," came the enigmatic response. "Did you know that the Anvarrid cut their palms as part of their marriage rituals? They mingle their blood, an ancient custom, although most don't make more than a tiny cut. That's what this scar reminds me of."

Shironne sighed. "Yes, Mama told me that too."

"Ah. Tell me, dear, what do you know about the history of my people and our fortresses?"

Shironne felt her brows drawing together as she tried to figure out where the doctor's seemingly rambling thoughts had gone. "Not much. I learned Larossan history, not the Six Families."

"Then let me tell you a few important things. The Founders built the fortresses, breathed life into them, and ordered them to watch over each Family. But like any other living thing, sometimes one of the fortresses becomes ill. For that reason, the Founders also created touch-sensitives, a small cadre of individuals able to communicate with the fortress. A fortress could tell the sensitives what ailed it, and they, in turn, could fix it."

"It spoke to me," Shironne said, suddenly feeling breathless.

"Yes, Mikael told me you were quite startled."

"I didn't realize it was *alive*," she admitted. "I mean, legends say it's alive, but I never thought it would talk."

Deborah reflected mild amusement. "Yes. Most people assume it's alive in the same way that a mushroom or a potato is alive. Not very, I mean."

The mental image of the Family living in a giant potato floated into Shironne's mind, and she had to press her lips together to keep a laugh inside. This wasn't an appropriate time for humor. "But how do your people fix the fortress, then, if it can't tell you what's wrong anymore?"

"I'm told there are ways of working around that problem," Deborah said, "built in for the eventuality that the touch-sensitives—or *interfaces*, as they were once called—didn't survive. You know from your own experience that when such abilities first manifest, it can be debilitating. Many touch-sensitives starve to death before they learn to tolerate food again, and some simply never learn to cope, and choose to join the snow."

Join the snow was a Family euphemism. Shironne knew that because Mikael knew it. There had been a time when those who couldn't deal with life in the fortress would simply flee it in the winter and lie down in the snow to die. It was an ancient term, which carried a great deal of racial guilt behind it, because most people who did that had done so because they felt they were a burden to the Family. Shironne shook her head, not wanting to chase down the meanings of that at the moment.

"So we manage without," Deborah continued, "although the communication isn't as clear as it would be if a touch-sensitive was there to interface with the fortress. Languages are naturally limiting, I'm told, especially when it comes to Anvarrid. However, my point is that the Families very quickly learned that touch-sensitives have myriad other uses. Translating, interrogation, investigation. I believe you've done all of those for the colonel at one point or another. And you've seen that your talents can be used in the medical sphere as well."

Shironne thought she finally understood. "So you want me to be a doctor for the Family."

"Hmm . . . not exactly where I was going with this, dear, but I have to admit I wouldn't *mind* your help in the infirmary. Aron says you're well versed now in human anatomy, although you've generally worked with dead specimens."

"Then what?"

"You have abilities that are very useful to many people. Those talents, however, include the ability to walk into Mikael's dreams. You may not be aware of this, but he usually manifests a reflection of the victim's injuries. Almost as if he's a living record of that information, because he can't truly recall the dream himself, just as most of us forget our dreams."

Yes, there was a memory in Shironne's mind now of Mikael waking with blood soaking his shirt, of short breath and tight lungs and fear. He'd done that the last time, forcing other sensitives to endure it. He feared it would kill him one day. He'd feared that for a couple of years now, because it had been growing worse and worse. Her breath grew a bit short in response.

Another thing I shouldn't know.

Shironne took a deep breath. "You think I can help him, don't you?"

"I think that if you see into his dreams, he won't have any need to show them to anyone else. I hope that having someone to interpret his dreams will cause him not to reflect the victims' wounds."

"That would be better, wouldn't it?" she asked aloud.

"For Mikael? Without a doubt. Better for the sensitives in the fortress as well. But . . ." She paused, as if about to say something terrible. "He struggles to escape his dreams, like he can't let go of the victim, and I fear that one day he'll follow one down into death."

And she suddenly grasped *exactly* what the doctor intended with this conversation. For Deborah Lucas, it wasn't about Shironne coming to help the Lucas Family with their lonely fortress. It wasn't about aiding their doctors or finding murderers for Colonel Cerradine. Her powers had a more important use.

The doctor didn't care about helping the rest of the world nearly as much as she wanted Shironne to save Mikael Lee from his own dreams.

And Deborah was pressing her—gently—to determine whether she would be there the *next* time Mikael Lee had a terrible dream. She couldn't actually ask that, though. It was forbidden. The very question implied a relationship between Shironne and Mikael that was unacceptable in the eyes of the Lucas Family. To them, Mikael was an adult, and she was a child.

For four more months.

Shironne shifted in her chair. "You want me to walk into his dream to stop him from getting lost and hurting himself."

"Yes," Deborah said. "But you need to consider whether you want to risk this. After the last dream, some of the other sensitives had bruises and were short of breath. His dream affected them, and I can't guarantee that it won't affect you that way if you try to help him tonight. I would rather have had your mother here for this discussion, but I'll ask you, taking into consideration that among Larossans, you're an adult."

And she was quite desperate. Shironne could sense that, despite Deborah's calm voice.

"I have no doubts, ma'am. I want to help." No, that wasn't what the doctor needed to hear. Shironne lifted her chin, facing where the doctor sat. "I want to help Mr. Lee."

Relief surrounded the doctor like a fog, quickly settling away. "I am grateful, Miss Anjir."

Fear began beating at the back of Shironne's mind, a whisper from a room down the hall. Shironne shook her head to dispel it, but it continued to rattle away. "I think Mr. Lee is about to start dreaming," she warned. "He's frightened."

Deborah stood. "Then we should go see if you can break into his dream, don't you think?"

CHAPTER THIRTY-TWO

Shironne followed Deborah to a room farther down the hall. She sensed the colonel waiting wakeful in one corner. Mikael's mind fluttered in fear, like a bird in a cage.

"*Is* he dreaming?" Deborah asked softly.

"Not that I can tell," the colonel returned.

"He will be in a while," Shironne told them. "He knows that and he's panicking in his sleep."

"The sensitives told me that he *screamed* for a time before his dream began," Deborah said, placing Shironne's hand on the back of a tall chair. "Is he doing that now?"

Shironne sat down, trying to hear this the way her mother might have. "I suppose they might perceive it that way. If they don't hear him well, they probably wouldn't know exactly what's wrong. He just doesn't want to do this alone."

Her response started Deborah thinking hard again, the doctor's mind spinning down in tight spirals, hiding all her feelings inside.

Shironne slipped off one glove and touched a linen shirtsleeve that bore the sense of Mikael. She located his hand, gone chill in slumber. His knuckles were scarred, his hand calloused but clean. He had a scar slashing across his palm as well, rather like the one she had. She tried to wish reassurance at him. His anxiousness calmed then, as if he'd only been waiting for her to arrive.

He started slipping away from her, the dream pulling him down.

It tugged at her as well. Shironne slid with it, not aware when she passed into sleep.

. . .

Shironne stood on a cobbled street under the dim lamplight, clad in her worn pink tunic. She glanced down at herself, seeing orange petticoats, startlingly bright against the brown of her leather slippers. She glanced down at her gloveless hands. Her fingers looked slim and elegant, like Mama's. In her dreams they usually looked plump and shorter, the way she recalled seeing them last, before she'd lost her sight. She turned them over and saw that her left palm lacked the scar that should mar it. Mikael had never seen it, she realized.

I'm not seeing anything. This is what his *mind sees. This is what I look like to him.*

Then she shook her head. She wasn't here to stare at her hands.

Where is he? She should see Mikael somewhere, shouldn't she?

She glanced up and down the street. Nothing seemed familiar, giving her no answer. She supposed it could be the northwest quarter of the city, past where the wealthier Larossans lived; a newer section of town, with stone streets and sidewalks and gaslights—possibly the Seychas District. *Why here?*

Rows of houses three and four stories high lined both sides of the unknown street, close together and dark now. Little traffic moved on the street, only a few pedestrians bundled heavily against the chill wind. She spotted a couple of coaches heading away from her, and then turned about to inspect the other side of the street.

A man stood almost directly behind her. Shironne took a startled step back when she saw him, but he ignored her. He remained standing under the lamppost, appearing lost in thought.

"Who are you?" she blurted out, too surprised for courtesy.

He failed to react, as if unaware of her presence. She tried again, reaching out to shake his sleeve, and he ignored her. He must not be able to perceive her at all.

This had to be the victim. *I'm looking at a man who's about to die.*

Shironne swallowed, feeling her breath shorten. She couldn't save him, could she? Mikael watched in his dreams but couldn't interfere. All she could do was observe. Frustration welled through her, making her grind her teeth.

Who was he? His clothes told her nothing about him. They were casual, and not a wealthy man's, but well tailored. His face appeared more angular than those of most Larossans, that and his height hinting at some Anvarrid blood. Otherwise, she couldn't see anything distinctive about him.

He appeared to be debating something in his head, his eyes lowered. Shironne lifted her left hand to his cheek, lightly touching his unresponsive face, and his anxiety swarmed around her.

There were *two* men inside that worried mind. She sensed the one, his thoughts tortured by a decision he fought to make. Mikael's consciousness twined through the other's like two vines growing together.

The first man worried, thinking he needed to talk to her first before reporting it, that it would only be fair to discuss it with her. He didn't even know what he'd say, his thoughts argued. *Just come out with my suspicions?*

This was a soldier, even if he wasn't wearing a uniform.

Shironne lowered her hand, staring into the man's face. She wished he'd surrendered a name to her, so she'd have some idea of his identity. She tried again, drawing from his conscious mind only the same circular pattern of worry and responsibility.

She *should* be able to pull more out of him.

She hadn't touched him at all, she realized—she *couldn't*. She'd left her overly sensitive skin behind in that room where her body slept. She rubbed one hand along her tunic sleeve and felt nothing other than the normal texture of the wool, the embroidery and beading around the cuff. Her presence in this dream existed only through her link with Mikael, and he'd reached this man with his mind, not his skin. She could access only what Mikael was accessing.

Movement caught her attention, and another man passed them by in dark garb. He had a heavy coat pulled close around him and was apparently unaware of Shironne's presence. The first man stilled suddenly, his thoughts going awry, scattering like marbles dropped on the ground. His face went slack and his mouth fell open.

Shironne stepped away from him, perplexed. His left hand brushed his neck and he swallowed with a pained sound. Shironne backed farther away, frightened now.

He put his hand to his throat. A whisper feathered out between his lips, too indistinct for her to catch. She touched him again, but his mind only chattered with fright and anger.

He knows. He knew *exactly* what had just happened to him. He knew what *would* happen, just as it had to the others. The man in front of her knew he'd been chosen to die.

Who is he? He seemed so familiar, but she couldn't place him because it was Mikael who was touching him, not her. This new limitation frustrated her.

The creaking rumble of a coach approaching warned her. Shironne scrambled away to get out of its path, not certain what it might do to her dream-self. A lumbering traveling coach slowed to a halt only a few feet from where she stood. It bore no crest—the sort of vehicle a nobleman might use when he wanted his identity hidden.

The door opened and two men jumped down. Their victim watched them come, his knees giving out as they neared him. He slumped to the stone pavers.

Shironne gazed at them, trying to find something distinct about them in the gloom. Their faces and clothes told her nothing, as nondescript as their victim's. The victim's panic turned to frustration, leaking through Mikael across *her* senses. His captors raised him to his feet again.

A third man stepped down from the coach then, his presence drawing her attention as if he was now the center of the dream.

His features looked Larossan. She would guess his age to be

around forty, but she wasn't particularly good at that. A touch of gray marked his temples. He seemed a man accustomed to getting what he wanted. His clothes were of the finest quality, clearly better made than those of his two associates. The cut seemed odd to her, though.

He laid one bared hand against his captive's cheek. Then he looked at her . . . and, unlike the others, he actually seemed to see her.

Shironne forgot everything else when his dark eyes stared into hers. Mesmerized, she watched as the distance between them seemed to disappear. The rest of the dream slowed to a halt. The two other men dragging their victim to the coach appeared to stop, suspended in time, the horses unmoving.

The only sound she heard was her own terrified breathing.

The man reached out with his other hand, almost as if to caress her face. She wanted to back away but remained frozen there. One of his fingers slid down the curve of her bruised cheek.

I've come looking for you.

His lips moved, words coming forth that her ears didn't recognize. She was learning it thirdhand, like an old rumor, passed via the victim through Mikael to her. The words' meaning whispered into her mind all the same, things he wanted repeated. He wanted her to bear his warning, claiming that she alone would come out of this dream with the memories he wished. As if he *knew* her, as if he *recognized* her, he understood what she could do better than she did herself. The familiarity of his touch terrified her.

Shironne jerked away, almost shredding herself out of the dream to escape him. She fell to the pavers and then scrambled up. She ran to a nearby house and crouched down by the steps, making herself as small as possible, hoping to escape the man's attention.

He hadn't moved from where he stood. He watched as the others—three of them now—struggled to lift their burden into the coach. They climbed up, clambering over their victim's body. The older man turned, gazed at her again, and smiled.

Shironne ran, turning into an alleyway that was weirdly unformed. The buildings faded off into blackness, leaving her nowhere to go. Fear beat in her blood, so she leaned against the alley wall, trying to calm herself. Somewhere in the dream she still sensed Mikael's presence, but she didn't want to be where he was—not if that man was there.

She concentrated on keeping contact with Mikael in her mind, sinking down until she sat in the vague alleyway. Darkness crept about her, unformed spots in the fabric of the dream. This must be a place in the city Mikael didn't know, this alley, and therefore he couldn't dream it well.

She could feel Mikael's anger and fear coupled with the victim's desperate worry, ever present, the very air of the dream. Time passed, and his fear settled. The victim understood that Mikael would be there, watching over him.

And then she was sure. Even though she wasn't sensing the victim with her own mind, the perception she had of him through Mikael told her that this man, this victim, was Lieutenant Aldassa.

She put her head on her knees, unable to stop the tears. She couldn't do this. She couldn't bear to watch Aldassa die. How did Mikael live through this, over and over? She put a hand over her mouth to hold in her sobs.

If Mikael could do this, she could.

She was here to protect Mikael, and she had to calm herself to do that. Shironne reached into her tunic pocket, trying to find her focus so she could anchor herself to it, pull herself out of the dream. Only she didn't have it. The crystal was in the pocket of her blue coat, and Verinne had taken it away.

Her heart began to flutter. *How can I pull Mikael out of this dream if I don't have it?*

But the crystal couldn't exist in the dream anyway. Mikael didn't know she had it. So how had she used it to yank him out of his memories before?

It was the *idea* of the focus. She slid her hand into her tunic pocket and felt the cool edges of the stone under her fingers. She felt its clean lines and simple structure. She drew the focus out of her pocket and stared down at it. It had the shape her fingers remembered. It was blue, as her mother had said when she gave it to her long ago, and it glowed softly, a beacon in this dark alleyway. She cupped her hands around it, memorizing it, fixing it in her mind so that it would be a tool for her to use whenever she needed it.

She took a deep breath and forced away the victim's fear, Mikael's fear. She had to keep a level head if she meant to control this dream world, to be the witness they all needed, that Aldassa deserved. She had to get Mikael safely out.

She pushed herself to her feet. She wanted to be where they'd gone rather than abandoned in this chilly alleyway of Mikael's mind. She tried to make Mikael hear her, thinking that it was his dream and he *must* control it somehow. The world changed around her abruptly, showing her Aldassa being hauled from the traveling coach in a different dark alley.

Three men dragged him across the ground, his head drooping to his chest. One of their number stayed behind in the coach, his face reflecting anguish—the involuntary witness. The last man, the one who could see her, followed them at a distance, not taking part in the gruesome pageant. Shironne shrunk back into a doorway, caution overriding her need to witness the crime.

They were in the Lower Town now, a slum. The stench was less pungent in Mikael's dream, but distinctive even so. There were no streetlights here. The police didn't frequent this quarter, saving their efforts for those parts of the capital that made stronger demands. People here kept indoors at night, and those who didn't had ill reasons for being abroad.

She watched as they dragged the man down the stone embankment into the shadows of the Lower Town Bridge. The fourth man trailed behind them as if too fastidious to soil his clothes. He followed the others to the embankment but went no farther, waiting with one foot up on the stone wall, looking as if he'd merely gone for a moonlit stroll.

She didn't want to watch. Her heart fluttered wildly—the victim's fright, shared with Mikael and thus transferred to her—and she forced it back down. How much time passed she didn't know, but then the men returned from the embankment and strode into the shadows.

Was it over?

No, they were still in Mikael's dream.

He was trapped in Aldassa's dying body, counting on her to bring him back.

Forgetting her caution, Shironne ran across the dirt street and flung herself down the embankment, landing in the sludge that lined the edge of the river. Crumpled fabric lay near the flow of water and a rope snaked off into the darkness, tethering something away from the black water.

She screamed Mikael's name.

She heard laughter and turned back to see the last man standing on the stone embankment, limned by the faint moonlight. He smiled warmly, almost affectionately, at her, the way Father used to smile at Perrin.

"Remember," he said—a foreign word, but she knew it.

She grabbed for her sense of Mikael and the dream shredded, catapulting her back into blindness.

CHAPTER THIRTY-THREE

Mikael took a great breath, the air rushing into his lungs. He was alive, which he'd doubted a moment before. Shironne Anjir had called him back from death. He was safe.

Deborah was helping Miss Anjir sit on a chair next to the bed. The girl's hair was rumpled, as if she'd been sleeping. She clung to his hand, her face stricken.

And then it all returned to him, erasing the relief of having survived another dream. He rarely had memories of his dreams right away, but this time he was sure. The victim had been David Aldassa.

Mikael sat up and struggled to get to his feet, entangled in the heavy blanket Cerradine had thrown over him. He reached out for his jacket, determined to go out and see for himself, to find Aldassa, but Shironne's hands grabbed at his arm.

"No," she cried. "There's nothing you can do. It's over."

He almost pulled away from her in anger but saw tears in her eyes, his own regret reflected on her face. "I have to know."

"You already know it was him," she said. "It's too late."

Echoing him, his own helplessness turning on her. Mikael tried to control his pain, wanting not to inflict it on her further. He drew a sniffling breath, sat down on the edge of the bed, and rubbed his free hand over his face. He was always too late. That was his curse—to watch others die and never be able to save them.

"Who?" Cerradine asked.

Deborah waited on the other side of the bed. Dahar glanced at her and then shook his head in a puzzled fashion.

Shironne put her free hand over her mouth to stifle a sob, her dark eyes filling with tears. Mikael wished he could put his arms around her, but that wouldn't be appropriate, so he stayed the impulse. He looked back at Cerradine, whose expression betrayed only curiosity. "I think they took David Aldassa, sir."

Cerradine went still, olive skin paling. "No."

"He knew, sir. The victim knew I was with him. He wanted me to remember things, so he had to have known me."

"Are you certain?" Dahar put a hand on Cerradine's shoulder.

"He *knew* me." Mikael shut his eyes, trying to recall what had identified the victim as David Aldassa in his mind. "He worried about his daughters and his wife. It was him."

Cerradine turned away and leaned on one hand against the door.

A tear spilled from Shironne's eye and slid down her cheek. Cerradine's pain had to be tearing at her. Mikael could almost sense that.

"Do you remember anything?" Dahar asked. "Where? What did you see?"

Mikael closed his eyes, trying to answer the questions. Only the victim's emotions and sensations stirred in his mind. The details escaped him. Then he recalled there had been a second witness this time.

"I think it was the Lower Town Bridge," Shironne said unprompted. "It smelled, and the dirt near the embankments was slimy. The coach is big, but unmarked. Five men, all gone now. He knows about Mikael." She sounded exhausted. Mikael squeezed her hand in reassurance.

"He?" Dahar asked.

"The head . . . person of them," Shironne faltered, then went on. "He talked to me in some other language, but I understood him. He's been trying to reach Mikael, to talk to *him*, but he couldn't, so he waited for me. He *knew* I would be there, so he spoke through Mikael to me. Well, I guess through Aldassa and then through him to me. He says we know what he wants. He'll keep killing until he gets it and he'll get closer to home every time."

Cerradine looked around at those words, his face grim. He got up and began moving, gathering his coat and hat. "You are to stay with Deborah—do you understand me?" he said to Shironne, putting a hand on her cheek. "I don't want you out on the streets."

Shironne nodded. She was familiar enough with the colonel that his touch didn't disturb her. He'd done it to underscore his urgency. He'd wanted to be certain she knew he was concerned for her. "I'll stay with her, sir."

Cerradine drew on his coat, and Dahar did the same. Mikael moved to join them, but Deborah's hand came down on his shoulder, pressing him back to his sitting position on the rumpled bed. "I'm not letting you go until I know you're not hurt."

Mikael tore at his collar, opening the throat of his shirt so that she could see his shoulders. He didn't need to look down to know there was nothing there. He felt *normal*—or as normal as he would any other time he'd been woken out of a dead sleep.

Deborah's eyes scanned his bared shoulders and then flicked toward Shironne. "Go, then," she told him, "but don't forget you've left us here."

He glanced down at Shironne. She made a waving gesture with her hands, so he grabbed up his coat and headed out to join the colonel and Dahar down in the common room of the tavern.

"There was a rope," Shironne said just before he passed through the doorway. "They didn't want the river to wash him away, so he's tied there. Look for that."

Mikael nodded. She wouldn't see him, but she would catch the sense of it from his mind. He shook his head. This was a body none of them wanted to find. He only hoped he located David Aldassa before the colonel did.

. . .

Shironne felt Mikael's anxiousness abate some once he'd left the small room they were in. Once he was doing something, he felt better, a reaction she could well understand.

"Thank you," Deborah said softly. She touched Shironne's sleeve. "You seem to have found a way to keep him safe."

In the dream, she meant.

"The others," she went on, "don't understand the sort of risk that was for you. Especially the colonel. He's always seen this possibility as a way to fine-tune Mikael's dreams. To find murderers."

Whereas for Deborah, this exercise was more about saving Mikael.

"I want to find that man who killed Aldassa too," Shironne said.

"I know," Deborah said and then sighed. "For now, I need to decide what to do with you, Miss Anjir," the doctor said. "It's at least an hour before dawn."

Shironne lifted her head. "How long was I sleeping?"

"A few hours. Mikael's dreams aren't like normal dreams, coming and going. When he does this, he dreams for a long time. From the moment he contacts the victim until . . ."

Until they die. How long had she spent sitting in that dark alley of Mikael's mind? Hours? It had seemed to pass so quickly.

"Dahar brought some clothing for you to wear," Deborah went on.

Shironne wondered what manner of garments the prince—her uncle—would have thought to bring for her.

"I had to guess on your measurements, but I've had a great deal of practice. Why don't we take care of that, and then decide what's to be done?"

Dressing in unfamiliar clothes, even with Deborah's help, was a daunting prospect, but Shironne was too worn down to argue. She sighed.

"Are you skin shy?" Deborah asked gently. "I can leave if you prefer."

That was a term the Family used to describe members of a yeargroup who preferred never to be seen undressed, a rarity in most yeargroups, where they grew up in close quarters. "No, I'm fine. I have two younger sisters who don't believe in privacy."

Deborah chuckled but then sobered. She explained each garment—trousers, shirt, vest, jacket. The jacket and vest had hidden plackets. Shironne felt the linen of the shirt, finely woven and new. No dye.

She's brought me a uniform. A Family uniform. Her mother wouldn't like it, but she probably wouldn't like her daughter to wear an army uniform either. "It's brown, isn't it?"

"Yes. You are still a child, dear," Deborah said. "And before you point it out, I *am* aware that the threshold we've set for adulthood is arbitrary."

Shironne supposed they had to have some criteria. Perhaps Family children just matured later than Larossans. "I'm blind. That would surely make me a liability for the Family."

"I think that tonight you more than proved your worth, dear."

CHAPTER THIRTY-FOUR

Mikael wasn't certain how long he'd slept, but the patrons of the tavern's common room had all departed, leaving the place in relative quiet. It had to be well past midnight. Synen and a guest argued near the doorway, the guest complaining that comings and goings in the night had ruined his sleep. Not wanting to lose Synen's goodwill, Mikael offered to pay the man's lodging. Surprised at the sight of the two non-Larossan patrons in their Lucas Family uniforms—accompanied by an army officer—the man hastened to agree with the plan.

"Just send the bill to me at the palace," Dahar interrupted, sounding out of sorts.

Cerradine stood to one side, arms wrapped around his chest. He was clearly trying to calm himself, but Mikael suspected his emotions were leaking out, provoking Dahar's snappishness.

Synen nodded, not bothering to ask Dahar's name. He probably knew exactly who Dahar was. The placated guest picked up his bags and returned upstairs to finish his night's sleep. Synen turned to Mikael. "What are you up to, lad?"

"We need to borrow a few things," he said. "Do you have a wagon?" He'd seen one before in the stables in the tavern's back court.

"There's the hay cart we use in the stable," Synen said hesitantly. Mikael could tell from his dour expression that Synen suspected what they wanted it for. "You can take that."

"Could we also borrow a few blankets, and perhaps one of your stable boys as a driver?" Dahar asked, sounding more diplomatic now.

"A discreet one," Mikael amended.

Synen nodded, stroking a finger along his stubbled jaw. "I'll send my older son with you," he told Mikael. "Just keep him out of harm's way."

Synen went back into the kitchen to make the necessary arrangements. Dahar paced around the quiet common room, clearly upset, occasionally pausing to pick up an object and look at it.

Another patron came down the stairs then, gave them a startled glance, and crossed to knock on the kitchen door. Synen's wife emerged and the man asked that breakfast be sent up to him after all. Then he headed back upstairs, with only one perplexed glance at the common room's three occupants.

"This man," Cerradine said, "in the dream. Shironne said he knew about you, and he knew about her being in your dream. How is that possible?"

Mikael had been puzzling over that since she'd said it. "A lot of people know about my dreams and could have told the killer, but about her being *in* my dream? There are very few people who know that was planned."

"Myself, Cerradine, you, and Deborah," Dahar said. "And the girl, of course."

Mikael shook his head. "Plus Kai and Elisabet, who were there when we talked about it, along with anyone any of us have told."

"I didn't tell anyone other than Aldassa and Messine," Cerradine said.

Mikael shook his head. "The day before yesterday—or was it yesterday?—when I was on my way back to the fortress, I think someone . . . rifled through my mind. Deborah has a book that lists a type of Pedraisi witch that can do that. Just go in and look around. Not like a touch-sensitive, where I have to be thinking about a subject for her to be able to pick it up."

"Deb's mentioned that to me before," Cerradine said. "Mind Thief, I think."

"That's why I think it must have been me. I knew about the plan, and he just picked that out of my head, that Miss Anjir was going to try to see into my dream. He wanted to be seen."

Dahar picked up an empty glass from the bar and gazed at the maker's mark stamped into the bottom. "He's been stalking you."

"I think so. If he's from the original group of priests, then he's come all the way from the border to haunt my dreams."

"How would he know about you in the first place?" Dahar asked.

"He has Paal Endiren, sir. I'm sure of that now. So he could know everything Paal knows."

"And even though Mikael never worked directly with Paal, everyone in the office knew about his dreams." Cerradine turned to Mikael. "Shironne said he thinks you know what he wants. What is it, then?"

"I don't know," Mikael said. "How am I supposed to know?"

"If he rifled through your mind," Cerradine insisted, "then he must know whether it's in your head or not. You *have* to know."

Mikael chased down the logic of that. Had David Aldassa become a victim only so that the killer could reach him? "I swear, sir, I don't know what he wants."

Dahar came around and peered into Mikael's eyes. "Will he give us three days before killing again?"

The man had told Shironne the next victim would be *closer to home*. Mikael wasn't sure what that meant, but he didn't want to find out. "I don't know."

"Then find him," Dahar said firmly, "before we have to deal with another body."

How was he supposed to hunt these men? Aldassa, with all his squads of soldiers, hadn't made any headway on locating the killers. Mikael nodded anyway, and Synen returned then with a handful of blankets and his son, sparing him from protesting ignorance yet again.

The cart proved smaller than Mikael had hoped, but adequate for their needs. Synen's son drove them down to the river, Mikael sitting in the back with Dahar while Cerradine shared the seat with the young man.

Under the moonlight, a thin fog rose off the surface of the river, the normal smell kept at bay by the chill. Only light traffic flowed through the streets, mostly carters out early to get their loads through before dawn brought congestion to this part of town. In their heavy black overcoats, he and Dahar drew relatively little notice.

"You weren't broadcasting," Dahar said as they drove along the river walk toward the Lower Town Bridge. "Not at all."

Mikael cast a surprised glance at him, unsure of Dahar's expression in the dark. "Sir?"

"I told Deborah, but you were asleep. You weren't broadcasting anything. That happened when you were with the girl in my office as well. You kept disappearing from the ambient, almost as if the two of you had locked everyone else out. She stopped you from broadcasting."

His breath came a bit short—nothing to do with his dream, though. "She stopped me?"

"Yes. I don't know what that means, but it is . . . interesting. Khajurian does that when around her husband."

He felt slow-witted, but not enough that he didn't catch Dahar's implication. Khajurian was the king's daughter and was *bound* to her husband—their minds were profoundly linked, so much so that what one knew, the other did. It was the reason that Khajurian, despite being the king's only child, wasn't under consideration to be his heir. The phenomenon was rare but had been documented since the first days of the Anvarrid invasion. Hadn't Lucasedrion been *bound* to his wife? A fainter version of the situation had occurred among Anvarrid for centuries, but the Family had proven far more susceptible to an Anvarrid's *binding*, provoking a far deeper communion between the individuals involved.

Dahar was implying that he was *bound* to Shironne Anjir.

That was ridiculous. He'd never met her before this week. Didn't there have to be an exchange of blood? That was the source of the Anvarrid wedding ritual of cutting the bride's and groom's palms to combine their blood.

Mikael shook his head. It shouldn't even be considered. She was a child still, and as such, he couldn't discuss that possibility with her.

The Lower Town Bridge loomed in sight, spanning the man-made embankments of the river. One of the very first things built by the Anvarrid when they'd invaded, the old arch bridge was constructed out of stone stolen from the remains of even older structures, the shapes mismatched and jarring. Time had stained the granite abutments and embankments an unattractive orange-beige. Mikael had always wished the king would tear down the bridge and replace it. He suspected he'd feel that even more strongly after today.

They left the cart up on the river walk with Synen's son standing guard.

The water ran far below its normal level this time of year, exposing a wide swath of slime-covered sands. The bridge's abutments rose from the stone embankments on the sides of the river, the outer arches reaching over the partially exposed ground. The abutments that supported the central arch had iron rings fixed to their sides, with chains running through them so that fishermen could tie off their boats there. No one fished there this early, and Mikael really didn't want to consider the sort of fish one could catch in the foul water this far south into the city.

Lights on the bridge illuminated footprints in the mud past the embankments, signs of slipping and sliding, too many to gain a clear picture of what had happened there.

Peering out through the light fog, Dahar pointed to the abutment nearby. "Looks like a pile of clothes over there."

The victim had been dragged under the bridge where the moonlight didn't penetrate. Mikael gazed at the nearest set of chains that wrapped under the bridge. He could keep a hand on the chain and hope not to slip. The water ran silent and purposeful there, determined to escape the city. "Let me go down and look around, sir."

"I'll go," Cerradine said, stepping up onto the wall.

"Can you swim, sir?" Mikael asked.

Cerradine's dark eyes fixed on him.

"Let me do it, sirs," Mikael said. "I can swim out if I lose my balance. You can't."

Dahar raised an eyebrow but didn't argue. He started rolling out the old braided rope they'd borrowed from the stables instead.

Mikael stripped off his overcoat and jacket and handed them up to Cerradine. He took the rope Dahar offered and tied it around his waist, hoping it wouldn't snap if it had to support his weight. His teeth started to chatter. "If I go down, sir," he said, "don't try to come after me. Let me go."

Dahar turned a pinched look in his direction. "I'll do what I need to."

Mikael slid down the river wall and landed on the slimy, exposed bank. The footing was terrible, and his boots were going to be ruined. Keeping one hand on the wall, he made his way toward the bank under the bridge, where the shadows were still dark enough to hide a body from view on the street. He heard a carriage rattle past overhead, the sound echoing bizarrely underneath the old stones.

This time of year the water was low enough that the chain was several feet above the murky water. But under the middle of the bridge, a line was tied, straining off into the water.

Shironne had said something about a rope or line. That they'd tied the victim to keep him from getting dragged away.

Shivering now, Mikael made his way closer to the line. There were only a couple of feet of exposed mud under the bridge's footing, at a sharp incline. He slipped, and one foot slid in the river. Chilly water flooded into his boot.

Reaching down under the water, he found the line almost submerged in the muck. He worked a hand underneath it, feeling the tautness as the current dragged at the weighted end. He managed to haul the line above the water, but his feet slipped out from under him. He went down and swallowed a mouthful of river water when he gasped at the cold. He struggled back upright, coughing, using his grip on the rope to steady himself.

"What happened?" Dahar called from the river wall.

"I'm fine," Mikael yelled back. Dahar had to have sensed his momentary panic. He could swim, but he didn't want to in *this* water.

Dahar didn't seem appeased. He yanked on the old braided rope attached to Mikael's waist, taking up the slack. When Mikael got close enough, Dahar put out a hand and guided him out of the water, and then together they began to haul back the river's prize. The line stretched into the water, its burden visible even before they pulled the dead man out.

Mikael glanced up at Cerradine, who watched with anguish plain in his face. "Stay up there, sir. We don't need to risk you."

He hauled on the line and pulled the body onto the narrow strip of exposed bank; then he turned the body onto his back.

Mikael stared into the dark eyes of David Aldassa. He suddenly felt sick to his stomach, the death becoming all too real to him.

"Stop that," Dahar protested sharply.

"I'm sorry, sir," Mikael said, swallowing bile. He calmed himself, trying to get his stomach under control. The faint smell of sewage coming off the river didn't help.

He untied the braided rope from around his own waist and wrapped it under Aldassa's limp arms. Dahar and Cerradine used the braided rope to haul the body up next to the embankment, and then dropped it down again to aid Mikael in climbing up as well.

Shivering, he sat down next to Aldassa's body and dropped his head into his filthy hands. His slip had soaked him completely. He could hear Dahar moving about; someone wrapped a blanket around his shoulders. Cerradine silently wrapped Aldassa's body in a second blanket as Mikael stared into the dark rush of the river.

His nose had started running and he smelled and none of that mattered.

• • •

The Family uniform felt strange, the trousers different from the ones Shironne normally wore under her petticoats, closer fitting. Despite that, the lack of petticoats made her legs feel strangely bare and exposed. She recalled enough about Family uniforms to know they were similar to army uniforms, so Cerradine's workers wore this sort of clothing every day. *I can get used to this too.*

Deborah had left her alone for a time to speak with the innkeeper, bidding her to try to get some sleep. That gave Shironne time to turn her mind to her other problem instead.

For some time, she'd expected that once Perrin was safely married off, she would go to work for the army, much as she did now. Only *officially*, with a uniform and perhaps her own place in one of the buildings that rented rooms to army personnel. But if she was supposed to help Mikael Lee, that meant being near wherever he was. This arrangement at the tavern wasn't practical. It would be so much simpler if she lived nearer him. Like in the palace itself.

Or if he lived out in the city. Had Mikael ever contemplated leaving the fortress, going to work for the army instead, perhaps? She quickly dismissed the idea. He was too Family. He didn't even want to inherit his grandfather's position because it would mean giving up being Family.

And then she understood that he actually *was* in line to inherit his grandfather's position—the Master of Lee Province, much like a king, but on a provincial level instead. Mikael dreaded that fate with all his heart. Because it would take him away from everything he loved and make him an Anvarrid, and he was relieved that his grandfather wouldn't accept him because he simply looked too Lee, too much like his mother, who'd merely been a guard and had only been half-married to Mikael's father anyway.

And when Shironne reflected that she didn't know how someone could be *half*-married, the knowledge came to her that there was some manner of contract, and it had been legally binding only on his Lee mother, but not on his Anvarrid father.

How do I know that?

Mikael Lee was still *there*, at the edge of her thoughts. That was how she could pull those details from his mind.

She'd woken from his dream with her bare hand on his vest, wool old enough to bear traces of oil from his hands, residue from cleaning, and a touch of lemon, his heart calming under her touch. He'd drifted back to wakefulness more slowly, not noticing when Deborah helped her back onto the chair again.

Most people she could shut out as long as their emotions were mild. Even when stronger emotions came into play, she could usually force them away. Mikael seemed to be the exception. Her sense of his presence now occupied a small corner even when quiet, like a sleeping dog.

How long had it been that way, and she'd simply not noticed? Since she'd realized he was *in* the dreams, a presence that the victims could feel, watching over them to deal out justice later? How long had she been gleaning bits and pieces of memories from his mind?

We've found Aldassa. The sleeping dog suddenly bayed, thundering through her mind. *We're taking his body to the headquarters. We'll come back for you.*

Shironne felt her eyes sting with tears again. She'd known *that*, too . . . that he'd found David Aldassa's body, caught in the river's current but still tied to the footings of the Lower Town Bridge, just as she'd seen in his dream.

She hadn't wanted to know. She didn't want to, even now. Even though she'd known exactly why they'd gone down to the river's edge.

She wished she could shut him out, not share Mikael's vague sense of guilt, that feeling that he was responsible for David Aldassa's death, that he'd failed to figure out what the killer expected of him, and that he would be responsible for the next death as well if he couldn't figure out what he supposedly had tucked away in his mind, probably still in pieces, because that man believed he knew.

But it was hers too, that guilt.

. . .

Dahar's hand descended on Mikael's shoulder. "Come on. We need to get him out of here."

Mikael stood, his boots squishing. Dahar would want to get the body to the army's morgue as soon as possible, before people saw it and talk spread of another death. Dahar wouldn't want panic in the city.

Following Dahar's lead, he picked up one end of the wrapped body and lifted it up over the stone embankment. Synen's son came and helped, his face pasty but otherwise in control. Mikael climbed over the wall last, and they laid the body in the cart. This time Cerradine sat in the back with Mikael, one hand on Aldassa's body, while Dahar sat up front with Synen's son.

They drove in the direction of the army's headquarters, and Mikael held the blanket around him with one hand. They passed through the Lower Town's fetid streets, past the temple, and up toward the better parts of the city. Cerradine's eyes were fixed on Aldassa's body, making certain it didn't slide in the hay. When Mikael glanced back toward the river, he was the only one to see him.

In the pallid light of a streetlamp, Paal Endiren stood near the corner of the Black Street Temple, barely visible in the shadows.

Mikael pushed himself out of the back of the moving wagon and landed hard on one knee. Dahar yelled after him, but he waved Dahar off as he jumped to his feet and jogged back in that direction.

Endiren still stood at the far corner of the temple, arms wrapped about himself in the cold.

Then two men in brown tunics emerged from the shadows from behind Endiren. They grabbed him and started dragging him down the temple steps toward an approaching coach.

Mikael ran. He dashed through a hundred sets of chimes in the temple's white colonnade, setting them tinkling discordantly. When he reached the end of the colonnade, across the temple's wide steps, he saw that the men had reached the coach and were pushing Endiren into it. He barely fought them, as if he was simply too weak.

Mikael reached for his pistol, only to realize he didn't have any weapon with him, so he ran down the steps toward the coach. It began rolling again, the horses picking up speed as it headed deeper into the Lower Town. Mikael's wet boots slipped and he tumbled down the last few hard steps, rolled to his feet, and kept running.

But the coach was moving too quickly, its lead on him growing as the driver's whip cracked in the silence. Mikael followed as it turned a corner onto Fenless Street, but when he reached that corner, it was gone.

He stopped there, breathing hard. He pressed a hand against his stomach, suddenly nauseated by the exertion and frustration, making him break into a sweat. His breath steamed in the cold.

The colonel jogged up beside him. "What in Hel's name was that, Mikael?"

"That was them," he said without hesitation. "They had Paal Endiren."

The colonel cussed under his breath. "Where did they go?"

"They turned here, but by the time I got here, they were gone. There's no catching them now."

The colonel slapped a hand on Mikael's shoulder. "I'll get . . ."

Mikael knew how that sentence usually went. It was usually, *I'll get Aldassa to,* followed by whatever set of tasks needed to be done. Because Aldassa was Cerradine's right hand, or had been.

Face stiffly controlled, the colonel turned and headed back toward the temple.

CHAPTER THIRTY-FIVE

It wasn't dawn yet, but the army hospital was awake. Captain Kassannan greeted them at the hospital doors, his expression grim. Word had already flown through the square that they'd brought another body. Drained, Mikael just watched as two of the hospital's orderlies placed Aldassa's body on a stretcher under the hospital's lights.

Cerradine left the body in Kassannan's charge, going to break the news to Aldassa's wife instead. Apparently she'd been awake most of the night, terrified when her husband didn't return home after what should have been a simple errand, so she'd contacted Kassannan to see if he knew anything of her husband's whereabouts. Kassannan already wore white ribbons on his sleeve—he'd been prepared for the worst.

Once the body was out of the hay cart, Dahar headed back to the tavern with Synen's son. He intended to retrieve Shironne, claiming that since he was the girl's uncle, it would look better if she was in his company than in Mikael's. Mikael didn't argue. He had work to do here at the headquarters anyway.

"Why David?" Kassannan asked Mikael as they walked down the stairs to the morgue. "You dreamed it, didn't you?"

Mikael started at the question. "Yes. A message, we think. We don't know what it means, though. And Paal Endiren was involved. I saw him."

"In your dream?" Kassannan asked. "Or in real life?"

"Both."

Kassannan unlocked the door to the morgue and helped his orderlies open the elevator. Mikael sat on one of the chairs near the wall, staying out of the way as they carried the stretcher into the morgue and placed Aldassa's body on one of the tables.

Kassannan carefully removed Aldassa's boots and cut away his trousers. He'd known Aldassa far longer than Mikael had. They'd even fought on the same melee team, representing the army, when they were younger. This had to be almost as hard for Kassannan as it was for the colonel.

"I don't understand how Endiren could be involved in this," Kassannan finally said.

"I don't either. He was forcibly dragged back into their coach, so I don't think it was voluntary. He didn't look right." Mikael shifted uncomfortably, very aware of his still-damp trousers and vest. He should go back to the fortress and change, but he needed to go find whatever had provoked Aldassa's trek to the fortress to question Elisabet. That had to be important. Mikael was sure he would know it when he saw it.

The captain carefully surveyed the body, starting with the neck. Mikael already knew what he would find.

"You smell bad, Mikael," Kassannan commented.

"I went into the river."

"Swallow any water?"

"No. Yes, a bit."

"If it was Lower Town water, it'll probably kill you."

That was almost a joke, although the water had been foul. "How do you stay so calm?"

"This isn't David Aldassa, Mikael. David's gone. This . . . is evidence."

Mikael understood the idea, but he'd always had difficulty accepting it. "I can't help thinking it was my fault."

"Yours?" Kassannan didn't even look at him.

"I'm fairly sure the killer found out about him from me," Mikael admitted.

"Every person who's observed any part of the investigation will have seen David walking the banks of the river. He told me people crowded up on the river walk the other day." Kassannan took a damp towel and began wiping residue from the river off the body. "You're not responsible, Mikael."

"I should have figured it out. Supposedly, I have it all in my head." Mikael stood up and went closer, looking over Aldassa's still form. The captain had closed Aldassa's eyes. "What will happen to his family?"

Kassannan continued to work. "Liana will grieve. The girls will too. We'll take care of them."

"You make it sound simple."

"Simple? It is." Kassannan paused to look at him. "You cope, or you don't. I *know*, Mikael."

Kassannan had lost his own wife several months before. Mikael had known Hanna Kassannan, although not well. He'd dreamed her death too. "Of course, Aron."

"Truthfully it isn't that simple," Kassannan amended. "Every person deals with death differently."

Mikael stood over Aldassa's body with the now-familiar carvings running from shoulder to shoulder. This time, no matching ones marked his own shoulders. He didn't feel sick either. He felt *detached* from this death, despite the fact that Aldassa had been a friend. Mikael wondered if he'd lost something in the exchange. "Do you think the colonel would mind if I went through the files in Aldassa's desk?" he asked after a time.

"Not as long as you don't leave a stench behind." Kassannan crossed back over to the counter running along the walls and carefully extracted a piece of paper from the sliced remains of Aldassa's trousers. "I felt this when I cut these off. You might put it with the case papers."

Mikael opened the folded sheet of paper, trying not to tear the sodden page. The ink had smeared. He could make out very little, but he thought he saw the name Andersen. The paper itself looked familiar—one of the Andersen file pages, although from which specific file Mikael didn't know.

Sighing, he took one last glance at the body and left the morgue. He crossed the square to the administrative offices, breathing the chill morning air and feeling bone weary. A few soldiers greeted him solemnly, going on about their own errands. The chalkboard on which they tracked their betting on who might be the next possible victim had been wiped clean.

Mikael went and sat at Aldassa's desk. He closed his eyes, trying to draw on that bit of David Aldassa's psyche that needed remembering. What had David wanted him to know? There was something here he needed to see, something Aldassa *hadn't* shown Cerradine. Why?

Opening his eyes, Mikael surveyed the tidy desk. Aldassa kept things meticulously organized, every file where it should be, reminding Mikael of Kai's habits. Of course, if Kai wanted to hide something, he'd simply misfile it and then miraculously find it when needed later. Mikael wondered if Aldassa might not have done a similar thing.

Mikael hunted for the files that Kai had held on to, the bundle in which he'd hidden the list of the victims. He located them in the back of the box that they'd handed over to Cerradine only days ago. The only thing missing was the Andersens' spurious account of vigilantes tracking down the priests of Farunas.

He pulled out the drawer in Aldassa's desk where a neat alphabetical file held personnel records for different agents of the army's intelligence corps. He spotted a file folder of a different type from all the others, one of the folders the Daujom used. It was filed under A, for Andersen.

Mikael sat there and read as soldiers came and went in the hallway outside, and he realized the Andersens might not be liars after all.

CHAPTER THIRTY-SIX

Shironne felt what seemed like the thousandth thing this morning, trying to identify what the infirmarians put in their different salves. This tin held one made with beeswax, almond oil, comfrey, and rosemary—and about twelve other herbs and oils she didn't recognize. She could separate them from the others in her mind, only she'd never encountered them before and didn't know their names. It was soothing on her skin, fortunately, with no impurities in it.

It was Deborah's transparent attempt to keep her mind busy, Shironne knew. To keep her from thinking about Lieutenant Aldassa's death.

"Mr. Lee has reached the palace," she told Deborah when the elder approved her partial listing of the ingredients.

"How can you tell?" Deborah's voice sounded curious.

"He just wanted me to know, so we wouldn't worry." Once she'd wiped off her fingers on a damp cloth, Shironne tugged at the high neck of the jacket she wore, unaccustomed to having something so close around her throat.

"Ah," Deborah said. "How very polite. You can undo the top hooks, dear."

She did so. "I don't think he's in a mood for politeness."

Deborah took the tin of salve away and held out another for her to touch. Shironne carefully grasped the new tin. "Someone else handled this last."

"Yes, Jakob did. One of the engineers burned his arm, and Jakob used this."

Shironne touched a finger to its surface, finding a slick substance. "I don't know what that is, but it feels a bit like grease."

"It is a kind of grease, only purified."

Even purified, the texture still felt disgusting. "How . . . um, interesting."

"Clearly you think not, by your tone."

"I'm sorry ma'am. I'm distracted."

Mikael hadn't slept, she realized. Acknowledged, his thoughts tumbled past her, weariness making him incoherent. *He was well, although his throat ached, and he smelled, and they'd found Aldassa, and he felt like a traitor because he had to go looking for Elisabet now, and he'd seen Paal Endiren, which could only mean something bad and he wanted to sleep, and bathe, although the order should be the other way around because he would never go to his bed in all this filth.*

Shironne shook her head and forced Mikael's thoughts back into their corner of her mind. "They've taken the lieutenant's body back to the army hospital," she told the doctor. "I should go help Captain Kassannan."

"No, dear," the doctor said firmly. "Not until the colonel comes to take you home from the fortress himself. He's trusting us to keep you safe."

Shironne heaved a sigh. She was tired of everyone trying to protect her.

. . .

The plumbing in the palace mimicked that found by the Anvarrid when they'd first come across Below, but the water in Above was never reliably hot.

Mikael stood under the fall of lukewarm water, his forehead pressed against the chilly tiles. His throat felt sore. That wasn't from his dream, as it had been all the other times. He thought he had the beginnings of a cold. His side still ached from a bruise Eli had dealt him what seemed a century ago, he had a new bruise forming around the knee he'd bashed against the paving stones, and he had Kai to thank for the lingering soreness along his cheekbone and across the back of his skull. He wanted to sleep, but he had no time for it.

Pushing himself into action, Mikael scrubbed at his hands with a boar-bristle brush. He wanted to be certain he cleaned them well enough not to distress Shironne. This was, tradition said, the true reason behind the Family's fastidiousness. Touch-sensitives always knew how dirty things truly were.

He felt far better afterward, as he dressed in a clean uniform, arming himself as well. If the sentries inside the palace chose to be offended, he would deal with that later. He shoved his pistol into his sash and put a handful of spare cartridges in his jacket pocket. After slipping his knife into its sheath in the back of his sash, he belted on his sword, the first time he'd done so since coming back from Jannsen Province. Only then did he head downstairs for the infirmary, wanting to check in with Deborah before he hunted down Elisabet.

Deborah expected him, he discovered. She tossed him a horehound candy as he walked through the doors. He didn't have to ask how she knew his throat had begun to ache. Shironne sat on the edge of one of the infirmary beds, her feet not quite touching the floor. She wore a child's brown uniform, which served exactly the purpose Deborah intended—to remind him of her age.

At times, Shironne seemed so mature he forgot her status.

Her face turned toward him, and he knew she'd picked up that thought. She bit her lower lip but didn't say anything. Deborah must have lectured her about proper behavior for a child, or perhaps she merely reflected the doctor's somberness today.

"We found the body," he told Deborah.

She glanced up at him. She looked tired, his fault again. "Yes, I know. I'm sorry to hear it. Jon will be devastated. David's like a son to him."

Mikael nodded, feeling the guilt rise again. "He went to see Aldassa's wife already. He arrived back at his office before I left, but I didn't get a chance to speak with him."

"Dahar has gone down there to help out."

Mikael shot a look at Shironne, catching the edge of her frustration, that odd flash of emotion that he *knew* wasn't his. She wanted to be at the army headquarters too, he suspected. She placed a tin of unguent back on the cluttered table in front of her and wiped her hands on a towel, nodding as she did so.

"What did you need, Mikael?" Deborah asked. "Other than to tell me what I already knew?"

"I wanted to make certain you were all right," he said aiming that toward Shironne. "Also, I'm looking for Elisabet."

Deborah cocked her head but didn't ask him *why*. "Have you tried Kai's quarters upstairs? He's kept himself locked up for the better part of two days now."

Mikael had already tried there. He'd been very surprised to visit Kai's apartment in the king's household only to find Tova, not Elisabet, on guard duty. He couldn't ask Tova where to find Elisabet without doing so in front of Kai, so Mikael had left as quickly as he could. His appearance there had likely only served to alarm Kai. "I've already checked there. Elisabet assigned her Second to watch him today. Elisabet's not in her quarters either, ma'am."

Without answering, Deborah pointed past him. Mikael turned to see Elisabet striding through the doors of the infirmary. She stopped, and Mikael suddenly realized that Elisabet might not want to discuss her past in front of Deborah. "I need to talk with her," Mikael said. "If you'll excuse us, ma'am."

"Mikael," Deborah said softly, "don't make Kai's mistake."

Kai's mistake: trying to protect Elisabet when it wasn't needed. Elisabet was the closest thing Deborah had to a child of her own. She'd been under Deborah's care since she'd arrived at the fortress thirteen years ago. Mikael suspected Deborah knew Elisabet's secret, even if she'd never officially been *told*. As things were, he didn't think he had the right to feel betrayed.

For a brief moment, Shironne's bare fingers touched his hand. He thought apology at her, hoping that she'd not take his silence for unfriendliness. Then her fingers drew away from his, the brief moment of communion ended.

Mikael glanced guiltily at Deborah. "I need to go."

"Where?" Deborah asked, her eyes flicking in Elisabet's direction.

"I'm not sure, ma'am." Mikael turned and headed for the door, Elisabet preceding him.

In the somber gray hallway outside the infirmary, Elisabet turned an emotionless gaze on Mikael. "Kai has been trying to force me away from your investigation. I need to know what's happened."

Mikael hadn't expected her to say that. He didn't know why he'd expected some sort of denial, but then again, he'd underestimated Elisabet all along, hadn't he? "Perhaps if we went up to the office," he suggested, "we could—"

"The third place Kai will look, after my quarters and yours."

Mikael chose the mess hall instead. He located a quiet nook on the western end of the hall, shadowed from the main mess. He needed to talk to her without interference.

The scents of the impending lunch service surrounded them. His stomach started protesting its emptiness but Mikael ignored it. Their business was more important than his unpredictable belly. He sat down, hand on his sword's hilt to keep it out of his way. Across the small wooden table, Elisabet settled into a chair as silently she did everything. She wasn't wearing her overcoat, but she did wear full uniform, hinting that she expected to leave the fortress.

"I need to ask you some questions," Mikael said. When she nodded, he continued. "What did you do after they killed your family?"

"Lay on my back."

This was the curse of questioning people. Even if they didn't lie, they often withheld information, either to protect themselves or to protect someone else. This was where having an ability like Miss Anjir's would be terribly useful. He asked a clearer question. "Were you with your grandfather?"

"Yes."

Well, that told him how they had escaped the massacre. "Did the two of you pursue the killers?"

Her pale eyes stared down to the table. She didn't answer.

"Did your grandfather pursue the killers, Elisabet? Yes or no?"

"Yes," she said softly, her shoulders stiff.

"The Andersens claimed they found the bodies of nine of the priests scattered along the way to the border, shot. They followed the trail of two people who were in turn following the priests. Was that you and your grandfather?"

"Yes."

Mikael wished he could simply shake her until he got better answers out of her. "Did your grandfather shoot those men?"

A hint of fear showed in her eyes, something Mikael didn't think he'd ever seen. For a second he stared at her, trying to figure out what had prompted that fleeting expression and her outright evasion. "I've heard they killed David Aldassa," she said rather than answering.

She didn't want to blacken her grandfather's memory, he guessed. He would have to work back around to that question again to get a straight answer out of her. "Yes, last night," he said. "He intended to come talk to you. You were his First, so I suspect he felt he owed it to you to warn you before he went to the colonel with these same questions."

A yeargroup of children filed into the mess, preparing to start a lesson there. Mikael remained silent until the children and their sponsors passed to the far side of the hall. Elisabet's eyes met his.

"Aldassa suspected your grandfather killed those nine men," he said, "and that one or more of the surviving priests are here now, hunting you in some form of retribution."

Her brow furrowed. She stared at the table between them. Her hands clenched together, knuckles showing white.

"Paal Endiren was close to you when he lived in the fortress. I suspect he knew you well enough for you to have told him what happened. When he disappeared over the border into Pedrossa, somehow this priest got hold of him and found out you'd survived."

He was saying *I suspect* a great deal, which he didn't like at all.

"Paal knew," she acknowledged.

"How your family died?"

"Yes."

"And that your grandfather killed those men?"

"My grandfather's eyes were weak, Mr. Lee," she said, a touch of exasperation in her words. She looked at him then, her hard eyes bleak.

Mikael's hands went cold. *Surely Deborah doesn't know.*

"You were only eleven years old," he protested, thinking even as he said it that if he'd known who killed his father, he might have hunted them down himself. He'd been thirteen at the time.

She can never say it aloud.

It would amount to a confession, and he would be required to turn her over to Dahar. Now he understood why she never allowed Kai near her. Kai's political career wouldn't survive the stain of association with her, a vigilante who'd killed nine men. The senate—led by Lord Hedraya—would use her past as a reason to reject Kai as the king's heir. It didn't matter that she'd probably saved innocent lives, that her family was killed, or that she'd been a child. They would portray her as a cold-blooded murderer. She would likely be acquitted if tried, or the case even dismissed out of hand, but that wouldn't protect Kai. And someone *would* put the details together. Clearly, Aldassa had come close.

Mikael heard whistling, his agitation upsetting someone across the mess hall. Mikael counted to himself, trying to stop his anxiety from clouding the ambient.

He suddenly understood Elisabet far better. He suspected that, like the worst of his dreams that he tried to bury in the back of his mind, she kept the memories of that time closely locked away, hidden even from herself—a way to stay sane.

"I saw Paal Endiren this morning," Mikael told her. "I'm going to find him and bring him back here."

"Let me get my rifle."

He considered protesting, but Elisabet, of all people, *should* be involved in this now. He wasn't going to make Kai's mistake.

CHAPTER THIRTY-SEVEN

Mikael hadn't expected the conversation to turn quite the way it had. He'd thought he had it all figured out. Mikael fingered the butt of his pistol, trying to worry out all the changes this made in his world, and realized that, in the end, it made no difference at all. She was still the same Elisabet he'd known for years now.

She returned a few minutes later in full arms, her long, old-fashioned rifle in hand. Mikael wondered if it was the same rifle she'd had as a young girl.

"Where?" she asked.

"The old Larossan temple in the Lower Town, on Black Street. They picked him up there, and someone had to have seen where they went."

They ended up walking down into the city and taking a cab. Since Kai was the king's heir, a driver from the fortress would probably spill where they went should Kai ask. The last thing Mikael wanted was Kai pursuing them down into the city.

Elisabet didn't speak on the journey. One foot braced on the bench opposite her, she performed a meticulous check of her rifle. She cleaned the barrels and then counted her ammunition. Cold seeped into the silent cab as Mikael checked his pistol and settled his knife in his sash.

The cab stopped in the street outside the temple. Mikael stepped down, hand on his pistol, clearing the doorway for Elisabet. She jumped to the cobbles as Mikael tossed up a Family credit marker. The driver palmed it and shook the reins to get the horses moving.

It was late morning, and people rushed by on the street, some stepping back when they noticed two people in Lucas Family uniforms. The traffic in the street continued to flow, though, the attention they drew a fleeting thing. They edged their way to the side of the street, pausing to wait for a street cleaner's wagon full of the previous day's manure to pass.

This part of the city predated the Anvarrid invasion, many of the granite buildings more than two centuries old. The streets were filthy, this particular road favored by teamsters because it was one of the wider ones in this section of town.

Mikael glanced up at the temple, as always experiencing a feeling that the tall edifice loomed over him, intent on pouncing. In daylight, the Black Street Temple showed its age. It wasn't like the newer temples, built to mimic the palace's wide archways and onion domes. This was more of a vault of barrel arches—pre-Anvarrid architecture. A wide stone band around the base of the temple buttressed the arches but could use some repair, particularly at the corner nearest the street. The low colonnade through which Mikael had run earlier was now inhabited by priests in their simple red tunics and black trousers, ready to lay their blessing on those myriad chimes and sell them to anyone seeking the peace they were supposed to engender.

Mikael walked up the granite steps, Elisabet behind him. "He was standing right over here."

Elisabet came up next to him, watching his back, her eyes still focused on the activity on the street. "What was he doing?"

"I don't know. Maybe he got away from them. They had to drag him back." He peered around that corner of the temple toward the river.

"Paal!" Elisabet bolted down the steps and directly into the traffic on the street, darting between two wagons and disappearing from his view.

Mikael ran after her, hoping he'd not be hit. Horses balked, people yelled, and the traffic halted abruptly in her wake. Mikael made his way through the stopped vehicles. Elisabet stood in front of a wagon carting barrels. She gestured for the teamster to back the horses away and crouched down. Mikael knew even before he got there what he'd see.

Paal Endiren lay on the cobbles before the wagon team. Tortured breath rattled through his mouth, a gurgling sound that Mikael recognized. He'd heard it in his dreams before—the sound his father had made as his lungs filled with his own blood.

The dark-haired young man lying on the ground looked half-starved and far older than twenty-five, like he'd used up all his days at once. His brown skin had a faint bluish tinge, and he wore a jacket turned inside out to hide its gray color—a dead police officer's coat. Elisabet crouched next to Paal and gently touched his face. Mikael watched as Paal's mouth moved, but no sound came forth. A froth of blood and air stained his lips.

The teamster pulled his team farther back, and Elisabet sat down on the filthy cobbles next to Paal, holding his hand. Mikael stood over them, one hand on the hilt of his sword and his eyes on the growing crowd. He knew what Elisabet waited for. It wouldn't take long.

After only a couple of minutes, she pulled her hand from Paal's slack fingers and glanced up at Mikael. He knelt down, placed his hands under Paal's shoulders, and lifted. A wet, sucking sound came from the body, making Mikael's stomach heave. Elisabet helped him carry Paal to the steps of the temple.

The driver followed, his hands quivering. "I didn't see him. He jumped out right in front of my wagon," he insisted.

"Pushed," Elisabet said with a single shake of her head.

She'd been watching the street, Mikael knew. He spent a few

minutes reassuring the rattled teamster and finally sent the man on his way. Two police officers in gray jackets showed up a moment later and began objecting to their interference.

"He's Family," Elisabet told them and turned away, her face pale.

The officers continued to argue until Mikael finally persuaded them to arrange for Paal's body to be taken up to the fortress. When all was done, Mikael climbed the steps of the temple to join Elisabet, the noon hour past.

"What did he try to tell you?" Mikael asked.

"He said he was sorry." She paused, frowning. "So where do we go from here, Mr. Lee?"

"I don't know. Did you see someone push Paal?"

"It looked as if Paal fell, but I saw a man standing next to him, watching me."

"What did he look like?"

"Larossan, gray at the temples, fit, forty to fifty, about your height." She glanced at him and added, "Perhaps taller."

That answered Shironne's description of the priest. "Did you recognize him?"

Elisabet pursed her lips, her eyes unseeing. "I don't . . . remember much from those days."

He could hardly blame her for that. "I suppose we start hunting, then."

. . .

Cerradine had hoped a note would be enough. He should have known better. Still draped all in white, Savelle Anjir walked down the hallway and directly into his office, not even waiting to be announced.

She pulled off her white scarf and twisted it in her hands. "Where is she?"

Cerradine heard panic in her voice. He strode past her and closed the door. Dahar had gone to the hospital to talk with Kassannan again, so they were alone in his office. He put his hands on her shoulders to reassure her, but she jerked away from him. "She's safe, Savelle. Did you not get the note I sent?"

"Messine told me she was with your foster sister. Where? Where has she been all this time?"

He directed her to one of the chairs and leaned against the desk. "I'd trust Deborah with my life. Shironne is with her, up at the fortress."

"It's one thing for her to defy Verinne to help for a few hours, Colonel, but she's been gone all night. No investigation is worth compromising her reputation that way."

Anger flashed through him. She glanced up at him and he realized she'd felt it. He tamped it down. She couldn't know. "They killed David Aldassa last night, Savelle." He managed to say it without his voice breaking.

Her eyes closed, and she covered her face with her hands. She dealt with David every time she visited this office. "I'm so sorry, Jon."

How many times had he heard condolences already today? "His wife is expecting another child," he said, not sure why he told her. "They'd decided that if it was a boy they'd name him for me. David wanted me to have dinner at their house so they could tell me, but I was too busy."

His throat hurt. He closed his eyes, trying to will away the weakness. He felt her hand brush his cheek, and then her arms came around him. He buried his face in her neck, holding her to him. Bitter tears stung his eyes.

Cerradine controlled himself after a moment, regretting that he'd forced his emotions on her. He drew back, and the hand with which she'd cradled his head stroked along his jaw. He stopped it with his own hand and pressed a kiss into her palm, grateful for her sympathy.

She stilled in his light grasp, her dark eyes wide, sparkling with unshed tears.

He released her hand and ran one finger along her brow, the dark arch like a seagull's wing. Her freed hand wrapped around his neck, pulling him closer, and he kissed her. He knew he shouldn't, but he'd wanted to for so long. She held him tighter, caught up in his desire. He kissed her fervently, months of frustration fueling his ardor.

Only after some time did she protest, a faint attempt to push him away. "No, Jon."

Her halfhearted resistance could be overcome easily. She was a sensitive. His emotions could override hers, making her want him as much as he did her.

And realizing what he'd just thought, he let her go.

She brushed nervous hands down the front of her white tunic. He'd managed to loosen her hair from its chignon. It fell over her shoulder, a thick, straight fall of dark brown silk in which he wanted to bury his hands.

She moved away as if sensing his weakening self-control. "I'm still in mourning, Jon."

"He wasn't worth this sacrifice on your part." His breath came a little fast. He didn't expect her to answer.

"It's my choice, Jon." She touched the white ribbon wrapped about his sleeve. "I didn't realize you'd lost one of your men," she said, "but I feared for Shironne's safety."

"We would never have allowed her to be hurt," he said.

"A mother's fears aren't always rational. Verinne fell into spasms when she discovered Shironne missing. I had to leave Melanna and Perrin under Kirya's charge to come here."

He'd forgotten all of *her* problems in the interim. "Was your journey successful?"

She nodded. "My uncle and I reached an agreement about my father's estate. He will pay my household expenses until I no longer need the income, and then I will turn the property over to him."

That was an interesting compromise. It would provide for her and the girls, and she wouldn't have to pay taxes incurred on a property sale. "Very clever."

"Thank you," she said. "He's counting on my remarrying quickly, I'm afraid . . ."

He suspected his mouth was hanging open. "*How* quickly? Because . . ."

The office door opened and they both started. *The worst timing in the world,* Cerradine thought as Dahar stepped through the doorway. He and Savelle gazed at each other, both looking uncertain.

Resigned, Cerradine made the long-overdue introduction. "Dahar, I don't believe you've formally met Madam Anjir. Savelle, this is Dahar."

Seen together, one couldn't help but notice the resemblance between them, mostly around the eyes. Dahar smiled at her. "I've always wanted to meet you, you know, only I didn't know if you wanted the association."

Savelle flushed when Dahar took her hands. He'd forgotten that she was raised Larossan and didn't usually touch men outside her family. Then again, he was her brother. "It was a terrible scandal, my lord," she managed.

"A minor scandal at best, Savelle," Dahar said. "Our father was well-known for his wandering eye. You weren't the only such child. It's not as shocking as you think."

She shook her head, faint traces of tears making her dark eyes shine. "You haven't lived with the rumors, my lord."

"Please, call me Dahar. I grew up in the same yeargroup with one of my half brothers," he said then, surprising Cerradine. Dahar rarely spoke of the unlamented Stephan. The child of one of the king's quarterguards, Stephan had been a thorn in Dahar's side throughout their youth. "I do know what it's like, a bit. Besides, it was thirty-odd years ago. If someone casts that far back for dinner conversation, they must be very bored. Khader and I would both enjoy having you and your daughters visit us. Please, give us a chance to know you."

"A good idea, Dahar," Cerradine interrupted. "You could take her and the girls up to the palace now. No one need know Shironne wasn't with them the whole time."

Dahar agreed, willing to fall in with the plan. Cerradine thought it would answer for now, at least under mild scrutiny. "It will keep anyone from asking where she was, Savelle."

Savelle glanced back to him, brow furrowed. He'd asked her to go against her life's training. She lifted her chin then, meeting Dahar's eyes squarely. "I would be grateful for your help, my—Dahar."

Dahar grinned. "You did that very well, Savelle."

She flushed and looked down again. Her dark hair fell across her face like a curtain. "My hairpin appears to have slipped out," she murmured.

Cerradine spotted the long ivory pin on the floor near his desk and handed it to her. "If you recall . . ."

"I remember where it is," she said. "If you'll excuse me . . . um, Dahar, I need to replace this." She slipped out of Cerradine's office, leaving him facing an annoyed Dahar.

As soon as the door shut behind her, Dahar turned and gave him an irritated glance. "What was going on in here?"

Dahar would have sensed the emotions in the room the moment he entered. Cerradine knew he hadn't been controlling himself well at that moment. "There is nothing going on . . ."

"Hairpin," Dahar said succinctly.

Cerradine raked a hand through his hair. Of all the times for Dahar to get prickly about something that wasn't his business. "Take her back to her house. Pick up the two girls. It will give you the chance to get to know her."

"I have things to do today other than socialize, Jon," Dahar said testily.

"This chance isn't likely to come again, Dahar. Under that soft-spoken façade, she's as stubborn as a mule. Convince her that the scandal of being associated with your House won't kill her."

After brief consideration, Dahar agreed.

A soft knock sounded at the door. Dahar opened it and allowed Savelle back in. With her hair repinned and her tears wiped away, she looked elegant and serene.

"Amdiria will adore you," Dahar said warmly. He took her slender hand and placed it on his arm. "Now, shall we go pick up your girls? On the way you can tell me all about them."

Savelle smiled hesitantly at him, and Cerradine found himself hoping that the two of them would find some common ground.

CHAPTER THIRTY-EIGHT

Mikael settled on the spot he'd been standing in when the priest touched him. Their questioning of citizens near the temple hadn't borne any fruit, and this hotel on the corner of Strait and Cadij streets was the one location he had in common with the killer. If Elisabet could spot the man, they might have a chance to stop him before he killed someone else. Then again, they could wait here for days and see nothing.

But if the priest was searching for Elisabet, eventually he would come to them.

They were on the edge of the Seychas District where the architecture wasn't as old. The hotel had a decorative turret on each corner topped by a small dome, but the majority of the roof was sensibly sloped rather than flat, allowing snow to slide off in winter. The only flat space on the roof was a narrow walkway across the front. Elisabet leaned against the stone rail there, calmly observing the street four stories below as if she could watch forever, showing the patience of a hunter. "Stop moving, Mr. Lee," she told him at one point. "You're distracting my eyes."

Forced to settle in one place, Mikael waited in silence until the inaction began to prey on his nerves. "Did you learn to shoot to hunt?" he asked, distracting her ears instead.

"Yes."

"What did you hunt?" The only thing he'd ever hunted was other men. He'd never had cause to shoot an animal.

"Wild dog, Mr. Lee."

"To eat?" That sounded wretched.

"We had sheep. A pack of dogs can kill off a flock in a week. One of us always guarded the sheep."

Probably where they'd been when the priests descended on her family's home, like wild dogs themselves. "Ah, I didn't think dog would taste very good anyway."

"It tastes like dog, Mr. Lee."

He was too much of a city boy to know if that was a joke or not. Perhaps on a farm, he reasoned, one wouldn't want to waste food. "I'd rather not try it."

She shrugged, her eyes fixed on the street.

He scuffed one foot in the gravel atop the roof. "What happened to your grandfather? Did he return to the Family with you?"

"They shot him before . . . ," she began. "I buried him."

"And you came to Lucas Province on your own? And convinced the elders to take you in?"

"He said to do that when we were done. I didn't know what else to do."

Mikael took off his sword belt and laid that to one side. He probably wouldn't have known what to do either. "Does Kai know?"

"Kai's very intelligent, Mr. Lee," she answered, her eyes not moving. "He's put information together. He suspects."

Mikael understood the distinction. They both might suspect that Elisabet had killed nine men, but they didn't actually *know* it. "That's why he tried to keep you away from the investigation."

"Once he knew this was related to the massacres, yes."

Mikael rolled that around in his head. Kai *could* have put together the information from the facts that he knew. It would require several inferences, but Kai had been sitting in his quarters with nothing more to do than think. Someone in the twenty-fours had, no doubt, been feeding him news and rumor. What else had Kai figured out? Mikael wondered. He asked Elisabet, who gave a short laugh.

"He doesn't talk to me anymore, Mr. Lee."

"To whom does he talk?"

"No one, now. He has no one he trusts."

Which sounds about right, Mikael thought sadly. "Why not?"

"He doesn't know who he is any longer. He's heard rumors."

"Rumors?" Those would be the same rumors Jannika had mentioned, he had no doubt.

"About his parents. He's not been the same since. I don't know what to do about it. I can't erase them." She tensed, watching the street below. She half raised the rifle and then lowered it again, resuming her resting stance. "I wish I could. There are too many secrets."

They lapsed into silence again. He joined her in watching the street, knowing his observations served no purpose. *Shironne* had seen the priest's face. *Elisabet* had. He had only vague impressions and a description to work with.

No, he *had* seen the priest in his dream. Shironne couldn't have seen him otherwise. But his memory of the priest was buried and he could only hope he recognized the man when he saw him in daylight.

"He'll be better off once I'm gone," Elisabet said, surprising him. "Tova will be good for him. She's amusing."

Gone. She didn't mean she was leaving, he realized. "After this . . ."

Her eyes not leaving the street, she shook her head. "I've escaped my fate for too long. There will be nothing after. Not for me."

Mikael didn't respond, shocked by her calm assumption that she would die.

• • •

The corpse had a terrible feel about it, even before Shironne touched it. It smelled of blood and filth. Chemicals permeated the skin, ones she didn't recognize, along with a bizarre tang of silver. She shuddered and reminded herself it was only a body. She felt Deborah's hand under her elbow, reassuring her. Her revulsion must have shown on her face.

Her mother and sisters *were* visiting the palace—Above—an introduction to the king's consort, Lady Amdiria. Shironne had joined them when they arrived, but the opulence of the king's household was wasted on her. She couldn't see the imported rugs or brocaded chairs or the consort's intricately embroidered robes. And while the lady herself seemed very likable, Shironne had been uncomfortable the whole while.

Sitting about in a fine room was no more useful than identifying unguents in the infirmary. The feeling that she needed to be doing something had prickled along her spine, from the moment Deborah escorted her to her mother's side, throughout what seemed like an interminable meal where Perrin spoke incessantly, and up to the moment Shironne begged her mother to let her go back to the infirmary. A runner—an impatient young man named Eli—had escorted her back down to Below again. She'd arrived there just before Deborah learned that a second body had been brought to the fortress.

Paal Endiren. Mikael had watched him die. Not in a dream, but on the street in the Lower Town.

Shironne stood now in one of the cold rooms, the same place where Iselin Lucas had lain. She and Deborah were alone, although the doctor's young runner waited outside in the hallway, presumably to carry Deborah's pronouncements back up to the palace.

Shironne reached out a hand, touching clothing worn for many days. Sweat, dirt, and a clinging sense of horse pervaded the fabric. There were traces of skin, dirty water, urine, and bits of food gone rancid. She fumbled for a clean cloth, finally locating one in the jacket of her unfamiliar clothes. She wiped at her fingers, unable to keep the expression of disgust from her face. "Where is his hand?"

Deborah took Shironne's bare hand in her own, her concern and curiosity winging around Shironne's mind, distracting her from the feel of filthy clothing. Deborah's hand lay atop hers on the man's, the doctor's living thoughts drowning out any impressions she received from the body.

This performance *fascinated* her, Shironne realized. "I need you to take away your hand, ma'am."

Deborah's hand lifted, carrying away with it the strength of her curiosity.

Shironne shivered, pulled instead into the fleeting remains of the dead man's memories, still potent. They'd had little time to fade or freeze. "He wanted to die. He's wanted to die for a long time now, but they wouldn't let him. He wanted it to be over."

That remained foremost among the memories in the decaying mind, repeated so many times that the leaves in the piles all seemed to tell her the same thing.

She pulled herself away from the memories and simply felt the flesh with its sickening chemical saturation. It had run rampant through the body, seeping into all the tissues, evident even in the man's sweat. Whatever it might be, it had made him a slave to them.

She moved her hand back to the filthy tunic, feeling past the clothes into the broken chest, searching for more information. He'd drowned in his own blood, a swift suffocation. Broken bows of ribs on the right side of the body arced into the lungs. She could sense far away in his abdomen the shattered pelvis and torn innards that would have brought a slower death had he survived the other. He couldn't have survived both injuries. Even if he weren't injured, his blood seemed all wrong, as if there were many poisons in him already. She told Deborah what she thought, and the doctor agreed.

"He's very thin," Deborah said regretfully.

His skin had a dry, papery feel to it. He was dying an old man's death at only twenty-five. "What could have done this to him?"

"He appears to have been addicted to a drug called blue sky."

"How can you tell?" Shironne asked.

"There's a bluish tinge to his skin, a pervasive one. Even touches his corneas."

"It turned him blue?"

Deborah seemed sad. "Only a faint hint of blue. I've seen this before in the City Hospital. I can only speculate as to whether he made this choice himself."

Shironne puzzled over that. "You think they drugged him to keep him under control?"

"It's possible. Paal rarely came to the infirmary when growing up, but I have difficulty imagining him as one who would turn to drugs. Then again, I didn't know him well."

Shironne laid her hand on his and concentrated on sifting through the memories left behind. Most she found were blurred memories of captivity. All the while, he'd been aware of what happened to him, locked inside his own mind, unable to escape.

He'd wanted to die, if only to escape the endless guilt. He'd wanted not to lead them where they wished to go. He'd wanted to apologize to Elisabet for betraying her, for falling into the wrong hands, and he wanted never to have met the man who stole everything, every confidence, every secret he'd ever held. Shironne feathered through the leaves of memory, finding Paal's regrets everywhere.

She worked them, reshaping his memories in her own head until they made sense. "He was captured," she told Deborah. "I think *they* did this to him, the drug, but I'm not certain. They captured him, and the man—the one who touched Mr. Lee, the one from the dream—stole his memories. Paal thought he'd betrayed Elisabet."

Deborah said nothing, her mind whirling in escalating worry.

Shironne lifted her hand from the body. "They brought him here to see her."

"Paal never tried to contact anyone at the fortress," Deborah said, her voice strained. "Elisabet would have told me."

"That's not what I meant. The priest didn't know what she looks like. He'd seen her, sort of, in Paal's mind, but that's not the same as actually seeing someone. The impressions we have in our minds are often . . . warped. Besides, all Family look alike to some people. Same uniform, same hair. So they were keeping Paal around to point her out, to verify her identity."

The chill in Deborah's mind mimicked the temperature in the room. "I need to talk to Dahar. Dear, if my runner takes you back up to the infirmary, can you wait for me there?"

Shironne agreed, thinking that Deborah would place her only in safe hands. Deborah led her to the door of the cold room, where a second man waited with the runner to prepare the body for burial, a calm and anonymous presence.

While Shironne rubbed at her hands with a warm, damp towel, Deborah instructed the runner. She hurried away afterward, able to move faster without a blind girl in tow. Shironne pulled on her gloves under the runner's curious gaze, wondering what he would make of her.

"What would be the best way to do this, miss?"

He had a pleasant voice and seemed quite tall. Taller than Mikael, certainly. Maybe as tall as the colonel. "Perhaps I could put my hand on your arm," she suggested.

He lifted her left hand, set it on his sleeve, and carefully led her down the hallway in the opposite direction from which they'd come. Judging from the arm under her fingers, she added *muscular* to her mental description, making him a very large young man, fitting with what she considered the stereotype of Family. He thought very little at her beyond mild curiosity, his mind carefully trained. He paused. "How do we negotiate the stairs, miss?"

"How far away is the first step?"

"About two feet."

Shironne instinctively grabbed for her petticoats to lift them and remembered then that she didn't have any. Flustered at her mistake, she started up, one hand against the wall, the runner following behind her. His mind laughed at her, though not in a malicious fashion. She felt the railing end and stepped out onto the first landing, then followed that around to the next stair.

She talked with him, stopping only twice to catch her breath as they made their slow progress up the stairs. In a day or two, she would be sore. Once they hit Five Down, there were more people going up and down, so Shironne stayed near the wall, trying to keep out of the way of faster-moving feet. The sound echoing in the well gave her an idea of the stair's shape, making it easier for her to negotiate the steps.

By the time they reached One Down, she knew Gabriel the runner far better. Like her, he was a sensitive. Eli, the runner she'd met upstairs, was his cousin. Gabriel was a runner downstairs, in Below, because sensitives weren't permitted to serve duty outside the fortress. For their own protection, of course. The next year, when he was a seventeen, he would begin his three years of required service as a sentry. That was when he would first be allowed to serve aboveground. And after those three years he could decide what he wanted to do with his life, whether to continue to serve as a sentry, or to take a different position within the Lucas Family. Shironne couldn't imagine spending most of her life down here, but Gabriel seemed to think it perfectly natural.

They eventually reached the infirmary, easily identifiable to her now by the smells alone. She located one of the bunks and settled there, resigned to waiting again. She sighed.

"You become accustomed to it," Gabriel said.

"To what?" she asked.

"The endless waiting to be treated like an adult."

"You don't find it annoying?"

He sighed. "It's the way it is. The rules are there to protect us, even if we chafe at them. I just try to keep that in mind."

His acceptance of the label of *child,* as if he couldn't imagine it being any other way, fascinated her. Shironne opened her mouth to say that but heard voices in the hallway outside the infirmary and whistling from a sentry. She knew now what that meant. Someone had let their emotions slip out of control. The sentries whistled to protest such lapses.

She felt Kai approaching then, the thunder of his worry making her teeth hurt. He wasn't as loud as Mikael, but his sullen nature made him harder for her to bear. She rose and backed away until she hit a table or shelf. She stood there, pinned against it by Kai's anxiety.

"Where's Deborah?"

He spoke to Gabriel, she realized. Could Kai even see her? She could be standing behind a partition or screen and not even know it.

"She's not here, Master Kai. I don't know where she's gone." Gabriel's voice sounded even. "Please calm yourself, sir."

It was the rule down here. *Stay calm, or risk upsetting everyone around you.*

Kai's frustration didn't diminish. Shironne stood motionless, hoping not to attract his attention, but his focus switched to her anyway. The force of it frightened her, as if he stood next to her and grasped her by the arms. She heard him approaching and shrank back.

"Where did Deborah go?" he asked.

"She went to find Dahar."

"Why?"

"I'm not sure."

Kai grabbed her arm, the heat of his hand seeping through the fabric of her sleeve. He didn't hold her tightly enough to bruise, but she wasn't going to get away from him. "I heard that David Aldassa is dead, and now Paal. Is that true?"

Kai wasn't angry with her. He reserved all that anger for himself. Shironne nodded jerkily.

"Please," he said, voice lowering, "just tell me where she's gone."

Elisabet. He was afraid for Elisabet's life. "No one told me," Shironne protested.

A feather of frustration broke through his fear. For a second Shironne thought he was going to start shaking her. As if recognizing that impulse, he abruptly let her go, embarrassment flashing across his mind.

"I need you to help me," he said in a calmer voice. "The sentries told me she left with Mikael. I need you to find them."

"How can I find them? I don't know where they went, Mr. Lucas."

Kai stepped away, giving her breathing space again. "I know what you are," he said. "I *know* you can find him."

CHAPTER THIRTY-NINE

Kai's certainty surprised Shironne. How did he know she could find Mikael? She hadn't told anyone that. And she wasn't even sure she could, not from so far away. She put her hands to her head, concentrating. At the edge of her awareness, she sensed him, far away and to her left. She tried to orient herself but had no grasp of direction in this vast underground building.

"I think he's that way, Kai, but I don't know how far." She pointed, feeling foolish.

He said nothing about her use of his name. "Would it be easier if you were outside the fortress?"

Easier than what? "I suppose so."

"Then come with me." His hand grasped her wrist over her jacket sleeve.

"No, I can't," she protested, and then recalled her earlier frustration. If she was out there, could she help find the killers? She wasn't sure whether Kai, in his current fury, would be helpful or not. But she might be.

"You can't just take her, Master Kai," Gabriel added his objection. "She's to wait for Elder Deborah, sir."

"I'm her cousin. She'll be safe with me." He hauled Shironne toward the door of the infirmary.

"You shouldn't do this, Kai," a woman's voice said then.

Shironne had been so caught up in the whirlwind of her cousin's emotions that she'd not even noticed Kai had a companion. She could hear the unfamiliar woman walking behind them now that she focused on it. She hoped the woman would temper Kai's recklessness.

"I didn't ask your opinion, Tova," Kai said rudely.

So much for that hope, Shironne thought. Tova had to be standing in for the missing Elisabet, Kai's shadow now.

Kai dragged her through the halls far more quickly than the runner had only a few minutes before. He hurried her up the stairs and through doorways until Shironne felt a touch of wind, surface air. The breeze caressed her face, warm enough now that it was afternoon. She had flagstone under her feet, so they were behind the palace. She could sense Mikael thinking, puzzling at something.

"He's in that direction," she said, pointing without any orientation at all. She had no idea where they'd stopped, which made her uncomfortable. If Kai abandoned her, she'd be lost.

Kai called out to someone, requesting that they bring around a coach. He pulled Shironne along with him, clearly intending to keep her with him until he actually found Elisabet. Shironne stumbled, only to be caught by the worried Tova. A coach approached, the team harnessed in record time, or else the palace kept them standing by. Kai paced while Tova apparently inspected the coach, and then he lifted Shironne up into it like a rag doll. He climbed up and sat down next to her. Tova entered last, closing the door carefully behind her, exuding a hint of panic.

"Who are you?" Tova asked her after a moment of silence in which the coach began to roll out of the courtyard.

Shironne almost answered before Kai's hand descended on her arm to prevent her.

"Don't ask, Tova. What are they doing?" he asked Shironne instead, ignoring his guard.

"I don't know. Mr. Lee is thinking hard, but I can't tell what about."

That answer appeared to be acceptable. "How much has he figured out?"

"I can't know what he knows," Shironne protested. *That isn't true, though, is it?*

"Yes, you can." His voice reflected no doubt. "Anything that's in *his* head, *you* know. The more you're around him the faster the barrier will fail. Damn, I should have figured it out as soon as I recognized you."

Recognized her? They hit a bump in the road and Shironne grabbed at his arm for balance. "What do you mean?"

Kai seemed to consider her question. She felt his anger subside. He permitted her to keep her grip on his sleeve. "You have no idea what's happened to you, do you?"

"I don't know what you're talking about. Tell me," she begged, hoping that Kai, in his sullen bluntness, might.

"You're the little girl from the fair. I was there. Mikael didn't do it intentionally, you know. Your blood, his blood, it runs in both Houses. But the barrier between you will fail, and he'll drown you out." He said that last with regret, as if pronouncing a death sentence.

"I'm not afraid of Mikael," she insisted.

Kai made a scoffing sound.

"Why do you dislike him so much?"

She knew she'd been incredibly rude the moment she said it. Hurt feelings welled up in him, quickly controlled, things she suspected he never said aloud. Shironne pulled off one of her gloves and laid her hand next to his, not quite touching. His mind responded with wariness, as if she'd offered him poison. Then she felt a light touch as his calloused fingers brushed over the back of her hand.

She felt his pain in the whirling birds in his head. His thoughts flew past, all afraid to be touched or heard, for fear someone else might think him ungrateful, or spiteful, or undutiful. He tried so hard to please everyone, and in the end, no one was satisfied.

Shironne kept her hand under his, snatching at all the disappointments in his life. *Nothing ever goes the way I plan. I shouldn't be the king's heir. The king should have chosen Sera. Sera, at least, is Dahar's child. Everyone knows that, just as everyone thinks I'm not.*

And Dahar wants Mikael to marry Sera. That would make Mikael his son after all. He'll have the son he'd always wanted instead of the one his wife forced on him. Everything comes so easily to Mikael. Everyone loves him, even Shironne, and he'll destroy her someday. Elisabet likes him, taking Mikael's part in arguments, protecting him. She told him her secrets, ones she's never admitted aloud to me . . .

Kai held to Shironne's hand in a strange sort of confessional, a sort of apology meant to be heard by Mikael as well. He'd never planned to cause trouble for Mikael, but he often had, his temper and jealousy getting the better of him.

Overlying all was Kai's fear that Elisabet would die, that he would never have another chance to convince her. He'd been in love with her since the first time he laid eyes on her, when he was only twelve and named the First of his yeargroup. But every time he thought she cared for him, in the next instant she would be cold and distant.

"She won't marry you," Shironne whispered to him, not for Tova's ears. The hand on hers tightened, anger flaring through the contact. "You're the king's heir and you can't afford to be associated with her."

His mind turned that over, not mistaking her words. "Three years, little cousin, and still she won't let me close to her. She doesn't care for me."

"No, she does." Shironne felt certain about that.

"How would you know?" he asked, not allowing himself to believe.

She thumbed through the pages of her memory, wondering where she'd found that knowledge. It was *his*, not hers—*Mikael's*. She recalled Mikael talking to Elisabet in a common room, although she'd certainly not been there. "He knows, Kai."

Her cousin let go of her hand, taking away the myriad touches of his mind. Then she realized he'd kept from her what she'd originally asked.

"What did you mean about me and Mr. Lee?" she asked.

Kai repeated his earlier words. "You know what he knows."

"I heard the words the first time you said them. What do they *mean?*"

"You're *bound* to him. He knows what that means, but you're a child." He locked his emotions away, thinking fast about his plans, leaving her with only Tova's worry to battle.

Shironne took her hand from his arm and put her glove back on. She felt about until she located a hand strap. Exhausted, she leaned her head against the wall of the coach. She could ignore Tova for a time.

She didn't understand what Kai meant, although he appeared to think she should. The word *bound* meant something to him, something beyond ropes or chains. It had to do with her inability to completely shut Mikael out of her mind. *The barrier between you will fail . . .*

She listened for Mikael. Shironne could almost hear him, fretting that Kai would hate having Tova as his guard if Elisabet died, that Kai could never forgive Tova for being the one who lived.

• • •

The sun began to set, the shadows stretching along the rooftop. They'd had a long, chilly afternoon. "Do you feel someone watching us?" Mikael asked, voicing the concern nibbling at his mind.

"Yes," Elisabet said. "But I can't see them."

Mikael watched with sudden dismay as a coach turned into the alley north of the hotel and stopped near the stables. As he could see only the roof, he didn't actually recognize the coach. He didn't need to. He could tell Shironne was inside, even without seeing her.

You shouldn't have come here, he thought at Shironne. He sensed her regret and decided she hadn't wanted to come. Mikael tapped Elisabet on the arm, and her eyes turned toward the stone pavement below.

She shut her eyes and sighed. "I should have never left her in charge of him."

Tova must have given in to Kai's demands, something Elisabet would never have done. Tova stepped down from the coach and looked around. Kai didn't wait for her permission. He jumped to the ground after her and then helped Shironne down.

Mikael swore under his breath at Kai's recklessness. He shoved his pistol in his sash. "I'll go down and talk to him," he told Elisabet.

"Leave the access door open," Elisabet ordered. Her eyes focused on the street below, her rifle trained on the pedestrians hurrying by.

Mikael took the stairs at a run and strode through the red-draped lobby of the hotel, shouting a quick apology at the owner. He'd make amends later. He came down the front steps just as Kai and his companions emerged from the alleyway, about twenty feet away. Kai was hauling Shironne through the press of people on Cadij Street in Mikael's direction. Tova followed a few steps behind, one hand to her pistol.

He didn't see the first blow fall, but people suddenly flooded off the sidewalk and into the path of oncoming vehicles. Screams erupted ahead of him. A rush of pedestrians trying to escape forced him back. Mikael struggled free of them just as a shot rang out, causing people far and near to scatter. A man in a brown tunic fell into the street—Elisabet's work.

No second shot came. Mikael finally shoved through, getting close enough to understand why. Kai stood motionless on the sidewalk. A well-dressed man stood next to him, one hand lifted almost casually to the side of Kai's neck. Even from where he stood, Mikael could see the glint of metal in the fading light.

Mikael studied the expression on Kai's face. Kai knew he'd made a mistake and was trying to *think* his way out of this.

Where is she? He couldn't see Shironne at all. He could feel her fear, but his angle prevented him from seeing her, so he stepped closer. The man next to Kai turned and smiled at Mikael, a self-satisfied expression on his face. He looked Larossan, shorter than Kai by several inches, with light brown skin. His dark hair and dark eyes matched those of most of the other pedestrians, but Mikael *recognized* him. A frisson of Shironne's remembered fear ran through him. Something *beyond* sight told him this was the man from his dreams—their killer priest.

The man gazed serenely back at Mikael. He spoke, and Mikael

watched as his lips moved, not comprehending the words, his admittedly limited grasp of Pedraisi failing him.

"He says not to move," Mikael heard Shironne call out. He craned his neck and spotted her several feet behind Kai's captor, sprawled on the ground with Tova lying facedown halfway across her legs. A second man squatted near her, a knife in one hand and the other hand at her side, pressed against Shironne's bruised cheek. Tova didn't move, either unconscious or worse.

Shironne's face betrayed her fear. Mikael froze as it wrapped around him, tendrils of her terror snaking into his mind, making his stomach heave. He shut his eyes for a second, trying to calm his breathing and in turn to calm her.

Tova was *bleeding* on her.

Hot human blood soaked into her borrowed trousers, carrying with it all of Tova's fading anguish and her fading life. It dragged at Shironne, and Mikael could *feel* it through her, the strength of blood far more powerful and personal than mere touch.

Traffic on the street had halted completely, some people abandoning their carriages and coaches and taking refuge in the building entryways and behind stairs. Mikael could hear sobbing somewhere, and tortured breathing, which he suddenly determined came from the man lying in the street, the one Elisabet had shot.

The priest spoke again.

"He says you know what he wants. Don't shoot again." Shironne yelled. She was interpreting the priest's words through her contact with her captor, Mikael realized.

He took a step closer, no more than ten feet away then. Kai's eyes met his, his face a mask of calm acceptance. The priest stared past Mikael toward the hotel, waiting for Elisabet.

CHAPTER FORTY

Mikael counted the odds. The priest had two hostages. The object the man held to Kai's neck wasn't a knife. It looked more like a syringe. There was poison in the man's hand, a poison strong enough to kill Iselin Lucas inside an hour.

And Kai is expendable to them.

Elisabet was their target, and once they had her, they didn't need Kai. From the lack of concern the priest showed for his companion dying in the street, Mikael reckoned the other Pedraisi were expendable to him as well.

He heard Elisabet coming down the steps behind him. He saw and *felt* Shironne's cringe as the touch of the second man's hand relayed his triumph at the sight of their quarry. Elisabet walked forward until she stood at Mikael's side.

"Get them out of here," she whispered. She handed him her rifle, her eyes meeting the priest's. Mikael wrapped his left hand around the rifle's warm barrels, casting a quick glance at Elisabet. Her chin lifted. Only cold disdain showed on her face—no fear.

Mikael turned his attention back to Kai just in time to read what Kai intended. "No!"

It took only a slight movement to close the distance, Kai's neck pressing into the syringe in the man's hand. He gasped, then let his weight take him down to his knees, pulling the man off balance. The metal syringe hit the sidewalk and skittered away.

Elisabet drew her pistol. The priest's eyes turned in her direction, but he didn't appear concerned as he slowly straightened. He drew a gun out of a pocket, pointed it at Kai, and spoke again.

"Kai might live," Shironne interpreted. "That's true . . . or at least this man believes it."

But Family were more susceptible to poisons. After Iselin's death, Kai knew that. He'd done his best to remove himself from the calculations. *Damn him.*

The priest spoke again.

"He says he can still kill him," Shironne called out.

Kai's balance failed and he toppled to his side, unheeded now by his captor. The priest's eyes locked with Elisabet's. She met his gaze squarely, and he spoke directly to her.

Shironne didn't repeat it this time, her face paling.

Mikael could feel her fear, coursing through his head as if it were his own. His heart raced. The priest had threatened to kill Shironne, and she'd refused to relay the threat. The man crouching next to her slapped her, hard.

"There's no need," Elisabet said coolly, and handed Mikael her pistol. Her eyes flicked in his direction. "Take care of Kai. Get them *all* back to the fortress, Mr. Lee. Step back. Choose the right time. This is my responsibility. No one else should pay."

Elisabet walked away from him, stepping into the street. A man ran out of the alleyway, and the one guarding Shironne abandoned her to join him. Each took one of Elisabet's arms, walking her away toward a coach that stood among the halted traffic.

Choose the right time. The sparring advice repeated in his head. This wasn't the moment, not with Kai barely breathing on the sidewalk. First priority had to go to him, Mikael knew, not Elisabet. The Anvarrid always came before Family, and Kai *was* the king's heir apparent and a member of the Royal House. It didn't matter what Kai wanted, or what Kai believed about himself.

Mikael crouched down and laid the rifle on the ground.

The priest began backing away toward the coach, his eyes watching the pistol in Mikael's hand. He cast a quick glance at the man dying in the street and turned his gun toward Shironne. Pinned under Tova's weight, she couldn't escape him.

Mikael raised the pistol, but the priest pointed his gun directly at Shironne's head. Mikael stopped moving then. "Stay away from her!"

No matter how poor a shot, he can't miss at that range.

Mikael watched, helpless, as the priest grabbed the back of Shironne's jacket, dragged her out from under Tova's body, and held her like a shield in front of him. He edged toward a coach that had lumbered into motion, approaching from the other side of the street. The legs of Shironne's brown trousers were stained almost black with Tova's blood.

Shironne's terror beat around him, and Mikael did his best to ignore it. He began closing the distance, one cautious step at a time. *Don't do anything stupid,* he warned her.

Mikael stepped over Kai's prone form.

His eye on Mikael, the priest looped the hand with the gun around Shironne's shoulder so that the gun touched the side of her head. The coach trundled nearer, within thirty feet now. The priest used his teeth to yank the glove off his other hand.

As soon as Mikael saw it, Shironne began struggling. Her fear redoubled around him, a numbing haze, making his teeth hurt and his stomach turn.

The priest slid the gun into his jacket and hooked his fingers into Shironne's jacket. He held his bare hand only inches from her face, glanced at Mikael, and smiled. He had a much better threat now.

Mikael stopped. Shironne went limp in the priest's grasp, terror on her slack features. The coach drew to a halt only feet away from them.

The priest looked at Mikael, his dark face unreadable . . . and touched his hand to Shironne's cheek.

She screamed, a cry that seemed to sound in Mikael's head more than his ears. A sense of violation flooded through Mikael's senses, just as horrifying as it had been the day before when it had been his own. The priest dug through Shironne's mind, amused and leisurely about it.

Unable to move, pinned in place by her terror, Mikael felt Shironne pushing him away from her, trying to protect *him* from the priest's touch, to block him out. She closed her thoughts down into a box with sharp crystal edges. Her fear still hazed his mind, but Mikael could no longer sense *anything* beyond that.

The priest backed the final few feet toward the coach, dragging a now-silent Shironne with him, and Mikael followed helplessly. They would take her with them. They would hold her hostage, knowing he would be helpless to do anything while she remained in their control. They would take her away from him.

One of the men in the coach lowered the step and the priest shifted his grip on Shironne to lift her up. Shironne's fear abruptly turned to fury, flinging Mikael free from the haze of her panic.

Mikael shook his head, as if waking from a dream. He couldn't sense her now at all. Something indefinable went on in her mind, directed at the priest, and he'd been thrust away from her—completely locked out—whether by her or the priest, he didn't know.

Then the priest abruptly shoved Shironne away from him, shock on his face. She slumped to the ground, and the priest jumped up onto the coach's steps. The others pulled their master inside and shut the door, and the coach rolled away, leaving Shironne lying like a broken doll on the pavers.

Mikael ran to her. She didn't respond to his touch, looking almost as if she'd fallen asleep, but he knew better. He picked her up and carried her out of the street, alarmed by the lack of any sense of her in his mind. She still held herself locked away from him.

He set her down on the sidewalk pavers next to Kai and brushed dirt from her cheek. "What have you done?"

He didn't want to leave her there, but people were returning to the street. A crowd gathered in front of the hotel, pushing and craning to get a better look at the bodies.

Take care of Kai. Get them all back to the fortress, Mr. Lee. Elisabet had been right; he had to get Kai out of the confusion first.

Kai's dark eyes met his, angry even in the midst of his struggle to breathe. Mikael turned him so that he lay on his back, and the harsh sound of his breathing eased. Kai mouthed something at him, but Mikael couldn't make it out.

"I didn't understand," he said, forcing himself to be patient. At the moment, he wanted to strangle Kai more than anything else.

Kai tried to form the words again, his lips barely moving. *Go after her,* Mikael made out.

"I have to get you out of here first," he told Kai, scanning the gathering crowd for a responsible face. "There's a coach from the palace down the alley to the north of the hotel. Would someone fetch it?"

People glanced at one another. A young boy bolted in that direction.

Kai's fingers scrabbled at Mikael's boots, a forceless touch. He whispered again that Mikael should go.

"I'm not leaving, Kai. I'm going to check on the others and I'll be right back. They're bringing the coach."

A Larossan man shouldered his way through the crowd on the sidewalk, his dark face concerned. "I'm a doctor," he told Mikael. "What's happened here?"

"Do you know Deborah Lucas?" Mikael asked.

"Yes, she volunteers at the City Hospital." The doctor knelt next to Kai, pressing fingers to Kai's neck.

Reassured by that faint verification, Mikael went and retrieved the metallic object from against the wall. It looked like one of the infirmary's syringes, only smaller and all metal. "Would having this help?"

The doctor glanced at it uncertainly and asked if that was how the poison had been delivered. When Mikael nodded, he took it with careful fingers and stashed it in a coat pocket.

Mikael left Kai in the man's care and crossed to where Tova lay in a crumpled heap on the sidewalk. He turned her over, knowing before he did so that she was dead. A long, slender knife emerged from the side of her neck. Blood stained her chin and cheek where her face had lain across Shironne's legs. Her wheat-colored braids were tipped in red.

A guard, first and foremost, must be willing to die. Mikael knew that from his own service as a guard. He wondered if Tova had ever given it serious consideration. Mikael pulled her hood over her bloodstained face, hoping the gawking crowd would be respectful.

The man in the street was dead too, lung shot. A bloody froth marked his lips. He'd drowned in his own blood, just as Paal had—a touch of retribution for Elisabet.

Mikael glanced up and saw the doctor still kneeling over Kai, so he dragged the dead man's body out of the street and arranged it on the sidewalk next to Tova's. He retrieved Elisabet's aged rifle and went back to Shironne. She lay motionless, only a few feet from Kai. Mikael knelt and touched her cheek, alarmed by her listlessness. No sense of her remained in his mind.

A pair of policemen finally arrived on the scene, arranging to control the passersby. People began to return to their wagons and carriages, and traffic struggled to resume its normal flow.

The coach from the fortress drew up. The palace groom jumped down from the tail, and he and the doctor lifted Kai carefully onto the coach's floor. The doctor offered to accompany Kai back to the fortress. Mikael agreed, desperately relieved to have the man's assistance. The groom promised Mikael that they would get back to the palace safely. At this point, there wasn't any more that he could do for Kai. It was up to the infirmarians now.

He knelt next to Shironne, uncertain whether to send her to the fortress with Kai or to keep her with him. He pulled off a glove and touched her pale cheek, unnerved by the isolation he now felt from her—a *lack* of sensation, like the day he'd cut off his braids.

Mikael waved for the driver to head back to the palace without him. He thanked the doctor again and took one last look at Kai, saying a quick prayer to Father Winter that Deborah could keep him alive. Anvarrid *were* harder to kill, which might give Kai the edge he needed to fight off the poison. Mikael watched the coach roll away. Then he turned back to the girl lying on the sidewalk.

Ignoring a policeman's questions, Mikael lifted her into his arms and retreated to the steps of the hotel. He settled there in the twilight, holding her in his lap, wondering how he could rouse her. He didn't care if people stared.

Mikael lifted her chin to look into her face. It felt as if she was slipping away from him, so he laid his cheek against hers, closed his eyes, and tried to *call* her, to act as her anchor just as she had been his in his dream. How had she done that?

CHAPTER FORTY-ONE

Shironne hid in the far corner of her mind, in a cage built within her focus. It wasn't the real focus, but the one she'd created in her mind, a crystalline hall not unlike that alleyway in Mikael's dream, unclear because it was merely a place to hide, not a place to *be*. She was afraid to have Mikael learn what she'd done and what she was.

The priest had touched her, sifting through her mind as he'd done with Mikael, with David Aldassa, with Paal Endiren. He had peered into every secret she had, drawing out what he willed, from her most private memories to her vaguest childhood recollections. She had clutched her secrets close, but he'd mocked her inability to stop his invasion of her thoughts. He wanted to know exactly what she was, something even she herself didn't understand.

The priest now knew her more intimately than anyone else alive did, and she felt unclean. He'd called her *cousin*, recognizing within her common blood their common powers. He'd wanted to take her with him, not just as a hostage as Mikael feared. He'd found her interesting in many ways.

From far away she felt Mikael's touch, reassuring her, needing her to come back to him.

She couldn't go back.

It had taken only a second to make the leap from recognizing what the priest did to her to understanding *how* he did it. She'd simply not been trying hard enough. She could have anything out of Mikael's memories she wanted, and that was unfair. Not just Mikael either—*anyone* she touched.

That ability had lain disguised, explained away as touch-sensitivity. Surely her father had known, though, from the first, what she could do. That was why he'd never touched her save with a gloved hand. He'd known what she was because it was what ran in *his* family.

It had taken only a second more to turn her newfound knowledge back on the priest.

Now she knew Gajaya Ramanet, the High Priest of Farunas, far better than anyone else ever had. She had riffled through the leaves in his mind, able to pick and choose among his memories, reading what she wanted.

She didn't know which was worse: to have run her fingers through his mind or to have done exactly what he had done to others. She felt corrupted, as if she'd submerged her hands in the foulest water of the river near the sewage outlet.

Mikael's call continued. *I don't care what happened. I want you to come back. I need you. I'm losing time and I need you to help me now, because every minute Elisabet gets closer to death.*

Mikael didn't even know the truth about why.

She ran her hands through his memories and saw that Elisabet hadn't told him everything. It didn't upset him when she did that, because he had nothing to hide from her.

Eventually, he told her, *you'll know all my secrets anyway. I don't care.*

She didn't frighten him. He would forgive her for what she was.

She knew then exactly what *bound* meant.

Shironne made herself feel again, forcing herself outside of her hiding place. She felt his cheek pressing against hers, warm in the chilly air, perspiration on his skin and a fine grit of dust from the rooftop where he'd wiped a gloved hand across his face. A faint roughness told her he hadn't shaved. A hint of soap clung to his skin. He smelled of wool, starched linen, perspiration, and lemon again. The wind carried the scents of horse and dirt and the taste of coming rain.

The aftertaste of blood floated on the air, sharp and metallic in her mouth. She felt it on her legs, Tova's blood on her borrowed trousers, soaking through to her skin. *Blood—so much more personal than almost anything else.* She could bear it, but only just.

His arms tightened around her, trying to reassure her. She turned her face into the wool of his coat, hiding her tears.

"It doesn't matter," he murmured next to her ear. "I trust you. That's the difference. I trust you."

That was the hardest part, to know that he trusted her. Tova was dead, and Mikael still trusted her. "I shouldn't have led him here," she whispered into his jacket.

"No. Kai shouldn't have asked. Tova should have stopped him. It's not your fault." Mikael set his hands on her shoulders, holding her back so he could look at her. His dusty fingers brushed across her cheek, wiping away her tears. It merely left other dust behind, but he didn't truly understand that. Not yet.

His mind said he would have liked to stay this way, with her held comfortably in his arms, for the remainder of the evening, only he had to go after Elisabet, and he had no way to know where to look if she didn't, and he could only hope that she did, because Elisabet's time was running out.

"He meant to take her to the river," she said.

"Where on the river?" Mikael asked, his voice betraying his urgency now that she'd chosen to rejoin the hunt.

She'd been through the priest's mind. She had a vague sense of him moving slowly through the city. She raised her hand and pointed the direction. "He knows I've been in his head, so he'll change where he'd planned to take her. We'll have to *follow* him."

Mikael pushed her up to her feet, then rose himself. He led her down the steps to the edge of the street. A man spoke to him—a policeman, she knew from Mikael's mind—and Mikael answered, bidding him to send the bodies back to the fortress.

He hailed a cab. When one stopped, he lifted Shironne into it and settled across from her. It smelled, the straw on the floor sticky under her boots. She could feel Mikael's foot on the edge of the bench on which she sat, bracing him as the cab began to move.

She heard the mechanical sound of Mikael checking his gun. He had more than one, she decided as a different sound, a clicking one, heralded a second weapon.

"Can you hold the rifle?" he asked.

She wanted to wipe her face, but this took priority, so she extended her hand. He placed the barrel of a rifle in it, held perpendicular to the floor of the cab. Heat clung to the weapon, and a very fine burned dust. She realized this must be Elisabet's, not his—Mikael wasn't partial to rifles. He didn't *like* guns at all, although if he had to kill someone, that was his first choice.

"Are we still going in the right direction?" he asked.

She nodded and heard him shift, the sounds of fabric moving. His mind whirled; he was counting cartridges, not getting stuck on five this time.

"Yes." She didn't know what to do. She was worse than useless.

"We need to head for Miller's Point," Mikael yelled out at the driver. He turned back to her. "How is killing Elisabet going to set things right?"

"It's because he didn't kill her before," Shironne said, trying to sort through what the priest had in his mind. Even at the best of times, motives were never entirely pure. She'd looked into enough people's minds to know that. "He thinks that spoiled all the sacrifices afterward, and that's why his god allowed Elisabet to kill his father."

"I don't understand," Mikael insisted. "She wasn't there."

"Yes, she was. She was the first."

Mikael stilled in his preparations. "What?"

"They sacrificed her first."

. . .

Mikael looked up from the pistol to Shironne's pale face.

"Elisabet was one of the sacrifices? How could she have survived that?" He recalled that she'd said something about lying on her back the day after the massacre of her family, but it was amazing that she'd survived. She had to have lost a lot of blood.

"*He* didn't know. Paal Endiren didn't either, but he knew Elisabet had the scars. Paal knew that about her. That's how the priest found out she was still alive." Her face had a perplexed expression, as if she was searching through the corners of her mind, trying to locate the facts she wanted. "He questioned Paal when they captured him. That's why Ramanet came hunting Elisabet. He didn't know she'd lived until he touched Paal, and then he figured he knew why his father failed. He blames her for making everything in his life go wrong. He wants to make sure she dies this time. Part of that is to fix the magic that went wrong, but a large part of this is just about revenge."

That didn't surprise him. "You got all of that when you touched him?"

"I know . . ." Her chin quivered, but she pressed on. "I know how to do it now. I could do it before, only I didn't really know I was doing it. I thought I was just . . . doing the other . . . the touch-sensitive thing."

What runs through the mind of the corpse?

Deborah had suspected this. That was why she'd given him that book—to warn him about Shironne's abilities. Shironne looked upset when he thought that, as if she feared he would run away from her.

"I don't care," he reassured her.

She clung to the rifle as if that alone kept her upright. She hadn't had much sleep the night before either, he knew.

"I'll be fine," she said. "He thought his god was pleased, letting him find *me*. That it was a sign of his approval. That he's chosen the right path. He meant to take me with him."

Mikael wiped his hand on his sleeve and then reached across to touch her cheek. Redness showed where the other man had slapped her, overlaying the fading bruise. "How, exactly, do you mean that?"

"He wanted to collect me, like a pressed flower." She shivered when she said that.

He thought of those menageries from the book. If they still existed, someone would surely want her. "I won't let them take you."

"He noticed you in the dreams through the victims, only he couldn't talk to you. You weren't listening to him in the dreams. That's why he had to find you in person and figure out what you knew. That's when he learned about me. He wanted to capture me, because he would get a lot of money for me and . . ." She drew a shuddering breath. "He knew that I had to be related to him, and he thought he might even get to . . . keep me. He thought . . . he thought he would get you too, because he thought you would follow him if . . ."

"I would have." Mikael knew that much was true. He wished calm at Shironne, assuring her, "Anyone takes you, I'll come after you. I promise."

He stuffed Elisabet's pistol into his sash next to his own—one cartridge in each and a handful in his pocket.

"Here, give me that rifle," Mikael said. She held it out to him.

The driver hit a bump and Shironne tumbled onto the dirty straw on the floor of the cab. Mikael helped her back onto the seat, guiding her gloved fingers to a hand strap. He lifted the flap on the window and saw they'd reached the end of the warehouse district and were heading toward the river. The driver started bringing the horses up to speed.

"Can we beat them there?" Shironne asked.

"No." He'd spent too much time dealing with Kai. Mikael braced a foot on the opposite bench again and inspected the rifle, uncertain about using Elisabet's weapon. It had an unusual double-barreled, double-trigger design. It must be particularly true or Elisabet wouldn't have kept it. Both barrels were loaded; she must have reloaded while coming down from the roof.

He had four shots without reloading, then, and no spare cartridges for the rifle. He'd left his sword sitting on the hotel's rooftop. He cursed inwardly. He was going to have to rely on his marksmanship, not one of his stronger skills. He would have felt a lot better having the sword even if he didn't get the chance to use it. As he was struggling out of his overcoat, he asked, "Are you certain we're going in the right direction?"

She shook her head. "It's not like with you. I knew *exactly* where you were, but I only have a vague sense of where he is."

Mikael felt a perverse flash of satisfaction. He didn't *want* Shironne to be able to find the priest easily. That should be reserved for him. That had been his logic for dragging her along, though, he thought guiltily, placing her in just as much danger as Kai had. "I shouldn't have brought you."

Her look went mulish. "You are *not* leaving me. You can't find him on your own anyway."

"True." He drew the sheathed knife out of the back of his sash and handed it to her.

"If I need this, I'll be in more trouble than I can handle." She took the knife, inspecting it with her fingers before slipping it under her own sash.

"I'd still rather you had some way to protect yourself. It's better than being a pressed flower."

CHAPTER FORTY-TWO

The cab slowed suddenly, the driver applying the brake. If Mikael hadn't had his foot braced where it was, he'd have been on the floor. He threw open the door and glanced out at the riverside, eerie under the falling darkness. He'd been to Miller's Point before, so the terrain was moderately familiar. Mikael jumped down, caught Shironne as she came to the door, and set her on the ground beside him. He kept a firm grasp on one of her hands as he snagged the rifle's strap and slung it over his shoulder.

The cab driver, spooked by their surroundings, refused to remain behind. Mikael didn't have any more credit markers, so he tossed his hooded overcoat up to the man instead. He told him to take it to the fortress for his pay, giving him a string of instructions for the sentries at the fortress gates as well. The driver turned the cab in a wide circle, heading away from the quiet riverside.

The moon shone through breaks in the low clouds that had drifted in. Mikael didn't trust the illusion of emptiness. Tall grasses and reeds grew out in the shallows, so there were numerous places to hide. Much wider here than it was in the pinched confines of the city, the river flowed slow and shallow.

Shironne stripped off one of her gloves and shoved it into the pocket of her jacket.

"Which way?" Mikael asked. "River's in front of us."

"Downstream, I think. Can you try to be quieter?" she asked. "You're drowning him out."

Mikael turned away from her, frustrated. The last of the twilight was fading. He suspected that in a quarter hour he wouldn't be able to see at all. If the clouds obscured the moon, they had no chance of catching the man. Mikael closed his eyes, praying for time as quietly as he knew how.

"Definitely this way," Shironne said.

Shironne pointed downstream, toward the city. Mikael took her gloved hand and drew her to a pathway that followed the river's bank. Shironne tripped over a stone, but Mikael kept her moving.

They crossed a rocky patch and she stopped, forcing him to halt as well. Her fingers wrapped around a handful of grass growing higher than her head. "Wait. Someone was just here." She led him off the pathway into the grass, stumbling as she headed for the river.

Harvesters had cut the reeds there down to stiff woody clumps no higher than Mikael's knees. In the absence of the reeds, the men would have few places to conceal themselves along the riverbank, only the trees growing twisted among the rocks.

They hit a shallow eddy and Mikael cut straight across, ignoring the water. He dragged Shironne through the reed stumps, his boots squelching in the soggy earth. When they hit a patch of dry ground, Mikael ran, hauling her along through the saw grass there. The moon had come out again, showing him a curve in the river ahead.

"Farther down," Shironne said breathlessly. Suddenly she yelped and her hand jerked away from his.

Mikael skidded to a stop in the gravelly soil and spun back. He didn't see her. She'd tumbled down into the tall grass, hidden from him. He could sense her frustration, coupled with her firm resolve not to panic.

"I'm caught on something," she yelled. "Go! You're running out of time."

Judging her urgency, Mikael ran on. The saw grass gave way to bare silt again. He turned the bend of the river and spotted figures poised on the bank under a willow.

Two lanterns cast a glow around where they held Elisabet on her knees under the naked branches of the tree. They'd stripped her to the waist, her skin a pale blur. One man held her arms behind her, keeping her immobilized. A second man crouched before her—the one who'd held a knife to Shironne's neck. His blade flashed as he traced letters already written in scars across her skin.

A third man stood at the river's edge, arms folded over his chest, chin thrust out and arms folded as he watched the other two work. *Ramanet*, just as Shironne had noted, letting the others do his work for him.

The man's dark eyes lifted, too far away for Mikael to make out his expression. Mikael yanked his pistol from his sash and fired even as the man moved, diving toward the river's surface. Ramanet disappeared under the water.

Mikael ran for a tree near the pathway. He'd lost his advantage; the two other men were moving. The one who'd held Elisabet's arms let her go, and she slumped facedown into the water. Jerking the rifle from his shoulder, Mikael crouched behind the tree, pulled back both hammers, and aimed.

He chose the man who'd wielded the knife, squinting to make out the man's dark face. He fired and the man dropped to the dirt. The second man hid behind the tree now, but not well enough. Mikael fired the second barrel. The man lurched away from the tree and collapsed.

Mikael tossed the rifle away and ran to pull Elisabet out of the water, drawing her pistol from his sash as he went.

The first man managed to rise, one hand held to his side. He caught sight of Mikael then and set a foot on Elisabet's bare back, forcing her head under the water.

Mikael dropped to a knee and took his third shot. He scrambled back up when the man fell to the ground and ran the last few yards to Elisabet's side. She lay facedown in the water, unmoving. Terrified, Mikael grabbed a handful of braids and hauled her out. Elisabet gasped, her eyes unfocused.

Relieved, Mikael dragged her back from the water's edge. He laid her next to the tree's trunk and, deciding she could wait for a moment, checked the two men he'd shot.

The first was dead, shot through the cheek. The second lay on his side on the bank, blood bubbling out of his mouth. Mikael turned him over onto his back, reckoning that the man didn't have long to live. Satisfied that neither posed a threat, Mikael returned to where Elisabet lay.

Blood from her right shoulder washed across her chest but didn't obscure the scars. The knife man had gotten through only the first four letters of his epitaph, matching the new cuts to old scars stretched by time. A jagged scar ran across the width of her chest beneath her breasts. No wonder she'd always moved a little stiffly.

"Too stubborn to die, aren't you?" he said, amazed an eleven-year-old could have survived such injuries. Mikael untied the ropes binding her hands.

"You're a lousy shot," she mumbled and then coughed.

He propped her up so that she leaned back against the tree. Elisabet didn't seem to be drugged—Ramanet must not have had another dose with him—but Mikael suspected she had a concussion. She must have given them a fight once they got out of reach of Kai. Her shirt, vest, and jacket lay among the tree's gnarled roots. Mikael grabbed up her shirt, folded it into a pad, and held it against the new wounds.

He lifted her left hand to the makeshift bandage. "You've got to hold this. The two here aren't a threat."

"Where's Kai?" she said, grabbing at his hand with bloodied fingers.

"Sent him back to the fortress. It's up to Deborah now." He grabbed her jacket and draped it over her shoulders. He reloaded her pistol and placed it in her other hand. She lifted it into her lap.

"Now I need to find that priest," he told her.

She nodded wearily. "Go on."

. . .

Shironne cursed the wires holding her foot hostage, some sort of bizarre contraption left on the shore just for someone who couldn't see to step into. She worked at the wires with her hands and finally got the foot free, cutting her leg in the process. Blood smeared her fingers, but her leg didn't hurt too badly, whatever she'd done.

Once her own frustration bled away, Mikael's anxiousness swelled back through her consciousness to replace it. He'd found Elisabet and had her safe. *Two men down,* he thought very loudly in relief, *one to go.*

I'm coming for you, Mikael thought in her direction. *I need you to help me find Ramanet.*

He'd never be able to see her where she sat. She called back and struggled to her feet, his anxiety making her heart pound. She listened to the river. She'd gotten turned around when she rose. She sensed him off to the right. Instead, she'd shouted in the wrong direction.

She turned carefully to keep her feet away from the wire snare. "Mikael," she yelled. Her own breathing sounded harsh in her ears, and overly loud.

. . .

Mikael heard Shironne call his name. He headed that way, but something pale blurred into his sight as another man appeared from behind the same tree he'd used as a shield moments before. The man moved to block Mikael's path, a long, slender knife in his hand.

It wasn't the priest—too young and too big.

The man lumbered closer and swung the knife in a wide, unpracticed arc. Mikael suddenly realized who he was. He'd forgotten to count the coach's driver among the priest's followers.

"I don't have time for this," he yelled at the man, who kept coming closer anyway. Mikael reached for his knife only to find nothing there. He'd given it to Shironne.

Seeing his moment of confusion, the big man charged.

Mikael jumped back and away, anxiousness flowing through him. He spotted Elisabet's rifle lying where he'd dropped it in the grass just past the tree. He scrambled in that direction, the driver coming after him.

Mikael dove, grabbed the barrel of the rifle, and swung it about, staying low. The rifle's butt hit the man midstride, catching him on the shin. The driver stumbled back, yowling in pain.

Mikael moved his grip to the rifle's locks and shoved the butt into the driver's face. It connected with a satisfying crunch. The man dropped his knife, his hands going to cover his eyes. He sobbed like a child and hunched away, blood streaming from a broken nose.

Mikael swore under his breath. He didn't have the time to be fighting a driver. He stepped up and swung the rifle once more, hitting the back of the man's head.

The driver dropped like a rock.

• • •

Shironne called Mikael's name again but he didn't answer. She could hear the river to her left. She took a hesitant step in his direction, and then another. A few more and she squelched into the chilly water. It ran into her boots. She didn't dare move quickly to escape it or she might misjudge and fall into the river, so she paused there, trying to decide what to do.

At a distance, she heard the sounds that reminded her of the melee she'd seen when she was a child—Mikael was fighting with someone. His mind was busy, thoughts locked away, but an aggressive eagerness ran through him, sweeping into her mind as well.

Her hands clenched into fists. Her breath came short and blood pounded in her ears. Sweat trickled down her spine. Then the sounds of struggle ceased.

"Shironne?" Mikael called after a second, worried again.

Someone grabbed her jacket and jerked her toward the river.

She lost her footing and fell to her knees in the water, gasping as her bared hand rubbed against the not-quite-dried blood on her trouser legs.

Shironne screamed in fury, Mikael's ferocity still running through her veins like fire. She knew who held her. Ramanet had his hands on her. He was stronger than she was, dragging her away from the bank. With one arm, he pinned her to his chest.

She kicked at him, screaming. She jabbed an elbow toward his solar plexus like Hanna Kassannan had taught her, but she didn't know what she hit. His grip loosened for an instant, though. She plunged back into the water, and it closed over her head.

All sensation stilled in an undefined, icy world that dragged and pulled at her. Terror pounded through her. She didn't know which way was up. She held her breath, knowing she couldn't do it forever.

. . .

Only a few feet from the bank, Mikael saw the priest turn Shironne loose. The man stood chest-deep in the river—more than deep enough for the current to carry her downstream.

Mikael dropped Elisabet's bloodied rifle and ran into the water, following his sense of her panic. Several yards away, her head broke the surface of the water.

"Put your feet down," he yelled at her.

One arm flailed out of the water, her fear unabated.

I can't calm her down, not when I'm terrified myself. Mikael dove into the deeper water and managed to grab one of her legs. Her other boot caught him on the jaw, but without force. He yanked her back to him, trying to get his feet under him at the same time.

Shironne's arms wrapped around his neck. Mikael worked an arm about her waist and levered himself up. She coughed wretchedly against his neck, shivering.

The priest stood only a couple of feet away, a gun in his hand. He leveled it at Mikael and reached for Shironne's sleeve, rattling off a command in his own tongue. Mikael understood the word *girl* but nothing else.

"Let him take me," she whispered and then coughed again.

"Absolutely not." Mikael took a step back, wishing reassurance at her now. "Don't worry."

Shironne had been right about the man. Ramanet always had others do things for him. He'd pulled the gun from below the waterline. His cartridges would surely be ruined now.

Mikael held Shironne close, fumbling at her waist with his free hand. She still wore his knife in her sash. He wrenched it free and began edging toward the bank.

Baring his teeth, the priest pulled the trigger.

Nothing happened.

"You're not going to get your prize." Mikael carried Shironne toward the bank, keeping an eye on the priest the whole time. At this distance and in the dark, he didn't think he could throw the knife with enough accuracy to guarantee a kill. He would have to go after Ramanet again and make sure the man died this time.

The priest grimaced and leveled the gun at him again.

Ignoring him, Mikael set Shironne on the bank. "Stay right here," he ordered.

A shot sounded and a bullet whizzed past his ear. Mikael dropped to the sand, covering Shironne's body with his own.

CHAPTER FORTY-THREE

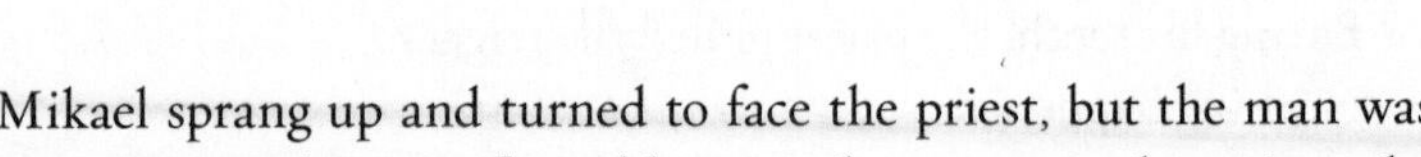

Mikael sprang up and turned to face the priest, but the man was gone again. The river flowed by in its hurry to get down into the city, carrying Ramanet away.

"I was waiting for you to get out of my way, Mr. Lee." A dozen feet back from the shore, Elisabet rose from a crouch, her pistol in her hand. She had managed to don her jacket somehow and had it almost completely buttoned. She dug a cartridge out of a pocket and calmly reloaded. "The body, Mr. Lee," she said. "I'll watch the girl."

Under her guard, Mikael stood and surveyed the river. Already yards downstream, a pale shape floated on the surface of the water. It was only a matter of time until the air buoying the body escaped and it sank.

Mikael ran along the bank until he could see the body more clearly. It snagged on something under the water and stalled in its passage. Mikael waded out and grabbed an arm.

He hauled the body out of the water and turned it over on the bank. Ramanet's dark eyes gazed up at the cloudy sky, all his elegance gone. His mouth hung slackly open. A small hole, almost centered on his forehead, oozed dark blood. Another bullet had torn through his shoulder. Mikael guessed that was his own lousy shot.

Mikael stared at the dead man for a second, thinking that Ramanet had been right in a way. Everything they'd attempted *had* failed because of Elisabet. Despite everything he had done, all the bloodshed, now he was just another corpse on the bank of the river.

He checked one last time to make certain the man was dead, hoisted the body over one shoulder, and carried it up to the path where Elisabet and Shironne waited for him. He wasn't certain which of the two was holding the other up.

He laid Ramanet's body on the ground at Elisabet's feet. Shironne slipped out of Elisabet's grasp and knelt next to the body. Realizing what she intended, Mikael squatted across from her. "Are you sure you want to do this?"

"The longer I wait, the more the memories will fade. I didn't think to look for it before." She caught her lower lip between her teeth, looking exhausted. "If he knows how to save Kai . . ."

Mikael took her hand and laid it against the dead man's cheek.

. . .

Shironne felt herself falling through Ramanet's mind, as if the shelves that had held everything in place had failed, falling haphazardly about like a ruined library. This was death, the loss of control of everything that made up one's mind.

But she found what she was looking for, the years-ago memory of Gajaya Ramanet watching his father sacrificing on the bank of the river. The centenary sacrifices—a hundred dead, one for every promised year of power. And then the shooting started. He'd seen his uncles, his cousins, cut down by an unseen army. When his father fell, he knew they'd failed, and he fled back across the river.

After that failure, he needed something special to catapult him into a position of power. Nothing came until the day he was asked to question a Larossan spy, and he found that elusive lever. The spy had seen scars whose pattern Gajaya remembered all too well.

And the woman who bore them could only be one who'd escaped the death his clan had spread along the border. She was a marksman, with an old rifle. *That woman* was why his father had died in shame on the bank of the Sorianas River.

Shironne sat down among the disordered books, searching through them for the truth of why Ramanet had pursued this path of death. She found a thousand motives written in those pages, some strong and others pallid, a maze of self-deceit and frustration that led back to the simple fact that his family name had been ruined, and this was his way of trying to mend it.

And finding a missing Ramanet girl—one who had to be descended from Nyassa, his cousin who'd shirked her duty and fled across the river to escape an unwanted marriage—that had to be a sign that his god approved.

Shironne set aside the man's book of his god, a book that was mostly a book about himself. Her own perception of the true god probably couldn't stand too close an examination, something she should consider later.

She looked instead for his more recent decision, whom to kill and when, and tucked that information away within the pages of one of her own books so she would remember it for the colonel. She found a book with everything Ramanet knew of the poison he'd used on Kai, what he'd perceived as an improvement on his father's plans. Snail poison, imported from the drowning islands far to the south.

That was what she'd come after, wasn't it?

Then she looked into his book that delineated everything he knew about his powers, the history of his clan, and how they'd used their powers through the centuries. It was likely half legend and half lies, but she took that information and hid it deep inside, to view someday when she felt more ready than she did now. She wasn't sure that day would ever come.

For a time she simply remained there in his dead mind, watching it crumble about her, the wood of the shelves rotting and collapsing. It was tempting to stay there to watch it all crumble down until it was dust and, after a few days, was nothing. But she pulled away, imagining that she wrapped her hand around her focus, and threw herself back into the real world, where Mikael waited and worried.

Shironne drew her hand from the cooling flesh under it. "I'm done."

. . .

"Why are *you* not injured?" Deborah asked Mikael in a vexed tone. "Usually you show up with blood all over your face, dear."

Three coaches had arrived by that time, dispatched from the fortress as soon as the sentries received the message Mikael had relayed via the cab driver. A dozen lanterns cast a glow about the area, illuminating a bustle of activity. Sentries wrapped the three priests' bodies under the watchful eye of the Family's battle master. Mikael directed him to where he'd left the driver whose nose he'd broken, uncertain whether the man was alive or not. He was simply too tired to care.

The doctor had patched up Elisabet first, judging her the worst off. Deborah crouched next to Shironne now, bandaging her cut ankle. Shironne sat mute under the doctor's ministrations, a blanket wrapped around her shoulders. She'd been quiet since her foray into the priest's mind, not ready yet to tell Mikael all she'd learned. Mikael thought he understood; he never told anyone *everything* about his dreams. It was too personal.

"Is Kai going to be all right?" Mikael asked.

"We're not certain," Deborah said. "Jakob is with him."

"Shironne says you have to keep him breathing," he told her. "If he keeps breathing, he should live."

"I suspected that might be the case, but I'm glad to have it confirmed, dear." Deborah used a clip to secure the bandage about Shironne's ankle. "We have ways to do that. Kai's tough."

"You must not have wanted to leave him."

She licked her lips. "His father and sister are with him, and all the twenty-fours want to sit with him. They don't need me there. At least here I can be *doing* something."

Mikael spotted Colonel Cerradine emerging from his own carriage. Cerradine grimly surveyed the bodies now laid out on the ground. As Mikael came near, he flicked a blanket back over the face of the priest, Ramanet.

"Is this him? Are we sure?" Cerradine asked, frowning.

"Yes, sir." Mikael squatted down across from him. "Shironne read his memories, sir, but she's really too tired to—"

"Is she hurt?" Cerradine interrupted.

"She cut her ankle," Mikael told him. "She'll be fine."

He shook his head. "Her mother is going to kill me," he muttered. "Did she find out why he . . . why David's dead?"

"Ask her later, sir, not now. She's done too much already." Past wanting to argue, Mikael headed back to the coach.

Inside, Elisabet leaned against the bolsters, Deborah next to her. Elisabet had a mild concussion after all. Mikael had no fear that she wouldn't survive it. What *did* scare him was learning that Elisabet had shot past his head when she couldn't even focus her eyes properly.

Shironne waited for him next to the coach, sitting with her arms wrapped around her knees. In the light of the lanterns, she looked half-asleep already. Some people did that—fell asleep after a crisis. Mikael reached down, helped her up, and lifted her into the coach. He settled next to her across from Deborah. Shironne's fingers wrapped around his, and her head drooped against his shoulder.

"I think it would be wise to get you cleaned up before your mother sees you, Miss Anjir," Deborah told her.

"Yes, ma'am," Shironne said, her eyes drifting shut.

Mikael put his arm around her, only to keep her from falling off the seat. He felt too worn and filthy to sleep. Shironne, evidently, did not.

CHAPTER FORTY-FOUR

The moment they arrived at the palace, Deborah put Shironne back into the hands of Lady Amdiria's staff. The consort's quarter-guards spirited Shironne away to the upper levels of Above, where her mother and sisters waited.

Mikael decided to go down to Below, to the infirmary, to check on Kai and Elisabet. Cerradine located him there, anxious for his promised explanation. Since Mikael would rather the colonel interrogate him than Shironne, he sat down with a cup of hot tea to answer the colonel's questions.

When he'd finished, Cerradine walked with him past the empty rows of beds to the back room where Kai lay. His breathing sounded ragged and whispery. Dahar sat next to the bed, his head lowered to his hands. Cerradine went, crouched down by his chair, and spoke to him quietly. Deborah walked up behind Mikael and set a hand on his shoulder. When Kai fell ill, she took it nearly as hard as Dahar did. "Will he make it?" he asked.

"It's been three hours and he's still breathing. I think he has a good chance."

"Is there anything I can do?"

Deborah shook her head, edging past him to peer in the doorway. "Thank you for offering, dear. Bringing Elisabet back alive was the best thing you could have done for him."

"Dahar looks terrible," Mikael whispered.

"I know. He would give his life for Kai's. It's killing him not to be able to do anything."

Cerradine spotted Deborah then and rose to talk with her, pulling her just outside the doorway again. "Dahar needs you to stay with him, Deborah."

"I have other patients." Deborah protested. "I have to keep an eye on Elisabet. She has . . ."

"Someone else can take care of Elisabet," Cerradine interrupted. He touched Deborah's cheek, giving her a stern look. "He needs you right now more than you need your pride."

Frowning, Deborah pulled away from his light touch, but after a moment she crossed to stand next to Dahar's chair. From the doorway, Mikael watched as Deborah whispered something meant only for Dahar's ears. He held one hand to his face, his shoulders shaking. Deborah wrapped her arms around him, and he pressed his face into her body, stifling his sobs.

Suddenly feeling like an intruder, Mikael turned away but saw Jannika standing in the entryway of the infirmary, hands folded tightly before her. He took a couple of deep breaths, knowing his control was already frayed. He went to talk to her anyway. Her expression seemed neutral, but as Mikael got closer, he could see her clenched jaw.

"Is it true?" she asked. "They said you killed the men who killed Iselin."

"Between Master Elisabet and I, we got all of them."

Jannika nodded once, turned halfway away, and then glanced over her shoulder with glistening eyes. "Thank you."

He never knew what to say when someone thanked him for ending another person's life.

"What I said before," Jannika added, coming back to take his hand, "about not seeing you again. I didn't mean it. I was letting the ambient move me, and I said things I shouldn't have."

He was glad of that, at least—that she didn't hate him. But he knew what she wanted him to say, and he couldn't. "The time's not right anymore," he told her. "Too much has changed for me, and—"

"And you're expected to marry the prince's daughter anyway," Jannika finished with a rueful shrug, revealing that she'd known about Sera all along.

"It's not that," he began, but couldn't think of where he could take this conversation that wouldn't end up with him in trouble.

He closed his eyes for a moment and concentrated, and realized that Shironne was sleeping, somewhere far above the fortress. *That* was what would keep him from pursuing Jannika . . . or marrying Sera, for that matter. There was a profound link between him and Shironne Anjir, and even though he wasn't ready to marry anyone, that tie warranted careful consideration. He liked Shironne Anjir—he had from the moment he met her. It would be easy to fall in love with her. As things stood, that path was forbidden. She was a child, and not Family, and he had no idea what she wanted for herself other than to be *useful*.

He schooled his thoughts to calmness again. "I need to take some time to consider what I intend to make of my life."

Jannika shook her head again. "And I'm not going to be part of it, you mean."

As much as he hated to say it, he did so anyway. "No, I don't think so."

She turned his hand loose, lips trembling, but leaned closer and kissed his cheek. "If you need someone to talk to, I'll still be your friend."

Then she turned and walked away, leaving him feeling like a traitor. He went and sat with Elisabet in one of Deborah's other back rooms instead, watching her sleep. Her yeargroup was notably absent, mourning three of their members already: David, Paal, and now Tova. Mikael wasn't sure whether they'd stayed away by choice, or if Deborah was holding them at bay. He hoped the latter.

Elisabet's blond hair streamed unbound across the pillow. She wore one of the infirmary's shirts in place of her ruined one. It covered both the new injuries and the old, although Mikael spotted a bandage around one exposed wrist. Her face was bruising now, more evidence that she'd fought her captors.

Mikael wondered vaguely what she'd been like as a girl, before the priests of Farunas had come to her home and destroyed her family, if she might have been cheerful and friendly like Shironne. He doubted it. She had come out of that experience a blade forged in steel, but she had to have been made of iron before that.

Elisabet woke at one point and regarded him blearily, which told him that Deborah had dosed her. "Mr. Lee? Is he . . . ?"

"He's still alive," Mikael told her. "They think he'll live."

And shockingly, Elisabet began to cry.

CHAPTER FORTY-FIVE

The rain had passed when Shironne woke, feeling as if it had all been a dream. A chilly finger jabbed at her cheek again. "Hurry, wake up," Melanna whispered.

The heavy bedding tucked tightly about Shironne held her captive. She struggled into a sitting position, trying to recollect where she'd washed up last night. The weight on the bed bounced away, Melanna going to tell Mama that she'd finally awoken.

Shironne recalled ending up in this incense-scented bed somewhere on the third floor of the palace. Lady Amdiria's two guards had placed her in a room not used for years. They'd found her a nightdress, made for Lady Sera but never worn, and even dug up new linens for the bed. Then she'd had a hot bath. Isolated from everything by the muffling water, she usually didn't care for baths, but this once she'd relaxed in its comforting warmth; *safe*, unlike the cold grasp of the river.

Her cousin Kai would survive. Shironne knew that without asking, because Mikael knew it. She had a distant sense of him now, busy with some errand or assignment. He'd gone down into the city, she realized, tying up loose ends.

Her mother entered the room, and Melanna jumped up on the bed again, exuberant in her curiosity. Mama sat down next to her and took Shironne's hand in her own. The familiar scent of vanilla and sandalwood surrounded her.

"Are you all right?" Shironne asked, sensing her anxiety.

It frightened Mama to have everything spun so far beyond her control, Shironne could tell. Savelle Anjir could no longer deny her relationship to the king—not given the fact that they sat in the king's household in the palace and that her daughter wore a princess' nightgown.

Shironne fingered the gown's silk embroidery. She wanted to reassure Mama but couldn't think of anything to say that wouldn't sound childish.

A brisk presence entered the room, one of the guards returning. Perrin trailed her. Even from the doorway, Shironne could feel her sister's confusion and exultation. Now that Perrin knew of their royal uncle, she was probably going to be insufferable.

The quarterguard took command of them, driving Perrin and Melanna back into the sitting room and bullying Shironne out of the bed. Half an hour later, Shironne had been tidied, dressed up like a doll in more of the absent Sera's unused garments, and set down to a very belated breakfast in the next room over. Since she'd never eaten dinner the day before, she slowly consumed most of the meal laid before her, Melanna cheerfully joining her in a second breakfast. Fortunately, someone had told the kitchens to keep their presentation simple.

When Shironne finished eating, she spent a long while with her mother and sisters, relating some of what had passed the day before. The story made Perrin afraid and grateful it hadn't been her. Melanna enjoyed the tale, particularly relishing the fact that Shironne had turned the priest's gift back on him. Clearly, she didn't understand the implications of it.

Her mother worried, being wise enough to know that Shironne had left a great deal unsaid.

Afterward Melanna insisted that Shironne finish her book with her. With nothing better to do than wait, Shironne sat next to her, listening to her sister's childish voice as she struggled her way through the very last chapter. Rather predictably, their hero won out and then swore his undying love for the wailing heroine. Shironne suppressed laughter at the disgusted tone of Melanna's voice.

Later in the afternoon Dahar arrived, the colonel behind him. Both men radiated exhaustion, which made Shironne want to return to the bedroom and crawl into the overlarge bed with its clean sheets.

"Eli, would you take the two young ladies out to the courtyard?" Dahar suggested to someone outside the room. "Perhaps you could show them the gardens."

The self-satisfied runner Shironne had met the previous day—Gabriel's cousin, Eli—entered the hall, immediately capturing Perrin's attention. He asked if Miss Perrin and Miss Melanna would come with him. He must be handsome, or Perrin wouldn't be so eager to go. Her sisters followed him from the room. Shironne felt gratified they hadn't sent her away, a tacit admission that they didn't consider her a child, or not *too* much of one.

"We do have a few things we need to discuss," Dahar said then.

Shironne grasped her mother's hand, and even through her gloves read her mother's resignation.

Her mother sighed. "Very well."

"I don't know if you are aware," Dahar began, "that your husband's mother came from the same clan as the priests of Farunas. We aren't certain how close their relationship actually is."

"Shironne told me," Mama said. "I'm not surprised—that Tornin might have had such an ability, even if he denied it."

"He would have gathered information by touch, Savelle," Cerradine said. "A sensitive would probably have noticed if he tried to tamper with them, but others wouldn't."

"I know," she whispered. "I've . . ."

Shironne didn't say anything. She'd always suspected Mama knew far more about Father than she'd ever admit.

Cerradine went on. "Our concern is that we don't know whether any of the priests sent word back to their clan about Shironne and her powers, or if your husband told anyone before he died. I'd like to keep my people where they are in your household until we've had time to assess the risk that they might come after her."

Shironne didn't flinch. She'd known from the moment she'd touched Ramanet that it was a very real possibility.

"We could move your family here, into the palace," Dahar offered. "This wing is mostly empty. The House of Valaren also owns several estates, if you'd like to leave the city for a time."

Her mother considered the offer, mind spiraling in uneasiness. "There will be talk," she said hesitantly.

"Doubtless," Dahar said. "My aide has gone down to speak with the editors at the various newspapers. He'll make certain Shironne's name stays out of the press, I promise."

Ah, so that's where Mikael's gone.

Her mother reflected relief. "Thank you."

The colonel came then and took Shironne's hand, suggesting in a whisper that they leave her mother and Dahar alone for a time. He led Shironne from the room under the curious attention of the quarterguards and down many stairs until they came to the stone steps that led from the back of the palace down to the courtyard. Shironne could smell the stables and sun-warmed stone.

"I'm glad Kai is doing better," she said when they stopped on the landing.

The colonel laid her hand on the wall, indicating they should wait there. "Yes, I don't know how Dahar would manage losing him."

While Kai would be physically well soon, Shironne doubted his heart would heal quite so quickly. "He'll blame himself for Tova's death," she said.

"He should," Cerradine said bluntly. "He could have caused yours as well. There's enough blame to go around for everyone this time, except for you."

"Kai thinks . . ." She wasn't sure if she should broach the topic, but she did anyway. "Kai doesn't think that Dahar is his father. Is that true?"

Cerradine sighed heavily. "I don't know."

The way he said that suggested that he didn't *know* but had a strong opinion on the matter anyway. Poor Kai. "Wouldn't it be better if he knew for certain?"

"There are times when people want to bury the past," the colonel said. "When it's painful, and can't be changed, why spend time fretting over it?"

"Like knowing the truth about my mother's family? Or my father's family?" She didn't know what to make of the fact that she had relatives in Pedrossa—relatives who might have a power like hers. Who might consider her worth stealing.

"I see your point," the colonel said. "Yet it's never mattered to Dahar."

It did to Kai, though.

Shironne sensed Mikael's approach then, as he came through the back doors of the palace. She suddenly divined why the colonel had brought her out to the steps.

"I'm going to go up and check on your mother. Make certain she hasn't strangled Dahar," the colonel added with a chuckle. "I'll leave you in Mikael's hands for now. We should be ready to leave in, say, a quarter hour or so?" The colonel walked back into the palace, abandoning her there on the steps.

CHAPTER FORTY-SIX

Mikael stood only a few feet away, broadcasting relief at the sight of her. He took in her borrowed finery, thinking loudly that the Anvarrid-style dress dragged on the ground, made for someone taller with a straighter figure. Her hair had been carefully plaited and bound up, he noted, with ribbons that actually matched her clothes for a change.

"You look much better," he said politely. "I hope you're rested. You kept falling asleep last night." He took her gloved hand and drew her down to the second landing. He sat with her on the steps, much as they had that first day she'd come here. "I guess I'm supposed to be saying good-bye," he told her. "I probably won't see you again for a while."

Because of the rules. Because they forbid him to associate with a *child*.

"I'm not one of your people," she attempted. She could almost feel his apologetic smile.

"That doesn't excuse me from obeying the rules," he said. "It's been overlooked so far because Cerradine needed us working together. Otherwise we would have been prevented from meeting." Hurried thoughts rushed through his mind, of things he shouldn't consider. "I put you in a great deal of danger, but I couldn't have found Elisabet in time without you. I wanted to thank you for your help."

Through her light touch, she could sense the ache in his knee and his sore jaw. He seemed to have a sore throat now, too. All she had was a tender cheek and a cut on her ankle. "I wanted to."

"That might have been because I badly *wanted* you to help," he said. "I have the ability to overrun people's wills, particularly sensitives. I took advantage of that, and I'm sorry."

He surprised her with his remorse, as if he'd *forced* her to help him. "I know who I am when I'm alone," she said. "I never answered your question, but I gave it a lot of thought while I sat in my room the day before yesterday."

"And?" He truly wanted to know her answer.

"I'm just me. People have ideas of what they want me to be like, and it's easy for me to be what they want when I'm near them, but at heart, I'm still myself. It's easy for me to be around you because we're both a lot alike to begin with. I get into a great deal of trouble without your prompting. You didn't force me to be different from what I already am."

He didn't speak for a long time, thinking that any changes he'd forced on her had already happened. They *had* to have met before, his mind rambled, and the damage had been done then, changing her life irrevocably. "I hope that's true," he finally said, not believing his words.

Shironne sighed. "I wish I could be around the next time you have a dream. Perhaps I can locate a mirror in it."

"What?" She'd surprised him with the change of topic.

"To find out what I look like."

"You *saw* yourself in my dream?"

"Yes. Well, part of me. I wore the tunic I wore the first day you saw me, and I could see my hands—which was strange. I've not seen them in so long. Actually, I saw what *you* think my hands look like. You didn't know about the scar on my palm, so when I looked down, it wasn't there."

"What scar?" he asked, a strange tension in him now.

"I have an old scar on my palm."

"May I look at it?"

It seemed a reasonable request, so she tugged off her right glove. She felt his leather-gloved hands taking hers, curiosity in his mind.

He turned her hand over, exposing her palm. "Do you know what that scar looks like?" he asked.

Shironne blushed. The scar cut across her palm, straight and shallow, just like an Anvarrid wedding mark. "Yes, I know."

He asked himself how she'd gotten it, thinking loudly that it was a common place to have a scar, his mind simultaneously whispering the opposite.

Embarrassment rushed through her. It had been such a childish incident. She hated admitting it. "It happened when I was eleven. It's embarrassing, so please don't laugh."

"I would never do that," he said, his undertone revealing amusement anyway.

She snatched her hand away. "Oh, very well. My mother took us to the summer fair. She wanted to find out what Dahar looked like. She'd never seen him or even a likeness of him, so she took Perrin and me and we went to the melee because she'd heard he was one of the judges."

He knew of the incident. She could tell that from his mind. "You know what happened, don't you?"

"You fell over the railing into the arena. Were you terrified?"

Then she knew.

She'd landed atop a fallen fighter. He'd tried to catch her, but there had still been a small knife in his hand. It had actually taken her a moment to notice that her hand was cut, but he'd wrapped her hair ribbon around it and lifted her back up to her mother.

That had been Mikael Lee.

"No, I wasn't," she finally answered him. "It was an *adventure*. I was scared when the other fighters came in our direction, but you didn't let them get near me. I could sense that you wanted to keep me safe."

He laughed softly. "Do you remember anything else?"

Shironne remembered the incident as vividly as if it had been yesterday. "Oh yes. It was the first time I had ever seen anyone Family up close. You had blood on your face and a helmet on, but I remember your eyes. You had beautiful eyes. I fell in love with you a little bit," she admitted. "I *was* eleven."

Shironne tried to fit that memory of startlingly blue eyes together with what she knew of Mikael Lee now, wishing she'd seen his face better that long-ago day. She pressed her lips together, fighting back a sharp pang of regret. She would never know now what he looked like.

"They teased me mercilessly for a long time after that," he said. "They made jokes about little girls falling for me."

"I'm so sorry," she said, although it wasn't quite true. She *was* sorry they'd teased him.

Mikael laughed again. "No harm done. I wondered about you from time to time—if you were all right. I didn't know it had left you with a scar."

"It's not important."

"Let me see your hand again." He carefully took the tips of her fingers and touched them to his left palm. He'd removed his glove.

His thoughts winged around her, telling her that he looked at his scarred hand sometimes and wondered about the girl from that day. He didn't actually remember it, but he'd ended up cutting her somehow, not intentional at all, but quite permanent. His blood and hers, across the knife in a strange parody of an Anvarrid wedding ceremony, but without the grand temple, only the sand of the fairground arena.

He turned his hand, twining his fingers with hers. His thoughts tumbled into her consciousness, mentioning things he should not: that they were *bound*; that the tie wouldn't be broken by anything save death, but he could go far away and not trouble her overmuch; that perhaps she might not mind his presence; that she was too young to have all her choices taken away from her. His hand pulled away then, ending her closer link with him.

Shironne heard boots clicking in a familiar stride, the colonel coming down the steps again. Mikael rose and helped her to her feet. She replaced her glove, annoyed that *everyone* considered her too much a child to know her own mind.

No, he didn't. That wasn't what he thought. Instead, Mikael feared that, as Kai had warned her, he would overwhelm her mind, stripping her of everything that made her who she was, making her just a reflection of him. He feared that he would destroy her, and that was why he'd said he could go away.

But that assumed she was weaker than he, that he was too powerful for her to handle. "I don't need to be protected from you," she whispered.

He knew *exactly* what she meant. She could tell that.

"Take care," Mikael said softly, his words sincere. He placed her hand on the colonel's sleeve. His footsteps went away, up the stairs to the palace, and she knew he didn't look back.

She tried to recall what he'd looked like that day on the fairground, but only his eyes formed in her mind. She would walk in his dreams again someday, though, and perhaps then she would see the face of the Angel of Death.

Read on for an excerpt from
J. Kathleen Cheney's

THE GOLDEN CITY

Available in print and
e-book from Roc

Thursday, 25 September 1902

Lady Isabel Amaral plucked another pair of drawers from the chiffonier and tossed them in her companion's direction. Oriana caught the silk garment and folded it neatly while her mistress disappeared into the dressing room.

Oriana laid the drawers in a pile with the others, surveyed the collection spread across the bed, and shook her head. Even after two years living among humans she was still bemused by the number of layers a proper Portuguese lady must wear. Chemises and underskirts, drawers and stockings and corsets: they all lay neatly prepared to pack away, none of them meant to be seen. It was a far cry from the comfortable—and less voluminous—garb Oriana had grown up wearing out on the islands that belonged to her people. She rarely noticed her heavy clothes any longer, but seeing all the lace-bedecked items displayed on the bed before her, Oriana found the quantity of fabric in which Isabel swathed herself daily rather daunting.

What was missing? Even with all that lay in front of her, Oriana was sure Isabel had left *something* out. She puffed out her cheeks, mentally cataloging the garments on the bed.

She wished Isabel hadn't waited so late to inform her of the plan to elope. If she'd known in advance, she would have packed Isabel's best clothes neatly. She could even have sent a couple of trunks ahead via train to the hotel in Paris. Being rushed at the last moment was her own fault, though. She'd made her disapproval of the match known early on, and Isabel probably wanted to avoid an argument. But it was also Isabel's style to wait until the last moment. That made everything more of an adventure.

Unfortunately, adventures didn't always turn out well . . . particularly if one didn't have the proper undergarments.

Aha! Oriana suddenly placed the oversight. "You haven't any corset covers."

Isabel peered around the edge of the dressing room door and waved one hand vaguely. "Pick some for me. I only need a couple. Marianus will buy me new ones after we're married."

Isabel disappeared back into her dressing room, leaving Oriana shaking her head. She had to wonder if Marianus Efisio knew he would be spending the next few weeks shopping. While Isabel's family possessed aristocratic bloodlines tracing all the way back to the Battle of Aljubarrota, they had very little money. Everything supplied by the various milliners and dressmakers who'd rigged Isabel out in style had been bought on credit. Isabel's mother was counting on her beauteous daughter's marriage to a wealthy husband. Luckily, Mr. Efisio did meet that requirement.

Unluckily, he was already promised to another woman: Isabel's cousin Pia.

It was an arrangement made when he was just a boy and Pia an infant. Even so, it wasn't fair to simply ignore the arrangement. At any rate, Oriana didn't think so.

Isabel had waved away Oriana's concerns, claiming that Mr. Efisio wasn't suited to Pia's placid disposition. The elopement would cause a scandal, and Isabel's rarely present father would be livid. Nevertheless, Isabel's popularity in polite society would help her survive the disgrace. In time, Mr. Efisio would be forgiven for breaking his betrothal, particularly if Pia were to marry well. He had money, which always seemed to temper society's disapproval.

Isabel was like a tidal wave, though. She always did as she wished, and the gods would merely laugh at anyone who stood in her way.

Clucking her tongue, Oriana sorted through the contents of the rickety chiffonier's top drawer and selected the two best corset covers. She'd just laid them neatly on the bed when Isabel emerged from the dressing room, her arms overflowing with skirts and shirtwaists. She dropped them atop the garments Oriana had already folded, and a narrow line appeared between her perfectly arched black brows. "Am I missing anything else?"

"A nightdress," Oriana answered. She eyed the wreckage of her neatly folded stacks. Isabel probably hadn't even looked before dumping the clothes she'd carried. *Oh, well.* There was nothing to do but start over. Oriana nodded briskly and lifted the top skirt off the pile.

A knock came at the door, and she jumped. She instinctively hid her bare hands in the fabric of the skirt. She was usually so careful, but she'd taken off the mitts that normally hid her fingers so she could help Isabel pack. Then she realized she was wrinkling the skirt terribly and forced herself to let it go. She took a calming breath, hoping her voice would sound normal. "Who is it?"

"Adela, Miss Paredes," one of the maids responded from the hallway. "I have what my lady asked for."

Oriana cast Isabel a questioning look. What was Isabel plotting?

Isabel hurried to the bedroom door herself. Oriana stayed by the bed and shoved her hands behind her back. Other than Isabel, no one in the Amaral household knew her secret. Oriana wanted to keep it that way.

Her webbed fingers would give her away, and being caught in the city would mean arrest and expulsion, if not worse. They were her great flaw as a spy. She'd finally made the decision to have the webbing cut away, as her superiors insisted, and *had* planned to take her half day off this weekend to have it done. But Isabel's sudden decision to elope had fouled those plans. Oriana hadn't decided if she was vexed . . . or relieved.

Isabel opened the door only wide enough for the maid to pass her something and closed it quickly. She turned back to Oriana, a mischievous grin lighting her face, and held up a pair of maid's aprons and two crumpled white caps. "See what I have?"

Oriana stood there with her mouth open. Why would Isabel ask for *those*?

Isabel rolled her eyes. "A disguise," she explained. "See? If we wear black, we can put these on over our skirts and we'll look like housemaids."

Well, the only thing more scandalous than engaging in an elopement had to be exposure while doing so. The disguise *would* make the two of them less noticeable at the train station; most people in Isabel's circles didn't notice servants. Surely none would comment on a couple of housemaids dragging luggage about for their mistresses, even this late in the evening.

"I understand," Oriana said, trying for an enlightened expression. The black serge skirt she currently wore would pass for a housemaid's, but her white cambric shirt and the blue vest wouldn't. "I'll need to change my shirt, but it should do."

Isabel tossed the aprons atop the chiffonier and grinned. "See? It will all work out."

"I'm certain you've planned for everything," Oriana allowed, inclining her head in Isabel's direction.

A dimple appeared in Isabel's alabaster cheek. "When it comes to marriage, one must."

Oriana laughed softly. Isabel always had a clever retort on her silver tongue, a talent she envied.

She regarded the pile of garments atop the bed and tried to think of the best way to tackle the task ahead of her. An open trunk waited on the old cane-backed settee at the foot of the bed, although she would have to fold and tuck judiciously to get all these garments into it. She would likely have to add a portmanteau as well. Mr. Efisio had gone ahead to Paris, but he had ordered his coach to pick them up no more than a block away. She could carry their luggage to the coach in two trips if needed.

Isabel watched, tapping one slender finger against her cheek. "Now, what have I forgotten?"

"Nightdress?" Oriana reminded her.

"Oh, I mustn't forget that." Isabel dashed back to the dressing room.

Oriana folded the blue skirt from the top of the pile and set it in the trunk, located the shirtwaist Isabel wore with it and tucked that in next, and then headed into the dressing room to hunt down the matching jacket. She found Isabel standing before the full-length mirror in the cluttered dressing room, holding up a nightdress. It was her most daring, a white satin that bared much of her bosom like an evening gown.

Isabel glanced over one shoulder at Oriana, her face glowing with excitement. "Do you think he will approve? It's not too shocking, is it?"

Isabel was blessed with an ivory complexion and thick black hair. She had delicate features, delicate hands, delicate feet. Her hazel eyes had been the subject of many a wretched suitor's poem, and her rosy, bow-shaped lips had earned their own paeans. She was everything that Oriana wasn't—beautiful by any standard. A good thing too, as Isabel's sharp tongue and cutting wit might have earned her enemies were she less lovely. But she'd gathered a court of suitors and held them fast while waiting for a man of both adequate means and malleability to come along. Mr. Efisio had never had a chance once Isabel made up her mind to have him.

Oriana's eyes met Isabel's in the mirror. "I'm certain he'll like it, shocking or not."

"Good." Isabel smiled contentedly at her reflection, but turned back to Oriana, her face going serious. "I know you don't approve. I'm grateful you're coming with me anyway."

Oriana opened her mouth to apologize for her earlier arguments with Isabel over Mr. Efisio's fate, but paused. She still didn't approve. She nodded instead.

"I do love him," Isabel said then, the first time she'd told Oriana so. "Have you never been in love?"

Oriana gazed down at her folded hands, her throat inexplicably tight. She was only a few years older than Isabel, but her situation in life had never been amenable to courtship. How many times had her aunts pointed that out? Unlike women within human society, among her people a female often remained alone; there simply weren't enough males. Those females not meant for a mate were destined to serve their people instead, as Oriana did.

That thread of Destiny that bound her soul to some other's? Oriana didn't think it existed. She had resigned herself to that years ago . . . or she'd thought she had. Seeing Isabel so excited about her upcoming nuptials made Oriana wish she'd been one of the *others*—those for whom Destiny had chosen a mate. "No," she admitted when she found her voice. "I've never been in love, so I suppose I can't understand."

Isabel's brows drew together. "Do your people believe in love? Or are your marriages all arranged, like Pia's?"

Oriana mulled that over. "We believe we are destined for one in particular, or—"

"Then perhaps you just haven't met him yet," Isabel interrupted with a blithe wave of her hand.

Apparently Isabel believed that if *she* were to have a husband, then everyone must. At least Isabel's interruption had saved her from admitting aloud she was destined to be forever alone. Oriana nodded again, as if she agreed. She was realizing she did that quite often.

Isabel surveyed the mess on the bed with narrowed eyes, plotting how to subdue it, no doubt. "Now, why don't you go pack your own bag, Oriana? I'll finish up in here."

Oriana cast a glance back at that chaos and suppressed a shudder. Isabel would simply cram her clothes into that trunk. As she wasn't taking a maid along, Oriana would end up ironing everything later. She hated exposing her delicate hands to all that heat, but she would do so to help Isabel start off in her new life properly. One last thing she could do to repay Isabel for her kindness.

She tugged on her black silk mitts to hide the webbing between her fingers. "I'll be back shortly, then."

ABOUT THE AUTHOR

J. KATHLEEN CHENEY is a former mathematics teacher who has taught classes ranging from seventh grade to calculus, with a brief stint as a gifted-and-talented specialist. She is the author of the Novels of the Golden City, including *The Shores of Spain*, *The Seat of Magic*, and *The Golden City*. Her short fiction has been published in such venues as *Fantasy Magazine* and *Beneath Ceaseless Skies*, and her novella *Iron Shoes* was a Nebula Finalist in 2010.

CONNECT ONLINE

jkathleencheney.com
facebook.com/j.kathleen.cheney
twitter.com/jkcheney